Janet
Dailey

TREASURY
EDITION

Janet Dailey

TREASURY EDITION

Harlequin Books

TORONTO • NEW YORK • LONDON
AMSTERDAM • PARIS • SYDNEY • HAMBURG
STOCKHOLM • ATHENS • TOKYO • MILAN

These books by Janet Dailey were originally published as follows:

NO QUARTER ASKED
Copyright © 1974 by Janet Dailey
First published by Mills & Boon Limited in 1974

FIESTA SAN ANTONIO
Copyright © 1977 by Janet Dailey
First published by Mills & Boon Limited in 1977

FOR BITTER OR WORSE
Copyright © 1978 by Janet Dailey
First published by Mills & Boon Limited in 1978

Story Illustrations by Wes Lowe
Printed and bound by Kingsport Press Inc.

ISBN 0-373-65101-5

Printed in U.S.A.

CONTENTS

NO
QUARTER ASKED
Page 9

FIESTA
SAN ANTONIO
Page 195

FOR
BITTER OR WORSE
Page 383

No Quarter
Asked

Stacy's world collapsed with the death of her father. She needed time to adjust, to sort herself out; to decide what she wanted to do with her life.

The secluded cabin in a Texas valley seemed a perfect place to think. But all her hopes of peace and serenity vanished when she met the arrogant rancher Cord Harris. Especially when Cord said, "Go back to the city, where you belong."

It was exactly the wrong thing to say to Stacy. It made her fighting mad—and stubbornly determined to stay!

CHAPTER ONE

STACY stared out the window at the traffic rushing between the concrete buildings below. The sombre grey and brown tones of the towering structures reflected the depression that hung so heavy on the young girl's shoulders. A little sigh escaped her as she let the curtain fall back in place and turned to face the ageing man behind the desk.

'Mr. Mills, you were Daddy's friend. You should understand more than anyone why I have to get away by myself to sort things out. Why does it have to make any difference if it's in a New York apartment or a cabin in Texas?'

'It's because I was your father's attorney and closest friend that I wish you would think it over a little more ' the lawyer replied, removing his black-rimmed glasses and absently wiping them with his handkerchief.

'I'm not trying to run away,' Stacy ran a gloved hand nervously over her arm. 'I just need time to see where I fit in again.'

'Look, Stacy, any other young girl in your shoes would be going to Europe or the Islands. You're a wealthy girl now. I can understand that you aren't particularly happy with the way you acquired your money, but the death of someone dear always involves a difficult adjustment. You've always been so independent, even headstrong, that I don't see why you insist on burying yourself out in the country.'

Stacy Adams looked hesitantly at Carter Mills, Sr., wondering how she could make him understand why she had to go. Her father, Joshua Adams, had respected this man and trusted him as few men are ever able to in their lifetime. *Her father*. The words caught in her throat. Stacy glanced down at her blue suit and the gloved hands clenched so tightly in her lap. Her mother had died shortly after Stacy was born, leaving her globe-trotting husband with the unfamiliar and frightening task of raising their child. Refusing the generous offers from friends to care for Stacy, Joshua Adams had filled another suitcase with nappies and powder and carted the year-old girl off on his next foreign assignment. Life for father and daughter had been one long world tour with brief respites in New York to catch their breath before starting out again, as he built his reputation as a freelance photographer.

Loving memories whirled through Stacy's mind, most vividly, her seventeenth birthday three years ago, when her dad had smuggled a puppy into a plush New Orleans hotel. Cajun, he had called the pup, in honour of the Creole country of his birth. The wiggling, playful dog had swiftly grown into a husky German Shepherd, devoted entirely to his young mistress. Her father predicted that Cajun would protect Stacy better than any guardian angel. Stacy wondered if her father knew how right he had been, because it was Cajun who had pulled an unconscious but unharmed Stacy from the wreckage of the chartered plane before it burst into flames. The pilot and her father didn't make it.

As she tried to blink back the tears that clouded her eyes, Stacy raised her head to meet the lawyer's affectionate gaze. Her brown eyes grew misty with the threatening tears, as her mouth curved into a painful smile.

'I take it back, Stacy. Perhaps going out there will help you face your problems. Joshua loved the West and never turned down an assignment that would take him there.' Carter Mills, Sr., rose from his chair and walked around to where Stacy was seated. 'But remember you're still a young woman, barely twenty, with a lot of the world ahead of you. He wouldn't have wanted you to miss any of it—not the good and definitely not the bad.'

Stacy grasped the hands he offered and rose, her trim, tailored suit enhancing the feminine figure underneath. 'I knew you would understand and see why I have to do this.'

'There's at least one young man that I know of who's rather upset about your leaving,' Carter Mills commented. 'But you can't blame my son for wanting to escort you around our more fashionable clubs. And you can't say you don't belong there, not with the inheritance your father left you.'

'I'm afraid I haven't accepted the idea that I'm comfortably wealthy yet. Before I was happy just to be with Dad, travelling wherever the wind blew—maybe I inherited his itchy feet. Out there with just Cajun, Diablo, and miles of space, I should be able to decide about the future,' Stacy concluded as she reached for her purse.

'Are you taking that fool horse, too? I had hoped you'd sold him long ago,' exclaimed the lawyer with no attempt to hide his concern. 'I don't mind telling you that I think you're making a grave mistake taking him.'

'Oh, Diablo isn't as vicious and unruly as you would like to believe. He's high-strung, that's all!' Stacy smiled. 'You know very well that I'm an excellent horsewoman. Dad would never have allowed me to have Diablo if he didn't think I could handle him.'

'I realize that, but I'm sure it never occurred to him that you would be taking that horse out in the wilds with you,' Mr. Mills replied gruffly.

'No. I'm sure Dad probably hoped that I would settle down and take my place in society, so to speak. But I'm not ready for that yet. Maybe I never will want to be, who knows?' she said, then added, 'I really should be going.'

'What are you doing with the apartment while you're gone?'

'I decided to just lock it up rather than let it go,' answered Stacy, a shadow of pain clouding her eyes momentarily.

'Just as long as you know you're always welcome at our home. And if there's ever anything you need, don't hesitate one minute,' Carter Mills said.

'I won't. Carter Jr. is taking me to dinner tomorrow night for one last fling with civilization. He seems to think that I'm going to the darkest regions of Africa,' Stacy smiled, touched by the sincere concern extended by the lawyer. 'Thanks for everything, Mr. Mills.'

Stacy smiled as she walked out of his office into the reception room. Mr. Mills couldn't help but have misgivings about her impending trip. She wasn't going to an exactly remote area, but she would be reasonably isolated. When his son Carter had told him about Stacy's decision to rent a hunting cabin in the Apache Mountains of Texas for the spring, he had immediately checked into the situation as a personal friend. But he honestly could find no real flaws with her plans, except that she was going alone.

Stacy entered the lift with a lighted 'down' arrow

flickering above it. Mulling over her plans, she was unaware of the interested looks she received from some of her fellow passengers. The sprinkling of freckles across a too-straight nose usually dismissed her, in a stranger's eye, as average. But second glances noticed the gleaming brown hair framing her oval face and the dark brown eyes, now shadowed by her grief, with their naturally thick lashes that combined to give her a refreshingly wholesome aura.

On the ground floor, Stacy proceeded to the street where an incessant tide of pedestrians awaited the commands of the red and green globes. Swept along by the flow at the crosswalk, she let herself be led by the steady stream until she reached the parking lot where she had left her car. Preoccupied with her memories as she was, her hand caressed the steering wheel for a second before accelerating into the traffic. The luxurious sports car had been the last present her father had given her.

Looking back, Stacy realized she should have recognized the import the expensive gift carried. She had always assumed that, although she and her father lived very comfortably, their financial condition was dependent on her father's income. The discovery that her father's death had left her independently wealthy still seemed a dream. Stacy didn't know what she would have done if that had not been the case. She possessed a smattering of knowledge about everything, but she had forgone any further schooling to travel with her father.

Arriving at her apartment building, Stacy entered and took the lift to the fifth floor. Silently she walked down the corridor to her apartment and hesitated as she reached her door. Depression spread over her as she inserted the key and opened the door. She was immediately greeted by an ecstatic German Shepherd yelping his pleasure at her return.

'Cajun, you brute, did you miss me?' Stacy smiled sadly, cradling the enormous head in her hands as she looked at the unmasked adoration in the dog's eyes. 'What would I do if you weren't here?'

The telephone jingled dimly, stirring Stacy out of her thoughts. Bending a nyloned knee on the flowered couch, she picked up the receiver.

'Yes?'

'Stacy? Carter,' came the masculine voice on the other end. 'Dad said I just missed you.'

'I left there around four,' Stacy said, glancing at her watch as she sat on the couch.

'How's everything going?' A touch of concern peeped out of the light tone.

'Fine, really. I was just going to finish up the last of my packing, except for the few odds and ends that will have to wait,' Stacy said, adding with a little laugh. 'I even packed some dresses in with all my riding clothes. I'm planning to live it up in some little cowtown!'

'Just as long as you don't meet some tall, dark, handsome cowboy and ride off into the sunset on his trusty steed,' Carter mocked, 'I won't mind.'

'I wouldn't worry. They don't make cowboys like they used to,' Stacy chuckled. 'On our last trip west, all I ever saw were sunburned, middle-aged men with families to support.'

'Are you still driving down?'

'Just Caj and me. Diablo's going by train as far as Pecos. I'll pick him up there and go on to McCloud. The cabin's about thirty miles from town, so I'm really not too far from civilization.'

'I'm glad you didn't ask me to go along. All that solitude would drive me up the wall. I don't see how you'll be able to take it for more than a week. How different can one mountain be from another?' Carter teased.

'Maybe you're right, but I'll have to find that out for myself.'

'Can't talk you out of a thing, can I?' the voice in the receiver said. 'Listen, I have a brief to work on tonight, so I won't be able to come round. We still have a date for tomorrow night. Seven sharp, right?'

'Right,' Stacy agreed.

'Okay. Take care and I'll see you tomorrow. 'Bye!'

'Good-bye, Carter.'

The click of the phone echoed forlornly in the crushing silence that followed. Refusing to give in to the melancholy that the empty room emitted, Stacy rose from the flowered couch to enter her bedroom. She would do that last-minute packing she had mentioned, filling the void intensified by the phone call with a bustle of activity.

The next night Stacy was just fastening the clasp on her onyx pendant when the doorbell rang. She surveyed her reflection one last time in the mirror. The sleeveless, peach-coloured dress with its V-neck and pleated skirt set off the copper tan of her skin and the golden highlights in her hair, that was pulled back in ringlets, Grecian style. Taking a tissue, Stacy blotted her peach-tinted lips and applied a little gloss before allowing a satisfied smile to light her face.

When she opened the door to admit Carter, her dark eyes were flashing with pleasure. 'I didn't keep you waiting too long, did I?'

The tall, fair-haired man grasped her hands and pushed her away from him. His blue eyes answered her sparkle with a shine all their own. 'May I say what you already know? I wouldn't have minded waiting longer if I'd known what a vision I was going to see. Shall we go?' he asked, placing the crocheted stole Stacy handed him around her shoulders while brushing a light kiss on her hair. 'I've made reservations for eight at the Meadow Wood Country club.'

'Marvellous,' Stacy smiled.

The two chatted amiably on their way to his car, but once inside the conversation abated. Carter gave his full attention to the traffic around him while Stacy unobtrusively studied his silhouette. He was a good-looking man with light brown, almost blond hair and clear blue eyes. Six years older than Stacy and just entering his father's law practice, Carter was considered quite-a catch by many of her acquaintances. His attractive fair looks were a perfect foil for Stacy's brown hair and eyes.

There had never been any avowals of love or promises to wait between them. When Stacy had accompanied her father on his travels, she had sent Carter funny postcards of wherever she was and called him when she got back in town. Carter dated other girls when she was gone, but never anyone as regularly as Stacy. The two families had been pleased with the budding relationship of their children, nurturing secret hopes of an eventual marriage.

Stacy smiled, watching the competent hands manoeuvring the car into a parking lot. Their relationship could never be considered as brother-and-sister, she thought, even if it hadn't reached the heart-pounding passionate stage yet. They were both enjoying the other's company while waiting for love to come their way. Some day, she supposed, they would marry. They would have a good life. They got along together too well for it to be any other way. But not yet, not yet.

'Besides,' Stacy thought, 'I'm still naïve enough to wish for a love that will sweep me off my feet, even if it is only fairy-tale stuff.'

'Dreamer, are you going to get out of the car or just sit there?' Carter asked, laughing down at the girl as he stood holding the car door open for her.

'I'm sorry—I was off in another world.'

'Well, come back. Tonight is my night and I plan to make the most of it,' he smiled as he escorted her to the club entrance.

His arm rested lightly around her waist as he opened the elaborately scrolled doors of the private club. Carter ordered their drinks while Stacy gazed at the unique furnishings. The bar was decorated in an exotic jungle-type atmosphere with leopard and zebra skins adorning the walls.

When the waitress returned with their drinks, Stacy caught Carter looking at her with a sombre expression on his face.

'Why so grim? I thought we were going to celebrate tonight?' Stacy chided.

'Sorry, I was thinking about that vacation you're taking. Stacy, Dad isn't too happy about it, and neither am I. If anything happened to you out at that godforsaken cabin, it could be weeks before anyone finds out,' he said earnestly.

'Please, let's don't talk about it tonight. I've made up my mind that I'm going and that's all there is to be said,' she replied a little sharply because of her own apprehension. 'It seems everyone knows what's best for me but me.'

'Did it ever occur to you that this time they might be right?' A hint of disgust was in his voice. 'You seem to think that because you've travelled all over the world you can handle anything that may happen.

Why, you're no more experienced than some country girl! All your father showed you was the world from the sheltered side of a camera lens. You have no idea what it's like to be on your own.'

'Just because I've seen war and hunger and famine from his view, does that make it any less real? I know what life is about. And I know what I'm going to do with mine, so there's no need of discussing it any further,' Stacy retorted..

'Will you stop being so stubborn for once and listen to reason?'

'I told you the subject is closed.'

'Then let's dance,' Carter suggested roughly as the combo started playing a slow tune.

Stacy rose, pushing her chair back from the table. Carter held her elbow firmly, directing her to the dance floor. When he took her in his arms, both expressions were a little grim.

Stacy laughed, 'Oh, Carter, I'm sorry. I really didn't mean to lose my temper. Please don't let's argue tonight.'

He smiled down at the girl's pleading eyes. 'Okay, we'll consider the subject closed. We'll just enjoy our evening together.'

Later when their reservation for dinner was called, the couple entered the dining room and were escorted to a small table for two secluded from the rest of the diners. When the final course was over, the couple settled back contentedly with their coffee.

'That was a delicious meal,' Stacy said, accepting the light from Carter for her cigarette.

'Umm. But the partner is even more delicious.'

'Thank you, kind sir.'

'Did you want to go back into the bar and dance, or would you rather go somewhere else?'

'No, let's stay here. I really enjoy this atmosphere and besides, I don't feel in the mood for a discotheque tonight,' Stacy replied.

'Good, neither do I. There's some talking I want to do and I'd hate to shout it over the din of some rock band.'

'Please, not another lecture about my trip,' she begged. 'You promised there'd be no more discussion about my going to Texas.'

'And I have every intention of keeping my word. This is something entirely different. Shall we go?'

'Yes.'

Stacy waited for Carter at the entry way to the lounge while he paid the bill. They found a table over in a corner and ordered drinks. At the beginning of a slow ballad, they wound their way on to the floor. Holding Stacy a little away from him, Carter gazed down into her brown eyes and smiled gently.

'Remember after your father's funeral the comment Dad made about you being one of the family?'

'Yes,' said Stacy, returning the serious look on her partner's face.

'I want to make it legal. I want you to be my wife,' he said, their steps almost ceasing. 'I'm not trying to talk you out of your trip, but while you're thinking about the future, I want you to include me. Stacy, I care about you—I love you and I want to watch over you for the rest of my life. We've never talked about the future before and it's time we did. Before, we were both too young. I still had law school to finish and you still had some growing up to do. Well, they're both done now and this is the time to start planning the rest of our lives.'

'Carter, I don't know what to say. I don't know if I'm ready to settle down. I don't know——'

'Don't say anything. I know it's awfully soon after losing your father. You're bound to be confused, so I'm not asking for an answer yet. When I think you're ready, I'll ask you again properly. Until then I'm just asking you to remember that I love you and want to marry you while you're out there in that Texas refuge,' Carter said quietly, gently kissing the top of her forehead.

He drew her once again into the circle of his arms, and they continued their dancing in silence while Stacy mulled the proposal over in her mind. She shouldn't have been surprised by it, but she was despite her earlier thoughts on the same line. Returning to their table after the song was over, they sat quietly without speaking.

'You mentioned you were shipping Diablo to Texas. I was going to ask if you wanted to take my grey,' said Carter. 'He's definitely more manageable than that red devil of yours.'

'I don't expect to have much trouble with Diablo, but thanks for offering,' Stacy said, smiling at her date. 'Besides, he's already on his way to Pecos, so I'll just stick with my original arrangement.'

'What time do you plan to leave tomorrow?' Carter asked.

'I hope to get started by midday.'

'It's rather late now. I don't want it to be said that I kept you from your beauty rest. I think you'll have plenty to think about tonight. At least I hope so,' said Carter, casually referring to his earlier proposal.

They talked little on the way home. Stacy nestled down in her seat and gazed out the window at the neon world before her. Pulling into the parking lot of Stacy's apartment building, Carter turned the car motor off, then instead of getting out of the car, he sat quietly in his seat looking at the brown-haired girl beside him.

'I won't be able to come over tomorrow and tell you good-bye, so I'll wish you my good luck now,' he said, drawing her over into his arms.

Stacy tilted her head back and awaited his kiss. His lips were firm and gentle as they pressed down upon hers. He held her body close to his as his hands caressed the tanned shoulders underneath her stole. Stacy's heart increased its tempo with the growing urgency in his kiss.

'Take that with you, Stacy, and let it plead my cause,' he finished.

Reluctantly Stacy stepped out of the car when he came around and opened the door for her. In silence, they walked into the building to the elevator.

'I'll leave you here. Stacy, come home soon,' Carter whispered to her, looking down affectionately at the freckled nose and wide brown eyes. Softly he dropped a kiss on her forehead and walked away.

Watching the slender, but muscular man leave, Stacy felt a cold emptiness chill her heart. She turned uncertainly to the yawning doors of the lift. Quietly she let herself into the apartment, questioning her decision to leave the only home and friends she had.

An hour later she had fallen asleep, once again resolved to carry through with her plans to journey to Texas.

CHAPTER TWO

'McCLOUD—10 Miles,' the sign read. Stacy arched her back, stretching the cramped muscles. Two and a half days of steady driving were beginning to tell. But she was almost there and the excitement of finally reaching her destination was starting to flow through her. She glanced briefly at her reflection in the rear view mirror. Only her eyes showed the weariness she felt from the long drive. The pale, lemon-yellow top that complemented her olive-green pant-suit looked as fresh as when she had put it on that morning. The matching jacket lay over the back of the passenger seat where Cajun was sleeping, his huge body contorted by the limited space.

The two-horse trailer specially designed for the Jaguar was pulling easily. Diablo had raised quite a fuss when she loaded him in Pecos, but had since settled down nicely.

The afternoon sun was glaring through the windshield of her car as Stacy reached for the sunglasses lying on the dash. It wouldn't be long now before she'd be in her Texas retreat. First she would stop in town to look up the Nolans, so they could direct her to the cabin and then pick up some groceries. With luck she should be cooking her supper by seven.

Ahead she could see the growing outline of the small town. As it drew closer, Stacy lowered her speed, taking in as much of the surroundings as she could.

She pulled into a petrol station on the outskirts of town. Stepping out of the black sports car, she snapped her fingers to the waking Shepherd to follow. Stiffly and a little sleepily, he joined his mistress on the concrete paving. Stacy glanced appreciatively around the station, noting the lack of litter and usual car parts. Although the building wasn't modern, it was in excellent repair.

A teenage boy walked out of the office area towards the Jaguar. His admiring glance at the lithe figure passed unnoticed by Stacy as she surveyed the town ahead of her, shimmering in the afternoon sun.

'Fill 'er up, miss?' the young voice drawled.

'Please. Check under the hood, too,' she replied, smiling at the gentle Southern accent.

Cajun went off to investigate a grassy lot next to the station while Stacy walked into the office to escape the sun. Inside, it took a minute for her eyes to adjust to the absence of the blinding sunlight. There were two men inside. One, the older of the two, was dressed in an attendant's uniform. The other, who had his back to Stacy, was dressed in blue Levi's and a faded plaid shirt. His dark, almost black hair was barely visible under the sweat-stained brown Stetson on his head. His tall, muscular frame blocked the attendant's view of Stacy until she stepped over to the counter where there was a selection of sweets.

'S'cuse me, Cord. Can I help you, miss?' the man inquired.

Stacy glanced up at the man facing her, taking in the smiling hazel eyes and his creased face, leathered by the Texas sun. She couldn't help but return the smile offered by the stocky man.

'Yes, I'd like one of those chocolate bars,' Stacy said.

'Sure thing,' the man nodded, turning towards the cash register with the coins Stacy had handed him for the bar. 'Don't think me nosey, ma'am, but from your accent, I take it you're not from around here?'

Laughing, Stacy replied, 'I never realized I had an accent, but I suppose to you I do. Actually I'm from New York, but I'm staying here this summer. I was wondering if you could tell me where I might find a family named Nolan. I've rented their hunting cabin,' she explained.

It was then that the second man turned to face Stacy, and she was surprised by the seeming antagonism in his eyes. Puzzled, she heard him mutter a good-bye to the man behind the counter and stride out the door to a jeep parked beside the station. Turning back to the counter, she attempted to shake herself free of that haunting expression in his eyes. What had she done?

'I'm sorry, what did you say?' she asked, realizing the attendant had been addressing her.

'I said the Nolans run the grocery store in town. You turn right at the next block, then straight for two more, then left. Theirs is the second shop from the corner,' he smiled.

'Thank you.'

'Miss, you were a quart low on oil, so I put some in. Boy, that's some car you got,' the young boy commented, coming inside, his allegiance switching from the attractive girl to the black sports car. 'I'll bet she really leaves 'em behind on the straight-away!'

'That's enough, Billy,' the older man put in, taking Stacy's money for the petrol and oil. 'I'm sure the lady appreciates the fact you like her choice of cars.'

Stacy laughed in return. 'Right now I'd better look up the Nolans or it'll be dark before I get to my new home.'

'Well, you just follow the directions I gave you and you can't miss it. Molly Nolan is always there in the afternoons, and I imagine she'll know where to run down her old man,' the attendant said as he walked along with Stacy to her car.

She whistled to Cajun and waved a good-bye to the two attendants as she drove out on to the highway. Stacy smiled to herself as she turned right at the next block. The people seemed friendly anyway. At least two of them were, she qualified. And she wasn't going to let a dark-haired stranger's seeming hostility spoil her first visit to the town. If he hadn't seemed so disagreeable, she probably would have considered him handsome, she reflected.

He certainly had the requirements—dark hair, brown eyes, and a tall, muscular build—but he had acted as if she carried the plague. There really wasn't any reason for her to keep dwelling on those unfriendly dark eyes; chances were she probably would never see him again. It was the clear-cut features of his face with their straight lines outlining his jaw, cheekbones, and chin that gave Stacy the feeling there was no 'give' in the man.

Reaching the corner of the second block, she spied the grocery store. Ahead of her was a space just wide enough for her to park her car and trailer. Cajun attempted to join her when she hopped out of the car, but she ordered him to stay. She glanced into the horse van at Diablo before continuing on her way to the shop.

It was a quaint little main street, covering all of two or three blocks. There was a drugstore on the corner, the grocery store next to it, a little brick post office after that, followed by a clothing shop and a café. 'It isn't a big town,' Stacy thought, 'but it's probably sufficient to serve the ranch community surrounding it.'

Pushing the door open, she entered the grocery shop. Behind a narrow counter was a small, matronly lady

Stacy guessed to be in her late forties. Her hair was peppered with grey which made her seem more motherly. The simple house dress covering the plump figure reminded Stacy of a kitchen filled with the aromas of fresh-baked cakes. When the customer the woman was waiting on left, Stacy stepped forward.

'Excuse me, are you Mrs. Nolan?'

'Yes, I am. Is there something I could help you with?' the woman asked.

'I'm Stacy Adams. I made arrangements to rent your cabin for the summer,' Stacy explained, smiling at the jovial face.

'Of course, how silly of me. I should have recognized you right off. We don't have many tourists stop in our store. You did say you'd be here on the first part of May, but it had completely slipped my mind,' apologized the older woman. 'I imagine you're anxious to get out there before dark.'

'Yes, I had hoped to stay there tonight, Mrs. Nolan.'

'Oh, goodness, call me Molly or I'll think you're talking to someone else,' she laughed. 'My husband will be here shortly and can drive out with you. We cleaned it all up last week, but it's still a little barren. You know how men are, if they got somethin' to sit on and a place to cook food, it don't matter if there's curtains at the windows or a cloth on the table.'

'I'm sure it will be fine. I hope you didn't go to too much trouble just for me,' answered Stacy, recognizing that the woman had noticed her city clothes and was concerned that Stacy was expecting something fancier.

'Excuse me,' a voice from behind Stacy said.

As she turned to move away from the counter, she found herself face to face with the broad shoulders of the stranger from the petrol station. Involuntarily her eyes rushed up to meet his. There was no flicker of recognition in the dark eyes, no spark of interest.

'Oh, Cord, I'm so glad you're here,' said Molly Nolan, coming around the counter to take his arm. A faint smile tickled the corners of his mouth as he looked down on the motherly figure. 'I want you to meet Miss Stacy Adams. She's rented the hunting cabin in the foothills of the east range for the summer. Stacy, this is Cord Harris, your official landlord. The Circle H headquarters is about ten miles from the cabin.'

Surprised by the unexpected encounter with the stranger a second time, Stacy murmured a polite reply to the introduction and managed to raise her eyes to meet his stony gaze again. This time there was no doubting the hostility and contempt in his eyes. Deliberately they searched her face and continued their way over her yellow top to her creased slacks and fashionable buckle shoes, before returning derisively to her face. The pant-suit that Stacy decided as being practical for travelling before suddenly seemed too chic, too elegant for this rough country.

Embarrassed, she felt the growing heat burning her cheeks. Angry that this Cord Harris had managed to make her feel artificial and cheap, she thrust out her chin defiantly.

'I hope you won't find our country too desolate and isolated for you,' the man went on, a trace of sarcasm in his voice.

'I'm sure I'll enjoy my stay here. Almost everyone has made me feel very much at home,' Stacy replied, attempting to curb the anger that trembled on the edge of her words.

'I'm sure they have,' inserted Mrs. Nolan. 'We don't have many pretty young things like you around here. Why, once the word gets around that you're staying

for the summer, our young men will beat a path to
your door!'

'I doubt that,' Stacy smiled, 'but it's nice of you to
say so.'

'Not worried about staying alone at that deserted
shack, are you?' Cord Harris interposed. 'After a few
nights alone out there, you'll probably welcome the
company of our young men.'

'It's possible, but unlikely. You see, Mr. Harris,'
Stacy was now indignant at the veiled cynicism, 'I
came here to be alone. I do intend to make friends,
but I don't intend to enter the social set.'

'"Intend," very cleverly stated,' the dark-haired man
drawled, meeting Stacy's flashing eyes with a cool gaze.
'It leaves you wide open to do whatever you please.
And somehow you don't seem the type to isolate yourself for any amount of time.'

'Now, Cord,' Molly Nolan put in, trying to quench
the unexpected friction between the two. 'I don't
think it's our place to judge Miss Adams or her plans.
You apologize for your rudeness.'

'If what I said was unfounded, I certainly do apologize.' His hand touched his hat brim, mockingly. 'I do
hope you enjoy your stay here, Miss Adams, however
long it may be.'

Nodding a good-bye to Mrs. Nolan, the arrogant
rancher picked up his sack of goods and went out the
door without allowing Stacy time to reply. Her fury
had reached the peak where words failed her. Never
had she met such an overbearing, insolent, and sarcastic man! Turning to the astonished woman beside
her, Stacy vented her displeasure.

'Who does that man think he is?'

'Oh, you mustn't mind Cord,' soothed Molly absently. 'He has a tendency to voice his opinion. Under-

neath all that bluster though, he's really quite charming.'

'You could have fooled me,' Stacy exclaimed. 'I wish he lived ten thousand miles away instead of just ten. What in the world did I do to warrant such an attack?'

'Nothing, dear, I'm sure. Maybe you just reminded him of someone else,' the woman replied bustling around to the other side of the counter. 'I imagine you'll want to do some shopping. My husband ought to be here any time now.'

Still fuming inwardly, Stacy took a trolley and started down one of the aisles. 'He may be my nearest neighbour,' Stacy thought, 'but I'll make a special point to avoid him from now on, though I would like to see that infuriating coolness of his upset once!'

After picking up all the supplies she felt she would need, Stacy returned to the check-out where she found Molly Nolan engaged in a conversation with a thin, balding man. Guessing that it must be Mr. Nolan, Stacy joined them.

'Well, dearie, did you find everything you needed?' Molly inquired, then turned to the man by her side. 'This is Miss Adams, Harry. This is my husband. He'll drive up to the cabin with you.'

'I'm happy to meet you, Mr. Nolan,' Stacy said, extending her hand to the little man before her.

'Molly said you was a pretty thing, but she didn't say you was this pretty. Ya shore are going to light this little cowtown up,' the bright-eyed man replied, eagerly shaking her hand. 'I hope the cabin will suit you all right, 'cause it shore ain't very fancy.'

'I'm sure it will suit me. I'm used to roughing it with my dad,' Stacy said, smiling at the man who was an inch shorter than Stacy's five-foot-four.

'Oh, is your father coming to join you?' Molly asked.

'No.' A flicker of pain haunted her face momentarily. 'He was killed in a plane crash a month ago.'

'Oh, I'm so sorry. I didn't mean to——' Molly started.

'No, you couldn't have known,' interrupted Stacy.

'What about your mother? Is she still back East? Does she approve of your gallivantin' off by yourself?' Harry Nolan asked.

'My mother died shortly after I was born, so I'm pretty much on my own now. But you needn't worry about me being alone, I brought my German Shepherd along with me. I'm sure he can handle any four-footed animal that would wander in, and the two-footed variety as well,' Stacy laughed, thinking about Cord Harris with a malicious satisfaction.

'Good dogs, them Shepherds,' the old man agreed. 'He'll watch out for you real good.'

'Naturally I hope he won't have to,' Stacy said, reaching in her purse to pay for the groceries. 'Well, Mr. Nolan, I'm ready to go whenever you are.'

'Where'd you park your car?' he asked.

'Across from the drugstore.'

'I'll meet ya in about five minutes with my jeep and you can follow me out,' he nodded, moving towards the door.

'Now if you need anything or get to feelin' you want some company, you just hustle yourself into town. Me an' my husband would love to have you any time,' said Molly after her husband had left.

'I'll remember. But I think for a while I'm just going to enjoy the peace and quiet,' Stacy replied, touched by the motherly concern.

'The folks around here are all pretty friendly and would be more than glad to help you out if you have any kind of trouble, so you just don't hesitate to ask anybody,' instructed the matronly woman. 'Peace and quiet's fine, but you mustn't shut yourself off completely. You just remember that you're always welcome here and don't be ashamed to ask for help.'

'I won't be. Thank you again. You'll be seeing me.' Balancing the sack of groceries in one arm, Stacy pushed the door open with the other. It was nice to feel so at home with people she had only met a few minutes ago. With the exception of a certain man, everyone had gone out of his way to help her.

Reaching the car, she put the groceries in the back, quieted the excited dog, and looked around for Mr. Nolan. In the van Diablo was starting to raise a little fuss. Walking back to the trailer, Stacy entered the van by the side door of the empty stall. The sorrel turned his blazed head to her and blew gently on her face. Softly she talked to him, trying to quiet him down. His ears flicked back and forth catching her words, but his eyes still rolled with unease.

Glancing up, Stacy saw Mr. Nolan drive up beside the Jaguar. As she emerged from the van, the wizened old man crawled out of his jeep and joined her beside the trailer.

'All set to go?' he asked.

'Yes, just making sure everything was secure in the trailer. I'm afraid my horse is a bad traveller,' Stacy explained, glancing at the tossing head of the sorrel.

'Mighty flashy-lookin' horse,' commented her companion. 'What breed is he?'

'Mostly Arabian,' Stacy answered, walking over to the driver's side of the sports car.

'Never cared much for them. Too flighty actin'. Give me a steady quarter horse any time,' the man answered a little gruffly. 'Well, we best get goin'. The road's not in too bad a shape, so you should be able to keep up with me easy.' He started the jeep and moved off.

It wasn't at all difficult to follow him. They drove through a few blocks of homes before taking a gravel road heading north from town. The road soon entered the foothills and finally into the mountains themselves. After they had gone about twenty miles, the jeep turned on to a side road that was little more than a worn track. Stacy refused to let herself dwell on the jolts her Jaguar was taking and prayed that the low-slung sports car wouldn't get hung up in one of the ruts, while she was trying to concentrate on the bouncing rear end of the jeep in front of her. She glanced in the mirror anxiously at the horse trailer behind her. Diablo would really be a bundle of nerves by the time she got to the cabin.

The pine woods were so thick that she couldn't see to either side and with the sun setting, the rays filtered through the trees only in patches. The trees thinned out ahead as she watched the vehicle in front go down a small hill into what looked like a clearing. Reaching the top of the hill, Stacy saw a luscious green meadow before her with a stream cascading through it. Off to her left against the back of a canyon wall was nestled a small wooden cabin with a corral and lean-to beside it. Looking to her right briefly, Stacy could see the mountain meadow wander into the arroyos beyond. Why, it was a valley, but more beautiful than any picture she had ever seen.

Harry Nolan had parked his jeep and was standing by the wooden porch of the cabin when Stacy pulled her black sports car to a stop in front.

'It's beautiful!' she exclaimed, as she got out of the car to gaze at the surrounding mountains.

'Yep,' the man replied, removing his straw hat to wipe his balding head with a kerchief. 'I'll show you around the inside. I think you'll find it comfortable.'

Smiling, Stacy followed the wizened figure into the cabin. The main room housed a fireplace with a large, stuffed deer's head above it. The hearth was filled with firewood with an ample supply piled beside it. There was one sofa in the room and an old rocker. The kitchen, consisting of a few metal cupboards over an old-porcelain sink with a pump-type hydrant, covered the west wall. Luckily there was a propane gas stove to cook on; Stacy was sure she could never have managed one of those wood-fired ranges. The table with its two chairs sat in the middle of the room. She could see Molly Nolan's touch in the red-checked tablecloth and matching curtains at the window.

The motherly woman was probably responsible for the pillows on the sofa and the horsehair blanket hanging on the far wall, too. Harry Nolan explained to Stacy how to light the kerosene lanterns and adjust the wick to give off the right amount of light without smoking the glass before he showed her into the bedroom. A big four-poster bed dominated the small room. The bed was covered with a large patchwork quilt that Stacy knew had come from the Nolans. Squeezed in a corner was an old set of chest of drawers. Behind the door was a place to hang her clothes.

'Oh, this is perfect,' Stacy smiled, surveying the two rooms excitedly. 'I can't think of anything that isn't already here.'

'Well, I'm glad it suits you. The missus will be happy to hear how much you like it,' said Harry, his bright eyes glowing at Stacy's enthusiasm. 'Now, if you'd like, I'll help you unload that horse of yours in the corral.'

Accepting Mr. Nolan's offer, Stacy manoeuvred the car so the back of the trailer was over to the gate that the short man had opened. Stacy set the brake and walked back to let the tail gate of the van down before she entered the empty stall beside the restless horse. Anxiously, the sorrel pulled at the rope that held him, interfering with Stacy's attempts to loosen it. She tried to quiet the nervous horse, but his feet increased their tattoo on the trailer's floor as his ears flattened against his head. Finally the knot on the end of the lead rope was loose. As soon as he found himself free, the red stallion half-reared, pulling the girl along with him out of the van. The whites of his eyes flashed menacingly as he danced down the ramp on to the solid ground of the corral. As quickly as she could, Stacy turned the horse loose to gallop around the corral.

The flighty Arabian circled the corral warily, his flaxen mane and tail whipping in the wind. Then his attention was caught by the stranger leaning against the fence rail near his mistress. Instantly he bore down upon the man, his teeth bared and his pointed ears snaked back. With surprising agility the lean man leaped away from the fence and the savage attack.

'Does he do that often?' Harry muttered.

'Fortunately, no,' Stacy apologized, waving the horse back to the centre of the pen. 'Once in a while he does strike out without any apparent provocation, though.'

Studying the spirited horse pacing up and down on the opposite side, head held high into the wind catching the various odours carried by the mountain breeze, Harry turned to Stacy. 'What's that scar on his neck? A rope burn?'

'I don't know,' she answered, noting the faint white line barely visible under the full mane. 'He had it when I bought him.'

Eyeing the slim figure speculatively, Harry demanded, 'Just how the devil are you able to handle him? He could walk over you like you was air.'

'Evidently we have some sort of understanding. Although sometimes I think he just tolerates me,' Stacy laughed, shrugging off the concern in the man's voice. Changing the subject quickly, she asked, 'Are there many trails around here accessible by horseback?'

'Plenty. Most of them either lead deeper into the mountains or into the valley, and a few of them branch out over to the Circle H,' replied Harry, gesturing towards the west.

'Where is the Circle H exactly?' Her hands shaded her eyes from the setting sun. That was one place she intended to avoid.

'This here's Cord's land that the cabin sits on. We just got a lease. It's an abandoned line shack that me and some of my friends use when we go huntin' and fishin'. But if you're referring to the ranch house, that's about nine, ten miles from here. Yep, he's got himself quite a spread. Runs it with an iron hand, he does. But the men don't mind 'cause they always know where they stand with him. He pays good money and expects a good day's work for it.'

Stacy could believe that. He probably rode around with a whip in his hand.

'Molly said you met him at the store,' the ageing man added. ' 'Course, you know he ain't married.'

Stacy made no reply as she watched the sorrel paw at some hay in the lean-to. 'Who could stand him?' she thought to herself.

' 'Bout six years ago, we all thought he'd got himself caught, but the girl up and ran off with some oilwell man. Never did much like the girl. She always thought she was so much better than the folks around here. He's better off without her,' nodded Harry, ignoring the bored look on the girl's face, and kept on talking.

Secretly, Stacy couldn't help but applaud the girl who had managed to set that arrogant cowboy back on his heels, but she didn't show it.

'He fixed up his grandma's hacienda on the place for her, piled a lot of money in it. He lives there alone except for his housekeeper.' Moving away from the fence, Harry started towards his jeep. 'Well, if I want to get home 'fore dark, I'd better mosey along. If there's anything you need, you be sure to let us know.'

'I will, Mr. Nolan. And thanks for all you've done. I really appreciate it,' Stacy said, shaking his hand warmly.

She stood in front of the cabin and watched the jeep drive off on the faint trail into the stand of trees. The solitude encompassed her as she lost sight of the jeep in the gathering shadows. Cajun came up behind her and shoved his moist nose in her hands. Kneeling down, she rumpled the hair on his neck roughly.

'I'm not alone, am I? Not as long as I have you around, huh?' Stacy smiled, and looked towards the cabin door. 'Let's go fix us something to eat.'

CHAPTER THREE

THE sun was streaming over the meadow when Stacy walked out of the cabin door to watch the golden haze cover the meadow. The valley was filled with the songs of birds trilling their greeting to the new day. The sun's rays were striking the rippling brook, turning it into a ribbon of shimmering quicksilver. Inhaling the brisk, clear air, Stacy emitted a satisfied sigh. Then, clicking to the Shepherd standing beside her, she walked over to the corral.

Two days had passed since she had first came to the mountain cabin. The first day Stacy had spent unpacking and settling in. The tack had to be cleaned, as well as the horse trailer and sports car that was dusty from travelling over the gravel roads. She had taken an evening ride down the meadow to give the moody sorrel some exercise and accustom him to the change of climate. The second day she explored the mountains to the east of her, spending most of the day away from the cabin. The scenery continually took her breath away. Never had she travelled so far without finding any trace of civilization except an occasional herd of cattle in the valleys below. Surprisingly enough the evenings had passed rather swiftly for the young girl. After cooking her meal, feeding the horse and dog, she had sat out on the porch until the evening light faded.

It was so restful that, for the first time in several weeks, Stacy felt at peace. Surrounded by the natural serenity of the valley, the worries and grief that had plagued her before seemed non-existent. Nothing mattered but being alive. She knew she had done the right thing in alienating herself from the rest of the world. But part of her never wanted to leave, even though she knew she would have to eventually.

Last evening she had written Carter a letter letting him know she had arrived safely and was settling in. This morning she planned to ride along the main road to find a rancher's mailbox so that she wouldn't have to go into town to post it. She hadn't noticed one on the drive to the cabin, but then she had been concentrating on the road and the vehicle in front of her.

Entering the side gate of the corral near the lean-to,

Stacy got the bridle out of the shed and started to approach the red horse who began retreating to the far side of the enclosure. Ignoring the flashing white feet and the small pointed ears that kept flicking back and forth, she walked up to the horse. Snorting, the sorrel lashed out half-heartedly with his front hooves and dashed to the other side of the pen. Arrogantly he looked back at Stacy, tossing his head defiantly.

'All right, Diablo, let's don't play hard to get this morning,' Stacy said, walking slowly towards the horse. 'It's too lovely a morning to work up a sweat catching you.'

The horse stood uneasily as she approached, still talking to him in her soft voice. He eyed her apprehensively as she stopped in front of him and extended her hand. Diablo stretched his small muzzle to her hesitantly and after a little investigation, blew into her hand gently. Docilely he submitted to the bit and bridle and stood quietly, the reins dangling on the ground, while Stacy fetched the blanket and saddle. Stacy never knew how Diablo was going to react to the saddle, sometimes he accepted it calmly and other times he acted like a yearling that had never seen one before. Cinching up, Stacy led the quiet horse out into the yard before mounting. Whistling to Cajun, she started her mount down the trail towards the main road. The sorrel pranced a little as the Shepherd ran alongside, but offered Stacy no trouble.

The sun's rays peeping through the cover of branches danced on the coppery red coat of the horse accenting the whiteness of the rider's blouse. Cajun raced ahead investigating all the sights and sounds of the trail. Acknowledging her sorrel's desire to run, Stacy nudged the horse into a canter. They continued at a ground-eating lope until they reached the main

road. Here Stacy slowed the horse to a trot, turning
him in the direction of town. Diablo resented the
slowed pace and began side-stepping and pulling his
head in an attempt to loosen the tight rein. She was
unable to admire the scenery as she fought to control
her horse. Cajun still led the way, but checked back to
make sure his mistress was with him. Stacy's whole attention was devoted to her mount that had begun to
rear and plunge around. It was then that she noticed
the saddle slipping. The cinch had loosened during
the ride from the cabin.

Pulling the horse to a stop, she dismounted. But
Diablo had abandoned the earlier docility at the cabin
and refused to let her near him. His white feet lashed
out, preventing her from approaching him. Slowly
Stacy tried to edge her way up the reins to the horse's
head, only to have him pull away with his superior
strength. Concentrating on trying to quiet the fractious horse, she didn't hear the car coming down the
road behind her until it was within a hundred feet. As
she turned to see where the vehicle was, Diablo bolted
past her, but was pulled up short by the quick thinking of the girl as she yanked the reins hard, forcing the
horse to turn in a half circle.

With the noise of the car and the normal misbe-
haviour of the animal, the sorrel became completely
unmanageable. Ignoring the car that had stopped just
a few feet away, Stacy concentrated on preventing the
horse from breaking away. With the endless open
space before her, she knew she would never be able to
catch him once he escaped. In the mood he was in now,
he would run for miles before stopping.

From the corner of her eye, Stacy recognized the
dark, towering figure that had climbed out of the car
and was walking towards her. Of all people it had to

be Cord Harris. He was the last one she wanted to see just now.

'Looks like you're having a little trouble, Miss Adams,' the low-pitched voice drawled.

'Brilliant observation,' Stacy said sarcastically, puffing from the exertion of holding the high-strung animal.

Walking up behind her, the man took the reins out of her hands and motioned for her to move back. At the sight of a stranger on the other end of the reins, Diablo renewed his battle for freedom, but he was no match for the determined man. Dodging the flying hooves, Cord grabbed the cheek strap of the bridle and hauled the horse down on all four feet. Gradually the sorrel settled down, tossing his head and snorting occasionally.

Stacy gazed at the broad, muscular shoulders underneath the tan jacket the man was wearing and watched as he ran his hand down the horse's neck. She couldn't imagine anyone being able to win in a fight with this forceful man. Just then he turned his head and met her searching gaze. As much as she wanted to, she couldn't keep from staring into the dark eyes that smouldered with a strange, deep fire. He was the one who broke the silence.

'I would recommend you get yourself another horse. He's more than a slip of a girl can handle.'

'Thank you, but I didn't ask for your advice, nor did I ask for your help,' Stacy retorted, hating the fact that she was beholden to this man.

'It didn't look to me like you were doing a very good job,' he replied coldly, his mouth turning up in a mocking smile. 'But then, maybe I had the wrong idea.'

'I would have been able to handle him if you hadn't

driven up in that noisy thing,' she said, gesturing defiantly at the sleek gold and brown Continental behind her, 'and worried him more than he already was.'

'I didn't realize I needed your permission to drive down a public road,' drawled Cord Harris, the sarcasm heavy in his voice as his eyes flashed at her. 'If your horse is scared of traffic, perhaps you shouldn't be riding him where he's bound to meet it.'

'I'm sorry, I shouldn't have said that,' Stacy said bitterly. He had done her a favour and she wasn't exactly behaving properly. 'He's a little temperamental sometimes, and this happened to be one of those times.'

'I hope they don't happen very often or I'll be finding you lying dead somewhere out on the range the next time he throws you.'

'Oh, he didn't throw me,' Stacy corrected. 'I got off to tighten the cinch.'

'Oh,' he said, a frown creasing his forehead as he turned to the saddle. 'I apologize to your horsemanship, then, because I assumed the two of you had parted company a little more dramatically.'

'No,' Stacy laughed, 'though I admit we have a time or two!'

She walked up to fondle the horse's head while Cord proceeded to tighten the girth on the saddle. Turning back to face the girl, he rested his arm on the saddlehorn. Self-consciously, Stacy felt his eyes on her and turned to meet them, but he turned away quickly before she could read the expression written there. When he looked back, his face revealed nothing of his thoughts and Stacy looked away this time, feeling herself redden under his eyes.

'Where were you heading, any place special?' he asked.

'I was looking for a mailbox,' Stacy replied hurriedly, trying to cover the sudden unexplainable blush.

'A mailbox!' Cord laughed scornfully. 'Just where did you intend to find a mailbox out here?'

'No, I mean a mailbox for a ranch where the mailman delivers and picks up their mail,' defended Stacy, her dislike for the arrogant man returning once more.

'Well, I'm sorry to disillusion you, Miss Adams, but there aren't any between here and town,' he said, one side of his mouth curling up in disdain. 'You forget that this part of the country lacks a few of the luxuries that city people consider necessities.'

'I didn't know,' she said hotly, her temper rising, 'and I don't think it's very amusing of you to degrade a person because of their ignorance.'

'I'm not trying to degrade you,' Cord said calmly, unruffled by the fiery figure standing defiantly before him. 'I'm merely pointing out that you would be more comfortable if you would go back where you belong.'

'Mr. Harris, I don't think it's any of your business where I may or may not belong, and I would appreciate it if you would get out of my way so that I may have the pleasure of bidding you good-bye!'

Glowering down at her from his greater height, Cord Harris seemed about to say something, but clamped his mouth shut in a grim line. Although already regretting her hasty words, Stacy felt compelled to raise her chin to emphasize her stand. They stood glaring at each other for a few minutes and then, without warning, the rancher swooped her up in his arms.

'Allow me the privilege of helping you on your way,' he said fiercely, holding her in an iron grip against his chest.

So astounded was she by his action that Stacy didn't even attempt to struggle but lay in his arms, her heart beating wildly. She realized that she was playing with fire, crossing this man. Effortlessly, he deposited her in the saddle of the sorrel, tossing the reins over the horse's head. Catching them, she looked down at his blazing eyes.

'That's what you wanted, wasn't it?' the mocking face said darkly.

Regaining some of her composure, Stacy retorted, 'As I said before, Mr. Harris, I didn't ask for your help.'

'You'll find people around here don't ask—for anything. If they want to do something, they do it.'

Diablo, sensing the tension in the air, began dancing about. Stacy could think of no answer to Cord's cryptic words and felt sure that anything she said would only make the situation worse. She didn't want to incur his wrath again. The consequences were too unpredictable with a man like him. With as much poise as she could muster she reined the sorrel around the imposing figure. She could feel his eyes on her as she urged the horse into a trot back up the road she had just come down. Burning in humiliation, she longed to gallop away from those haunting eyes, but her pride insisted on an orderly retreat.

Stacy had to steel herself to keep from looking back. Finally she heard the car door slam and the motor start. Immediately she kicked the sorrel into a gallop. She didn't allow the horse to slow down until they had reached the turn-off to the cabin.

By the time the three reached the house, Stacy's humiliation had turned to anger. He had no right to treat her like that! His overbearing manner was outrageous and interfering. He acted as if he had a right to tell her what to do. Fuming, she unsaddled the fidgety horse, flinging the saddle and bridle in the shed with an unusual disregard for their care. She stomped out of the corral, closing the gate vehemently, and continued her pace to the porch of the cabin. The dog sensed the mood she was in and scurried off to a corner of the building under the shade.

Disgustedly, Stacy sat in the chair on the porch and gazed moodily at the quiet meadow. She shuddered as she recalled Cord's arms around her. She could still smell the masculine odour of his cologne that was clinging to her blouse. If only she had struggled or fought with him or done anything instead of just lying so passively in his arms, submitting herself to his will! She could have at least scratched those rugged features or pulled his dark hair. Never again would she allow herself to be so weak-kneed in his presence. If she ever met him again, she vowed, she would tell him exactly what she thought of him.

The serenity of the valley meadow failed to comfort her wounded pride. The peace she had felt earlier in the morning was gone and the inactivity of just sitting only increased her agitation. Finally she rose and entered the cabin. It was almost noon, but she had no appetite. Grabbing her swim suit, she changed clothes and, with a terrycloth jacket over her shoulder, started down to the brook that ran through the meadow. Perhaps an icy dip in the mountain stream would cool her temper.

Not far from the cabin the stream widened just deep enough and wide enough to enable her to swim. Kicking off her sandals, Stacy dived into the water. Cajun had followed her at a safe distance and settled himself under a shade tree to watch over his mistress. She splashed around for nearly an hour before pulling herself exhaustedly on to the bank. Propping herself up against the tree with Cajun, she lit a cigarette and relaxed. The afternoon sun started making its way across the sky, but still the two sat under the tree. The exertion of her swim had calmed her nerves, but it hadn't taken away the loathing she felt for the arrogant rancher. She toyed with the idea of returning home, but dismissed it quickly when she remembered Cord Harris's mocking smile as he said, 'Go back where you belong.' Never would Stacy give him that satisfaction.

'We're going to stay, Cajun, and what's more, we're going to enjoy ourselves. No more are we going to avoid Mr. Harris's ranch. If he doesn't like it, well then, that's just too bad,' asserted Stacy, rising to her feet. 'Tomorrow, though, I'd better go into town and post that letter before Carter sends a search party after us.'

The two started back for the cabin, Cajun trotting contentedly behind the heels of his mistress. Stacy's spirits rose as she walked. Her stride had a little spring in it and her face wore a satisfied expression. She was convinced that any future confrontation with Cord Harris would not find her coming out second best.

The next morning Stacy overslept, awakening at the persistence of the Shepherd's nuzzling. Hurriedly she had dressed and made coffee. She had hoped to get an early start into town. Just as quickly she fed the dog and gave the sorrel some oats and fresh hay before donning the shirt that matched her yellow slacks. Ordering Cajun to stay at the cabin, Stacy hopped into her black Jaguar and started down the trail to the main road.

She increased her speed, as she turned towards town. This time she was able to look a little more at the view around her. The tall stone mountains seemed to rise out of the prairie as they reached for the sky, their peaks changing into a dark grey contrasting the tans and greens of the plains below. The panoramic view was breathtaking. An occasional greasewood tree dotted the horizon with an exclamation point.

As the car passed the bend in the road where Stacy had had her run-in with Cord Harris yesterday, its speed increased perceptibly. Stacy didn't want to be reminded of that episode and was glad that she could hurry by it. But her spirits were dampened by merely passing the place, causing her to ignore the scenery and concentrate on the road. It was difficult to escape the image of those dark, compelling eyes that had watched her so intently as she sat astride her horse the day before. Their sardonic gleam remained indelible on her memory along with the tanned, sculptured face and dark, almost black hair.

A little over a half hour went by before Stacy reached the town of McCloud. The streets were fairly quiet with only a few people walking from store to store. She parked her sports car in front of the post office. As she climbed out of the car she removed the letter from her purse before walking into the brick building. Nodding a good morning to the clerk in the mail room, Stacy dropped her letter in the outgoing mail slot. She started to leave and then hesitated. Turning around, she walked back to the counter in the mail room.

'Excuse me, is there any mail here for Stacy Adams?' she inquired.

'You're the young lady that rented Nolan's hunting lodge, aren't you?' the quiet voice drawled. 'Yes, you had a letter, but I gave it to Cord to drop off to you. You've met him, haven't you? He said he knew you and since he's your neighbour, it seemed natural.'

'You gave *him* my letter?' Stacy was astounded. 'He knew I would be coming into town.'

'Maybe it just slipped his mind,' offered the middle-aged man. 'He'll probably drop it over to the cabin today. People are pretty neighbourly around here.'

'In the future, please hold my mail here until I come personally to pick it up,' Stacy said, checking her rising temper. The clerk had obviously thought he was doing her a favour, so she really couldn't blame him.

'Yes, ma'am,' he replied, eyeing her quizzically.

With a quiet thank-you, Stacy turned away from the counter and walked out the door. Reaching the sidewalk, she stopped and hesitated for a minute. She decided that it would only be polite to stop in and talk to Mrs. Nolan and thank her for all the extra work she had gone to at the cabin.

As she walked into the grocery store, she noticed Molly talking to a young, red-haired woman with two spirited youngsters tugging at her skirt. When Mrs. Nolan recognized Stacy coming in, her face immediately broke into a smile that reached all the way to her eyes. The young woman beside her also turned to meet Stacy. Her smile held as much welcome as Molly Nolan's.

'Stacy, I was wondering how you were gettin' along,' the elder woman said, walking up to take both of Stacy's hands in her own. 'Cord said he met you on the road yesterday and you seemed to think you were doing all right.'

'Yes, I'm doing fine,' Stacy replied, biting her lip to keep from making a caustic comment about Cord Harris. 'And I love the cabin. Mr. Nolan told me about all the decorating you did to make it more feminine, and I want to thank you.'

'Well, don't thank just me, thank my daughter, too,' Molly said, indicating the redhead beside her. 'I'm glad you stopped in, because I was really lookin' for-

ward to you two meetin'. Mary, this is Stacy Adams, as
you must have guessed. And this is my daughter, Mary
Buchanan.'

'I'm so pleased to meet you at last. Mother has
talked of nothing else, but that "lovely young girl"
living all alone in the cabin, and she didn't quite do
you justice,' the young woman smiled, extending a
hand to Stacy.

'Thank you,' Stacy replied. 'Your mother has really
made me feel at home.'

'I think she'll always be the mother-hen type looking
after her chicks regardless of whether they're hers or
not,' teased Mary, smiling affectionately at the woman
beside her. 'As you must have guessed, these two Indians here are mine. This is Jeff and this is Dougal.'

Stacy knelt down to shake hands with the two young
boys.

"You're awful pretty,' Jeff said, scrutinizing the
golden-brown hair that fell becomingly around the oval
face smiling back at him. ' 'Most prettier than Mom.'

'Well, thank you,' Stacy laughed.

'You have conquered him,' Mary smiled, gazing at
her oldest son with pride. 'But then he always had
good taste. Takes after his father.'

'Naturally,' said Mary, 'and don't ever forget it!'

'That's Mom, always reminding me what a catch I
made, as if I would forget,' Mary grinned. 'Are you in
a hurry or anything? Why don't you come over to my
house for coffee?'

'That would be wonderful, said Stacy, warming to
the friendliness of the attractive woman. 'My car's
parked right out front and——'

'Good, we walked down here and now we can beg a
ride back,' Mary said with a bewitching smile. 'We
only live a few blocks away.'

'You two run along then,' said Molly Nolan, 'so I can get back to work. Take care of these two boys. And don't let them eat all that candy I gave them.'

Mary directed Stacy to her home, a beautiful ranch-type house with a large fenced yard. The boys brawled out of the car reluctantly, wishing the ride could have lasted longer.

'They really got a thrill out of riding in your car. They'll remember that for ages,' said Mary, opening the front door and waiting for Stacy to enter first.

'I enjoyed it, too,' Stacy answered as she followed the other girl into a big, spacious kitchen. 'As trite as it sounds, I love children.'

'Well, I'm not going to make that natural comeback of "wait until you have some of your own", because I love mine and wouldn't change them for the world,' Mary agreed, heating coffee for the two of them. 'Mothers that moan and groan about all the trouble their children make almost drive me up the walls.'

'I know what you mean, although I'm not too experienced on the subject,' Stacy said, sitting down at the table.

'Tell me, do you have someone waiting back home?'

'Sort of,' said Stacy, remembering Carter Mills and his recent proposal.

'Sort of? You mean, he hasn't popped the question and you've come out here to make him see how much he misses you?' Mary concluded as she joined Stacy at the table with the coffee. 'Cream or sugar?'

'No, black,' Stacy answered. 'He did propose before I left, but I'm not sure if I want to get married just yet.'

'Do you love him?'

'I suppose so. I've never dated anyone else but him. We just knew each other so well that——'

'I see what you mean,' Mary nodded. 'I suppose with

the loss of your father and all, you didn't want to make any rash decisions.'

'Partly,' Stacy sighed.

'Maybe being apart will help you decide how much you really do care for him,' suggested Mary, realizing that the girl beside her was confused. 'Fortunately, there never was any doubt for me as to how I felt about Bill. He's the doctor here. The minute he got into town and took over old Doc Gibbon's practice, I knew he was the man I wanted to marry. I was almost twenty-two by then and had dated my share of men.'

'I wonder if that's my problem. Travelling with my father on his various photography assignments the way I did, I was never in any one place long enough to meet people my age.' It was comforting to be able to confide in Mary, a comparative stranger. 'And when I got back to town I always had Carter to fall back on. I admit I did have a crush on one of the reporters Dad worked with,' Stacy chuckled.

'I guess everyone has those,' Mary laughed. 'I had it bad for Cord Harris. I used to chase him all over.'

'*Cord Harris?*'

'Yes. Every girl around here has fallen under his spell at one time or another. He used to be quite the playboy,' said Mary, a smile playing at the corners of her mouth.

'That woman-hater? I can't imagine him being polite to anyone!' commented Stacy.

'I assure you he's not a woman-hater. He's a little bitter after that dirty deal Lydia Marshall pulled on him. But it's only a matter of time before some girl breaks through that thin veneer of his, and then you'll see what I'm talking about. When he turns the charm on, nobody is immune,' Mary concluded with a shake of her titian hair.

'You're looking at one girl who is immune,' Stacy. said vehemently. 'He is beyond doubt the most arrogant, despicable man I've ever had the misfortune to meet!'

'I see he's made a distinct impression on you.' Mary hid a smile with difficulty. 'I think you may have judged him a little too quickly. Ignoring his superb good looks and his great six-foot-four frame, you'll still find he has all the requirements of a good husband and father. And if that isn't enough, he owns the biggest ranch around and runs it with a profit.'

'That's all well and good, but I still pity the woman that ever marries him. He didn't hesitate to form a hasty opinion of me, and I don't intend to turn the other cheek.'

'Whew! The sparks must fly when you two get together,' Mary exclaimed, amused and puzzled. 'Funny, I thought you two would hit it off rather well.'

'Well, we don't,' Stacy said, hoping to close the subject. She couldn't bring herself to confide in this understanding girl about yesterday's episode. The humiliation was too fresh in her mind to talk about.

It was the middle of the afternoon before she bade the friendly family good-bye and promised to stop the next time she came to town.

In less than an hour, the young girl was back at her cabin being greeted by the wildly thumping tail of the Shepherd. Happily the two entered the cabin. While Stacy was preparing their supper, she noticed a note on the table. Walking over to pick it up, she saw an envelope underneath it. Quickly she read the note.

'So sorry I missed you,' it read. 'I took the liberty of bringing your mail.

C.H.'

'The nerve of that man!' Stacy said aloud, ripping the note into shreds and throwing it into the fireplace. ' "So sorry I missed you." Hmph!' she muttered, returning to the stove. 'Well, I'm not!'

After eating, she took her coffee out to the porch and read the letter from Carter in the waning light.

CHAPTER FOUR

THE late afternoon sun cast a long shadow of horse and rider picking their way through the rocky foothills. The red horse pranced a little as a lizard darted across their path, but responded to the quiet words from the rider on his back. From an arroyo on their left came the German Shepherd to rejoin his mistress.

Stacy called a hello to the dog and urged the horse into a canter on to the opening flatland. A smile rose on her lips as she turned to survey her backtrail with satisfaction. To her there could be nothing as beautiful as this untamed land. She was glad she had finally decided to trespass on the Circle H home range. The scenery was fantastic in its undisciplined beauty. Pulling the stallion up near some greasewood bushes, she dismounted to sit in their shade and gaze at the panoramic view before her.

After removing the flat gaucho hat, she dusted her white blouse off. They had been exploring since midmorning and even though she could feel the tiring of her muscles, she was still exhilarated by the wonderful country she had seen. She glanced at her watch and knew that when she remounted she would have to go directly back to the cabin in order to make it before sundown. After dark she might have trouble finding her way back.

Her thoughts turned to the letter she received yesterday from Carter. She knew he wouldn't be so eager for her to return if he were here beside her to enjoy all this scenery. And return she would have to. She couldn't cut herself away from the rest of the world indefinitely. Nature in all its harsh beauty had brought this realization to her today. She had decided during her ride that she would return in two or three weeks. This would be her vacation. She was sure that was the way her father would have wanted it. She'd get a job somewhere, maybe in a travel bureau. If not she would find something else.

But marriage? No, she wasn't ready for that, she thought as she shook her head. She cared too much for Carter to grab at the straw of escape he offered her. When they married, or rather when she married, Stacy knew she wanted to put her whole heart into it and the family that would come. She could only hope that Carter would understand that she wanted herself whole again before they made any life together.

Standing up, she faced the gentle breeze ruffling her long hair and smiled as she inhaled the fresh air. Life was good and there wasn't any sense in worrying about things that hadn't happened. Crossing over to the sorrel, she picked up the reins. Remounting, she whistled to the dog and turned her horse into the mountains from which they had come.

The horse broke into an eager trot, refreshed by the brief rest in the meadow. Stacy captured his spirit and eased her hold on the reins. The horse immediately moved into a rocking lope. As they reached the rock-strewn foothills, his gait slowed to a fast walk as he picked his way. Cajun followed not far behind. Stacy turned for one last look at the grassland she had left.

At that moment, with Stacy turned and off-balance in the saddle, a rattlesnake resting underneath a near-by bush sounded his warning. Before Stacy could turn around, Diablo was screaming, rearing high into the air. His terror was beyond restraint as he shook his head violently, protesting Stacy's instant tightening of the reins. Spinning in a half rear towards the flatland, the stallion unseated his light rider completely. As Stacy lost her grip and tumbled off, the horse bolted, taking his avenue of escape.

Unable to break her fall, Stacy landed heavily on her shoulders. Her neck snapped back at the impact, striking her head on a rock. Pain seared through her body. Valiantly she attempted to fight the unconscious-ness that threatened her. She struggled up on one el-bow, catching a glimpse of Diablo streaking across the meadow with his tail high. Vaguely she recognized the Shepherd racing towards her before she succumbed to the promising relief of blackness.

Frowning, Stacy turned slightly to look where the voice had come from. With difficulty she forced her eyes to focus on the smiling face hovering above her.

'Where am I? My father, is he——' she started, her brown eyes glancing around the unfamiliar setting in panic. Then she closed her eyes and added, 'I remem-ber now. I fell.'

'Don't try to talk,' admonished the doctor. 'You've had a bad fall, but you're going to be fine. I'm Dr. Buchanan, Mary's husband.'

Attempting a smile at the recognized name, Stacy tried to speak. 'Is Mary here?'

'No, you're at the Circle H. Cord Harris found you

and brought you to his ranch. You owe him a great
debt.'

'No!' Stacy cried, feebly struggling to rise from the
bed. 'I can't stay here, I can't!'

'Now listen, young lady,' the doctor said, gently restraining her movement. 'You need rest. The best
place for you right now is in this bed.'

Pleadingly she looked into his face, her eyes clouding with tears as she desperately willed him to change
his mind. His returning gaze was adamant. Involuntarily her eyes turned to the doorway that was now
blocked by Cord. It was impossible to tell how long he
had been there, his fierce gaze taking in both parties.

'Oh, why,' she sobbed helplessly, 'why did you have
to be the one who found me?'

'I assure you I wasn't out looking for you,' was the
caustic reply. 'I found your horse running loose and
backtracked him.'

'That's enough talking,' interrupted Dr. Buchanan.
'It's time you rested.'

Not having the strength to fight either her unwanted
host or the doctor's orders, Stacy turned her face from
both of them and allowed the frustration and pain to
sweep her away. The two men's eyes locked over the
girl, the rancher's defiant and unflinching, the other's
probing and questioning.

'I think we should leave her to rest in quiet,' the
doctor suggested, gathering up his instruments.

It was late evening before Stacy woke again. She lay
quietly in the bed and studied her surroundings with
a little more interest. The bedroom was masculine
with heavy Spanish furniture and bold, definite colours. She couldn't help wondering if this was the
rancher's bedroom. It seemed stamped with the same

austere personality that branded Cord Harris. Dark mahogany beams coursed the ceiling, accenting the white, textured paint. The coarse-grained effect was carried through in the curtains with their loose-weave tweed in reds and oranges that was repeated in the coverlet on her bed.

Stacy pushed herself into a sitting position in the bed, fighting off the wave of nausea that followed the movement. She was wearing a nightgown. The realization shocked her as she looked down at the yellow bodice. How and when had she changed? Who had helped her? Her face crimsoned at the thought of the muscular Texan. It was even her own nightgown. How had he come into possession of it? Unless, of course, he had sent someone after her things. But he wouldn't dare have the nerve to touch her!

'Well, I see you've returned to us. I thought you were going to sleep all through the night,' came a low voice from the doorway.

Stacy's eyes snapped up to face her unexpected visitor, her cheeks still blushing. 'What time is it?' Stacy stammered, unnerved at seeing the man who had been occupying her thoughts.

'After eight,' Cord replied, pulling up a chair beside her bed and gazing at her intently. His voice held no trace of the sarcasm she associated with him as he asked, 'How are you feeling?'

'Better,' she replied, unable to meet his penetrating eyes. 'I want to thank you for all you've done. I——'

'There's no need. I consider myself lucky that I spotted your horse. I hate to think how long you might have lain out there before you were found.' His low voice still carried that gentle tone that was so unfamiliar to her and did such strange things to her heart. 'Here, let me fix those pillows for you.'

Self-consciously Stacy allowed him to add another pillow behind her head. Aware of his nearness, she glanced up to his face, taking in the clear cut of his jaw and soft firmness of his mouth, but refusing to look above the high cheekbones at the dark, unfathomable eyes. She caught the scent of his cologne which she remembered so vividly from their encounter on the road. It was difficult to ignore the muscular chest and arms encased in the crisp white shirt. Stacy was sure he could hear the wild beating of her heart and cursed the way his physical presence could arouse her.

'Isn't that more comfortable?' said Cord, reseating himself in his chair. A smile was showing faintly on his mouth as if acknowledging the girl's embarrassment at his nearness. He couldn't fail to detect the flush growing in her cheeks as she sat silently with downcast eyes. 'Perhaps, Stacy, we should try to begin again,' he said, his voice changing to an impersonal tone at her continued absorption with a bow on her gown. 'We got off to a rather bad start. The doctor feels that it's best for you to stay here until you can get back on your feet. As it will only be a temporary situation, it will make it easier for both of us if we ignore our personal feelings.'

Surprised at his open acknowledgement of the unspoken antagonism between them, Stacy looked up into the two dark eyes regarding her so thoughtfully.

'Well, are we friends?'

Hesitantly Stacy placed her slim hand in the outstretched palm. It was engulfed in the large, tanned hand. She felt he held it a little longer than was necessary, yet the suddenness of his release upset her. His brows were now contracted in that old familiar frown and his mouth curled in a whimsical smile as he rose and looked down at her. Once again his size and air of superiority overwhelmed her.

'I imagine you're more interested in getting something to eat than listening to me. I'll send Maria in with some soup and tea,' the dark figure said, moving towards the end of the bed. 'Oh, by the way, your dog is outside and your horse is bedded down in one of our stud pens. I also took the liberty of bringing a few of your things here from the cabin. I hope you don't mind.'

'No,' Stacy answered, surprised at the meekness in her voice.

'Good,' he said, a twinkle now in his eyes. 'In case you were wondering, Maria "prepared" you for bed.'

Indignation rose in her as the tall rancher left the room. 'He's positively insufferable!' she thought. How could she have been taken in by that initial gentleness? Just imagining how he must have been laughing at her all the while he was sitting there angered her further. He was right about one thing—for the time being, she had to compromise until she was on her feet again. The throbbing in her head forced her thoughts to change to quieter things.

By the time the robust housekeeper, Maria, arrived with her food, Stacy's composure had returned, though she was sure her cheeks still retained some of their unnatural colour.

'Ah, the leetle one is feeling much better, no?' smiled the jovial Mexican, placing the tray with a steaming bowl of broth on Stacy's lap. 'The head, eet does not hurt so much?'

'Only a little. The soup smells good,' Stacy replied, inhaling the invigorating aroma of the hot broth. She was hungrier than she had thought. Thankfully Maria left the room and Stacy was allowed to eat at her leisure. She had just finished the last of the tea when the Mexican woman returned for the tray.

'That was very good, Maria,' Stacy smiled, handing the tray to the waiting hands.

'*Gracias*. I cook good. Meester Cord, he say my cooking the best anywhere in Texas.' The large woman giggled at the audacity of the claim.

'Well, perhaps he exaggerated a little, but it was very good,' Stacy laughed.

'You get some more sleep now,' Maria instructed, helping Stacy settle back under the covers. 'We have you up in no time. Doctor say for you to keep warm and rest, but thees bed so beeg you get lost in it. I tell Meester Cord, but he say eet all right. Pooh! You should have a man to keep you warm, not a beeg bed.'

Stacy could feel herself blushing at the woman's advice. She remembered again her impression that this was Cord's bedroom. She had to ask.

'*Si, si,*' the big woman laughed. 'You theenk maybe he sleep here tonight. No, he thought eet better he sleep in office.'

Maria continued her laughing, her belly rolling with the force of her mirth and her fatty underarms bouncing as she carried the tray out of the room. Stacy glanced apprehensively around before putting out the light. Although fearful that she would be unable to sleep, she dropped off almost immediately.

The morning sun was dancing its patterns on the braided rug beside Stacy's bed. Maria had already brought in her breakfast and had helped her clean up. Rather than attempting to brush the hair around her wound, Stacy had merely pulled it back and tied it with a bow to match the bedjacket that had been brought along with her other clothes. She felt much better as long as she ignored the dull pain in her head and the sniffles in her nose. She was just examining the unusual scrollwork in the bedroom door when it opened to admit the smiling face of Cord Harris.

'Good morning. Maria said you were up.' His low voice was cheerful with no trace of sarcasm. 'Do you feel like a visitor?'

'A visitor?' Stacy echoed, trying to think of who would be coming to see her. 'Yes.'

'Okay, feller, come on in,' said Cord, swinging the door wider to admit a cautious German Shepherd.

'Cajun!' Stacy exclaimed happily as the big dog recognized the figure in the bed and bounded to her, his tail wagging happily. With his front paws on the bed, he proceeded to give her a thorough washing with his big tongue. 'Stop it, you silly idiot!'

'I think he's rather pleased to see you. He refused to eat this morning and wouldn't move away from the front door, so I decided the best thing would be to let him see for himself that you were all right,' Cord explained, still standing in the doorway.

'I hope he wasn't too much of a bother,' Stacy said after she had managed to push the Shepherd off the bed and on to the floor where he sat gazing at his mistress with undisguised adoration. 'I'm afraid we're rather attached to each other.'

'I have some work to do around the ranch, so I'll leave the dog here for company. I've instructed Maria to bring you some books from the library. I know we don't have the elegant surroundings you've been accustomed to, but if there's anything else you would like, just ask and we'll see what we can arrange.'

'Thank you,' she replied, wishing she could think of something else to say. 'Everything's fine, really, and I'll try not to be any trouble to you.'

'You won't be—at least, not any more than I can handle,' he replied. The mocking smile returned to his face before Cord left, closing the door behind him.

'Have you ever been "handled" before?' Stacy asked the Shepherd, wondering why Cord had developed such a negative attitude towards her. 'I imagine he thinks he can "handle" anything that comes along!'

A few minutes later Maria arrived with some novels and magazines. Stacy noticed a couple of her favourite books and settled back to read. The day passed rather swiftly. With each knock on the door she half expected to see the rancher appear. When Maria returned for the supper tray that evening and Cord still hadn't come, Stacy decided that he wasn't going to come. Strangely enough, she felt disappointed. She tried to attribute it to her loneliness and desire for company regardless of how arrogant he might be.

CHAPTER FIVE

WITH a contented sigh, Stacy rested her head against the cushion and gave the Shepherd lying beside her an affectionate pat. Her soft brown curls lay carelessly around her neck, touching the edge of the simple orange and yellow shift with its V-neck and capped sleeves. Her tanned legs glistened all the way down to the Roman sandals she wore.

A subtle application of powder hid the slight redness around her straight nose that was the last reminder of the cold that had racked her body with chills and fever the past week. Her recovery had been swift, thanks to the quick action of Dr. Buchanan who had been summoned as soon as the course of her illness became apparent, and had given her medication.

Stacy was so engrossed in her outdoor surroundings that she failed to hear the measured steps entering the cobblestoned veranda until they were a few feet from her. Instantly she recognized the deliberate walk; hadn't she listened for it enough times outside her bedroom door this past week? It belonged to Cord Harris. Looking up, she met the full gaze of the rugged man's dark eyes. Her own travelled over the blue turtle-necked shirt accenting his broad shoulders and muscular arms, then down the trim waist and narrow hips, taking in the black slacks tapering over his dress boots.

So accustomed was she to seeing Cord in ranch wear, Stacy was surprised that he wore the dressy sports clothes with such ease. Most outdoor men she had met always looked uncomfortable in anything other than their everyday wear. She couldn't help noticing that there was no tell-tale sunburn where the hat brim ended nor where the sleeve of his shirt started. He obviously found time to make use of the pool.

Uncomfortably aware that she had been staring, Stacy blushed. A tall glass of iced liquid was held before her by a large, tanned hand. Timidly she accepted it, and her half-raised eyes caught the bemused smile on Cord's face. Though he had noticed Stacy's scrutinizing stare, Cord made no comment as he pulled up a rattan chair beside her.

'You're looking very well,' he said gently, his eyes flicking over her face. 'I hope the drink is satisfactory. I don't know if it's included in the doctor's orders, but it can't do any harm.'

'Thank you. It's fine,' Stacy replied, taking a sip out of the tall glass. Her senses were tingling with the nearness of her host as the smell of shampoo and shaving lotion wafted over to her in the evening breeze.

'I imagine it feels rather good to get outside after being shut in for so long.'

'Yes, it does. You have such a beautiful view. You must be exceptionally proud of your home,' said Stacy, a nervous lilt in her voice. She felt an unaccountable need to keep the conversation going.

'The antiqueness of the hacienda doesn't offend you?'

'Oh, no!' she exclaimed, her eyes widening. 'It's lovely. You must have done a lot of remodelling.'

'Yes, we did. The original hacienda enclosed this area here. It served as a fortress against attacks in the early days. When I decided to remodel it, I eliminated the south and west wings. Even now there's more room than a bachelor needs,' Cord informed her with a smile.

'But when you marry and have children, it will be perfect,' Stacy said as she looked at the whitewashed adobe walls.

'Undoubtedly.' There was a coldness and withdrawal in his tone and his attention was riveted on a distant mountain.

'What I meant was the size——' she stammered.

'I understand what you mean, Miss Adams,' returning his dark, expressionless eyes to her. 'But I don't anticipate that prospect being fulfilled in the near future.'

Obviously he was referring to his star-crossed romance with the girl Mary had spoken about. 'You never know,' Stacy replied a little more brightly than she felt. 'I'm sure there are a lot of girls who are very anxious to change your mind, Mr. Harris.'

'Are you one?' A raised eyebrow disappeared into the black hair curling over his forehead.

'I wasn't referring to myself,' she replied a trifle indignantly.

'It's very romantic-sounding to marry a man who owns a spread the size of this one, but reality is quite another thing,' he continued. 'This is a hard, demanding land even in these advanced times. The hours are long and the results are unpredictable at best. A wife can expect to be alone a great deal, and isolated. As far as entertainment is concerned, it's non-existent with the exception of an occasional social gathering. The same with the large department stores you're accustomed to. Major shopping requires a trip to San Antoine or El Paso. The rigours of this life are more than a city girl would want to cope with.'

'I wasn't applying for the position, Mr. Harris,' Stacy retorted, rising from the chaise with a reddened face.

'Cord,' he supplied, towering over her as he rose. Taking her arm, he steered her towards the pool, his eyes sparkling with amusement. 'Come over here. I want to show you something.'

'What is it?' Her impatience was marked by the sharpness in her voice.

'Really, Miss Adams,' Cord said in a mock scolding voice. 'I would have thought you'd learned by now how to take a little teasing!'

'I have met certain egotistical men who would be vain enough to believe that all women fall at their feet!'

'As I have met women who feel they're the answer to every man's prayer and he should succumb to their charms.' The two had reached the opposite side of the pool and stood facing each other defiantly, his hand still upon her arm. The air between them crackled with the unspoken challenge. His voice was low as he turned to face the horizon. 'Continuing this subject would accomplish nothing. We both have our own views.'

'Precisely,' Stacy said crisply. 'Now if you'll show me whatever it is you wanted me to see, I'll return to my room.'

'You wouldn't be interested.'

'What was it?' Stacy asked, slightly curious despite her annoyance with the arrogant man.

'Only an old family cemetery. I'm sure some ancient gravestones wouldn't interest your sophisticated tastes,' Cord replied sarcastically, his back now turned to her.

'I would like to see it.'

'It's not necessary,' he answered, as if this was an attempt at an apology on Stacy's part.

'Mr. Harris, the last thing I would do is go to patronize you. You said earlier that we should bury the hatchet and be friends. Obviously your wounded ego can't comprehend anything but undying loyalty. Now I would like to see "your" cemetery. If you don't want to accompany me, tell me where it is and I'll go by myself.'

The biting tone of her voice turned Cord towards her, his cool eyes examining her face as if assuring himself of her genuine interest.

'It's only a little way from here, but it's uphill. I wouldn't want you to overdo it your first time out. Perhaps we should postpone it.' At the angry denial forming on Stacy's lips, Cord went on, 'But if you're sure you want to go, I'll go with you.'

'I'm sure.'

'Very well.'

He started to take her arm again, but Stacy shrugged him off and began walking in the direction he had

indicated. Cord followed a step or two behind as they
made their way up the knoll behind the house. The
incline was slight, but in Stacy's weakened condition
she found herself out of breath when they reached the
top. She managed to ignore the sardonic gleam in
Cord's eyes and pushed on towards the wrought iron
enclosure ahead.

The assorted crosses and gravestones were dwarfed
by a large monument in the centre. Years had weathered most of them, but Stacy noticed that the area was
well kept. The grillework, which should have rusted
from age, still had a certain freshness in its black ex-
terior and the ground had been seeded with grass, its
green blanket lovingly covering the graves in a spring
shroud. Cord opened the gate and Stacy walked inside.

The two walked silently on the trodden path
around the dozen headstones before coming to a stop
near the centre. Most of the dates were in the late
1800s and early 1900s. Four of the smaller crosses
marked children's graves. One stone was recent, dated
eight years ago and bore the words 'Stephen Harris—
Father'.

'Is that your father's grave?' Stacy asked quietly, the
word "father" bringing a melancholy to her voice as
the freshness of her own loss washed over her.

'Yes.'

'I didn't notice your mother's. Is she buried here?'

A shadow passed over his face as Cord replied, 'She's
buried back East with her family.' There was a briskness in his voice and a hardness in his eyes. 'She
couldn't stand the ranch and its demands on her and
my father. A few years after I was born she went back
to her family.'

'She left you?' Stacy asked, pity in her heart for the
now dead man and his abandoned son.

'Father gave her no choice,' Cord said, his steel black eyes on her face, rejecting the sympathy he saw. 'I doubt if you'd understand. This is a hard land. You must take what is yours and then fight to keep it. My mother was a pampered child used to being waited on, so the future that was offered meant nothing to her. She wanted the luxuries she was accustomed to and her demands never stopped, not on my father's attention or his money. There wasn't enough of either for her.'

'And the ranch came first,' Stacy murmured astutely.

'Do you see this marker here?' Cord asked, turning to the centre monument. 'Elena Teresa Harris, my grandmother. She was a Spanish aristocrat who fell in love with my grandfather, who was a struggling rancher at that time with a lot of dreams. She was a real woman. He had nothing to offer her but an old adobe three-room house, a few head of cattle and a lot of land that was dry most of the time. But it didn't matter to her.'

There was no denying the respect and admiration in his voice as he spoke. Momentarily he stepped forward and opened the gate for Stacy, following her out. Engrossed in their conversation, she accepted his hand on her arm as they walked to the edge of the knoll looking down on the ranchyard below. With his other hand, Cord pointed towards the western mountains, purpled in the twilight.

'The Mescalero Apaches used those mountains as a stronghold and raided settler and small ranchers at will. And the "Comanche War Trail" is not far from here either. At the turn of the century the Indian menace had ended and this western region was populated by cattlemen seeking these rich pastures where grass was so abundant. Most of the settlers ran more cattle than the land could support—overgrazed it. That's why there's so much desert land out here today.'

'Can't it be reseeded? Left alone to grow back?' There was concern in Stacy's upturned face.

'It's too late for most reclamation. Either the wind carries the seed away, or the rain doesn't come when it's needed, or it washes the seed away before it gets a chance to deepen its roots. Ignorance and greed do more damage to the future than they do to the present,' Cord answered grimly. 'But my father and grandfather realized this. In more than one way, I have them to thank for what I have today.'

'You must be very proud of them,' Stacy said with a smile. 'A lot of things have changed since your grandfather's time.'

'He was a cattleman, tried and true. He'd turn over in his grave if he saw sheep grazing on his land,' Cord chuckled.

'Sheep?' Astonishment was written on Stacy's face. 'You raise sheep?'

'Yes, I have a few hundred head of registered stock on the higher pastures.'

'You don't run them with the cattle?'

'Sometimes, usually in the summer when we move the cattle to the foothills. We also have some Angora goats, but they're in the experimental stages as far as our ranch is concerned. Quite a number of ranchers have had good success with them. And there's our quarter horses. We have two exceptional studs and several young breeding prospects. I've doubled the number of brood mares in the home herd. We have an auction on the grounds every spring, selling some of the yearlings and two-year-olds that we aren't going to keep or older brood mares we want to replace with new blood.'

'I didn't realize you had so many individual enter-
prises,' Stacy mused, awed by the size of the ranch's
operation. 'I suppose there are oil wells, too.'

'No civilized Texas ranch would be complete without them,' Cord laughed quietly at the dazed expression on his companion's face. 'We have four on the
east boundary. Only two are still in operation. Most
all of the ranch property is outside of the oil-producing
region.'

'I'm beginning to understand what the expression
"cattle baron" means,' Stacy commented, looking up
at the bronze face.

'Don't let the magnitude of all of it lull you into
thinking it's an easy life,' he warned her. 'As diversi-
fied as the ranch has grown, it's only increased the
work load and the difficulty of control.'

Stacy grimaced at his words. It was hard to imagine
this powerful man not in control. He was so sure of
what he wanted that nothing would dare stand in his
way.

'Looks like Dr. Buchanan's car driving in,' Cord
went on, watching a station wagon pull up behind the
house below. 'We'd better go down. Marie will probably have dinner ready shortly, anyway.'

Nodding her agreement, Stacy followed him down
the slope. By the time they reached the veranda, the
smiling face of the young doctor was there to greet
them. To Stacy's pleasant surprise, his wife Mary had
accompanied him. The happy red-haired woman
walked forward, arms outstretched to the younger girl.

'You look marvellous!' Mary exclaimed, clasping
Stacy's hands warmly in hers. 'Tell me, Stacy, how
have you two been getting along?' she teased in a low
voice. 'I don't see any battle scars.'

'Cord and I have buried the hatchet, haven't we?'

Stacy replied with a throaty laugh. Glancing at the tall figure standing beside the doctor, she continued, 'We found some common ground that we both agree upon.'

Only the rancher understood the oblique reference to their earlier dialogue about their opinions of each other. Coolly she met his dark eyes, keeping the smile off her lips with difficulty. But in Mary's matchmaking mind, a totally different conclusion was reached.

'Well, this is news,' Bill Buchanan remarked. 'The last time I was here, Stacy, you couldn't wait to leave.' With a grin on his boyish face, he added to Cord, 'Maybe my patient's suffering a relapse.'

'I think she's just recognizing some of the attractions that can be found here,' Cord replied, quirking his mouth into a smile. 'With a girl as pretty as Stacy, I'll have to act as a guide myself to keep the young men from falling under her spell.'

Stacy caught the emphasis on her name, realizing he had noticed she had used his Christian name for the first time. Deliberately she met his mocking gaze and taunting words.

Stacy couldn't explain, even to herself, why she had referred to the angry words they had had before. She had enjoyed the easy companionship on the hill and the informative talk. Why had she taunted him? Did she feel safer with his mocking words and sarcastic smile? Pointedly she turned the conversation to Mary's two children. Several times she felt Cord's eyes searching her face, but she deliberately avoided looking at him.

'I'm afraid we're rather poor hosts, Cord,' she murmured, trying to cover the confusion he was causing by standing so close to her. Unaccountably, her hand drifted on his arm. 'We didn't offer the doctor and Mary something to drink.'

There was a darting look of surprise in Cord's eyes as he looked at the upturned face, but it was quickly suppressed by a smile to his guests. Guiltily she dropped her hand.

'I'll have Maria bring us something. Anything special you'd like, Bill, Mary?'

'No,' Bill laughed. 'Anything tall and cool will do.'

Cord left them for a moment to arrange for the refreshments. During that time Mary and her husband seated themselves in two of the garden chairs while Stacy settled on the cushioned settee. A few minutes later Cord returned followed by the plump Mexican woman carrying a tray laden with drinks and hors d'oeuvres. To Stacy's chagrin, Cord sat on the settee with her. Her annoyance escaped the other couple's attention amidst the confusion of accepting the refreshments Maria offered, but the one-sided smile on Cord's lips indicated that he had noticed her dismay.

To Stacy's relief, the conversation remained on a light vein. Several times she was uncomfortably aware of the dark brown eyes studying her and the magnetic closeness of the outstretched arm on the back of the couch. Mary, with her naturally lively personality, monopolized most of the conversation with anecdotes of the children, but gradually the subject turned to Stacy and her accident.

'When Bill told me that day about your fall, I practically insisted on bringing you into town with us,' Mary chattered. 'But he assured me it was better to leave you here where you would have ample opportunity to rest.'

'Actually what I said was "peace and quiet",' inserted the doctor with a smile. 'That's something hard to come by in our house.'

'He's always complaining about the boys,' explained

Mary, 'but he loves them as much as I do. Anyway, I can see how right he was. You look the picture of health. Of course, with this kind of scenery who would want to stay in bed?'

There was a twinkle in Mary's eyes as she gave Cord a sideways glance. Hastily Stacy spoke up, not wanting the innuendo to go any further.

'This is a beautiful ranch,' she rushed. 'The whole land around here is fascinating. It reminds you what little time has passed since it was a frontier.'

'Texas history is fascinating,' agreed the blue-eyed doctor.

'Were you at the cemetery when we came?' Mary directed at Cord. Without waiting for his affirmative nod, she continued, 'I wish you could have met his grandmother, Stacy. She was a wonderful old woman. You never thought of her as old, though. She was much too vital and active. I was only nine or ten when she died, but I remember her so well.'

'Cord told me a little about her,' Stacy said.

'She was remarkable. Somewhere amongst all her Spanish ancestry she inherited a pioneer spirit that was indefatigable,' Mary went on. 'But there was a certain way about her—the way she carried her head or looked deep inside you—that reminded you of her blue blood. My mother always said Doña Elena was the only one able to handle Cord.' In a conspiratorial aside to Stacy, she added, 'He was really a terror as a child—fantastic temper!'

Cord chuckled at Mary's words. 'You forgot to mention Grandmother's temper. I've always thought she cared so much for me because I inherited her temper.' In a mockingly tender tone, he added for Stacy's benefit, 'Thank heaven, I've learned to control it.'

'I'm afraid, Cord, there've been a few times when

you've caused us to doubt your words,' Bill Buchanan smiled with a dubious shake of his head. 'Don't get me wrong, Stacy, I'm sure the right woman would be able to deal with him, but I would hate to be on the receiving end of his temper when it does go out of control.'

Embarrassed by the sly matchmaking of the married couple and the recollection of the controlled display he had shown that day on the road, Stacy murmured a vague response. Thankfully, she was interrupted by Maria announcing that dinner was ready.

'You will be joining us, won't you?' Cord asked. Mary began to make an excuse, but Cord interjected, 'I'm not taking no for an answer. It's too seldom we have social visits and we won't let you go away so soon, will we, Stacy?'

He extended a hand to her which she was unable to refuse without being obvious. Distracted by his touch, Stacy half heard the lighthearted banter and acceptance by the pair. She felt herself being ushered into the dining room behind them, the tall shoulder of the rancher brushing against her. Her muscles tensed as she stifled a desire to pull violently away from him.

She had baited him at first about their earlier quarrel and became a little personal, acting as hostess when she herself was only a guest. Playing the little charade had amused Stacy at first as she had enjoyed seeing the surprised look in Cord's eyes. But now she had the distinct feeling that he was laughing at her. Somehow he had succeeded in turning the tables on her, making her the brunt of the joke. And she wasn't enjoying it at all.

As if he had read her mind, Cord whispered to her as he seated her at the table, 'You should have checked the rules.'

Stacy's brown eyes looked apprehensively into his,

but she couldn't find any words to answer him. His expression as he seated himself opposite her at the head of the table was pleasant, but his eyes hardened speculatively as he watched her flushed cheeks turn away to respond to a question from Mary. Twice during the meal Stacy was forced to look away from the probing glance of the aquiline face. The dinner seemed to last so long that she was sure it would never end. She was so tense she felt she was sitting on a lighted powder-keg that would explode at any moment. But when Maria served the coffee and dessert the conversation was still on safe topics. A tide of relief washed over her at the end in sight.

'Hey, come back!' Mary teased, waving a hand in front of Stacy. 'Didn't you hear what I said?'

'I'm sorry, Mary, I'm afraid I was daydreaming.'

'I was wondering if your accident had changed your plans, about staying?'

'No, not really,' Stacy replied, avoiding Cord's interested look. 'I'll be staying a couple more weeks before going back.'

'I'm afraid our country is a little too hard on her,' Cord interposed with a smile. 'After all, Mary, we were raised here and are used to it, but Stacy is from the East. I imagine it's a little tame and boring around here.'

'That's not true at all,' Stacy retorted impatiently.

'It's just that there's no future here for you, isn't that it?' A sarcastic smile played on Cord's mouth.

'Yes—I mean no,' stammered Stacy, recognizing that she was under a subtle attack.

'Now, Cord——' Mary began.

'Surely you realize that the newness of the adventure has probably worn off for her,' he interrupted. 'After all, how many mountains do you have to see before you've seen them all? A lot of people have come West with grand ideas, only to run back when the inconveniences and isolation have become too much for them.'

'I don't mind all that,' Stacy denied. 'I love this country.'

'You know, Mary, it takes stamina to carve out a future in this land.' Cord was deliberately ignoring Stacy and addressing his remarks to the redhead on his right. His voice was low and vindictive. 'Luxuries become vastly important when you're suddenly denied them after having them all your life.'

'He's comparing me with his mother!' Stacy thought indignantly. 'You don't know what you're talking about,' she said, crumpling her napkin on the table.

'Of course. How stupid of me not to realize that appearances are deceiving,' the mocking tone in his voice and a sarcastic curl on his upper lip. 'I should have recognized that behind the high-fashion clothes, the expensive sports car and the blooded horse there beats the heart of a country girl, unspoiled by a life that's catered to her whims.'

The room was filled with tension as the two glared across the table at each other. Stacy longed to lash out at him, but she knew she would only be playing into his hands. She sensed the discomfort of the other two at the table. Somehow she managed a feeble laugh.

'It seems you have me figured out.' A weak smile on her flushed cheeks. 'I'm just a simple country girl.'

A flicker of admiration crossed the tanned face, replaced quickly by a derisive gleam.

' "Simple" is a particularly appropriate adjective, as it denotes showing little sense,' Cord replied. 'You showed a remarkable lack of it when you journeyed unescorted out here where you knew no one, and proceeded to live alone in a remote cabin, unprotected from possible molesters, and went out riding alone on a horse you couldn't control to places you didn't know. By a stroke of luck you're not lying dead out there now.'

'I don't think that your guests are interested in your opinions of me and my behaviour,' Stacy replied, pushing her chair away from the table.

In the living room, Mary caught up with her.

'What's up with you two?' she asked.

'We just don't get along,' Stacy answered, her hands clutched tightly to ether. She glanced nervously over her shoulder into the other room.

'You seemed so friendly when we first came that, to be honest, I'd hoped you two had made a match of it,' Mary went on.

'That's impossible!' Stacy exclaimed, disgust and anger in her voice. 'We mana e to carry on a civil conversation once in a while, but it always seems to end with us at each other's throats. It's useless to even pretend that we can stand each other. He's so cynical and self-centred that he insists everyone kneel at his feet, and he's not finding me so subservient.'

Immediately upon uttering her words, Stacy felt Cord's presence in the room. Defiantly she turned to face the glowering eyes. The tall man with his broad shoulders seemed to fill the room, diminishing everything near him.

'Our guests are leaving.' The dark figure finally spoke. 'Are you going to the door with them?'

Stacy turned without answering Cord and walked with Mary as she collected her purse and started towards the front door. Stacy's back prickled ominously, aware of the rancher walking directly behind her. Before reaching the front patio, Stacy murmured an apology to the girl beside her, speaking in a low voice.

'I'm sorry you were dragged into the middle of our fight, Mary. I so enjoyed your coming out here.'

'Don't you worry about it,' Mary admonished. 'It happens to the best of us. You just hurry up and get better.'

'I second that,' Bill added, putting his hand on Stacy's shoulders. 'Professionally speaking, get yourself another couple of days' rest and limit your activities. After that you can do as you want.'

Looking up at the pleasant face of the doctor, Stacy gave him a timorous smile. Her pleasure at the kindness of her new friends was overshadowed by the dark man who was standing so close to her that her whole being screamed its knowledge. With cheery good-byes, the couple walked down to their car. A little forlornly, Stacy watched as the car disappeared down the winding lane. Resolutely she turned to face Cord and his scornful eyes, only to find him gone. Glancing quickly around, she saw his familiar form striding towards the stables. Puzzled and relieved at the same time, she walked into the house.

CHAPTER SIX

FOR the past two days, Stacy had taken special pains to avoid Cord Harris. Her success was achieved with the co-operation of the rancher, who apparently did not want her company either. Digging the toe of her boot into the sandy soil, Stacy looked around the grounds hesitantly. The time had come to talk to him and she

wasn't looking forward to it at all. She had fully regained her strength and wanted to make arrangements
to return to the cabin. The last of her packing had
been completed after lunch, which left her with the
unpleasant task of finding Cord. The big German
Shepherd padded contentedly along at her side as she
wandered past the open doorway of the office. A glance
inside verified the inner feeling that he wasn't there.
With an impatient sigh Stacy continued to the stables.

'He's probably out on the range somewhere,' she
thought grimly, gazing out beyond the buildings.

At the corrals she noticed a horse and rider rounding one of the barns at a gallop. Not recognizing the
man, Stacy waited. Her curiosity was aroused by his
haste. Her ears caught the shouting of voices not far
from the stables and she turned to see the reason for
the commotion, but the buildings blocked her view.
The rider had just reined his horse to a stop by the
corral gate and dismounted.

'What's wrong?' she asked the cowboy.

'S'cuse me, ma'am, but I got to call the doctor,' the
man murmured, starting to hurry past her.

'What happened? Who got hurt?' Stacy cried, a hor-
rifying picture already forming of Cord lying unconscious on the ground.

'That red devil of a stallion slipped out of the stud
pen when Chris went in,' he answered, hurrying towards the open office door with Stacy right behind
him. 'The young fool climbed on his horse and tried to
rope him. The horse went berserk and attacked him.
Luckily the Boss and us was headed in from off the
range and saw what happened. Don't know how bad
the kid's hurt—can't get near him.'

'Diablo!' Stacy gasped, staring at the man reaching
for the phone to the office.

'The Boss is mad enough to kill that horse,' muttered the cowboy into the phone, not directing the sentence to Stacy.

As she heard the man reach the doctor, Stacy rushed out of the office towards the standing horse. She jumped on the buckskin and turned him towards the distant sound of voices. Her thoughts were barely coherent as she shouted to the Shepherd to follow and kicked the already winded horse into a gallop. She just knew she had to get there.

'Kill Diablo!' The words rang like a death knell in her ears. Confused, she whipped the horse with the reins as he bounded around the buildings and headed towards the mounted figures beyond. As she drew up by the two mounted horsemen, she saw a rider trapped under his fallen horse with her red stallion between him and the two riders. A rope was flying free from Diablo's neck as he eluded the ropes of the other two riders. His neck and withers were white with foam as he continued to lash out with his wicked hooves.

'What the hell are you doing here?' shouted Cord Harris as he sighted Stacy dismounting her horse. His face was contorted in anger as he swung his big bay around to face her. 'Get back to the house where you belong!'

'He's my horse!' shouted Stacy, turning away towards the stallion who was lunging, teeth bared, at the other mounted rider.

'You crazy female,' roared the rancher, reining his horse over beside her, 'can't you see that damn stud is loco?'

It was then that Stacy noticed the bullwhip in the angry man's hand, the end dragging in the dust raised by the bay's dancing hooves. Fire flashed from her eyes as she raised her head to meet his dark eyes.

'What do you propose to do? Whip him into submission?'

'If I have to, yes. That boy over there is hurt!'

'Get out of my way!' Stacy demanded. Pushing his horse away from her, she walked to face the red stallion.

A shrill whistle rang from Diablo as he pawed the ground and shook his flaxen mane at the solitary figure in front of him. Rearing, he flashed his black hooves through the air, his ears snaked back.

'Diablo!' Stacy commanded, attempting to pierce the frenzied mind of the stallion. 'Diablo, settle down!'

His ears remained flat against his head as he lashed out with his back feet at the Shepherd worrying him from behind. Stacy could see the fallen horse attempting to rise, only to fall back on its side. As the stallion started to charge at her, she called to him once again, her voice raising in authority. Stacy thought she saw his ears flicker up as he swept towards her. When he was just about on her, she stepped aside and he thundered by. Spinning around, he faced her, tossing his blazed head. Out of the corner of her eye, Stacy saw the two mounted riders moving. One was headed for the injured rider and Cord was coming towards the stallion, the whip rolled on the saddlehorn and a rope flicking the air in readiness.

'Diablo,' her voice changed to a caressing whisper, 'easy, boy, settle down. It's all right, baby. Come here. Come on!'

But the excitement and the almost forgotten memory of the scar on his neck was too much. The red horse couldn't curb the demon driving him. His delicate head bobbed up and down, the foam flicking off his neck. He recognized the girl in front of him, but he was filled with a new sense of hate and strength. Out of the corner of his eyes he caught the movement of horse and rider coming up behind him and danced around to face them. Stepping forward Stacy called to him. This time he spun swiftly around and raced towards her, his teeth bared and his head low. When Stacy attempted to jump out of his way, the stallion veered into her, jostling her to the ground with his big shoulder.

Breathless but unhurt, she raised herself up to see Cord streaking after the horse. He yelled at the other horseman and both ropes encircled the red sorrel at the same time. Screaming his anger, the horse attempted to charge the furthest rider, only to be brought up short by the rope dallied around Cord's saddlehorn.

'We got him, Boss! We got him!' yelled the other rider triumphantly, as the horse struggled futilely between the two ropes. It only took him a few minutes to realize he couldn't hope to win. Swiftly the two riders led him to the gate of the stud pen from which he had just escaped.

Dusting herself off, Stacy saw the third rider who had been sent to call the doctor kneeling beside the fallen horse and rider. Hurriedly she made her way over to them, arriving the same time as Cord. His expression was grim as he knelt beside the pain-racked form of the young cowboy.

'Take it easy, Chris,' Cord instructed. 'We'll have you out of there in no time. Doc's on his way.'

'My leg's broken,' groaned the young rider, gritting his teeth with pain. 'Get me out from under this damned horse!'

'Shortly, how bad's that horse's leg?' demanded Cord, directing his words to the dusty figure trying to quiet the downed gelding. The only answer was a negative shake of the head.

Without a word, Cord rose and walked over to his bay horse and extracted his rifle from the scabbard. Stacy stood numbly watching the action, unable to move or react. The loud report of the gun as it silenced the life of the injured horse deafened her. Overcome by shock and horror, she did not see the doctor arrive or the boy being carried away on a stretcher; the only thing she could see was the inert form of the dead horse. The tears glazing her eyes seemed frozen, too. At last her vision was blocked by Cord's dusty, sweaty form. Stiffly she raised her tear-filled eyes to his blurred face.

'Why?' she whispered, forcing the words through the lump in her throat.

'When Chris roped your horse the sorrel charged, knocking them down, breaking Chris's leg and his horse's, too. The doc says he's going to be all right, six weeks or so off the leg and on crutches for a month or more.'

'No,' Stacy mumbled, barely coherent. 'The horse! Why did you have to kill him? It wasn't his fault,' she sobbed. It was her first experience with what seemed to her brutality and she couldn't keep her eyes from straying to the dead horse.

'The horse?' exploded Cord. 'Do you realize that I could have lost a man? A human being! And all you're worried about is a horse!'

His anger pierced her shock and she turned to his face again and read the distaste and disgust that filled it. He didn't understand. She was upset about the rider, but she couldn't reconcile herself to the cold-blooded killing of the horse.

'But he's going to be all right, don't you under-

stand? He'll be back, but the horse is dead and you
killed him! As if it was nothing!' Her voice was shrill
with shock and near-hysteria.

'Nothing? Do you realize that I'm now without a
horse and a rider? Do you think it's going to be easy to
replace a man at this time of the year?' he roared,
grabbing her arm in a vicelike grip. 'I have you to
thank for that, you and that horse of yours!'

'Oh, sure, it's all my fault,' she cried sarcastically.
'Well, don't worry. I'll pay for the hospital bills and
any inconvenience this caused you.'

'You're damned right you will!' Cord replied. His
voice lowered threateningly. 'But your money won't
buy your way out of this one. You're going to take
Chris's place. For once in your life, you're going to see
what it's like to work to pay a debt.'

'What are you talking about?' Stacy asked, her body
now trembling with anger.

'You've gained a lot of sympathy with that poor
orphan act of yours around here. I bet it really broke
your heart when your father died and left you all that
money,' he replied, scorn and contempt deep in his
voice.

His words cut like a knife into her heart as the horrible accusation left Stacy speechless. Unconsciously
she felt the contact of her hand against his cheek. Her
palm was stinging as the deepening fire in his eyes
once again focused on her.

'So that's the way the little cat plays,' he murmured
through clenched teeth. 'Today you got away with it,
but I wouldn't try it again if I were you. You start to
work tomorrow,' he stated. 'And wear something practical, like jeans. We don't hold any fashion shows out
on the range.'

Her feet were rooted to the ground and the angry

tears in her eyes trickled down her cheeks as she watched Cord stalk away. Her hands were clenched into tight fists as she tried to find the words to scream after him. But her mouth refused to open and the words never came out. She stood there shaking with uncontrolled anger that gradually gave way to gasping sobs. Cord Harris had already mounted his horse and ridden off in the direction of the ranch house before Stacy moved from her position. Slowly she made her way in the same direction, her mind jumbled with thoughts of hatred for the rancher and compassion for the injured boy and the dead horse.

By the time Stacy reached the yards, the dust from the ranch car was halfway down the road. Silently she made her way to the hacienda, oblivious to her actual surroundings. Once inside the house and in her bedroom, Stacy sat on the bed and looked at the possessions she had earlier collected to leave.

With one hand she wiped the angry tears away from her eyes as she sat going over again their conversation. It was wrong to be concerned for the horse as opposed to a human being, but it had been the shock of the horse's death. Perhaps she was even wrong to accuse Cord of brutally killing the horse without a thought if he could be saved or not. But Stacy could find no excuse for his outrageous attack against her about her father's death. Besides, she had never told him that she was orphaned, though she had told the Nolans, but no one, certainly, knew about the money she had inherited! The anger in her heart faded away and was replaced by the crushing feeling of despair. How could she ever hope to convince him that this wasn't true? But why should she try? The confusion of her thoughts drove her to her feet and she paced the room. Resentment of Cord Harris boiled inside her.

Just exactly how was he going to make her stay against her will? He certainly couldn't force her to work. And besides, just exactly what did she know about ranching? Stacy stopped in front of the mirror, an idea forming in her mind. He couldn't stop her leaving because he wasn't even here. She glanced quickly at her watch and just as quickly outside. More time had gone by than she realized. The sun was already down and Cord must have been gone for at least two hours. If she intended to leave before he returned, she didn't have much time. Quickly she began gathering her belongings and setting them outside her room.

Naturally, he would accuse her of running away and refusing to face his challenge, but let him think what he liked. Unfortunately she had been forced to accept his hospitality when she was ill, but there was no need to stay any longer. It was enough that she had offered to pay the hospital bill for the boy and reimburse Cord for the horse. If financially she was unable to pay him, that would be the time to try to arrange some way to work the problem out. Even she had to admit that she was responsible for her horse.

Stacy had just slipped her fringed jacket on and picked up her purse and started out of the bedroom when she heard the big oak door close. Numbly she stood beside her luggage and stared at the tall form standing at the bottom of the stairs. Cord's features were hidden in the shadows, but Stacy could well imagine the dark brows gathered together and the clean, hard set of his jaw, and most of all the grim line of his mouth. Her eyes were wide and darkening with apprehension as she felt the trembling course through her body. Neither spoke as the tension grew.

'I take it you're planning on going somewhere?' came the low baritone voice.

'What if I do?' Stacy retorted defiantly, lifting her chin in challenge.

'Then I would suggest you forget it,' was the cool reply as Cord stepped out of the shadows. There were new lines on his face that Stacy hadn't noticed before, but there was no mistaking the hard quality in his voice. He cast one further glance at the luggage and the still figure above him. 'You might as well unpack.'

'You don't actually believe you can keep me a prisoner here against my will?' Stacy exploded, in anger.

He gave her one brief glance before replying. 'You're in my debt and it's up to me to set the terms of payment.'

The hopelessness of fighting this man raced through Stacy and her shoulders slumped slightly, acknowledging defeat. The fire went out in her eyes and was replaced with despair and confusion. Struggling, she attempted to take one last stand. 'I will not stay in that room one more night!'

A glint of amusement showed in his eyes before he turned his face away from her.

'As you like. There's a guestroom down the hall. Use it,' he paused briefly. 'In case you're interested, the boy's going to be in the hospital for a few weeks and inactive for a couple of months.'

Stacy felt the heat rising in her cheeks at her inconsideration for not asking about the injured rider's condition. Why did he always manage to make her seem so heartless? Frustrated, she gathered up her cases and stalked into the hallway, stopping at the first doorway on her left.

She was too upset to take in the surroundings of the room. Her anger was too close to the surface to allow her to dwell on anything but Cord's dark eyes and sculptured face. His cool indifference irritated her. All she had done was make a fool of herself and increase his belief that she was spoiled and selfish. Stacy knew she could expect no mercy at his hands. He expected her to take the rider's place regardless of her sex.

'Very well, Mr. Harris,' she whispered to herself. 'I can take anything you can dish out. No quarter asked.'

The sun had barely touched the sky the following morning when there was a loud knock at Stacy's door. Sleepily she raised herself up on one elbow and looked out the window and then over to the clock on the dresser. It took her a minute before she remembered the previous day's events.

'Yes?'

'It's time to get up,' came Cord's voice from the hall. 'That is if you want coffee and some breakfast before work.'

He didn't wait for a reply, but strode away from the door. Determinedly, Stacy clambered out of the bed. It took her only a few minutes to dress in her Levi's and shirt and to tie her hair back at the nape of her neck. A little smile played on her soft lips as she looked at the image reflected in the mirror. If Mr. Harris thought that blue jeans and a plain blouse were going to make her look less of a woman then he was wrong. She couldn't keep the pleasure out of her eyes as she surveyed her gentle curves. She checked to make sure her riding gloves were in the pocket of her suede jacket, picked up her hat and walked down the stairs to the dining room.

Unfortunately Cord wasn't there. Stacy queried Maria, who replied that Mr. Harris had already taken his meal and was out giving instructions to the men. Maria was plainly confused by the turn of events and kept casting puzzled glances at the young girl. When

Stacy finished her toast and coffee, Maria said that Stacy was to meet the Boss out in the yard.

Gratefully Stacy realized that most of the men had already gone. It would have been embarrassing to be subjected to the forbidding rancher's orders in the presence of his men. As it was, she recognized his tall form still talking to two men. His back was to her, so he didn't see her approach, but Stacy was sure he knew she was coming.

The two men standing with him attempted to ignore the approaching girl. The taller of the two was only a few years older than Stacy and obviously embarrassed by the situation. He kept his head down, his hat preventing Stacy from seeing the expression on his face. The other man was considerably older and wizened. The constant sun on his face had made his skin so leathery that Stacy was unable to judge his age. When she approached the group the older one met her gaze openly, compassion and sympathy etched in the eyes that squinted in the morning sun. It was a comfort to recognize an ally here.

'It's about time you got here, Adams,' Cord said crisply, turning his aquiline features towards her. 'I want you to go with Hank and Jim today to gather the stock cattle in the winter range,' he ordered, casting only a cursory glance at the petite figure beside him. 'Any other questions, Hank?'

The older man shook his head negatively.

'Okay, mount up.'

Stacy started to follow the two men as they walked to the horses standing saddled on the other side of the corral, but was called back by Cord. Turning to face the imposing figure, she took her gloves out of her jacket pocket and began putting them on her hands, hoping to stave off the nervousness she felt facing him.

'Yes,' she said, looking boldly into his face, her voice matching the crisp tone he had. used earlier. She was unable to read his dark expression.

For a minute he didn't answer, then he said, 'Hank will show you all that needs to be done.'

'All right,' she replied, disliking the searching eyes that seemed to probe deep inside her. 'Anything else?'

'No. Good luck.' His tone was indifferent and conflicting with his words.

Briskly Stacy turned from him and walked to where the two mounted riders waited. The one named Hank handed her the reins of a short-coupled bay pony. Silently she mounted and turned her horse to follow the other two.

Shortly after leaving the ranchyard, the younger of the two men rode ahead, leaving the wizened old cowboy alone with Stacy. Normally she would have been enjoying the early morning ride, but today's circumstances made her conscious of the humiliating position she was in. Pride forbade her to look at the silent, hunched figure beside her. For a time the two horses moved along at their slow, shuffling trot, until the rider beside her pulled his horse into a walk and Stacy's mount automatically matched the pace.

'Miss Adams,' came the questioning, rough voice, 'now it ain't none of my business and you can tell me to shut my mouth, but if we're going to be riding the range together, it gets mighty lonely if all you can talk to is yore hoss. Now, it ain't in me to question the Boss's orders, but me nor none of the boys hold you responsible for what happened to the kid the other day. It's gonna be a long day in the saddle, specially for a dude like you, but it shore does make the day go faster if there's a bit of jawin' goin' on.'

Stacy had the distinct impression that this was the

longest statement the man had ever made, and she smiled at his thoughtfulness. He was trying to put her at ease in his own clumsy way and himself as well.

'Thank you, Hank. I appreciate it more than you know.'

'Well, I been working on this spread ever since the Boss was in knee-britches, and I seen some strange things. But I gotta admit this is the first time we've ever had us a lady wrangler. An' the Boss says you gotta pull your own weight,' he said, shaking his head in confusion.

'I intend to, too,' Stacy replied, a grim look of determination on her face. 'I don't know anything about ranching or cows, but I can learn. At least I can ride and am in fair shape.'

'Well, now, miss, I reckon you can ride all right, but you gotta relax a little more. Ya ain't in no hoss show, so you don't have to worry 'bout how you look,' Hank said with a slight smile. 'An' I'd watch what you call cows. Safe thing is to call 'em cattle.'

'I stand corrected,' she laughed. 'Tell me, Hank, what exactly are we doing today?'

'We're gonna be rattlin' the brush for bunch-quitters mostly an' gettin' the herd ready for movin' to the summer pasture. Most of the men trucked their horses to the far end of the pasture an'll be workin' towards us with the main herd.'

'Trucked their horses?' Stacy asked quizzically, her brown eyes examining the weathered face of the cowboy.

'Yep. It's a modern West you'll find. Rather than spendin' a lot of time ridin' to where the herd is, now they jus' load the the horses up in trucks or trailers and haul 'em as close as they can.'

'It's a miracle they don't use jeeps to round them

up,' Stacy exclaimed half to herself, in amazement.

'A few years ago when we was really tryin' to gather all the scrub bulls an' strays, the Boss ordered a helicopter to search 'em out. Things have changed,' Hank muttered. 'Reckon we ought to catch up with Jim?'

The brisk morning air was beginning to warm with the rising sun. Already the morning dew was rapidly vanishing from the undergrowth wherever the sun's rays probed through the shade. The distant mountainous hills were cloaked in a golden haze that cast its shimmering glow upon the grassland stretched out below it. The morning air was bereft of any breeze and the stillness was broken only by the shuffling trot of the three cow-ponies and the occasional call of the quail. The three riders travelled several miles before arriving at the first barbed wire fence. They rode along the fence until they arrived at a gate. Stacy and Hank waited astride their horses while Jim manoeuvred his horse into position to unhook the gate and open it for the other two. After they had passed through, the young cowboy followed, closing the gate behind him.

'This is where we start to work, miss,' the wizened cowboy said, indicating the land spread out before them.

'But I don't see any cattle?' said Stacy, looking at the vacant pasture.

'That's the general idea. If they was right out in plain sight it wouldn't be quite so much work. But they seem to know every ravine and bush on the spread and that's where they plan to stay.'

'But I thought that you raised domestic cattle, a Hereford cross of some sort?' she queried, plainly puzzled.

'We do, but they been left alone. They're just about

as skittish of humans as the old longhorns that used to graze this land. Only difference between the two is these ain't half as ornery as them,' Hank replied, squinting his eyes to look over the land. 'We usually split up a bit here, but you stick close to me for a while, miss.'

The three riders loped off; the younger cowboy moved fifty yards to their left and they all began scouring the brush. It was hot dusty work for horse and rider, and it wasn't long before Stacy removed her jacket and tied it on the back of the saddle. Between the heat of the sun and the constant exercise, Stacy's bay began perspiring, too. They scared up a couple of head of cattle, as they worked their way along. Stacy began to respect the game horse she was riding. By mid-morning they had about fifteen head of cattle driving in front of them. Hank instructed the young girl to keep them going while he and Jim added other strays with them.

At first she thought he was giving her an easier job until she began breathing in the dust that the cattle were kicking up. She wasn't even able to relax on the horse. Every time she allowed her attention to wander from the herd that was the precise time that one of the animals decided to make another break for the open bush. The little bay instinctively gave chase and cut it back into the herd. Quite a few times Stacy was positive that the horse was going to spin around and send her flying in the other direction. Her legs were so weary from gripping his sides and her body so covered with dust and grime and sweat that she was sure that she wouldn't make it through the rest of the morning let alone the whole day. Each time one of the cowboys added another steer to the herd, Stacy could hardly stop from sighing outwardly. She had learned for every steer in the herd her horse had to cover twice their distance.

Her mouth was dry and gritty, but she was afraid to sip out of her canteen for fear that one of the herd would decide to leave. The girl was happy to see Hank ride up alongside, but trying to smile a hello was an effort. He didn't look at her directly, but Stacy could still recognize a ghost of a smile on his face.

'Mighty dirty work, ridin' drag on a bunch of scrubs,' he murmured in the air. 'We're comin' up on the water tank where we'll meet up with the chuck wagon for lunch. Reckon maybe you could do with a rest, huh?'

'I don't mind admitting that I could, Hank,' Stacy replied, feeling her lips crack as she spoke. Giving the little bay an affectionate pat on the neck, she added, 'I think he deserves one too.'

'The remuda will be there. His work is done for the day,' the cowboy answered.

'Oh, look!' cried Stacy, turning her attention to the left. 'Isn't that Jim coming?—and it looks like he's got a little baby calf across his saddle.'

The younger cowboy joined them with a new white-faced calf lying crosswise on his saddle with the mother following alongside, lowing soothingly to her youngster.

'He's darling!' Stacy exclaimed. 'How old is he?'

'Just a couple of days,' Jim replied, the shyness still evident in his failure to look directly at Stacy, but proud of her interest in his find. 'I found them out in the brush. The calf wasn't able to keep up, so I thought I'd give him a ride to the calf wagon.'

'Calf wagon? What's that?' Stacy asked, her attention diverted from the snow-white face.

'There's usually a bunch of these latecomers that are

too little to keep up with the herd, so we have a trailer we put 'em in until we reach the night's holdin' ground and then we mammy 'em up,' Hank replied, amused at Stacy's concern for the calf. 'Take the little critter on in, Jim, we'll be there shortly.'

'Isn't that what you call a dogey, a baby calf?' Stacy asked watching as Jim rode on ahead.

'A dogey is really a calf without a momma, but a lot o' people call all calves dogies,' Hank answered.

'The cattle have settled down a lot. It must be your being here. Before, every five minutes one was heading in a different direction,' Stacy commented, enjoying the conversation with the knowledgeable cowboy.

'Nope, it's not me. They smell water. We just happen to be going the same direction as them.'

The cattle and two riders topped a small rise in the ground and came upon a high plateau covered with tall stands of pampas grass and creosote bushes. Ahead Stacy could see the large water tank and windmill. Beyond that was a station wagon and several pick-ups and trailers. A look of astonishment crossed her dust-stained face.

'That's the chuck wagon?'

A dry chuckle escaped the old cowboy's throat. 'I told ya the old West was gone. They bring the food from the ranch house and trailer the remuda to the noon stop,' the old man smiled. 'You go on and ride ahead. These cattle ain't goin' nowhere 'cept to that tank. Rest while you can. We're gonna be hittin' the saddle for another long afternoon.'

Gratefully, Stacy reined her little bay out around the herd and set him at a lope for the waiting vehicles. She rode over to where a cowboy waited by the trailers. There were already several riders over by the station wagon; some were eating and some were just getting their food. Behind the trailers Stacy noticed a couple of Mexicans cooling off some cow-ponies with replacements picketed along the trailers. Slowly she dismounted. Her bones and muscles were so sore that she stood for a minute to adjust to the solid ground beneath her feet. Now that she was on the ground, she wasn't so sure that she could walk. She took a few careful steps in the general direction of the wagon and realized that she was going to navigate all right under her own power, so she joined the men at the station wagon where they were dishing out food from the rear.

The good-natured grumbling and banter that had been going on when Stacy rode up had stopped, and Stacy became uneasy. She had been so comfortable with the old cowboy, and so tired and hungry from the skimpy breakfast, that she neglected to remember her awkward position. With a red face and a trembling hand she accepted the dish of stew and beans with a thick slice of bread alongside from one of the cooks and a steaming mug of coffee from another. Nervously she turned around to search for a shaded place to have her meal. All eyes were on her as she turned; some looked away abruptly while others eyed her boldly.

'Ma'am,' came a hesitant voice from her right. Stacy turned and with relief recognized the young rider, Jim. 'If you like, you can join me. Not many shaded places left.'

'Thank you, Jim,' she said, looking for the first time into the hazel eyes of the young cowboy. 'I guess I did look a little lost.'

'Yes, you mustn't mind the men. They aren't used to seeing women around camp,' he replied, removing his hat to run his fingers through his bleached brown hair, There was a boyishness about his face that deceived his true age which was in the middle twenties.

In between bites of food, Stacy asked, 'Have you worked here long?'

'Off and on all my life. Got out of the service a couple years ago and went to college, but I work here in the summers for tuition money,' he replied, a look of seriousness crossing his face.

'What are you studying?'

'Forestry, conservation,' was the quiet answer.

'Are you planning to be a park ranger?' Stacy inquired.

'Hopefully. Mr. Harris has suggested coming back to the ranch, but I think I'd rather not. Initially I was going to be a vet., but I discovered that I was more interested in the agricultural and ecological side,' he answered, enjoying the interest Stacy was taking in him.

'I wouldn't let Mr. Harris's wishes interfere with what I wanted to do,' Stacy said, a trace of bitterness in her voice as she stabbed at a piece of beef in the stew.

'No, of course not,' came the low, mocking reply.

Stacy jerked her head up and practically choked on the piece of meat as she stared into the tanned face of the rancher. Jim scrambled to his feet in embarrassment.

'We were just discussing my college plans, sir,' he stated, his jaw clenched tight, defending Stacy in his own way from the sardonic smile of his employer.

Swiftly Stacy got to her feet to prevent any further remarks on her behalf. It was humiliating enough to have to look up to Cord, but to be seated at his feet was too much. Cord Harris shifted his gaze from the young cowhand to the hatless girl before him. Boldly she met his gaze, conscious once again of her dust-covered clothes and face.

'Perhaps you would like to go check on your horses

for Miss Adams, Connors,' Cord suggested with a definite tone of dismissal.

The cowboy cast a wavering glance at the girl at his side. Stacy smiled at him with a great deal more confidence than she felt. Her pulse was racing at an unsettling pace. Reluctantly Jim Connors left the two standing alone beside the trailer.

'You seem to have gained yourself an admirer.'

'Don't be ridiculous! He was only being polite. He obviously has been taught some manners—which is more than I can say for some people,' Stacy said scathingly.

'I see you've managed to survive the morning in fair shape.' Cord ignored her insult and leaned against the side of the trailer to light a cigarette. Unconsciously he held the match until it was cool, all the while his gaze travelling over the dirty face of the girl.

'Yes. I managed quite well. Surprised?'

'No. I imagine you could do anything you set your mind to,' he replied. 'I only wonder if you have the staying power.'

'Hey, Boss, is that the filly you picked up at the sale last week?' Hank walked up beside them, his attention fixed on a chestnut sorrel at the far end of the trailer. The horse didn't like being tied up and pawed the ground impatiently while pulling at the reins. 'Shore is a nice-looking thing.'

Cord's eyes never left Stacy's face. 'Yes, she is.'

Stacy could feel herself begin to blush, but she couldn't break away from the compelling eyes.

'Do ya' think she's gonna be able to settle down to ranch life?' Hank asked, and then addressed his next remark to Stacy, not noticing that she was paying little attention to him. 'She was raced a few times and she's used to a lot of fuss and bother. Spoilt, you might say.'

A mocking smile crossed Cord's lips as he watched the discomfiture registering on Stacy's face. 'It's hard to tell, Hank.'

'Shore seems awful fractious. It'll take a lot of patience to change this one's way of thinkin',' the old cowboy went on with a shake of his head.

'It will that,' Cord said with a throaty laugh. 'It will that. Well, mustn't detain you two any longer from your work. I'll see you later.'

With no more than a brief nod to Stacy and a friendly slap on the back to the cowhand, Cord strode over to where the young horse stood tethered, the secretly amused expression still on his face. Untying the reins, he swung his tall frame easily into the saddle as the spirited horse danced beneath him. He didn't even glance in their direction as he reined the sorrel over towards a group of riders talking over their last cup of coffee. Stacy couldn't hear what was said, but gathered it was an order to mount up, because shortly after they dispersed and walked over to where their ponies were tied.

Out of the corner of her eye, she saw Jim walking up leading two horses. He handed her the reins to a big Roman-nosed buckskin. Stacy could tell that Jim was embarrassed about leaving her in Cord's clutches, but at this moment the tanned face was still plainly visible in her mind and the delicious, throaty laugh was still echoing in her ears. Silently they mounted and rode over to join the grizzled cowhand, Hank, and get at the afternoon's work.

CHAPTER SEVEN

STACY had thought the morning long and arduous, but by six o'clock that evening she knew the true meaning of bone-weary. She yearned to give a cry of joy when she sighted the windmill that indicated the night's holding ground for the cattle.

Her failure to try to shirk her work off on to them had gained her both Jim and Hank's respect. Several times they would have taken over for her, but she hadn't let them. It would have been easy for her to trade on her womanhood, and they would have allowed it, in spite of their employer's order.

Hank suggested that she ride on ahead and get a cup of coffee for each of them, but she declined, saying with a tired attempt at a laugh that she was going to need help getting off her horse. At the moment it seemed almost too true to be funny. A short time later they hazed their small herd in with the main one settling down for the night about a hundred yards from the camp.

A sense of peace cloaked the riders as they rode back into the strange western camp of motorized vehicles where the odour of petrol and oil mixed with the smell of sweaty horses, cattle, and humans. Good-naturedly Stacy accepted the helping hand of the younger cowboy as she dismounted. She felt no self-consciousness as she limped her way to the station wagon and the promising aroma of coffee. Hank had arrived before the other two and was talking to the riders who had gathered around the lowered tailgate.

'Hank,' Stacy groaned, looking into the grey eyes, a

smile of mock pain on her face, 'I think you're looking at the very first bow-legged lady wrangler. I'll never walk straight again as long as I live, let alone be able to sit down!'

There was a considerable amount of sympathizing laughter from the group and, more important, acceptance. Accompanied by a goodly amount of jesting and joking, Stacy was presented with a steaming cup of the cook's java. After inhaling the steam rising from the cup, she emitted an audible sigh of appreciation.

'Cook, you are a master chef, but tell me, where is the bath water?' she exclaimed, and met with another round of laughter. 'Do you boys go through this every day?'

'Twice on Sunday,' one of them replied, and laughed at the expression of mock disbelief on Stacy's face.

'Spare me the details and help me find a way to sit down!'

Several of the riders stepped forward, including Jim Connors, and with exaggerated care lowered her to the ground. Despite her aches and pains, Stacy was beginning to enjoy herself, and so were the men. There had seldom been a woman in their midst and definitely none that had joined in making fun of herself and her situation. With a sparkle in her eyes, she started to make another comment to the men, only to notice that they had grown very quiet and were looking beyond her. Still in a jovial mood, she turned her radiant smile to include the object of their attention. Cord Harris's frame had cast its shadow over the group. His expression was a study of amused interest in the girl and the surrounding riders. Stacy couldn't say why or how she had the nerve to say what came next.

'Oh, Patrón, please allow this lowly peon to remain

seated in thy great presence, for I vow I couldn't rise if you commanded me.'

There was a chilling stillness as the men waited for their boss to answer. Stacy was horrified at her words, but it was too late to retract them. She held her breath along with the men. The low chuckle that finally came relaxed everyone and most of all the seated Stacy.

'Charlie, give me a cup of that brew of yours while I sit down beside this señorita,' Cord directed with a grin to the cook.

Someone had started a campfire, and Stacy fixed her attention on it rather than the disconcerting man beside her, trying to ignore the delicious chill that had quaked her body at his pleasant laugh. The sun was beginning to set now, casting its coloured shadows on the countryside, while the two sipped their coffee in silence. The cook brought them a plate of beefsteak and beans and refilled their coffee.

'Well, what do you think of the cattle drive?' Cord asked as they began eating their meal. 'Is it what you expected it to be?'

'No,' Stacy replied with a smile, 'not meant as a complaint, but it's a lot harder work than I thou ht.'

'So far you've come through with flying colours,' he said.

'Meaning you don't think I'll last.'

'Meaning I have no opinion except that you've done very well.' There was a mocking glint in his eyes as he went on, 'You really should do something about that temper of yours. You're a little too quick to take offence.'

'Perhaps I've had cause,' Stacy replied, her gaze still occupied by the flickering campfire flames.

'Touché,' Cord smiled, his eyes observing the still face. 'I imagine you're pretty tired after today's work.

The remuda hands will be heading back to the ranch house shortly. You can catch a ride with them, or wait a little longer and I'll give you a ride back.'

'Is everyone going back?' Stacy was astounded. 'You mean you just leave the cattle unattended to stray all over?'

'No,' Cord chuckled, 'most of the men will be staying and taking their turns at riding herd. They've brought along their bedrolls,' he added, indicating places where some of the men had already made them up.

'Then why am I going back to the ranch?'

'Because you didn't come prepared for staying overnight and because it wouldn't be permissible for a woman to spend the night out here on a trail drive,' Cord replied a little curtly. 'Plus you've only been out of a sickbed a few days. It would be foolish to overdo it.'

'Oh, but I'm just one of the boys, remember?' Stacy mocked, her brown eyes flashing bright sparks, magnified by the burning embers.

'During the day,' he qualified in his crisp tone.

'I'm staying the night here.' Stacy's voice was low and determined.

'You will be returning with me.'

'Then you'll have to carry me forcibly from here, and that would make quite a scene. But then you don't mind scenes, do you?'

'You're forgetting that you have no place to sleep,' Cord stated. 'Didn't you learn from your last experience what can happen staying out in the cold at night?'

'I'm quite sure I'll be able to make some sort of arrangement to borrow a blanket or something from someone.'

'Or perhaps share a bedroll?' was the sarcastic reply. 'I'm sure you'd have plenty of offers.'

'You dirty-minded beast!' Stacy exclaimed, forgetting the tired muscles in her body and bounding to her feet. The fury mounted in her face as she waited for Cord to join her. 'I don't know what kind of women you're familiar with, but let me assure you that I don't fit in that category!' Her voice raised as she struggled to keep control of herself. 'I don't have to listen to that kind of talk from any man!'

Cord grabbed hold of her arm, preventing her from running away from him. Trembling, Stacy stopped, neither attempting to pull away from his vice-like grip nor turning to face his cold dark eyes.

'Are you hoping one of your knights will come to your rescue?' he asked in a mocking whisper that she just barely heard.

Unable to reply, she stood immobile. Finally she heard a sigh leave his lips at the same time he released her arm.

'I believe an apology is in order. Therefore I apologize for the insinuations made and will make accommodation for you to spend the night here,' Cord said quietly.

Still Stacy did not turn to face him. There were hot tears of humiliation and hurt in her eyes as she felt his hands touch her shoulders and slowly turn her around to face him. With surprising gentleness his large hand cupped her chin and raised it up so that he could see her face. His own expression was hidden by the shadow of his Stetson hat.

'I guess we're both a little tired and on edge,' came the familiar deep voice. 'Get a good night's rest.'

Cord turned quietly and left. She was conscious of a feeling of emptiness as the chill of night stole over her shoulders and face where a moment ago his hands had been. The anger had vanished, leaving Stacy staring off into the dark after him. Uncertain, she turned back to the flickering campfire and the quiet figures of the ranch hands.

Jim Connors walked up to her from behind one of the trailers carrying a bedroll and a blanket. His bright, questioning hazel eyes searched her face, but Stacy accepted the bedding with only a quiet thank-you and walked over to the other side of the fire. Dully she watched some of the hands loading horses into vans and start pulling out. Involuntarily she searched the darkened forms for Cord and strained to catch the quiet conversation for the sound of his voice, but with no success.

She slipped under the covers of her bedroll and stared up into the dark blue sky overhead, plagued by a variety of emotions—hurt, anger, humiliation, resentment, but most of all a wonder and mystification towards this unpredictable Cord Harris. At last the tired muscles claimed her attention and ignorant of the hard ground and chilling air she drifted off to sleep.

She was sure she had just barely fallen asleep when a hand began gently shaking her shoulder. Her eyes fluttered open to a starlit sky. Stacy had difficulty focusing on the figure beside her in the absence of light. At first she thought it was Cord, but then she recognized the smaller build of Jim Connors.

'It's time to get up.'

'It's dark yet,' she muttered, sleep heavy in her voice.

'It's four o'clock,' the young cowboy answered lightly. 'We rise early around here. Breakfast is almost ready. Better get washed up.'

A moment later he was gone. Painfully Stacy rolled out of her bed, all of her muscles crying out for her not to move. It was all she could do to stand up. Stiffly she walked over to a basin of water warmed by the re-kindled fire. Gratefully she splashed the water on her face, enjoying the clean sensation it gave her skin. Awake now, she glanced around the camp with inter-est.

Everywhere there was activity. Horses and riders were walking along the outside of the camp and other riders were mumbling sleepily over their coffee and flapjacks. Over to the east, the sky was beginning to lighten with the coming dawn.

While she was eating the enormous breakfast Jim had brought her, Stacy saw the remuda trucks ap-proaching with a load of fresh horses for the day's work. Since Jim had already finished his breakfast he offered to get her a mount for the morning. A few min-utes later he returned leading a big, rangy sorrel and a smaller-built pinto. Quickly Stacy finished off the last of her pancakes and carried the plate and mug over to the station wagon. Several of the riders had already left when she returned to the waiting cowboy. Hank had joined him, mounted on his horse.

'Ready for another day, miss?' he asked, a smile spreading over his tanned face. Watching her slip her hat on, he added, 'Now a real cowboy puts his hat on as soon as he gets up.'

'I'm still learning,' she laughed in return, taking the pinto's reins from Jim. 'What's the agenda this morn-ing?'

'Gotta sweep the east side of the main herd for strays,' he replied, swinging his pony in that direction.

A groan passed Stacy's lips as she mounted her horse. It was a mixture of dismay at the orders and a rebellion of her sore muscles at returning to the saddle.

'Is Mr. Harris joining the drive today?' she asked.

'Oh, he stayed the night last night and took one of the watches,' replied the older cowboy. 'Imagine he's headin' the herd up now.'

'Oh,' Stacy murmured. The idea that Cord had spent the night in the camp was oddly disquieting to her.

'It's a gorgeous morning,' she exclaimed as her pony danced beside Jim's mount as if in emphasis of her words. The sun was climbing the sky now, chasing away the last vestiges of the night's shadows.

'It's spring,' the young cowboy replied, capturing the exuberance of the attractive girl at his side.

'And it's a beautiful country to be in, in spring!' she laughed. 'It makes you feel great just to be alive!'

'You really like it here—in Texas, I mean?'

'I love it,' Stacy answered, not noting his qualifying words. 'There's room here. I mean, you feel free. No one's crowding you. It's hard to describe.'

'I know,' Jim replied, his eyes studying her face. 'Let's ride over this way. I'd like to show you something.'

'What is it?'

'You'll see,' he said, looking ahead as they altered their course to the left. 'What brought you here to Texas?'

For a minute Stacy didn't answer, but there was something about the young man with his close-cropped brown hair that made her want to confide in him.

'My father was killed in a plane crash about a month and a half ago,' she answered quietly. 'We were very close. You see, my mother died a few months after I was born, so all there ever was was my father and me.'

Jim studied the girl quietly with his hazel eyes, but didn't interrupt her.

'He was a freelance photographer, quite famous in his field. From almost the time I could walk he took me with him on his assignments. I was never in one place long enough to make any real friends. Oh, there were a few that you always got reacquainted with when you returned somewhere,' Stacy added, her thoughts turning to Carter Mills, 'but it really all boiled down to each other. Dad had chartered a plane to fly us back to Washington after a trip into Tennessee. Over the mountains we developed engine trouble and crashed.'

There was a silence for a time while Stacy fought to control the lump in her throat. Staring in front of her, she began to speak again. 'Cajun, my German Shepherd, was along. I was knocked unconscious, but somehow he managed to pull me out of the plane and shortly afterwards it burst into flames. My father was still inside.'

'Your father was Joshua Adams,' said Jim.

'Yes,' she answered, a whispered hoarseness creeping into her voice. 'Afterwards I was confused. A lot of Dad's friends and colleagues offered to help, but I didn't really know what they could do.' A stilted laugh came from her lips. 'He always loved the West. I guess I came out here for two reasons, to be close to him and to find what I wanted out of life.'

'You've been here before?'

'Not here specifically, but Dad had assignments in El Paso several times and various other places in Arizona and New Mexico,' Stacy answered, then added with a laugh, 'I really didn't expect to spend my time chasing cattle!'

Understanding that she was trying to shake off the

sadness that talking about her father had raised, Jim Connors joined in with her laugh.

'No, I don't imagine you did. Hank and I were along with the Boss when he found you that morning on the range.'

'You were?'

'The Boss was fit to be tied when he found your horse,' Jim stated, smiling over at the girl. 'He was the first one to spot your dog and reach you. None of us had ever seen him in such a state before. He was snapping orders around so fast and wouldn't let anyone else near you but him.'

'He was probably afraid I'd sue him for allowing that snake to be on his property,' Stacy laughed, ignoring the inquisitive glance.

'You two don't get along very well,' Jim commented.

'It's not my fault. I think he just hates women in general,' she replied.

'No, I don't believe that,' the cowboy said with a dubious shake of his head. 'After his engagement to Lydia, I don't believe he's taken women at face value any more. He's forgotten the word trust.'

'Whatever his problem is, it's not mine.'

'The place I wanted to show you is right over here,' Jim said, turning his pony abruptly to the right towards a small hill. 'I was in a lecture class where your father was a guest speaker. I think you'll appreciate this.'

The two riders topped a small rise to view a meadow covered with a sea of blue flowers. They paused briefly on the hill as Stacy gazed awestruck at the beauty of the multiple blossoms waving brightly in the morning breeze. Mother Nature had covered the hill in a luxurious blanket of deep blue. In the distance they could hear the songs of birds bringing the earth alive on that hill.

'It's beautiful, Jim. What are they?' Stacy exclaimed at last.

'Bluebonnets.'

'Such a beautiful blue, almost purple.' Her gaze remained on the flowers. 'They put the sky to shame.'

'Shall we ride down?' he asked.

Stacy didn't answer, but touched the pinto's flank with her heel. Single file the pair rode down the hill to the meadow, stopping in the midst of the indigo profusion. Jim dismounted before Stacy and helped her off her pony. His hand remained on her elbow as they walked companionably amongst the flowers. Stacy couldn't resist picking a small bouquet and inhaling the sweet fragrance.

'I'm so glad you brought me here,' Stacy said, turning to face the young cowboy. She only had to raise her eyes a few inches to look into the light hazel ones.

The hand that had been on her elbow slipped up to her shoulder, and the cowboy's other hand moved to rest on the opposite side. The bouquet held in Stacy's hands was the only thing separating them when they both heard the sound of an approaching horse. Simultaneously they turned to face the hoofbeats. It only took Stacy an instant to recognize the rider sitting so straight in the saddle and the blood began pounding in her heart. Cord Harris reined his horse down the hill towards the couple, stopping just short of them.

'Am I interrupting something?' came the implying tone. Not giving either one a chance to answer, he rested an arm on the saddle-horn and said, 'Then let's get back to work and save the flowers for off-duty hours.'

Both Stacy and Jim mounted their ground-hitched

horses with a certain amount of chagrin, fully conscious of the accusing dark eyes. Once on their way again, the rancher nudged his horse between the pair as if separating two naughty children. Stacy's lips set in a grim line, resentful of the childish way Cord was treating them. He was unmindful of her displeasure. After they had left the meadow of bluebonnets, Cord turned his head slightly towards the quiet cowboy riding on his left.

'I want you to ride back to the main herd and help Jenkins on the point, Connors. I'll accompany Miss Adams back to where Hank is holding some strays,' ordered Cord in a tone that defied a negative answer.

The young cowboy reined his pony abruptly away from Stacy and his employer, dug his spurs into the horse's flank and was away at a gallop. Angrily Stacy turned on the forbidding form still beside her.

'You had no right to reprimand him. It was as much my fault as it was his.'

'I'm glad you see it that way. It's just what I was thinking too,' Cord replied, an amused smile on his lips, but flashing fires in his eyes. 'However, if it's any of your business, I was looking for him to tell him just that before I found him with you.'

Stacy was more than a little taken back. She had naturally assumed that Cord was disciplining her companion because of Jim's interest in her. The reddening of embarrassment flowed in her cheeks.

'But that doesn't mean I approve of you bewitching my men to such an extent that they forget to do their job.'

'I don't know what you're talking about,' Stacy muttered.

'You surely don't expect me to believe you were looking for strays on foot in that field?' he questioned.

'No, I don't!' answered Stacy exasperatedly.

'Then there really isn't anything more to be said, is there?'

'Yes, there is!' Stacy exclaimed. 'You don't have the right to tell me who I may or may not make friends with.'

'I have a great deal to say about it,' matching the angry tone in Stacy's voice. 'You are in my employ and as such, your actions become my responsibility. If I feel it's necessary, I'll dictate who you may associate with and who you may not.'

'Are you telling me I'm to leave Jim alone?'

'I'm telling you that you will not flatter my men and seduce them into having any romantic notions towards you. Is that plain enough?' Cord flashed.

'Perfectly!' she retorted, and kicked her pinto into a canter.

The two silent riders hadn't travelled very far from the meadow when they came in sight of the wizened cowboy driving a half dozen steers. With a wave of his hand towards Hank, Cord wheeled his horse away from the pinto and headed back across the range as Stacy fell in beside the wrangler.

Shortly before noon the small band joined up with the main herd. Stacy searched the riders around the main herd for some sign of Jim, but only caught a glimpse of Cord, which deterred her from looking more closely. She wasn't in the mood for another run in with him. Quietly she followed the wizened Hank to the encampment where they ate lunch and changed horses. Hot and tired, Stacy sat silently astride her horse in the noonday sun and waited for the veteran to join her. He ambled over to the ground-hitched pony beside Stacy and mounted.

'We'll be stayin' with the herd this afternoon,' he

stated. 'The two of us will be ridin' the right flank.'

Several times that afternoon Stacy caught sight of
Jim, but only once did he acknowledge her presence
with a wave. Stacy felt guilty for possibly getting the
young cowboy into trouble; she only hoped that Jim
wouldn't hold it against her. Of course he couldn't
very well rush over when he saw her—after all, he was
working. Twice she found herself looking around for
some sign of Cord Harris, but if he was taking part in
the afternoon drive, he escaped Stacy's eyes. Instead of
feeling relieved that his watchful eyes were not on her,
she felt empty.

At four o'clock the herd arrived at a stand of cottonwood trees that marked the course of a rushing stream.
This was the night's encampment. They drove the
cattle across the shallow water, bedding them down on
the opposite side. As Stacy followed Hank back over,
she looked wistfully at the swift-running water. What
an opportunity to wash some of the grit and grime
off!

All the hands had gathered around the cook wagon
where the coffee was fresh and hot. Stacy and Hank
dismounted at the remuda trailers and joined the
others. By tomorrow morning the herd would reach
the summer pasture and the drive would be over until
fall. Stacy stood quietly and sipped her coffee while
listening to the boasting and grumbling of the veteran
cowhands. Supper would be dished up shortly and she
wanted to go down to the stream before then. She finished the last of her coffee and handed the cup to the
cook. None of the group paid any attention to her as
she walked away towards the cottonwood trees.

Stacy strolled leisurely, following the river upstream. Five hundred yards from camp where the
stream widened as it made a turn, she stopped. This

was the perfect place to bathe, far enough away from camp to ensure privacy and far enough upstream for the water not to be muddied by the cattle crossing. Even an obliging tree had a lowhanging branch on which she could hang her clothes. Happily she swept the brown hat off her head and pulled out the rubber band holding her hair. Free from the confinement, the long chestnut hair fell caressingly around her shoulders as she sat down by the edge of the water to remove her dusty boots. Her toes wiggled happily in the coarse sand as their owner gazed blissfully at the beckoning water, glistening brightly with captured rays from the sun. Stacy hopped to her feet and made one last glance around her bathing hole to make sure there were no uninvited two-legged visitors, before shedding her blouse and jeans.

Clad only in her undergarments, she waded into the water. A small shudder ran through her at the unexpected coolness of the stream. She hummed merrily as she rubbed away the dirt and grime of the drive. Carried away by her enjoyment, Stacy failed to hear the sound of hooves muffled by the sand. A horse and rider came to a halt beside the overhanging cottonwood where Stacy had hung her clothes.

Still humming her happy tune, Stacy entered the shallower water and began wading towards the bank. Glancing at the tree, she stopped in the now waist-deep water, stunned by the sudden appearance of the horse and rider. Her surprise was quickly replaced by a self-consciousness of her scanty attire. Swiftly she lowered herself into the water.

'You could have had the decency to let me know you were there, Mr. Harris!' she exclaimed, her face red with shame as she addressed Cord's mocking face.

'I missed you at camp and came out looking for you,'

the deep voice replied, ignoring her angry criticism.

'Well, now you've found me, so kindly leave so I can get dressed.' Her embarrassment replaced by indignation.

'I'll wait for you over there,' Cord said, smiling, as he indicated a group of trees where his view of her would be obstructed. Amusement was all too visible on his face as he reined his horse around and left.

Hurriedly Stacy clambered up on the bank, chagrin and resentment hampering her. Trying to dress quickly, she struggled to pull the clothes on over her wet body. The sleeves of her blouse clung to her wet arms and with fumbling fingers she managed to get it buttoned and tucked into her Levi's. The boots slipped on easily even over the damp socks. She removed her hat from the tree and began running towards the place where Cord waited.

Cord stood silent beside his horse observing her approach. The haste with which she dressed and rushed to meet him had flushed her cheeks and her brown eyes were bright with tension and embarrassment. Stacy stopped a few feet in front of Cord and hesitated. Her eyes searched his face, desperately trying to read his inscrutable expression.

'Come on,' he said, 'I'll walk you back to camp.'

A little breathless, she fell into step beside him as he led his horse in that direction. The saturnine face never once turned towards her as they walked in silence. The strain was too much for Stacy. With her free hand she ran her fingers through her damp hair nervously.

'I was hot and dusty from the drive.' A hint of defiance was in her voice.

'The water certainly looked inviting,' Cord commented, refusing to take the bait of the unvoiced challenge she had made. 'To be honest, I was tempted to join you.' He searched her face, his eyes travelling from the damp tendrils of her hair around her forehead down her straight nose and coming to a halt at her moist parted lips.

Stacy knew they were very close to camp now. In her side vision she could make out the moving forms of the cowhands. She knew she should feel self-conscious at the possible observance of her and Cord, but she was only aware of the broad shoulders and the strong tanned face of the man beside her. He must have read the confusion and bewilderment in her gaze as she tried to fathom this change in his attitude towards her, for he abruptly released her arm and began their course once again for camp.

'I've never known a woman yet who could turn down a chance to freshen up,' Cord teased. For some reason that she could not or would not acknowledge, Stacy felt safer back on their old grounds of mocking banter.

'How can I properly seduce a man if I go around smelling like a cow?' she returned, a new lift in her walk and swing to her head.

'You have a very good point,' Cord agreed as they walked into the camp area. 'Go grab yourself a bite to eat, little one. I'll see you later.'

Stacy felt his hand touch her shoulder lightly as he moved away from her towards the horse vans. The warmth of his touch radiated as she visualized the imprint of his hand on her shoulder. Abstractedly she walked over to the group of men, conscious that her whole attention was focused on the retreating figure. Throughout the meal, she involuntarily watched for his approach. When he failed to come she was depressed. Usually she dreaded his presence, and here she was looking forward to it. What manner of man was

he that he could make her want to be with him and
hate him at the same time?

The cottonwood trees surrounding the camp hastened the darkening purple of the setting sun. Shadows
had begun casting their black forms through the camp.
The flickering fires seemed to grow increasingly
brighter. From the other side of the flame she recognized the figure of her riding companion of the morning. Jim seemed to be looking for someone as he stood
studying the various clusters of hands. Then he spotted Stacy and made his way around the campfire to
where she was sitting apart from the others.

'Hi,' the serious hazel eyes smiled. 'Been looking for
you.

'Work hard today?' Stacy asked.

'Not too. I'm sorry I had to leave you in the lurch
like that today,' Jim said, squatting down beside her.

'We didn't come to blows if that's what worried
you,' Stacy laughed. 'I didn't mean to get you into
trouble, Jim.'

'Seriously, Stacy, I like you. You know that, don't
you?' Jim asked quietly. When she failed to reply, he
added, 'Are you engaged or anything?'

'No.' Stacy avoided the turned head beside her. She
should have felt pleased by his affection, but she found
herself regretting the turn the conversation had taken.
'I like you, too, Jim. You're a very good friend.'

'That's the way I feel too,' he replied. 'I hope I'll be
able to see a lot more of you.'

'I hope so, too,' Stacy said. 'I've never had too many
friends.'

'Stacy,' affectionately, a calloused hand raised itself
and the fingers caressed her smooth cheek, 'you're
quite a girl. I bet you could turn a man down and
make him feel happy about it!'

CHAPTER EIGHT

'CONNORS!' snapped a voice a few feet away from the couple.

Both Stacy and Jim sprang guiltily apart at the biting tone as Cord stepped out of the shadows. Part of his face was still hidden by the darkness, but there was no doubting the leashed fury in the set of his jaws and the furrow in his brow. His dark eyes narrowed menacingly as he stared at the young cowboy.

'You have a unique talent for turning up when you're not expected,' Stacy accused, not liking his dictatorial manner.

'Obviously,' was the reply. Cord's penetrating gaze flickered briefly to Stacy and returned to Jim.

'Well?' he demanded.

'I have nothing to say, sir,' Jim answered, his chin jutting out as he met the censorious eyes.

Stacy could feel the resentment burning inside her. The way that Cord was humiliating Jim in front of her was unforgivable! His pride was being stripped away right in front of her eyes. How much did Cord think Jim could take? And why should it concern him that she had been talking to the cowboy?

Jim regarded Stacy silently. Finally he bade her good night and walked away. Furious at the tyrannical rancher, Stacy turned to face him, her brown eyes flashing as she trembled from the anger building up inside her.

'Just who do you think you are, Mr. Harris?' she cried. 'Do you get some kind of big thrill humiliating a man in front of a woman? Or do you just like everyone to know that you're Mr. Big Shot around here?'

'I don't see where it's any concern of yours what my reasons are,' said Cord, his voice still fierce with controlled emotion.

'That's a remark typical of you,' Stacy said bitterly. 'You consider yourself a law unto yourself, responsible to no one. Well, you're nothing! Do you hear me, nothing! Why, Jim is more of a man than you could ever hope to be. And furthermore, if you think you've succeeded in lowering him in my eyes, you're sadly mistaken. Before, I only considered him to be a friend, but now I can see that, compared to you, he's the only man on earth for me.'

'You admit, after all, that it is a man you want,' Cord retorted, a muscle in his jaw twitching in his own mounting anger. 'I seriously doubt if you would know a man if you saw one.'

'I know that whatever it is I'm standing in front of now, it's not a man!' she snapped, fully aware that she was pushing Cord too far, but beyond the point of caring. She enjoyed degrading this paragon before her.

The slender thread that had held his temper in check snapped as his face grew black with fury. Roughly he grabbed Stacy's arms, drawing her so close to him that she could see the throbbing veins on the side of his jaw. The iron grip of his fingers dug deep into her shoulders as she struggled uselessly against his muscular chest. He was much too strong for her. As one large hand moved, sweeping around her waist, the other grabbed her long brown hair, twisting her head back until she was forced to look into his face. Crushed against his chest, she stared tremulously into the now coal-black eyes.

'By God,' Cord said hoarsely, 'I'll not have you throwing yourself at my men. If it's an affair you're after, well, I'll take care of that right here and now!'

Slowly his face lowered down to hers as if enjoying the apprehension Stacy felt as she realized he was going to kiss her. Valiantly she tried to struggle again, but he restrained her easily. His arm tightened around her as if he meant to crush out every ounce of resistance. As his mouth pressed cruelly against hers, Stacy felt a fire of passion sear through her body. The fierceness of his kiss, meant to punish, hurt, and humiliate, stifled any effort she might have made to respond as the bristle of his whiskers scraped her skin. But the whirlpool of his nearness kept spinning in her mind and the throbbing of her heart must have echoed into his ears as it did in her own. When Stacy felt he would never let her go, Cord stepped away. The suddenness of his release jolted her off balance and she fell to the ground. Stunned, she lay there staring up at the towering figure.

'Never back a man up in a corner,' Cord said, the coldness back in his eyes. 'I told you once before to learn the rules before you played the game.'

'I despise you!' Stacy gasped, rising to her feet and flinging herself at him.

He caught her wrists easily and stared emotionless at the teardrops running down her cheeks. She kicked and scratched at him, but the attempts were warded off easily until she was finally exhausted by her efforts.

'You've beaten me,' she finally murmured, fighting the lump in her throat. 'You can always force me to do what you want, but you can never make me feel anything but disgust for you.'

There was no sign of self-reproach in his eyes as Cord looked at Stacy. As he lowered her imprisoned hands and released them, he stood silently searching her face for what Stacy didn't know.

'I know,' Cord finally sighed. 'I know. Come on, we'd better join the others.'

'Is that all you've got to say?' Stacy asked in a small voice, slightly astounded. 'No apologies? If that's the way you treat your women, I can see why you got jilted.'

Cord's face turned to stone at her words and his dark eyes bored deep inside her. Uncomfortably aware that she had trespassed on to something that was none of her affair, the numb Stacy stood there, tear-streaked and proud.

'I don't intend to apologize for my actions. I don't know what you heard about Lydia and me, but whatever it was, it's none of your business,' the cold, hard voice replied. 'Consider what happened tonight a lesson you should have learned long ago. You're not an unattractive girl. You're lucky that I haven't fallen under your spell or the outcome of tonight could have been quite different. Fortunately, I know you for what you are, and the cheap tricks your kind use to satisfy your egotistical craving for attention and admiration.' The sarcasm seeped through his words. 'The subject is closed.'

Stacy couldn't speak. She looked into his face, repelled by the disgust mirrored there. Bewildered, she offered no resistance when Cord took her arm and guided her back towards the campfire. Several times she stumbled on the uneven ground, but he never hesitated in his stride. Nor did he even glance her way; only the hand on her arm verified that he acknowledged her existence.

When they reached the campfire, he released her and walked on into the circle without her. Grateful to be away from him, Stacy slipped over to her bedroll, praying no one would speak to her or see her tear-rimmed eyes in the glowing firelight. Hiccupping silent sobs, she crawled into her covers. Cursing him for his unwarranted opinion of her, she snuggled inside the blanket for comfort, but her body and mind retained the memory of the strength and warmth of his arms and the brutality and fire in his kiss. Vainly she rubbed her lips with the back of her hand, but the memory was indelibly marked. Sleep crept up silently on her exhausted body.

The morning sun shone brightly down on Stacy astride the little bay horse she had ridden the first day. She could take no interest in the surrounding country as she rode along the flank of the herd. Listlessly she sat on the pony and let her gaze blur in the multitude of cattle.

Last night in her dreams she had relived Cord's embrace, but this time it was filled with passion and desire. She had returned Cord's kiss with equal fervour. The dream was almost more disquieting than the actual kiss. Afterwards she had clung to him, driven by a desperation that he would reject her. She felt she had somehow betrayed herself in that dream. She hated Cord Harris and everything he stood for. The shame and guilt she felt for the imagined kiss far exceeded the humiliation the actual kiss had filled her with the night before.

The pounding of approaching hooves aroused her from her thoughts. Looking up, Stacy recognized Jim Connors astride the galloping horse. He waved and rode by to pull up beside Hank. They exchanged a few words between them, causing an embarrassing flush to flood Stacy's cheeks as she wondered if they were discussing her. If it had been one of the other days, she would have dropped back to join them, but she was afraid to face them today for fear they could read in her face the events of the night before. A few minutes later Hank rode up beside her.

'We'll be reachin' the pasture in the hour,' said Hank. 'The Boss told Jim this morning that as soon as we got to the summer pasture you were to go back to the ranch house.'

'Why? Did he say?' Stacy asked, dreading the prospect of meeting Córd Harris again.

'Nope. One of the hands will be there with a pick-up and you'll ride back with him. And the Boss wants you to go to his office as soon as you get there,' Hank replied, the same searching look in his eyes. 'You had another go-round with the Boss last night, didn't ya'?'

Stacy started to deny it, but knew she couldn't fool the sharp-eyed cowhand and nodded affirmatively.

'You two do rub each other's fur the wrong way,' he smiled with a shake of his head. 'Jim said the Boss come up on you two last night.'

'I suppose he jumped all over Jim this morning?' Stacy remarked bitterly.

'Jim figured he would, but he didn't say a word about it, in fact he even put Jim in charge of one of the brandin' crews,' the veteran smiled, watching Stacy's face closely for her reaction.

'He did?' The amazement was written on her face. 'Probably his way of apologizing,' she reasoned to herself.

'I imagine you're thinkin' me to be an ole gossip, but are you sweet on Jim or somethin'?'

'No,' said Stacy, a hint of a smile appearing on her face. 'We're friends. He knew my father, or met him at a lecture.'

'Good,' the old cowboy grinned with a satisfied gleam in his eyes.

'Good. Why?' Curious at his unusual remark.

'Ain't his type. You need somebody stronger to hold you in check. Fire and fire always makes a bigger flame.'

'I didn't know you mixed matchmaking with philosophy, Hank,' she laughed. 'Tell me, do you have someone in mind?'

'I do, but I ain't tellin'. You'll know soon enough,' Hank answered mysteriously. Kicking his horse, he added over the din, 'Better get back to work.'

Laughing, Stacy joined him, the gloom of the morning fading in the wake of the sagacious cowboy. When the last steer had been chased through, Hank motioned towards a waiting pick-up, indicating that that was the one Stacy would be taking back to the ranch house.

She rode over to the remuda trailer and dismounted. Dodging the milling horses and riders, she made her way to the truck. The driver opened the door for her and motioned her inside. Stacy exchanged a few pleasantries with him, but the growing anticipation of meeting Cord after last night's episode gradually silenced her. Her imagination had all sorts of reasons for his wanting to talk with her. If she was lucky he might want to put an end to the bargain they had made.

Driving into the yard, Stacy noticed an unfamiliar gold-coloured Cadillac parked in front of the hacienda. Even though she wasn't familiar with all the vehicles of the surrounding neighbours, she was sure she had never seen any car like that before. A curious sense of foreboding filled her as the pick-up pulled up beside the house gates to let her out.

Tired and filled with dread, Stacy walked with her bedroll and hat in one hand and suede jacket in the other. As she opened the door she wished she had a chance to clean up and change before meeting the formidable Cord Harris, but knew that he expected her as soon as she arrived. Resentment flared briefly within her, as she recognized that he wanted her at a disadvantage. How could she appear cool and in control if she looked like a dirty urchin?

Stepping inside the cool interior of the entry way, she became aware of voices in the den. Uncertainly she stopped before the closed door and tried to recognize them, but the thick oak door muffled the sounds. 'Maybe he's busy and doesn't want to see me now,' she thought. No, she might as well get it over with. Resigned, she placed the items in her hands on the bench outside the room, gave a few brisk brushes at the dust on her jeans and blouse, smoothed her long hair back to where it was caught at the neck, squared her shoulders, and knocked at the door.

'Come in,' came the muffled reply.

With more confidence than she felt, Stacy opened the heavy door and walked into the room. Cord stood directly in front of her beside his desk. There was a nonchalance and ease in his carriage that intensified her nervousness.

'Come on in,, Miss Adams,' Cord instructed with a slightly imperious wave of his hand. His mocking eyes flicked over her dishevelled appearance and he added, 'I see you've just got here.'

'I understood you wanted to see me right away,' Stacy said defensively, looking the tall figure in the eye. 'If you're busy I can come back later.'

'No, that won't be necessary,' he said. His gaze left her to travel casually to the tall-backed chair in front of the desk. 'You don't mind waiting a few minutes, do you?'

For the first time Stacy's eyes searched the room for

the second voice she had heard outside. So intent on meeting Cord was she that she had momentarily forgotten her curiosity about the owner of the Cadillac outside. A movement in the chair captured her attention. The over-sized leather chair with its back to Stacy had hidden its occupant from her view. Now she saw the slender, stockinged legs, the high heels and the polished nails of a feminine hand. As the graceful figure rose from the chair, Stacy felt the quiver of a premonition flow through her. The woman was strikingly beautiful. Her hair was jet black and drawn back into a chignon, emphasizing her high cheekbones and creamy skin. Her eyes, as they turned to survey Stacy, were as black as her hair and sparkled with a subdued fire. She was several inches taller than Stacy and managed to give the impression that she was looking down that graceful nose at her. The dark eyes glowed with pleasure as the woman looked at the bedraggled appearance of the other girl.

'You are going to introduce us, aren't you, Cord dear?' the strange woman asked in a clear, melodic voice.

'Of course,' he replied, his eyes never straying from Stacy's blushing face. 'Lydia, I'd like you to meet Miss Stacy Adams. She's been helping me around the ranch here, as you can tell. Miss Adams, this is Lydia Marshall, a very old friend of mine.'

Murmuring an incoherent hello, Stacy nodded. Lydia—that was the woman Cord had been engaged to! Conscious of the significance of the two being together, she flashed a questioning look at Cord. His face maintained the same mocking expression that she had become so familiar with these past weeks. The gleam in his eyes that she had previously attributed to his satisfaction at her untidy appearance held something more. Maybe they were back together again, but what of Lydia's husband? A thousand questions raced through Stacy's mind as she tried to concentrate on the conversation between the two, but the only thing that remained implanted in her mind after Lydia left the room was the silky voice of the dark-haired woman.

Stacy stared at the closed oak door trying desperately to shake the chilling dread that grew within her.

'I said would you like to sit down, Adams,' the deep voice repeated in a slightly louder tone.

'Of course—I'm sorry,' Stacy mumbled, further embarrassed by her inattention. She walked over and sat in one of the straight-backed chairs beside the desk. Cord had already seated himself behind his desk and was shuffling through a few papers.

'She's a very beautiful woman. Did her husband come with her?' Stacy blurted out before she realized it.

'No,' Cord replied, a whisper of a smile in his eyes and a smug satisfaction on his lips. 'It seems Mrs. Marshall is getting a divorce.'

'Oh,' Stacy managed in a very small voice. Why did it upset her that the two were obviously getting back together?

'Now to get at the reason I called you in here,' he started briskly. 'It's quite clear that our previous arrangement is not going to work, at least not the way I planned.'

'I'm still willing to write you a cheque for any of the damages that I've caused,' she volunteered, sitting nervously on the edge of her chair. 'I quite understand that you wish to be rid of me now, and I assure you the feeling is mutual.'

'I'm afraid you misunderstand,' he said, raising one eyebrow. 'I still believe you should work your debt out. What's obvious is that you can't take the place of one of the men, or even half of one. Therefore I propose that you handle something more in a feminine line.'

'I don't quite understand what you're getting at?'

'As I mentioned to you once before, each spring I have an auction where I sell some of my registered quarter horse stock, Texas-style. That means a barbecue and a party.' Cord's eyes were sparkling as he watched the dawning comprehension on Stacy's face. 'I'm sure with your country club background you'll be able to organize this year's activity, which will leave me free to take care of the ranch.'

'How many people will be here?' Stacy asked, ignoring the veiled sarcasm in his last statement. 'When is it going to be?'

'Before the day's over, I imagine several hundred people will have been here at one time or another. The date is set for June the ninth, almost four weeks away,' he answered, studying her face thoughtfully. 'Now, if you think it's too much for you——?'

'Not at all,' Stacy said defensively. 'But I must admit I'm curious why you didn't ask Mrs. Marshall to act as hostess and co-ordinator for you.'

'It's really none of your business, the reasons for my decision to use you, but I've already said that I wanted you to work your way out, and this seemed the only alternative.' His voice had grown cold at her presumptuous statement. 'And Mrs. Marshall is going through a difficult adjustment and shouldn't be expected to supervise the preparations for a gathering of this size with the emotional pressure she's presently under. Besides, it wouldn't exactly be proper for Lydia to do so at this time. Of course, I doubt if you would realize that.'

'I didn't know that other people's opinions bothered you,' she retorted, stung by the masterly way he was protecting his former fiancée.

'It depends a great deal on the people involved,' Cord's icy voice replied. 'There are some people whose reputation I wouldn't want damaged, and there are some people who aren't going to be around long enough to worry about.'

'If you're making some subtle reference to me, I would prefer that you speak your mind,' Stacy said angrily. 'You've acquired some ridiculous idea that I go around flirting with every man I meet. At least I don't go accosting guests staying in my home!'

'I thought you'd have better sense than to bring that up,' Cord snapped in a dangerously low voice. The muscle in his jaw twitched its familiar warning sign again. 'Last night is better forgotten. Most women would have had enough pride not to have brought it up again.'

'I don't happen to be most women!' Stacy retorted, rising agitatedly from her seat to stand with her hands clasped tightly on the back of the chair. 'Evidently you expect me to forget it with a snap of my fingers.'

'Frankly, I don't care whether you forget it or not,' Cord said, looking up at the slim figure. 'Unless, of course, you want a repeat performance.'

'That's the last thing I would ever want from you!' Guilt burned across her face as she remembered her response to his kiss in her dream.

'Very well,' he said, closing the subject and turning his attention to a sheaf of papers in front of him. 'Here are some of the arrangements already made for the sale which you should make yourself familiar with. You may use this den as the centre of your activities. I won't be disturbing you since I take care of most of my paper work in the office. Quite likely there'll be a few details you will want to go over with me. You can contact me at that time. I believe that's all.'

His cold tone of dismissal froze the angry words in Stacy's throat. She stood by the chair for a moment, but he didn't raise his eyes from the stack of papers. Briskly she turned on her heel and strode out of the room, giving the heavy oak door an added impetus as it closed. Gathering her belongings in the foyer, she stalked up the stairs to her room, where she flung her bundle down on the floor and stared at her glowering reflection in the dresser mirror.

An hour later, as Stacy was walking out of the bathroom after showering and changing her clothes, she met Cord in the hallway.

'I neglected to give you the keys to your car,' Cord said briskly, his cool, dark eyes taking in the freshness of her appearance. 'You'll be needing transportation, so I had one of my men bring it over from the cabin. It's in the garage.'

'How thoughtful of you,' Stacy replied sarcastically.

'I also had a typewrter installed in the den,' he added, his eyes narrowing at her tone. 'I believe that should take care of the things you'll need.'

'I'm quite sure everything is satisfactory,' she said, starting to brush past the handsome figure. But his muscular arm shot out and blocked her passage. Stacy's flashing eyes looked up at the darkening face.

'You can wipe that expression off your face,' Cord stated threateningly. 'A good thrashing would do wonders for a spoiled brat like you.'

'Violence is your solution to everything, isn't it?' she answered, not flinching under his penetrating gaze. 'Now, get out of my way and let me by.'

Shaking inwardly, she pushed his arm out of her way and walked briskly down the stairs. At the bottom of the steps stood the dark beauty of Lydia Marshall, her black eyes icy cold as she watched Stacy walk past her. The ice vanished as Cord made his way down the steps behind Stacy.

'There you are!' Lydia said in her saccharine voice. 'I was beginning to wonder if you'd forgotten me. I fixed us a drink. I hope I've remembered how you like them.'

Lydia's voice fluttered after Stacy like a flaunting red cape, but she didn't wait around to hear Cord's reply. Hurrying blindly into the den, Stacy leaned against the closed door and waited for the trembling in her knees and the pounding of her heart to return to normal. Why did she let Cord arouse her this way? He never acted the same way towards her twice. One time he was teasing and friendly as he was when he had found her at the river, and the next time he was violent and abusive, as when he had kissed her so brutally. And today he was the Don, condescending and dictatorial, making sure she knew where her place was. As far as Stacy was concerned Cord deserved the icy Latin beauty of Lydia Marshall with her sickening, ingratiating airs. Oh, how Stacy wished for the steadiness of Carter Mills. She was growing extremely weary of being a barometer of Cord's emotions.

Discouraged and weary from the last three days of riding, she crossed over behind the desk and sat dejectedly in the chair and studied the stack of papers in front of her. The image of the tanned hands shuffling through them crossed her mind. Absently she shifted through them, her attention straying at first until the magnitude of the party with all its details began to sink in.

Horror-stricken, she sat in the big swivel chair and went through the papers once more. If he hadn't been so antagonistic she would have explained that she had never given even a dinner party for more than twelve people in her life. What was she going to do now? The memory of his derisive, mocking smile flitted in front of her as she saw herself trying to explain to him.

'Oh, how he'd like that,' Stacy thought. 'It would really please him to see me fall flat on my face. Well, that's not going to happen. I'll have to work a lot harder than I thought, but if I'm lucky, he'll never see the few mistakes I'll make.'

With renewed confidence she tackled the stack of papers again and began to sort a plan out in her mind.

CHAPTER NINE

THE red sorrel tossed his flaxen mane in the air and snorted his displeasure at the firm hand curbing his pace.

'Easy, Diablo,' Stacy quieted him, but he continued to pull at the bit.

Maybe a good gallop would release some of her tension, Stacy thought. The row she had had with Cord earlier that afternoon had taken its toll on her patience. Two weeks had passed since he had put her in charge of the sale festivities. the co-ordination of all the various activities was a full-time job and exceedingly trying for someone who had never done it before, despite the assistance from the wives of the permanent hands. Stacy had been pleased with the job she had done thus far. She also had the feeling that Cord was satisfied with her work, too. Not that it really mattered what his opinion was, she told herself. But this afternoon when she was going over some of the correspondence with him regarding the preparation of the auction itself, Cord had asked her for the printer's proof of the sales catalogue. Stacy knew nothing about it and confessed her ignorance of it to him.

She could still see the thundering expression on his face when he heard her words. She burned at the memory of his scathing remarks. If only she had been able to explain to him her inexperience in arranging such affairs, but the humiliation had burned too deep to allow any room for further scorn. The man was so callous that he couldn't possibly possess anything that even remotely resembled a heart.

Cord had been gone almost every day since the initial meeting when he had turned the preparations over to her. Sometimes during the day he took time to confer with her, but their conversations were limited strictly to the auction. Stacy didn't know if the ranch work was pressing or if he was merely avoiding spending any time with her. Lydia breezed in several times looking for him, occasionally condescending to consult Stacy for Cord's whereabouts, conveying the impression that he was helping her with the technicalities of her divorce. Usually she found him somewhere, since Stacy often saw them from her window, Cord's head bent low to catch some confiding remark the raven-haired woman made, her arm resting possessively on his. Stacy normally turned guiltily from the window, blushing as if she had been caught in the act of eavesdropping on an intimate conversation. Other times she watched until they were out of sight before returning to her work with an odd sense of depression about her.

She was positive that Cord's continued absence in the evenings was caused by Lydia. Strangely enough Stacy found herself either missing him or dreading his arrival, and she refused to let herself delve into the reasons for her contradictory emotions.

Several evenings Jim Connors had joined her on the veranda, and they had chatted away, discovering many interests in common. Stacy enjoyed the easy companionship of the young cowboy with his ready laughter and undemanding company. It was a vast difference from her tempestuous relationship with Cord Harris. With Jim she felt comfortable and at ease, not worrying about each little word she said and how he was going to interpret it. The friendly relaxed atmosphere that surrounded her when she was with Jim reminded her of the way she had relied on Carter Mills.

Carter. He seemed eons away. Had it only been such a short time ago that she had been with him? His last letter had been chatty and full of interesting tidbits of various mutual acquaintances, but it also held an underlying current of concern that Stacy couldn't ignore. She knew he was waiting for an answer from her, one that she couldn't give. She had difficulty even recalling what Carter looked like; all she could summon up was a blurred image of short, sandy hair and shining blue eyes so unclear that it could have been Jim she was picturing rather than Carter. Maybe the resemblance between the two was the reason she was so drawn to Jim. Stacy really couldn't say. But she had no desire to think on it. She probably would have been better off if she had never come out here, but then she never would have fallen in love with this wild, rugged country. Even in her present circumstances, Stacy enjoyed the closeness of the demanding landscape. Gone was the overcrowdedness, the smog, and the endless blare of traffic; in its place was endless space, fresh air, and the muffled calls of God's creatures.

With a glance at the sinking sun, Stacy remounted the rested horse and turned him towards the ranch house. Her wandering thoughts were brought up short by the knowledge that she had to return before the sun was too far down.

All too quickly they reached the stables. Stacy dismounted and led the docile sorrel through the fence gate to the stable area. Humming contentedly, she didn't hear the approach of the wizened Hank.

'You shore are mighty cheerful,' Hank crackled behind her.

The sudden voice startled her. 'Hank! You shouldn't do that!' she admonished with a shaky laugh. 'You practically scared me out of my boots!'

'You looked so happy and contented that it seemed a pure shame to spoil such a pretty picture,' he grinned.

'I thought only the Irish had kissed the Blarney Stone. Seems you people out here must have one of your own,' she teased, a sparkle lighting up her brown eyes.

'Pshaw! Ain't nothin' fancy about tellin' a pretty girl she's pretty when all she had to do is look in the mirror an' see,' Hank replied with a grunt.

Warmed by the affection of the gnarled man beside her and the caressing rays of the firey-bright sun, Stacy had a tremendous urge to spread her arms and envelop the great wild, rugged land that had captured her so completely. Instead she raised her face to the gentle breeze and inhaled the fragrant perfumes it carried.

'I love this land!' she exclaimed, ending in a regretful sigh. 'I'm going to hate leaving all this behind.'

'I thought you didn't like it here?' Hank commented, turning his head away to hide the twinkle in his eye.

'I've never seen anything like it. At times it's so harsh and desolate, but the beauty is still there. Oh, ño, Hank, I don't like it, I love it!'

'Humph! If you're so fond of this place, why leave it? Why don't you just move to some part of the country around here?'

'It wouldn't be the same,' Stacy replied with a gentle shake of her chestnut hair.

'What's so special about this place, anyway?'

'It's a hundred different things. The sun wouldn't set quite the same. The hills wouldn't be the same colour,' she explained hesitantly.

'The sun sets the same anywhere,' Hank snorted. Then he turned to her rapturous face, not even trying to hide the gleam in his eyes and added, 'What about the Boss?'

'What do you mean?' Stacy queried, stiffening at the reference to the enigmatical Cord Harris.

'Ain't he a part of all this?'

'Of course not! He's——'

'He's the only reason why you're wantin' to stay here at all,' Hank grinned, hurrying on before Stacy could voice the protest forming on her lips. 'Quit kiddin' yoreself that you're only here to work out the trouble yore horse caused.'

'He won't let me go,' Stacy cried.

'You won't let yoreself go,' Hank answered. 'Face it, girl, the only hold he has on you is your heart. You love him. I've known it for a long time.'

'No,' Stacy said weakly as the gruff words sank in.

'Reckon it's about time the cat was let out of the bag. If you got any guts at all, you'll admit it to yourself.'

Stacy stood speechless after the retreating figure. In love with Cord Harris? Impossible! Why, he was the most arrogant, rude, hateful person she had ever known. She hated him! Memories raced through her mind—the racing of her pulse when he entered a room, the torment and pain of his mocking smile, the burning of her skin at his touch. Stacy groaned, remembering the black hair with its wayward lock that fell on to the tanned forehead and the dark, flashing eyes that so many times threatened to consume her with their fire, and the finely chiselled cheekbones with their shadow of a beard, his mouth that had bruised and battered her with his kiss when all the time she had been seeking it, waiting for it.

Impatiently the stallion turned and whickered to the slim, freckled figure. Numbly she led him to his corral. stumbling several times, unable to focus on anything but the vivid picture of Cord etched in her mind. She loved him! This torment that possessed her when he was near was the desire to love which was antagonized into hate by his rejection. As she turned the sorrel loose in his paddock, Stacy allowed the realization to wash over her. How could she have been so blind not to have recognized it before? A bubble of elation filled her as she raced to the hacienda. A flush filled her cheeks; a glow lit her brown eyes; and a smile spread across her face with the warming knowledge of her discovery. Stacy Adams loved Cord Harris, her heart chanted. She wanted to scream it to the world. Breathlessly she threw open the heavy oak door and rushed into the silent hall.

The emptiness stopped her. He wasn't here. He had left with Lydia this afternoon after Stacy had quarrelled with him. The desolation swept over her. How could she have forgotten Lydia with her raven hair and porcelain skin? The divorcee with her dark beauty had returned to Cord, returned to accept the love he had once laid at her feet. It was she he cared for, not Stacy. The excitement of her new-found love had allowed Stacy to forget one vital thing—Cord despised her, despised everything she stood for!

'Get hold of yourself, Stacy Adams,' she scolded, wrinkling the golden freckles on her nose at the self-pity that wanted to swallow her. 'Your father didn't raise a quitter. Cord thinks you're a feckless girl without an ounce of sense to your name and concern for no one but yourself. You've got to show him before it's too late that he's wrong. At least you can fight for him. You can give that raven-haired witch a run for her money!'

With grim determination Stacy swept aside the waves of melancholy. First things first and the first was washing the dust off from her ride and after that she would dress for dinner. Tonight she'd wear her backless jersey culotte dress with the bold turquoise and emerald design. She had brought it along on a whim, but now she would put it to use.

A spark of combat gleamed in Stacy's brown eyes as she undressed swiftly and stepped under the biting spray of the shower. 'Cord,' she let the name roll lovingly from her lips. It had the sound of a man, the tensile strength of a whip cracking overhead. The rugged land of Texas had bred a man to match and conquer its harsh terrain. Remembering the strength of his hands, the steel of his arms and the solidness of his broad shoulders, she felt a quiver of passion course through her. If only she could look into his dark eyes and see a desire and a love for her there, how perfect her world would be.

By the time she had stepped out of the shower, she

had recaptured the earlier enchantment of her new emotion. With a youthful resiliency she had bounded back with a sureness based on faith rather than common sense. Briskly she rubbed the rough terry towel over her body. Singing happily to herself, she returned to the bedroom where she proceeded to dress with a great deal more care than she had ever bothered with before.

Finished, she stood before the large dresser mirror inspecting her reflection with a critical eye. The brilliant blues and greens of her dress offset the light golden tan of her arms and the sun-bleached highlights in her hair. With a final glance at the satin shoes peeping under the floor-length skirt, she winked a compliment to her reflection and left the room.

With a regalness of carriage that denied the flutterings in her heart, Stacy descended the stairs. The plump Mexican housekeeper was setting the table in the dining room. The confidence in Stacy's face took a little dive when she saw only one place setting. She almost asked Maria when Cord was expected home, but pride wouldn't let her concede the possibility that he wouldn't be returning early. Her inquiries on previous evenings had always been met with a negative answer and she couldn't bear to hear one tonight.

'The señorita looks lovely tonight,' Maria bubbled with her usual wide smile. 'You have a date with Jeem, maybe, no?'

'No,' Stacy smiled as she tried to steel herself against the trembling in her body.

Quietly she seated herself at the empty table and tried to eat the attractive dishes placed before her. But the anticipation that consumed her didn't leave any room for food even though she tried valiantly to show an interest in the fruit salads and cold meats that

Maria had prepared so painstakingly for her. Finally, after picking away at a pineapple confection for several minutes and not tasting a bit of it, Stacy pushed herself away from the table. It was no use. The tension and apprehension of waiting had stolen her appetite. She was just too excited to eat. Nervously she rose from her chair and began pacing by the table.

'Do you not feel well, señorita?' the Mexican woman asked, standing in the doorway of the dining room.

'It was really a very good meal, Maria. I just don't have any appetite,' Stacy apologized, not wishing to hurt her feelings.

Maria seemed to accept Stacy's explanation and began clearing away the dishes. Stacy watched for a minute, trying to gather the courage to ask Maria if she knew where Cord was.

'You perhaps would like your coffee out on the patio?'

'Yes, that would be nice,' Stacy murmured absently. Quietly she started to walk from the room, then stopped and in a nonchalant voice asked, 'Do you expect Mr. Harris home early this evening?'

'Oh, no. He went to a cattlemen's dinner. He usually very late,' was the reply before Maria bustled off to the kitchen.

Dejectedly Stacy walked through the living room to the large glass doors that led on to the veranda. The hope had washed out of her eyes as she slid the doors open and stood on the cobblestone floor outside.

The loneliness seemed to seep into her bones, quelling all the hope and confidence she had summoned. Restlessly, Stacy walked farther out and leaned heavily against a pillar supporting the balcony above. She struggled desperately to fight the dejection and listlessness that was surrounding her. The pool shimmered darkly in the dim light, a hint of ominousness in its depths. She gazed in the direction of the family cemetery on the gentle knoll above the house, hidden from direct view by the adobe walls. Silently she whispered a prayer to Doña Elena, Cord's grandmother. If she understood how much Stacy loved this country and her grandson, perhaps the ghost of this Spanish woman would intervene on her behalf. But no, that only happened in dreams. Wishing Cord by her side could not make it so.

Absently Stacy heard the sound of steps on the patio. Assuming it to be Maria with her coffee, she remained leaning against the pillar, not wishing the Mexican woman to see the tears that threatened to roll down her cheeks.

'Just put the coffee on the table, Maria. I'll serve myself in a minute,' Stacy's voice was uncommonly low, her throat choked by the emotion she couldn't control.

'The coffee's already here. You don't mind if I help myself before it gets cold, do you?' came the reply.

'Cord,' she whispered faintly. For a moment, she was afraid her legs wouldn't hold her. In that brief moment he rushed to her side.

'Stacy, are you all right?' His hands seized her shoulders roughly.

'Yes, yes, I'm fine. You startled me,' Stacy replied shakily, refusing to look into the probing dark eyes for fear they would see the naked love she felt.

'For a minute there I thought you were going to faint. You were as pale as a ghost. Are you sure you feel all right?' The concern still in his voice as his tanned hands remained on her arms.

His nearness overwhelmed her. She was so conscious of the rich black cloth of his suit, the brilliant whiteness of his shirt, and his face just inches from hers, that she couldn't look up. She couldn't let him see what he was doing to her. Her eyes concentrated on his left hand, the strong fingers, the dark, curling hairs peeping out from the cuff of his shirt.

'You're hurting me!' Her voice came out weakly as her body threatened to sway against the massive chest that presented itself so invitingly.

'I'm sorry,' Cord said, moving abruptly away from her, a briskness returning to his voice. Stacy glanced up, but his eyes were hidden in the night's shadows and she was unable to determine his reaction. Did he consider her a silly city girl afraid of the dark? 'I didn't realize I was holding you so tightly,' he finished.

Firmly Stacy got hold of herself. She mustn't act like a coltish schoolgirl. After all, this was what she wanted, a chance to be alone with him. The trouble was her tongue was twisted up with the love in her heart. How much easier it would be just to tell him she loved him. Casually she walked up to the edge of the veranda to join him.

'Care for a cigarette?'

'Yes, thank you,' Stacy replied, watching the masculine hands holding the cigarette case as they removed another filter-tipped cigarette and lit it for her. The sudden flare of the lighter illuminated the rough features of Cord's face, outlining the lines of tiredness etched around his mouth.

'Maria didn't expect you back till much later. She said you were at a cattlemen's dinner. Have you eaten?' she asked, trying to keep too much concern from showing in her voice.

'Yes,' he replied noncommittally.

'Are those type of things usually over this early?' Stacy asked, desperately trying to keep the conversation going, hoping he wouldn't notice her nervousness.

'No, it was still going on when I left.' His reply was abrupt and gave Stacy the impression that he didn't feel like talking.

'I imagine you're rather tired. Perhaps you'd rather I left so you could relax?' she suggested, willing the pain to leave her heart.

'You're extremely solicitous tonight,' Cord replied, an eyebrow raised quizzically in her direction. 'Yes, I am rather tired, but no, you don't need to leave. If you want to make yourself useful you can pour me a cup of coffee.'

Without replying Stacy walked over to the table. As she stood bathed in the light from the living room, Cord's low voice carried to her, 'You look very becoming in that frock you're wearing.'

'Thank you,' she murmured, trying to still the trembling that ceased her hand.

'Were you expecting company tonight?' His voice had changed from an indifferent tone to the familiar mocking one.

'No,' Stacy said too swiftly, trying to cover the embarrassment that his observation had caused. If only he knew that the only person she expected was him! 'I just felt like slipping into something different.'

Cord walked over into the light near Stacy. She handed him his coffee, her own dark eyes flicking up to meet his as she did so.

'I was hoping you'd be up,' Cord said briskly, moving out of the light where she couldn't study his expression.

'Oh,' Stacy cursed inwardly at the breathlessness in her voice.

'I wanted to apologize for this afternoon. You're doing an excellent job on the barbecue and I was unreasonably harsh.' He seemed to hesitate as if waiting for a reply, but no words came from her lips. 'No harm has been done, and the fault was mainly mine for not advising you about the catalogue.'

'No,' Stacy rushed, 'I should have realized that——'

'Whoa!' Cord laughed. His warm deep mirth thrilled her. 'Let's close the conversation before we start a mutual admiration society.'

'But that's just what I want to do,' Stacy thought as she joined the laughter. She felt rather than saw the tension ease out of him as he turned and flicked his cigarette off into the dark. She watched the arc of the glowing embers as it sailed through the air to be lost in the shrubbery. Her long fingers stubbed her own cigarette out in an available ash tray. Cord had moved over to the pillar where Stacy had been standing when he had arrived. She wandered a few feet to the other side of him, her own cup of coffee held caressingly in both hands, enjoying the feel of its warmth to her palms.

'Oh, the stars are out!' she exclaimed as she looked into the velvet sky at the brilliant array.

'Now you've seen stars before,' the mocking voice said.

'Yes, but you see, when I was looking out here earlier, there were only one or two dim stars and now there's hundreds,' Stacy explained, radiant with her enthusiasm. 'It seemed so lonely with no moon and just a couple of stars, but now it's magnificent.'

'Tell me something, Stacy,' he said, leaning lazily against the pillar, his dark gaze surveying the lithe form beside him, 'are you really what you seem? One time you're a dewy-eyed girl enraptured with a flower or a moon or something, another time you're a hot-tempered Irish colleen fighting me tooth and nail, then you're a cool, sophisticated debutante acting out a part like earlier tonight in your fine satin gown. Which one is the real you?'

'Will the real Miss Stacy Adams please stand up?' she laughed, not wanting to face the serious eyes. But when he failed to join in with her joke, Stacy added as truthfully as she could, 'I suppose I'm all those things.'

Her eyes tried to read his expression, but his face was in the shadows. He stood quietly for a time until the silence became too much for Stacy and she nervously walked over and placed her cup near the coffee urn.

'Stacy?' There was a hesitation in Cord's use of her name that she couldn't identify.

'Yes?'

'Would you come here a minute?' If only she knew what made his voice seem so different, almost unsure. 'I'd like to ask you something, if you don't mind.'

Stacy's heart beat wildly as she moved beside the tall figure leaning negligently against the white column. He didn't turn to look at her, but continued to gaze out into the night.

'How can a man go about asking a woman who has had all the material things she's ever wanted and whose beauty ensures her all the attention she could ever desire to share her life with him?' Cord's voice had a briskness of controlled emotion that wrenched at Stacy's heart.

With difficulty she suppressed a strangling gasp. 'Oh, dear God,' she thought, 'he's asking me about Lydia.'

'What can I offer her? A life in a country that she must dislike? A monotonous existence?' he went on derisively. 'Just exactly who does the giving and who does the taking in that kind of a situation?'

'I—I would think offering her your love would be enough,' Stacy stammered, pain racking her body in silent sobs, her mind reeling and tormented with doubts.

His dark head twisted sharply to scrutinize her face which she had turned to look out into the night so that the grief that was filling her eyes would be hidden.

'Would that be enough for you?' his low voice asked, but he didn't wait for a reply. 'And just how would you let your man know?'

'It would be enough for me if the right man asked,' Stacy answered, a calmness settling over her heart, knowing his love would be all she would ever ask. She turned to face him, and a serenity radiated from her face as she added, 'And if he loved me, he'd know.'

A dark hand reached out and imprisoned her wrist, pulling her over beside him. Her breath came in rapid gasps as the dark, fiery eyes bore into hers.

'If he was unsure, how would you go about telling him, Stacy?' Cord's voice vibrated near her hair. She felt his left hand slip behind her waist, coming to rest on the bareness of her back, its contact searing through her body. His right hand released her wrist and travelled up to her white throat to caress the side of her neck just below her ear. She knew she had only to lift her head slightly to his face, but she couldn't. Very gently, his thumb slid under her chin, forcing her head up. Stacy's eyes didn't travel any farther than his mouth that was slowly descending upon her own.

At the first touch of his lips upon hers, she stiffened, not wanting to give in to their gentle demands. But soon, as Cord's ardour continued, she succumbed rapturously—begging, then demanding, the passion coursing her body at the answering hunger in his embrace. Who would have dreamed that Cord would kiss her in this way? Lydia, yes, but Stacy? Lydia! With a start Stacy came to her senses. Cord wasn't kissing her, not with this much passion. He was pretending she was

Lydia! Briskly she broke from his arms, standing terrified in front of him, ashamed of what he must surely guess. His face was at first soft as he looked down at her until the panic-stricken expression on her face registered. Immediately Cord's eyes blazed with fire as he turned abruptly away, his immense chest rising and falling at a rapid rate.

'We seem to have got carried away by our conversation,' he said roughly, removing a cigarette from his case and lighting it.' 'Our thoughts were obviously far apart.'

With an audible sigh of relief, Stacy realized he was mistaking her submission and acceptance of his kiss as a pretence that for her, he too was someone else.

'Luckily we both know what we feel towards one another, so there isn't any need to feel embarrassed,' he added, refusing to look at the unmoving girl beside him.

'No, thank goodness,' Stacy replied with a shaky laugh. 'It could have proved very awkward otherwise.'

She moved a step away from him, her body still trembling uncontrollably from his kiss, the initial magic of his lips destroyed by the knowledge that she was only a substitute for Lydia Marshall.

'I imagine it's getting rather late,' Cord said quietly. 'I suppose we ought to be turning in.'

'I am rather tired,' Stacy replied, grasping the straw he offered. 'I'll see you in the morning.'

With as much poise as she could muster, she walked out of the veranda into the living room. Cord followed a few paces behind, but as he entered the living room the phone rang. At the bottom of the stairs, Stacy heard him answer it.

'Harris Ranch, Cord speaking.—Yes, Lydia, I left the meeting a bit earlier than I'd planned. I intended to call you but——' Stacy didn't wait to hear more.

With a cry, Stacy rushed up the stairs. She couldn't bear to hear him talking to Lydia. It was going to be difficult enough to face him tomorrow without increasing her pain tonight.

CHAPTER TEN

THREE days had passed since that fateful evening with Cord. There were faint circles around Stacy's brown eyes and a slight drawnness in the full mouth, indicating the sleepless nights and tension-filled days. Cord had repeatedly ignored her, no longer checking with her every day as he had done before. In fact, twice when Stacy had been out walking and had seen him in the distance, he had changed direction to take himself out of her path. A crushing sense of defeat had closed in on her as she realized that he couldn't even stand to see her.

Abruptly, Stacy rose from the desk, refusing to let the melancholy within her interfere with her work. The sale was only a week away and there was a great deal still to be done. She was grateful that her time would be so occupied with the auction that she wouldn't be able to dwell on her own problems.

There was a light rap at the door to which Stacy called out for whoever was there to 'come in'. The oak door to the den swung wide to admit the vivacious form of Lydia Marshall.

'I'm not interrupting you, am I? Because if you're very busy, I'll just stay a minute.' An effusive quality in her low voice caused Stacy to cringe inwardly.

'No, not at all,' Stacy replied quietly, taken aback at the unexpected arrival. 'What can I help you with?'

'Nothing really. I just thought you might have time for some coffee and a little chat.'

'Certainly,' Stacy agreed, wondering what in heaven's name they were going to talk about. 'Just a minute and I'll ask Maria to bring some coffee. Would you care for a roll or anything?'

'I hope you don't mind, but I already asked her to bring some on the chance that you would be free,' came the quick reply, followed by a throaty laugh that grated the back of Stacy's neck.

'How thoughtful of you,' Stacy answered with a smile that didn't quite reach her eyes. Seating herself in the chair behind the desk, she continued, 'It's seldom that I have the time to take a coffee break. It will be a pleasant change.'

'I thought as much,' said Lydia, rising from her chair as the plump Mexican woman entered the room carrying the coffee service. 'I'll take that, Maria. I didn't order any sweet rolls. Did you want any, Stacy? I have to watch my figure, so I decline.' At the negative nod of Stacy's head, Lydia dismissed the rotund woman with a curt 'thank you'.

The proprietorial air that Lydia had adopted irked Stacy, and with difficulty she managed to accept the cup of steaming coffee offered her.

'Oh, before I forget,' Lydia exclaimed, reaching down beside her chair for her purse, 'I was by the printer's, and I remembered Cord mentioning something about needing the proof for the catalogue so I picked it up. I hope you don't mind. He mentioned how hard you were working, and I thought I'd save you a trip into town.'

'Thank you,' Stacy said coolly, accepting the pamphlet. 'Unfortunately I still have to go into town for some other things. I'm sure Mr. Harris will appreciate it, though.'

'Well, I knew how upset he was over it,' the smiling Lydia went on. 'I hope he didn't get too difficult. I know what a temper he sometimes has.'

The familiarity oozed out of Lydia's red lips, no doubt making sure that Stacy fully understood just exactly how friendly Lydia was with Cord. An anger slowly began to burn within her.

'Naturally, he was upset,' Stacy said firmly, 'as I was, but everything's under control now. It was merely a lack of communication.'

'I'm glad to hear it.' An icy glare was in Lydia's black eyes. 'I offered to help with some of the work, but Cord assured me that, at this time, it wouldn't look right. Besides, he thought you were doing an adequate job.'

Stacy's cheeks flamed at the emphasis of the word 'adequate'. The sickening knowledge that she had been casually discussed during one of their conversations lay heavy within her. The solicitous tone of Lydia's words coated the coldness that was enveloping her heart with a bittersweet veneer.

'Mr. Harris indicated that your present—er—circumstances wouldn't allow you to take too active an interest in the actual arrangements of the affair,' Stacy murmured quietly, wondering where she found the voice to speak at all.

Lydia's dark eyes narrowed as she smiled and said, 'Then Cord did explain a little of the problems we face.' With a disconcerted sigh, she went on, 'It's common knowledge how we've always felt for each other, despite my foolishness that got me into this mess. I wonder now how I could have been so naïve as to trade in all this for a sun that shines the same on the Riviera as it does here. I assure you, Stacy, it's a crushing blow to discover that to your husband you're no more than another possession to be dressed and displayed like a masterpiece by Renoir. If I hadn't known that Cord had promised that he'd always be here, I don't know how I would have made it this far. I guess it's knowing that my future is secure once again in Cord's hands. And it's just a matter of time and it all will be made official.'

Stacy didn't know if she could take much more of this conversation. She didn't want to know all their 'wonderful' plans. It was all she could do to contain herself and not jump up and pace the floor in desperation. Why was Lydia discussing this with her at all? Aloud Stacy managed to say something about how wonderful it was that everything was working out for them.

'Yes, it is,' Lydia replied, but her eyes were studying the flustered Stacy coldly. 'I'm so glad you see it that way. As attractive as Cord is, a lot of girls in your place would have developed a crush on him.'

'Mr. Harris and I rarely discuss anything but business,' Stacy answered numbly, trying to keep the emotion out of her voice. 'It would require a great deal of imagination to read more into his attentions towards me than actually exists.'

'You do understand I would dislike seeing you hurt accidentally when it could be so easily avoided. I know Cord feels a certain responsibility for you, and I wouldn't want to see you interpret it wrongly,' Lydia smiled smugly as she rose to place her coffee cup near the silver service. 'Well, I really mustn't keep you any more. I know you have a lot to do, and if I can help you in any way, please call me.'

'Of course,' Stacy replied, the smile on her lips stifling the pain in her chest, knowing that Lydia was the last person she would look to for assistance, and had the distinct impression that Lydia knew it.

Glumly she stared at the catalogue proof in front of her. Mechanically she leafed through the pages, her mind racing back to Lydia's words. 'Cord feels a certain responsibility for you, and I wouldn't want you to interpret it wrongly.' If only she could! If only she could read more into his actions than what they were. Responsibility? He had always acted as if she was a liability. It was a miracle he considered her at all.

Arousing herself from her thoughts, Stacy began rummaging through the drawers of the big oak desk looking for the copy of the proof supplied to the printer. She finally found it in one of the lower drawers and began the task of proof-reading the long list of quarter horses complete with their registration numbers, sires, and dams. It was tedious, but at least it required her full concentration and the floating image of the rugged Cord couldn't distract her. Flipping one of the pages over, Stacy straightened with a start. Mixed in among the papers was a piece of stationery with the letterhead of 'Lindsey, Pierce & Mills, Attorneys at Law'. The words fairly leaped off the page at her. Shocked, she glanced at the signature at the bottom of the letter. 'Carter Mills, Sr.'! What was a letter from Mr. Mills doing in Cord's desk? Drawn by the unexpectedness of the familiar letterhead and signature, Stacy began reading.

It was addressed to Mr. Cord Harris, Circle H Ranch, McCloud, Texas, and started out 'Dear Mr. Harris':

Miss Stacy Adams, the daughter of a client, has

rented a cabin located on your property. In writing this letter, I am stepping out of my sphere of authority. I would like to impose on you by asking that you keep a close watch over her.

The recent death of her father, a close personal friend, has left Miss Adams without any living relatives. Her father left her a very substantial income so that she is financially secure for the rest of her life. Unfortunately she has been very pampered in the past. Despite my protestations she has insisted on this self-imposed exile to recover from her grief. A stubborn and strong-willed young woman, her cosmopolitan raising has not prepared her for the rigours of western Texas, nor the dangers a young woman alone may face.

She has refused to discuss the length of her stay, insisting that it is indefinite. I would appreciate it, if it is at all possible, Mr. Harris, if you could persuade her to return. If she will not, I ask you to accept responsibility for her. I have enclosed a cheque which I hope will cover any inconvenience caused. I remain

> Sincerely yours,
> Carter Mills, Sr.

'No!' Stacy whispered, staring' at the scrawled signature at the bottom of the page. The red-tinged eyes that had shed tears so readily before were as dry as her lips as the horrible truth began to dawn on her. The letter explained so many things. Why Cord had been so hostile the first day they met, advising her that she should return to the refuge of the city life she was accustomed to. Why he had felt so responsible when she had taken that fall off Diablo and insisted that she stay at his ranch to recover. And when she was well,

the episode with Diablo had conveniently given him
an excuse to keep her here. It was also the reason he
was so concerned about one of his hands taking ad-
vantage of her. It was all so clear now. He had under-
taken the job of guardian when she came and that was
all she meant to him.

Lydia's words washed over her again, 'Cord feels responsible for you'. 'Oh, God,' Stacy thought, 'he must
have told her, too.' Her humiliation grew clearer and
clearer. How he must wish she was gone! Shamed and
hurt, Stacy rose from her chair and stumbled around
the desk, groping for some release from her misery. No
tears fell on the drawn, pinched face as she made her
way out the front door. The hurt went too deep to be
salved by the shedding of a few tears. Waves of nausea
swept over her as she stared numbly at the buildings
and surrounding hillsides. A hesitant breeze fingered
the tendrils of her chestnut hair as she stood immobile
on the concrete walk.

A plump brown hand touched Stacy's arm. 'Are you
okay?' came the concerned voice of the housekeeper.

Slowly Stacy turned and managed a weak smile before she replied, 'Yes, I'm fine, Maria. I just needed a
breath of fresh air, that's all.'

'You don't look so good,' the Mexican woman shook
her head as she followed Stacy into the house. 'Maybe
you should take a little siesta?'

'I'll be all right,' Stacy returned a little impatiently.
More quietly she added, 'I'm fine, really. It was just a
bit stuffy in there.'

Pride and a sense of fatalism squared Stacy's shoulders as she went back inside, opened the door of the
den, and entered. An unnatural calm had settled over
her that walled the pain apart from her consciousness.
If she could maintain this stoical control of her emo-

tions, she would be able to face the long week that lay
ahead of her. At her first opportunity, she would an-
nounce to Cord that she would be returning East as
soon as the auction was over. That would release him
from any false sense of responsibility that he felt and
remove her from his life for ever. Bleakly she replaced
the lawyer's letter in the lower drawer and began
mechanically rechecking the catalogue.

That evening Stacy was on her way down the stairs
when she saw Cord talking with Maria in the foyer.
The starchy freshness of his blue shirt and the sharp
crease of his darker blue trousers indicated his plans to
be gone that night. Still possessed by the stupor that
had engulfed her earlier, she walked up to him.
Poised, she stood waiting until his conversation with
Maria was finished.

'Did you want to speak to me?' Cord's voice re-
sounded harshly in her ears.

'Yes, if you can spare the time,' Stacy returned just
as crisply, ignoring the uncontrollable racing of her
heart. His dark eyes rested inquiringly on her pale,
drawn face.

'What is it you wanted?'

'I merely wanted to let you know that as soon as this
auction affair is over, I'll be returning home,' Stacy
answered quietly but firmly.

An eyebrow raised sharply as his brown eyes hardened speculatively. 'This is rather sudden, isn't it?' he
said, and without waiting for her reply, added, 'I take
it you're not asking my permission.'

'No.'

'I see,' Cord snapped. The sharp coldness sent an
involuntary shiver through the haggard Stacy. 'I didn't
expect you'd last this long.'

The morning sun was high over the mountains before Stacy wakened the next day. She had cried herself to sleep the night before, but with sleep had come the endurance to face tomorrow. Mechanically she removed her dress, crumpled from being slept in, showered, dressed, and went downstairs for breakfast. As she gazed out the window of the dining room, the distant hills beckoned her. It was the week-end and there wasn't much Stacy could do for the auction. She decided to spend the day riding the hills. She wasn't up to another confrontation with Cord and this would be by far the easiest way to avoid him. With instructions to Maria to fix her a cold lunch, she hurried upstairs to change into her riding skirt and boots.

A few minutes later she was walking out of the front door, her hat swinging from one hand, her lunch in the other. There was no lightness in her step, but her stride was firm. Reaching the stables, she walked to the paddock where the sorrel was held. Diablo danced forward to meet her and nibbled playfully at her arm as she put on his halter.

She waved a greeting to Hank riding by the stables. Thankfully he was busy and didn't stop to chat. His eyes were far too sharp and she didn't want to be put through another ordeal. The niggling sense of defeat was too painful a reminder without talking about it.

Diablo was full of fire, prancing and side-stepping in defiance of his rider's efforts to hold him at a walk. Four people walked around the corner of the stable. Stacy's attention was concentrated on holding the spirited sorrel and guiding him to the pasture gate. She managed a cursory glance in their direction. Two ranch hands were walking in front of Cord Harris and Lydia. A stifled oath came from Cord as he pushed past the hands and ran towards the mounted rider.

The sudden movement towards Diablo startled the sorrel, spooking him into a half rear as he tried to turn in the direction of the approaching figure.

Before Stacy could utter a protest, Cord was by her side, grabbing her by the waist and pulling her off the horse while the other hand had a tight hold on the reins of the panicking stallion. Setting her roughly on the ground, he ordered one of the hands to hold the horse.

'What in the hell were you doing on that horse?' he blazed.

'I was going for a ride, if it's any of your business!' Stacy retorted, her own temper rising at the undignified treatment she had just received.

'You're damn right it's my business!' Cord raged, grabbing her wrist and twisting it to force her closer to him. 'Isn't one fall enough for you, or would you rather get killed the next time?'

'That was an accident. It would have happened no matter what horse I was riding,' her own eyes flashed in anger. 'I own that horse. He's mine, and you have no right——'

'I have every right in the world as long as I'm responsible for what happens to you while you're on this ranch,' Cord interrupted coldly, releasing her wrist with a scornful sweep of his hand. 'And as long as you're on this ranch, you're not going near that devil.'

'Thank heavens, I won't be here long!' Stacy returned sharply. Her anger was reaching a point where the powerful, intimidating man did not awe her. 'And you'd better think of a way to keep me away from that horse, because he's mine and I intend to ride him any time I please!'

In the background Stacy could see the contemptuous eyes of Lydia Marshall mocking her childish display. But her irritation with Cord's dictatorial manner and his overworked sense of responsibility ignored the malice that glinted through the black eyes. Approaching the small group from the hacienda was a tall man dressed in a blue sport outfit. There was something familiar about his walk, but Stacy's attention was directed back by Cord's voice.

'I'll lock you in the house if I have to, but you're not riding that horse. There's plenty of other mounts available if you want to ride,' Cord answered, his voice lowering in an attempt to curb his anger.

'No, thank you,' Stacy said sarcastically, turning sharply on her heel to walk in the direction of the dancing stallion.

The raised voices and angry tones had incensed the hot-blooded horse and his flashing white feet drummed the ground in a staccato rhythm. A rolling white eye glanced back to catch a flicker of movement. Pulling at the lead rope held by the ranch hand, Diablo reared slightly and just as swiftly came down and lashed out with his back feet at the unidentified person behind him. But just as quickly, Cord reacted, pulling Stacy away from the menacing hooves.

Holding her back and shoulders tightly against his broad chest, he muttered in her ear, 'You are the most stubborn woman I've ever known!'

The sudden and unexpected physical contact with Cord swept Stacy's breath away. She felt her knees trembling and her heart racing away with his nearness. She could only hope he would attribute it to the close call she had with the spirited horse. She was too weak to step away from him, cherishing the strength of his arms and the mild aroma of cologne from his freshly shaved face. Cord turned her around, keeping his hands firmly on her shoulders. His expression was grave as he unhurriedly surveyed the pallor in her face.

'I've never met anyone in my life who needed a good spanking more than you,' he growled, releasing her and turning to the waiting group.

'Hear, hear!' came the laughing agreement of the stranger standing beside Lydia.

The happy baritone voice broke through the mist of tears that had taken possession of Stacy's brown eyes. Of course! She should have recognized him. With a broken sob, she rushed past Cord to the waiting stranger.

'Carter, Carter! I'm so glad to see you,' she cried, throwing herself in the young man's arms. Her voice was slightly muffled as she pressed her head against Carter's chest, but her unexpected greeting had brought Cord up short.

'Hey there, honey,' said Carter, surprised at the affectionate welcome he was receiving. Instinctively, his hand reached up to stroke the top of her head. 'If I'd known I'd be welcomed like this, I would have come a long time ago!'

Brushing away the tears that had trickled down her cheeks, Stacy stepped away and looked up into the gentle blue eyes. The suddenness of Carter's appearance combined with the unsettling contact with Cord had robbed her of her control. She realized that Carter had misinterpreted her welcome, but she was too relieved at having someone she could depend on here. His presence represented a refuge from the storm of emotions that was buffeting her around to the point of exhaustion.

'I take it you two know each other,' Lydia commented dryly, breaking the silence that had settled over the small group.

Embarrassed by her emotional greeting, Stacy

blushed slightly before turning to introduce Carter. She stammered an introduction to Lydia, overlooking an arched eyebrow and smug smile on the woman's face. Lydia offered a smooth manicured hand to Carter and one of her intense gazes while Cord stepped forward to complete the circle. His dark eyes were icy cold as Stacy started to introduce Carter to him, but Carter interposed before she could begin.

'Mr. Harris, I'm glad to meet you,' said Carter, grasping Cord's right hand firmly. 'I never thought I'd see the day that anyone would be able to refuse to let Stacy ride that horse and make it stick. I want to thank you for myself and my father for looking after her so well.'

'I won't mislead you by saying that it was an easy job. Miss Adams is a very strong-willed girl,' Cord answered dryly. 'Will you be staying long?'

'Only as long as it takes me to convince Stacy to come back with me,' Carter smiled, glancing tenderly down at the chestnut head beside him, 'hopefully, as my fiancée.'

CHAPTER ELEVEN

STACY had been covertly watching Cord's face, protected mentally by the young man standing beside her, but at Carter's statement Cord's eyes flashed their fire upon her.

'Isn't it wonderful, Cord?' Lydia gushed, her malicious eyes flicking over Stacy briefly before she smiled up at Cord and took his arm. 'What a romantic conclusion for a reunion! It's really just perfect, isn't it?'

'Yes, it is,' Cord agreed, but his voice sounded husky as if he was struggling to control his temper.

No one seemed interested in Stacy's answer to the public proposal, not that she would have offered one if she had been asked. But it grated her that everyone was taking an affirmative answer as a matter of course.

'Carter, I'm in charge of the annual sale of registered quarter horses that Mr. Harris has every year. It's this coming Saturday. Will you be able to stay until then?' Stacy asked, anxious to change the subject.

'Oh, Stacy, you don't have to let a little thing like that stop you,' Lydia inserted quickly before Carter could answer. 'I'm sure it would be perfectly all right if I stepped in for you. After all, it would be an emergency of sorts.'

The last sentence was directed more or less at Cord. Stacy had the distinct impression that Lydia was only too anxious to get her out of the way and the sooner the better. It was all Stacy could do to keep a sigh of relief from escaping her lips when she heard Cord's reply.

'It's too late to make any replacements. The sale is too close and it would mean unnecessary confusion. I don't believe it's all that vital that Miss Adams return immediately,' Cord answered, his cold eyes turning on Carter as if daring him to disagree.

'No, of course not,' Carter added hurriedly. 'As a matter of fact, Dad gave me a week to persuade you to come back with me. We'll just call it a little vacation.' The young lawyer exchanged a conspiratorial smile with Stacy before turning back to Cord. 'Is there a hotel in town where I could stay? I'd like to get settled in.'

'There's no need to stay in town,' Lydia began.

'No, you can stay here,' Cord interrupted, silencing the polite protest Carter had started to make with a wave of his hand. 'There's plenty of room at the hacienda. If you'll excuse us, I have some work to do, and I believe you mentioned that you had a luncheon engagement, didn't you, Lydia?'

With a firm hand on Lydia's elbow, Cord manoeuvred her away from the standing couple. Silence descended over Carter and Stacy as he surveyed her quietly.

'You never did answer my question. It wasn't exactly a question, though, was it?' the soft voice asked. 'Don't answer it now either. I'll ask it again later when the setting is a little more romantic. Right now you can direct me to my room and tell me all the "tall Texas tales" you've learned.'

With a nervous laugh, Stacy joined hands with Carter before moving towards the hacienda. Eagerly she related the happenings since her arrival, many of them taking on a humorous aspect on their recounting. Entering the adobe building, she ushered him to one of the spare rooms down the hall from hers, after suggesting that he meet her at the pool in half an hour.

Stacy was floating lazily on her back in the pool when Carter surfaced from his dive beside her. The pair swam round for an hour before pulling themselves up on the side, happy and exhausted.

Stacy studied Carter's lithe, tanned body through lowered lashes. His light, almost blond hair was still wet from the swim and his smooth, unlined face seemed unusually young when she compared it to the rugged, sculptured features of Cord. Soberly Stacy realized Carter wasn't as indomitable as he had seemed before, but she had fallen easily into their old comradeship, unable to let him know the change that had taken place in her, the difference in her thinking.

'I know about the letter your father sent to Mr. Harris before I came out here,' Stacy said quietly, and noticed that Carter had the grace to redden.

'You understand that Dad was concerned about you,' Carter commented, squinting his blue eyes at the sun. 'As it turned out, we can be glad he did. I didn't know anything about it until after you were hurt.' Turning to study Stacy, he asked, 'What made you stay here—this auction?'

With as little detail as possible, Stacy explained the incident with Diablo, glossing over as much as she could Cord's antagonistic attitude towards her. Mischievous amusement spread over Carter's face when she finished, taking an impish delight at the implied humiliation.

'Imagine you out there chasing cows! That's too much!' he chuckled.

'Well, it wasn't too funny at the time,' Stacy retorted, unable to keep from bristling at his teasing. 'You don't exactly have a choice when Mr. Harris issues an ultimatum.'

'I rather got that impression this afternoon,' Carter said, sobering slightly, but a devilish gleam remaining in his blue eyes. 'I don't think patience is one of his virtues.'

'Hardly,' Stacy replied grimly. 'And he certainly doesn't have any patience where I'm concerned. I still think it was beastly of your father to write that letter, especially without telling me. When I remember some of the terrible things I said and did because I thought Cord was nothing but an arrogant tyrant who enjoyed ordering people about——'

'You mean he doesn't?'

'No. That is——' she stammered, struggling to find

the right words to explain her change of attitude without giving her true feelings away.

'Never mind,' Carter laughed, rising to his feet. 'I don't care what he is or does. He managed to keep you off that horse and in one piece until I could collect you. For all I care he could be Billy the Kid. Now, I'm going to change before this Texas sun of yours turns me into a lobster.'

The following night, as Stacy dressed for dinner, she dreaded the evening to come. She had hoped with Carter here that she would be able to put Cord in the back of her mind, but Cord had very successfully squashed that. Since her brief conversation with Carter alone the previous afternoon, Cord had been around constantly. If he didn't actually take part in their conversations, he was in an adjoining room. Either way his presence thwarted any attempts for privacy that Stacy and Carter might have made.

Carter had jumped at the dinner invitation when Stacy passed it on to him. His enthusiasm coupled with her earlier agreement left no way for her to back out. The anguish Cord's nearness would surely cause made her wonder if she derived some sort of bizarre pleasure from her torment. Each day that went by brought her closer to the time she would leave for good, thereby turning each glimpse of the virile man into a cherished memory to last the eternity she would be alone.

Willowy and delicate, like something out of a misty dream, Stacy descended the stairs to where Carter Mills and Cord Harris waited in their white dinner jackets. Carter didn't speak, but the admiration in his blue eyes sparkled a compliment that was more eloquent than words. Hesitantly Stacy looked into Cord's face for an affirmation of Carter's approval, but the dark eyes were masked and his opinion unrevealed, while the agitated twitching of the jaw muscle marred the still, stone-like quality of his brown face. Regretting that she had sought his praise, Stacy turned back to her escort.

'Are we ready?' she asked.

'And willing,' smiled Carter, possessively clasping his other hand over the delicate one on his arm.

A sleek and shiny brown Continental was parked in the drive. Stacy slid into the back seat behind the driver and waited nervously for Carter to walk around the car to join her. Apprehensively she glanced into the rear-view mirror to meet Cord's dark, enigmatical eyes that quickly looked away. The fair lawyer climbed in beside Stacy while Cord started the motor and manoeuvred the luxury car out of the drive. The conversation was sketchy during the journey to Lydia's, with Stacy too conscious of the dark head in front of her to do anything but pretend an interest in the scenery racing by.

'You're very quiet tonight,' commented Carter after they had parked and Cord had gone into the house to collect Lydia. 'Is something wrong?'

'No, of course not,' Stacy returned, a grateful smile on her face for the concern in Carter's eyes. How could she explain that the proximity of the driver upset her? 'I enjoy looking at the land, especially when the sunset is so close. It gives everything a mysterious peace.'

'That's my girl,' Carter muttered with a mocking shake of his head. 'Here she sits beside a man who's travelled halfway across the country to see her and she's admiring the scenery.'

'Oh, Carter, you know I'm glad you're here,' Stacy laughed, fully aware of the comfort his presence was to her.

'But I wonder if you're glad because it's me or because it's an old friend.' A sadly, serious expression was in his blue eyes as he gazed at her astutely.

Stacy's protest was arrested by the approach of a white-jacketed Cord with Lydia clutching his arm. There was a satisfied smile on his face as he gazed down at the chic woman. Stacy's heart experienced a painful tug as her brown eyes flashed a jealous green. Lydia's raven black hair fell loosely about her creamy white neck, accenting the sensuous décolleté of her lilac satin gown hanging precariously by two slim rhinestone straps.

As pleasantries were exchanged, Lydia glanced at Stacy's ring hand and then looked at Carter petulantly. 'I thought we were going to have something to celebrate tonight. Or did you forget to bring a ring along to make the announcement official?'

Carter managed a joking, noncommittal reply which escaped Stacy, whose attention was caught and held by Cord's intense gaze in the mirror. She felt the colour rising in her cheeks at the inquisitive and derisive expression in his deep brown eyes. Unwilling to take part in the conversation between Lydia and Carter, Stacy again forced her attention outside the glass windows. She managed to keep the jealousy and bitter pain from showing itself for Cord's mocking eyes to see.

Arriving at their destination, Stacy became enchanted with the rambling two-storey building nestled in a sylvan setting of pine trees and lush greenery. As the foursome entered the restaurant area, the host greeted Cord by his first name and ushered the group personally to a secluded table.

Carter held out the chair on Cord's left for Stacy, his hand lingering briefly on the filmy silk covering her

shoulder. The reassurance of his touch quieted the
nervous tremor in her heart. With a still hand, she
raised her champagne glass with the others as Carter
made a toast.

'To Texas.'

'And the happy reunion of those who've been separated,' Lydia added, her gaze taking in Cord's profile
possessively before turning to include the other couple.

Stacy was relieved when the dinner was served and
over. At least in the lounge the entertainment would
force conversation to the minimum. Leaving the table,
Stacy and Carter followed the other couple into the
lounge. Stacy's eyes were riveted on Cord's dark hair
curling above the collar of his white dinner jacket. As
if conscious of her inspection, he turned, gazing mysteriously for a moment into her startled brown eyes
before speaking.

'I hope you won't be too disappointed in the band.
The group is mainly Mexican in extraction, so you'll
find the music has a Latin-Western flavour rather than
the beat you're accustomed to.'

Inwardly Stacy flinched at the subtle undertone of
censure that laced Cord's words. His opinion of her
was so low already that it seemed useless to protest this
statement. Without replying she and Carter followed
them to a table. As soon as the cocktail waitress had
taken their order, Carter asked Stacy to dance. She
quickly obliged, happy to leave the disconcerting company of Cord and Lydia. Three guitars played the
strains of old ballad to the gentle tempo of drums.
As she matched the familiar pattern of Carter's steps, a
spray of confidence returned to Stacy.

'What's the matter with you tonight?' Carter asked
suddenly, his blue eyes examining her face intensely. 'I
have the feeling you're afraid or hiding something.'

Startled by his unexpected frankness, Stacy missed a step. A numbness seized her throat as hundreds of protests flashed through her mind, but before she summoned one, Carter went on.

'I don't think I want you to answer me. I think you'd lie or maybe not tell me the whole truth.' His tone was extremely serious. 'It would hurt too much either way. Stacy, if you ever want to tell me what's wrong, I'll be here no matter what.'

'Carter, I——' Stacy began, tears of misery welling in her brown eyes.

'Sssh! We won't talk any more. Maybe later when we're alone, but not now,' he whispered in her hair, and drew her closer into the comfort of his arms.

When the last strains of the ballad faded away, the group struck up a bouncier tune and the young couple remained on the floor. The knowledge of Carter's affection gave Stacy a crutch to cling to and the ability to return to the table with a more sincere smile on her face. Despite the invisible support of Carter, the evening dragged. The mocking tone and twisted smile of Cord whenever he addressed her made Stacy nervous and the triumphant glitter in Lydia's eyes fanned the ache that throbbed so close to the surface. The envious lump in her throat swelled whenever she watched Cord dancing with the sultry black-haired woman. Towards the end of the evening, Carter asked Lydia to dance, leaving Stacy alone with Cord.

'They dance well together,' Stacy commented with an attempt at nonchalance as she watched Carter and Lydia fall into step. Cord gleamed back at her, an unamused smile that flickered briefly with an emotion that Stacy couldn't quite recognize.

'Jealous?' the low baritone voice spoke. 'Lydia is a very beautiful woman.'

'No, of course not,' Stacy returned, but there was a tremulous catch in her voice as she spoke. She was jealous of Lydia, but not for the reason Cord was thinking.

'Shall we dance?' Cord asked softly as he rose and stepped behind her chair.

Naturally she would refuse. Why punish herself further by being held in his arms when he desired another? What could it possibly accomplish but more heartache? But not a word of protest had passed her lips as she found herself in his arms on the dance floor. There was no retreat now and the glow that radiated unconsciously from her upturned face laughed at the recrimination of her conscience. The firm hand on the small of her back was strangely exciting and the tender brown eyes that looked down upon her made her heart race with uncontrollable happiness. At this moment it didn't matter whether he was dancing with her out of pity or courtesy. Her hand tightened imperceptibly in Cord's and with a gentle smile in his eyes he drew her closer to his broad chest until her brown head nestled against his shoulder. Ignorant of the melody of the song the band was playing, the conversation of the dancers around them, oblivious to anything but the thrilling nearness of Cord, Stacy danced in silence, capturing the sensation of the rhythmic sway of his hips, the gentle pressure of his body against hers, the firm clasp of his hand and the caress of his breath on her hair.

The dance over, as if by previous arrangement, Cord immediately suggested calling it an evening. Torn apart by the emotions that threatened to surface from his nearness and the hopelessness of her love, Stacy quickly agreed.

The ride home had been a silent one. Looking back on it two days later, Stacy tried to analyse the reason. Carter had been unusually quiet. In the past they had often spent hours without talking, but this time there was an uneasiness about him, as if he was grappling with a problem he didn't know how to handle. And Cord had answered Lydia's sentences so abruptly that even she fell to silence. It had been a relief when the Continental had finally turned into the ranch drive and Stacy had escaped to the sanctity of her room.

Carter had been his old self the next morning, laughing and joking as before. After volunteering to help Stacy with the auction arrangements, he had pitched in with a familiar gusto, running errands into town, checking with Hank regarding the yearlings, and taking some of the more time-consuming tasks off Stacy's hands. Cord had reverted to his old habit of unexplained absences. The past two days he had practically avoided Stacy and Carter, joining them only once for dinner Monday evening and leaving immediately afterwards. He had not mentioned where he was going, but later that evening Stacy had seen a light burning late at the ranch office. Lydia hadn't been over either, which surprised Stacy as the divorcee had almost become a fixture at the ranch since her return.

Removing the paper from the carriage of the typewriter, Stacy forced her thoughts to return to the business at hand. Her morning had been consumed with last-minute requests for circulars of the auction. This one was finally the last. Slipping the information into an envelope and stamping it, she placed it with a stack of similar letters that awaited Carter's return from the stables. If she was lucky she would have time for a cup of coffee and a cigarette before she had to meet the wives of the ranch hands to go over various details they would be responsible for during the barbecue.

Leaving the den, Stacy walked towards the kitchen to help herself to some coffee. But Maria appeared in the archway between the dining room and living room carrying a small tray with a steaming cup of coffee and a sweet roll on it.

'You are a life-saver,' Stacy smiled. 'I was just going to the kitchen to get myself a cup.'

Maria bubbled her pleasure before adding, 'Weel the Señora Leedia be joining you?'

'Lydia?' Stacy's tone puzzled.

'*Si*. She just drive up een her car. I theenk perhaps she dreenk too.'

'I don't know——' Stacy began, but was interrupted by the opening and closing of the front door.

'Stacy, good morning. I'm so glad to see you're not busy,' Lydia smiled, entering the living room as Maria left. 'I hoped to have a little chat with you today, but I was afraid you'd be all tied up with Saturday's affair.'

'I'll have to be running off in a few minutes,' Stacy replied, not anxious to have another 'little chat' with Lydia. Their previous discussion was regrettable enough without enduring another.

Gracefully Lydia seated herself in the chair opposite Stacy, smoothing the skirt of her elegantly styled sundress before speaking. 'I don't see any engagement ring. Surely you've put that poor boy out of his misery by now.'

'If you mean Carter,' Stacy said coldly, incensed that Lydia was meddling in something that was none of her business, 'I've been rather busy lately. There's no rush, is there?'

'I wouldn't let him get away from you, if I were you.'

'That's the point, though, isn't it? You're not me.'

Lydia's cold eyes flickered ominously for a moment at Stacy's words.

'That's true, but I do have a better view of the situation than you,' she suggested solicitously.

'Why don't you come to the point?' said Stacy, irritated by the phoney concern that Lydia was attempting to project. 'We could talk in circles all day. Fortunately I have better things to do.'

Surprised at Stacy's unexpected audacity, Lydia rose from her chair, walked behind it, then turned her dark head with its glistening coronet of braids towards her.

'You're quite right,' her tone was sarcastic and contemptuous. 'There's no love lost between us, so why pretend? My point is really quite simple—don't withhold your answer from Carter in the hope that Cord will come through with a better offer, because he won't. Do you think that Cord is so blind that he doesn't realize that you've fallen in love with him?'

'Afraid of a little competition, or is your hold so slight over Cord that you can't take the chance?' Stacy retorted, standing to meet the glare of the older woman's challenge.

'Don't be ridiculous!' Lydia exclaimed. 'A more mature woman would be able to recognize the difference between affection and pity. You moped around all Sunday evening and then lit up like a Christmas tree the minute Cord danced with you. Can't you tell that he feels sorry for you, that his over-active sense of responsibility forces him to do these things? I don't know where your sense of pride is or whether you haven't outgrown that cow-eyed teenage stage yet, but either way your presence has managed to influence the plans that Cord and I have made. As ridiculous as it sounds, he doesn't feel he should make his true feelings known for fear of hurting you.'

'As I told Cord and I'll tell you, I'm leaving right after the auction,' retorted Stacy. 'I'll be returning with Carter, so that should end your concern. In a few more days I'll be out of your lives for ever and you and Cord can do whatever you like. In the meantime, I prefer that you leave this house now and stay out of my way in the future,' Stacy's voice trembled with controlled anger. But the truth of Lydia's words cut deep.

The click of triumphant heels echoed through the living room as Lydia left. Numbly Stacy heard her satisfied tone as Lydia exchanged greetings with Carter just entering the house. Walking into the living room, Carter studied Stacy for a second, noting the clenched fists at her side.

'What happened? She looked as if she just tried on the glass slipper and it fitted.'

'Really?' Stacy remarked with unnatural bitterness. Seeing the formation of a question in Carter's eyes, she hurried on, 'I have a meeting now. There's some mail lying on my desk. Will you see that it gets out today?'

Gathering her notebook, she hurried out the door.

The following evening Stacy and Carter went for a late ride after dinner. On their return Stacy chattered away happily with Carter refreshed and relaxed by the sunset ride.

'If you don't mind, I'm going to wash off some of your precious Texas dirt,' said Carter as they reached the front door of the hacienda. 'I'll meet you on the patio for a drink in half an hour.'

'A deal,' Stacy smiled, preceding him upstairs to her own room.

A short time later she joined him on the veranda. He was sitting quietly on one of the settees rubbing the ears of the German Shepherd abstractedly as he stared off into the deep ebony of the night. Seeing his mistress, Cajun pattered happily over to her side as Carter rose to meet her. Taking the hand extended to her, the chestnut-haired girl contentedly let herself be drawn into the settee beside h'm.

'It didn't take you very long,' Carter smiled. 'I thought I'd be able to sneak in an extra drink before you got here,' indicating a tray of tall glasses on the side table.

'At least you saved one for me,' Stacy teased, cradling an icy drink in her hands as she gazed into the midnight curtain of evening. 'It's a gorgeous night. I wonder where all the stars are?'

'If I were a proper lover, I would say they were all in your eyes.'

'Oh, Carter!' Stacy laughed protestingly, leaning against the back of the cushion.

Tenderly he cupped her chin in his hand, his face sombre in its study of her sobering expression.

'I wish I could say that and know it to be true,' he said, releasing her and rising abruptly.

Stuffing his hands in his pockets, Carter walked over by the pillar and gazed into the distance. Stacy fidgeted nervously with the pocket on her orange and yellow shift. The truth of his statement brought back the despair she fought so hard to subdue.

'Do you know how I've planned for this evening ever since I arrived?' A strange, bitter quality was in his voice that Stacy had never heard before. 'Here we are, all alone with not a soul to bother us. The setting is perfect, the black night shutting out the world, a couple of stars winking their encouragement, and a beautiful girl, her dark eyes filled with anticipation at the words that are to be said.' The light brown head turned to look back at Stacy. 'Only your eyes aren't.

filled with anticipation, are they?' He looked down at her.

Salty tears trickled down her cheeks to her tightly pressed lips as she bent her head from his accusing blue eyes.

'I was going to do it all properly tonight—get down on my knee and say, "Stacy, I love you and I want you to be my wife",' said Carter, his voice almost a monotone. 'Corny, isn't it? I love you, but you see, I'm a proud man. I don't want to possess something that doesn't belong to me. I suppose there are men who would have asked you anyway and taken the chance that they wouldn't be turned down. I'm not asking for an entirely different reason. I'm afraid you might accept, and I couldn't live with you knowing that you're in love with some rancher in Texas.'

Shame and humiliation shook Stacy's slim shoulders at the pain and bitterness she had brought into Carter's world. Rousing out of his mist of self-pity, Carter looked at the silent, sobbing form and walked over to where she sat, a hand moving unsurely towards her head.

'Oh, Stacy, why, why does it have to be this way?' His voice choked as he swept her off the chair into his arms.

'Carter, I wanted to tell you, but I couldn't,' she moaned into his shirt. 'I couldn't hurt you, not when I knew what that pain was like.'

'It'll be all right,' he smiled, drawing comfort from the easing of her pain. 'You know the saying "It only hurts for a little while." '

'I wouldn't have said "yes". I wouldn't have done that to you.'

'No, I think I knew that,' holding her away from him as he wiped her moist cheeks with his hand. 'Inside I knew you were made of a stronger stuff.'

'You will stay,' Stacy asked, 'and take me home after the weekend?'

'Of course. Don't you know, my pet, that you can use me any time?' Carter grinned, his smile taking the sting out of his words.

'I don't know what I would have done if you hadn't come when you did. I hadn't the pride to leave nor the strength to stay,' she confessed, nestling under his arm as they walked towards the yawning light from the glass doorway.

A troubled sigh echoed her words as Carter stepped forward to open the door. Hesitating just inside, Stacy turned to wait for him. He had stopped a step behind her, his attention riveted ahead of her. The brittle iciness of his blue eyes startled her and she turned to where he was looking. Cord was standing slightly to her right, a book in one hand and a cigarette in the other. His dark eyes were narrowed in an inscrutable expression as he looked passed Stacy to Carter. Abruptly, Cord turned his head and walked over to an ash-tray where he snubbed his cigarette out viciously.

'You young people are turning in rather early tonight, aren't you?' he taunted.

'It's been a hectic day,' Stacy murmured, starting to the stairway.

'All the arrangements are going along smoothly for the sale on Saturday, aren't they?'

'Of course. If you'd like to go over them now——' Stacy began, stung by the hint of neglect in his words.

'No, that won't be necessary,' Cord interrupted, his dark eyes examining the pinched lines in her face. 'There's time enough in the morning.' His tone curt and dismissive.

'Good night, Mr. Harris,' Carter offered, a little sarcastically.

'Yes, good night, Cord,' Stacy hastened at the sharpening of the rancher's eyes.

'Good night.' His voice followed them out of the room.

CHAPTER TWELVE

'HELLO!' came the call from the hill.

Stacy looked up in answer to see Carter's long legs carrying him down towards her. 'Hi yourself,' she replied with a grin.

'I should have known I'd find you down here,' Carter reproached. 'Don't you realize what time it is? You've been going since eight this morning.'

'It's only half past seven and I have a few things to finish up before tomorrow,' Stacy replied, ignoring the mild rebuke in his voice. 'Linda and Diane decided to set up the tables tonight instead of tomorrow morning. I thought I'd give them a hand. Did you get the things from Molly that Mrs. Grayson needed?'

'And delivered to her already. She shooed me out before I even got to sneak a taste of her famous barbecue sauce,' Carter concluded with a mock grimace. 'What's left to do?'

'Nothing, I hope,' Stacy answered with a nervous look around at the long row of folding tables. Waving a good-bye to the two women who were walking away, she turned to Carter apprehensively. 'Tomorrow will tell the tale. All my mistakes will be blatantly obvious.'

'Where's that girl who always rolls with the

punches?' Carter teased with a twinkle in his eyes. Wrapping an arm around her shoulders, he turned her towards the hacienda, adding, 'Day's done. Let's go and have something cool to drink.'

Stacy laughed in spite of her nervousness. A little relaxation would be in order, especially in the face of the ordeal ahead of her tomorrow. A twinge of pain laced her brown eyes as she considered what this week would have been like if Carter hadn't come. Studying his tanned face out of the side of her eye, she examined the new lines at the corner of his lips. Outwardly there was no change in Carter's attitude towards her and no reference had been made to Wednesday's ill-fated evening.

'Regretting the end coming?' Carter asked quietly, his hand squeezing her arm in comfort.

'No,' Stacy sighed. 'I'll be better off when I'm away from here.' 'And only haunted by Cord's memory,' she added to herself.

The couple skirted the front entrance, going directly to the patio at the side of the adobe structure. While Stacy settled herself on one of the chairs, Carter entered the house to get the drinks. The lowering fiery globe of the western sun failed to lighten Stacy's darkening brown eyes as she gazed around her morosely at the surroundings that had become her home these past few weeks. Drawn by a compulsion she didn't understand, she found herself staring intently at the knoll rising above the house. Distantly she heard the phone ringing in the living room and Carter answering it. Numbly she rose and began walking towards the small hill and the as yet unseen cemetery at the top. She didn't hear Carter call her name nor see his still form standing on the cobblestoned veranda with their drinks in his hands.

She didn't stop until she reached the black, wrought-iron fence that enclosed the graveyard. Ignoring the smaller crosses and markers, she made her way directly to the stone bearing the words 'Elena Teresa Harris'. Slowly she knelt in front of the tombstone until a denim knee touched the earth. One brown hand reached out tentatively and traced the letters gently. Two bright tears trickled down her cheeks as Stacy tried to draw comfort from those Cord had loved. Grief and anguish gripped her heart as she leaned against the silent grey stone.

Again Cord's voice echoed in her ear, but this time it sounded so real that she turned her brown head to look. Her eyes had to be playing tricks on her, for there before her stood Cord. It had to be a dream because when she looked up into his face there was the most peculiar light in his eyes. Suddenly Stacy became conscious of the encroaching shadows among the graves. Looking quickly to where the sun had been, she saw only a crimson glow marking its departure. She wasn't dreaming! The realization that it really was Cord standing before her jumped into her eyes as she turned back to face him. At the change in her expression, the large muscular arm that had started to extend itself towards her returned to Cord's side as she hastily scrambled to her feet.

'What are you doing up here?' Cord questioned, a hint of the softness remaining in his voice as he surveyed the pained, almost guilty look on her face.

'I came up here to——' The truth of her intention almost escaped her lips before Stacy could stop it. Nervously she glanced to the grey stone that marked the grave of Doña Elena before her eyes slid to the marker beside it. 'Your father's grave,' she ended lamely, conscious of the narrowing eyes upon her. 'I was remembering my father and somehow I thought coming up here would make him seem closer.'

Whether he accepted her muffled explanation or not, Stacy couldn't tell. Gripping her arm in his hand, he steered her out of the small cemetery without any further comment. Uneasily Stacy glanced into his face. Whatever he was thinking wasn't reflected there. The few minutes of silence were unbearable for her.

'How did you know where I was?'

'Your boy-friend saw you walking this way,' Cord answered, sarcasm seeping through his voice as his long strides carried them down the hill.

'Oh,' Stacy added faintly, as the steel grip propelled her before him.

She permitted herself a quick look down to the veranda before returning her concentration to the uneven ground beneath her. When they reached the edge of the cobblestones, Cord released her arm as if in distaste. A tight-lipped Carter handed Stacy her drink, his blue eyes examining the white pallor of her face.

'Are you okay? Where were you?' he asked quietly.

Stacy managed to nod an affirmative to the first question before Cord interrupted her. Swallowing a big drink from his glass, he stated in his derisive mocking tone, 'She was using my father's grave as a stand-in for her own.'

Carter's blue eyes studied Stacy's intently for a brief second before dismissing the explanation. But Cord wasn't finished.

'Giving in to self-pity is a luxury that this land doesn't allow, not for the people who live here.' The cold harshness of Cord's dark eyes penetrated Stacy's heart, sending the blood rushing to her face from the wound.

Cord turned away and started walking towards the

area north of the stables where the preparations for the barbecue were going on. Stacy and Carter followed a few steps behind. None of the three spoke on the way. Cord seemed to ignore the fact that they were behind him and Carter only glanced Stacy's way once.

The trio passed the long lines of tables gleaming eerily in the waning light and continued towards the red glow emanating from a nearby stand of greasewood trees. Cord slowed his pace so the three approached the fire at the same time. A long pit had been dug in the grove and a fire started in it. In the hazy glow, a form moved to shove another log into the fire. Stacy recognized Hank with a smile.

Adjusting her eyes to the flickering light, she studied the ingenious arrangement of the barbecue with interest. Curiosity overwhelmed the feeling of tension that had previously held her silent. 'Are those old beds the meat's on?'

'Army cots,' Cord smiled in answer. 'We wrap the legs in foil to retain the heat. The hands take turns tending the fire through the night and basting the meat with barbecue sauce.'

'Heavens!' Stacy exclaimed as she saw the enormous amount of meat on the metal slate. 'Aren't you going to have too much to eat?'

'We Texans have big appetites,' Hank snorted. 'We don't mess around with those tiny sandwiches like folks back East. If yore gonna sit here and watch the fire, I'll get some other things done,' he finished. As he turned away from the fire, he added to Carter, 'Might as well come along and give me a hand, I ain't as young as I used to be.'

Without waiting for an answer he tottered off into the dark. A twinge of fear clutched Stacy as she realized that Hank intended to leave her alone with Cord.

She knew Carter was staring at her, waiting for her to say something to indicate that she didn't want him to go. She couldn't think of anything to say. With a stifled exclamation, Carter stalked off through the trees after Hank.

Cord was the one who finally broke the silence, his low voice drawling out, 'Well, you'll be leaving in another day. I suppose you're starting to look forward to it.'

'Not really,' Stacy answered truthfully in a quiet and unemotional voice. 'I've really enjoyed myself here.'

There was a slight pause as if Cord was mulling over her reply. 'I imagined you'd be glad to be going back where you belong.'

Involuntarily Stacy stiffened at Cord's phrase. A flash of her old anger returned at his pompous attitude of always knowing what would be best for her. She quelled the urge to make a retort and continued gazing into the fire.

'Have you and Carter set a date for the wedding?' Cord asked, flicking a twig into the fire.

'No. That's something we'll probably do when we get back,' Stacy replied, not letting the hurt seep into her words. Her pride said it was better to let him think that there was going to be a wedding.

'You'll send me an invitation?'

'Of course,' she answered, straightening her legs and leaning back on her hands as she scowled into the fire. 'Are you going to send me one to yours?'

'Mine?' Cord queried, straightening slowly at her words.

'I forgot I wasn't supposed to know,' Stacy answered airily. 'Though why you wanted to keep it from me, I don't know. It's pretty obvious the way Lydia's always over here that there's more than just the burning embers of an old flame.'

'I see,' an amused expression on Cord's face as he stared at the charred legs. 'I suppose Lydia told you.'

'More or less,' she replied. 'She did all but write it on the wall,' she thought to herself. 'Now that you're released from your responsibility for me, you can go your merry way and I can go mine.'

Seeing his dark head turn towards her in surprise she added, 'I know about the letter from Carter's father too.'

'Carter's father? And how do you know?'

'You left the letter in one of the desk drawers. I must say you went to great lengths to see to it that I kept under your watchful eye. It's too bad you didn't let me in on it. We might have got along better if I'd known what was going on.'

'It didn't occur to me. You were a very headstrong girl. I only hope that Carter is successful in combating your more egocentric ideas.' Cord seemed to be secretly amused, which greatly irritated Stacy.

'Carter understands me,' she replied forcefully, lifting her chin defiantly.

'Oh, I'm sure he does,' Cord laughed. 'It's too bad he doesn't have more control over you.'

'If he had, I never would have come here and all this would never have happened.' Stacy's voice trailed off as a hint of melancholy crept into her voice.

'No, it wouldn't have,' Cord agreed quietly, falling silent with her.

The crackling of twigs and rustling branches sounded the return of Hank and Carter.

'Ready to head back?' Carter asked her.

'Might as well,' said Cord, rising and extending a

hand to Stacy before Carter could intervene. 'It's going to be a long day tomorrow.'

The ranchyard was packed with vehicles of every description from elegant El Dorados to broken-down ranch pick-ups. The auction itself had been over for two hours and the exodus of cars had just begun.

Stacy surveyed the long table that had been heaped with food earlier. So little was left of the vast quantities of meat, baked beans, potato salad, coleslaw, and breads that she sighed with relief that the appetites had been gauged so accurately. Already her group of ranch wives had started to clear the tables of left-over food.

'Are you through for the day?' Molly asked, a plump arm reaching out to fill the iced tea glasses.

'I've just been fired,' Stacy laughed, 'and ordered to join the fun.'

'Good. It's mostly all neighbours left now,' said Mary, hooking an arm in Stacy's and propelling her away from the table. 'You're going to witness a good, old-fashioned party.'

'Hey, where are you taking my hostess?' came the questioning laugh from behind them.

Halting abruptly. Stacy paled at the possessive tone in the voice. With a trembling heart, she felt the masculine hand rest on her shoulder.

'Cord!' Mary cried, 'It's about time you got around to your guests. You've been with those horses all day.'

'I see you've managed to extricate Stacy,' he replied, smiling down at the silent form beside him. 'You did a wonderful job, Stacy. I'm sorry I haven't had a chance to tell you earlier or to give you a hand which you didn't need.'

'Thank you,' Stacy stammered, a flush filling her

cheeks at his unqualified praise. 'But everyone has been good to me. I'm sure they covered a lot of my mistakes.'

'You're too modest,' Molly admonished. 'With someone as sweet as you, people just naturally take you to their heart and do everything they can for you.'

Tears pricked the back of Stacy's eyes at the woman's words. Knowing this to be her last day here, Stacy replied softly, 'You've all made me feel as if this is my home and I'll never forget any of you for that.'

Cord's hand tightened on her shoulder and the sudden pain forced Stacy to look into the tanned face. The questioning and confused look in his dark eyes rested on her face momentarily before turning to the other two women.

'This evening's party is doubling as a farewell party for Stacy. She's leaving us in the morning,' Cord stated grimly.

In the midst of the barrage of protests and objections, Stacy experienced a pang of regret at the ambiguous statements she had made about her leaving, always saying 'some time after the barbecue'. If only they knew how little she really wanted to go!

'Why are you leaving so soon?' Mary asked. 'I thought you'd be staying at least another week.'

'Carter has to be back the first of the week, so we decided to go together,' Stacy explained, ignoring the chill coursing through her as Cord removed his hand from her shoulder. 'We can share the driving and the trip won't seem so long.'

'The two of you are going alone?' Molly asked, frowning a little as she glanced at Cord.

'Tch, tch, Molly, you're showing your age,' Cord mocked. 'Remember this is the enlightened generation. Our moral codes are a little old-fashioned for them. Excuse me, I think it's time I mingled with some of the other guests.'

Despite the light tone of Cord's voice as he had chided Molly, Stacy caught the underlying thread of bitterness in his words. Embarrassed by the implication, she faced the two women self-consciously, ignoring the retreating broad shoulders moving through the crowd.

'Have you decided to marry Carter?' Mary asked lightly as the sounds of guitars and fiddles drifted towards them.

'No,' Stacy replied without thinking.

'Speak of the devil,' Molly muttered as Stacy glanced around to see the sandy-haired Carter walking towards them. 'So you're taking our favourite girl away from us tomorrow,' Molly scolded.

'How else will I ever get her all to myself?' Carter asked, wrapping an arm around Stacy's shoulders. 'Besides,' he added, noting the hidden pain in Stacy's eyes, 'a change of scenery might be advantageous.'

Stacy missed the glance exchanged between mother and daughter as she looked up into Carter's questioning, blue eyes.

'If you ladies don't mind, I think I'll dance with our hostess,' smiled Carter, possessively moving Stacy in the direction of the strumming guitars.

At the edge of the dance floor, he turned her into his arms. He allowed a few steps to the tempo before speaking.

'What happened back there? I saw Cord leave before I arrived.' His blue eyes studied the troubled look on her face. 'What did he say to make you look like that?'

'It wasn't anything he said,' Stacy murmured absently, catching sight of Cord watching them from the fringe of the crowd. 'It's me, I guess,' she sighed, forcing her eyes to Carter. 'I just don't want to leave. I know it's the right thing to do.'

'Stacy, are you even sure you're in love with him? If I thought I had a chance——' Urgency crowded out all caution as Carter gripped Stacy's shoulders. 'Marry me, honey. I can make you happy, you know that.'

'No, Carter.' The chestnut head shook negatively, agitation and indecision in her voice.

'He's so much older than you. How do you know you're not using him to replace the father you lost?' Carter's voice grew desperate and demanding. 'If I hadn't let you come out here, we'd have been married by now. Can't you see that, Stacy? You need an anchor. Let it be me. Say you'll marry me, Stacy, say it now before you regret it the rest of your life.'

'No!' Stacy fairly shouted, trying to stem the whirlpool of persuasion Carter's words were drawing her into. 'No,' she repeated more emphatically, turning from his arms to face the happy dancing throng before them.

'Think about it, Stacy. How can you be sure?' Carter rushed.

'There you are, Stacy,' came a masculine voice. 'Don't you know it's not proper for the hostess to run off in the middle of the party?'

Through blurring eyes, Stacy recognized the stocky form of Bill Buchanan.

'Doctor!' a frantic trill to her words as he grasped her outstretched hand.

'You don't mind if I steal her for a dance, do you, Carter?' Bill asked, a merry twinkle in his eyes. 'I'm too old to stand in line, and when the rest of the men get a good look at her that's just what I'd have to do.'

The doctor whisked Stacy into the clearing where a

lively tune was filling the air. As Stacy matched his bouncy steps, she momentarily glanced back to where Carter was standing. Her attention was caught by the tall figure standing steps away from him, separated only by the same trees in which she and Carter had sought seclusion moments ago. Forgetting her partner completely, Stacy stood motionless as terror raced through her at the realization that the turbulent fury flashing through Cord's eyes could only be caused by his overhearing her conversation with Carter. Suddenly Cord was moving through the dancers towards her. Hurriedly Stacy turned to her partner, ignoring his puzzled expression as she frantically hoped to lose herself among the other couples.

It was too late. The firm brown hand was gripping her shoulders as Cord expressed an abrupt apology to Dr. Buchanan and, without giving Stacy an opportunity to protest, forced her through the whirling couples. Away from the crowd, Stacy attempted futilely to pull away from Cord's hold.

'Let me go!' she cried desperately.

'Just shut up,' Cord replied sharply. 'You've done too much talking already.'

'It's none of your business what happened between Carter and me.' Stacy's temper flashed in her brown eyes.

'I'll decide what's my business.' The muscle in his jaw twitched as Cord turned her towards the hacienda.

'What do you want from me?' Her voice trembled.

'Some straight answers for a start,' said Cord firmly, his voice threateningly low as a couple crossed in front of them.

Walking on to the veranda, Cord muttered an imprecation as he caught sight of guests gathered by the pool. Without a hesitation in his stride, he turned her towards the knoll above the house. Realizing they were headed for the cemetery, Stacy glanced back at him suspiciously.

'Why are we going up here?' she demanded, slightly winded by the swift pace he was setting.

'It's probably the only place on this damn ranch where there aren't any people,' was the curt answer.

Reaching the top of the rise, he moved ahead, dragging her behind him, until they were out of sight of the people below. They stopped a few feet from the iron fence. Releasing her arm, he took hold of a breathless Stacy's shoulders.

'Why did you lie to me and let me believe you were going to marry Carter?' he demanded.

'What does it matter?' Stacy moaned, trying to wrench herself free of his hold.

'Do you want to go back? Do you want to leave here?' When she failed to answer, he shook her. 'Answer me!'

'No!' she sobbed, fighting the answers he was seeking and the truth she couldn't bear him to know. 'Please, Cord, don't!'

'Why don't you want to leave?'

'B-because——' she stammered. 'Oh, Cord, please let me go.'

'Stacy, I can't, not this time.' His voice was suddenly tender and pleading. 'Not until you tell me the truth. This time you've got to tell the truth.'

Tears ran unchecked down her cheeks as she gazed into his tanned face with disbelief. Desperately she searched for assurance that the loving tone she had heard was not a mockery. He pulled her closer, as one side of his mouth lifted in encouragement. He whispered, 'Don't look at me like that until you've answered me. Why don't you want to leave me?'

'Because——' she began, a flush filling her cheeks as a warm glow spread over her. 'Because I love you. Cord, I——'

But his lips silenced the rest of her words. All resistance was gone as previously checked passions were unleashed in a burning embrace. When at last the fiery urgency was satisfied Cord's lips left Stacy's to travel to her eyes, cheeks, the curve of her neck as he whispered his endearments in the glory of love.

'Oh, Cord, Cord, I can't believe it,' Stacy gasped, thrilling at his every touch. 'You really love me?'

'I've loved you for an eternity.' His deep voice choked with emotion like hers.

'You were so hateful to me,' she accused, amidst another shower of kisses meant to silence her.

'I fell in love with you the day I found you lying unconscious on the plains. I knew then if anything happened to you my life wouldn't be worth living,' Cord's voice was husky. 'When you recovered and said you were leaving in a few weeks, I knew I had to find a way to make you stay, to make you love this land as I do.'

'I do, Cord, I do,' murmured Stacy.

'I know. I've never told you how proud I was of you and the way you took your place with the men on the drive and did your share of the work, except on occasions,' he grinned.

'Were you jealous of Jim?' Stacy teased.

'I was jealous of anyone who touched you. Even your letters from Carter irritated me,' he confessed.

'Look at the way you paraded Lydia around. She told me you were going to marry.' Stacy's upturned face was earnest as she added, 'That night on the veranda I thought you were pretending I was Lydia.'

'How I wanted you that night, darling.' His calloused hand traced the curve of her cheek. 'When you recoiled from me——'

'Not from you, Cord. Never from you.'

'Oh, the tangled webs we weave,' Cord smiled.

'If you hadn't overheard my conversation with Carter and forced me to admit to you my love, would you have let me leave tomorrow?'

'I would have shown you no mercy, Miss Adams,' Cord mocked gruffly.

'No quarter asked,' Stacy replied with a smile, lifting her face for his kiss.

'And none given, Stacy,' Cord murmured, inches away from her lips. 'Now that you're finally mine, I'll never let you go. And there'll be no fancy wedding. We're going to be married as soon as we can. You understand that,'

'Yes, Cord, yes,' Stacy answered fervently, yielding once again to his embrace.

FIESTA
SAN ANTONIO

Fiesta
San Antonio

The heavy gold band on her finger proved it was actually true. She was now Mrs. Colter Langton! And in return for the solution to her problems, she had a bargain to keep.

It wouldn't be easy. Hard and unfeeling, Colter had warned her. "I don't particularly like myself," he said. "It's just as well you know now the kind of man I am. That way you won't expect much from our marriage."

If Natalie had secretly hoped that something would grow between them—the dream almost died with his words....

CHAPTER ONE

THE black velvet sky was studded with diamond stars, a cloudless Texas night, warm and languid. But there was a crackle of excitement in the air as the eyes of the crowd lining the banks of Paseo del Rio focused on the river parade.

A man stood in the crowd, but he was not a part of the festive throng. Tall, whipcord-lean, he stood aloof, expressing an aura of detachment. The cold, chiselled lines of the handsome face belonged to a man who rarely smiled, who had found no reason to smile for a long time.

Thick light-brown hair fell with careless attraction over his forehead, the slight waves streaked with burnished gold from long hours in the sun. The teak-dark tan of his complexion emphasised the impression that the face had been carved from wood, dispassionate and indifferent, without a soul. His eyes seemed to hesitate between green and blue, but there was always a frosty tint to their colour.

A gaily decorated barge floated under the stone footbridge, its bright lights blazing for the benefit of the crowd gathered along the river's bend at Arenson River Theatre. A murmur of appreciation rippled through the spectators. The young girl standing in front of the man glanced quickly at him, her blue eyes feverish with excitement.

'Look at that one, Daddy,' she breathed in awe. 'Isn't it beautiful?'

'Yes.' There was a suggestion of an impatient sigh in his clipped agreement, but the girl's attention had returned to the parade.

His gaze flickered uninterestedly over the float and back to the child in front of him, a single, long brown braid nearly touching the waistband of her dress. How old was Missy? Colter Langston wondered idly, then silently cursed that he couldn't remember if his own daughter was ten or eleven.

He snapped a gold lighter to his cigarette, the brief flame throwing his arrogant features into sharp relief, inhaled deeply, then cupped the burning tip in his hand. What was he doing here? His eyes swept the crowd in contempt. People stood elbow to elbow, craning their necks for a glimpse of the floats when they could have remained at home and had an unobstructed view of the parade on their television sets.

'Observing the Fiesta is not participating.' Unbidden Flo Donaldsen's statement came to him.

Yes, it was his aunt who was to blame for his presence in the crowd, his aunt and the prickles of conscience over the years of his neglect of Missy. Not neglect, Colter corrected silently. His daughter had never wanted for anything. She had beautiful clothes, plenty of food, a home. He had never sent her off to any boarding school. She had lived under the same roof with him since the day she had entered this world. What more could the child want from him? he thought impatiently.

This shy, quiet withdrawn child with her thin, sensitive face was his daughter. Yet Colter Langston felt no surge of emotion at the knowledge. He cared for her—as much as he could, but there was no bursting warmth of pride to fill the emptiness within him. With his usual cynicism, he decided that parenthood was vastly overrated.

Grinding out the half-smoked cigarette beneath the heel of his boot, Colter Langston glared resentfully at the slow-moving minute hand of his watch, knowing the parade had barely started and wishing it was over. There was an ominous tightening of his lean jaw as he realised he had committed himself to accompanying Missy to all the activities of Fiesta week, the celebration marking Texas's independence of Mexico. The River Parade was the first major event and he was already bored. Idleness didn't appeal to him.

With a self-mocking movement of his mouth, he admitted that there was little that didn't bore him. An only child, a son, born the heir to the vast Langston holdings in the Texas hill country north of San Antonio, he had been denied nothing as a child, a wild teenager, or a young man. Now, at thirty-four, he realised his senses were satiated. Life held no more illusions. Sex, love, marriage, all were coldly dismissed. The happiness and satisfaction that were supposed to exist in those items were the products of writers' and poets' imaginations. Colter had tried them all and found them wanting.

For the last five years, since his father's death, he had been the sole owner of the Langston Ranch and its numerous investments. The power of the Langston influence was his to command and he was accustomed to being obeyed.

Matt Langston had taught him that every man had a price, monetary or otherwise. Colter had admired and respected his father, but they had never been close. His mother had died when he was six and he had only photographs to recall what she looked like.

As for his wife Caroline, she had married the Langston name. It hadn't taken Colter long to realise that. The daughter she had died giving him within the first year of their marriage had been her means of cementing a permanent link with the Langston power and wealth. Her diary had callously stated that she had never loved Colter, only his money and name. Looking back, Colter realised that he had never loved her, only the perfection of her beauty. He had married her to satisfy the lust she aroused while adamantly withholding herself.

He had never loved anyone, not even himself. No one loved him. Missy tried, just as Colter had tried to love his father. Perhaps the one who came closest to caring for him had been his aunt Flo. When his mother had died, Matt Langston had brought her widowed sister to Langston Ranch to look after his son. She had stayed on to care for Missy.

But no longer. His mouth moved into a grim, forbidding line. At the end of this month, Flo Donaldsen was leaving, figuratively if not literally. She was a strong, proud woman who spoke her mind and Colter had received an unfaltering share of it before he and Missy had left for San Antonio.

'I don't like what you've become, Colter,' she had told him. 'You are cold, insensitive and sometimes cruel towards other people's feelings. You show more kindness and attention to your horses than you ever do to your own daughter, and it isn't right! You're cynical! Your heart has turned to stone—if you ever had one. Missy needs her father, not an ageing aunt. And if you can't be the parent she needs, then you should provide her with a mother. You'll not shirk your responsibility off on to me any longer. According to your father's will, the cottage by the creek is mine whenever I want it, along with a pension. I'll be moving into it at the end of the month.'

Colter hadn't argued. Eventually he knew he could work his way around her. He had no qualms about using the affection she held for him and his daughter to gain what he wanted. Yet he had to admit that perhaps Missy deserved a mother.

Deirdre would relish the role. Granted he found her company to be stimulating and enjoyable, at least for the time being, but Colter knew that Deirdre only tolerated his daughter. The sensually attractive redhead was a man's woman, definitely not the domesticated type. When the physical attraction Deirdre held for him passed, as it undoubtedly would—as it had with all the other women he had known—she would probably take her vengeance out on Missy. No, he would not marry Deirdre.

Candy tossed from a float landed at his feet, missing the outstretched hands that tried to intercept it. As Missy bent to retrieve it, a set of small fingers reached it first. A pair of dark brown eyes peered through the mop of thick brown hair falling over his forehead, their expression reluctant and hopeful.

'Was this yours?' The little boy's clenched fist opened to reveal the paper-wrapped candy, offering it hesitantly to Missy.

Colter watched the movement of his daughter's mouth into a refusing smile, noticing her lack of inhibition towards the child who was half her age.

'No, you can have it,' Missy assured the little boy.

The tiny palm remained outstretched as the boy fixed his gaze longingly on the candy. 'Nonnie said I wasn't supposed to take things that belonged to someone else, and I'm not supposed to take things away from girls.'

Missy cast Colter a shy, adult smile before turning a solemn face back to the boy. 'You found it, so you can keep it.'

Bright brown eyes studied her face for an instant longer, then small fingers closed protectively over the candy. For precious seconds he held it in his fist before he reverently began unwrapping the paper.

'My name is Ricky,' he said importantly after he had carefully placed the candy in his mouth. 'What's yours?'

'My name is Missy and this is my father,' she replied.

The boy named Ricky had to tilt his head way back

to look up at Colter's face. One corner of Colter's mouth turned up in wry amusement at the open inspection he was receiving. He rather liked the boldness of the boy's look, forthright and not easily impressed. Nor intimidated, it seemed.

'I don't have a father,' Ricky announced, 'but some day I'm going to have cowboy boots, too.'

The two thoughts did not correlate for Colter, but obviously they did for the boy. Briefly Colter wondered whether he and Missy would have been closer if she had been a boy instead of a girl. He doubted that. He would probably have been irritated by the constant demands of a son.

'Did your mother bring you to the parade?' Colter heard Missy ask.

He was a bit surprised at her interest in the boy. She had never seemed to display much interest in the other children she went to school with, although she had seemed fond of little Josh Harris. Still, Colter had presumed she was a loner like himself, the one trait they shared.

'Nonnie brought me,' Ricky nodded, adding with a shrug, 'but I think she got lost.'

'Are you sure you're not the one who's lost?' Missy smiled.

'I don't think so.' A small frown drew his brows together. 'I know where I am, but I don't know where Nonnie is. So she's the one who's lost,' he reasoned.

It was Colter's turn to frown as he saw his daughter touch the little boy's arm and bend slightly towards him in a solicitous movement.

'Yes, but you see, Ricky, your Nonnie knows where she is, but she doesn't know where you are. I'll bet she thinks you're the one who's lost,' Missy explained.

The corners of his mouth pulled down. 'I'll bet she'll be mad again,' Ricky sighed.

'Where did you last see her?'

Colter guessed the trend his daughter's questions were taking and the last thing he wanted to do was become involved in a search for the boy's mother. If the boy was lost then it was his mother's fault for not keeping a closer eye on him.

'Over there somewhere.' The boy's hand waved in the general direction of the footbridge. 'I was thirsty and she was going to get me a drink.'

'And you were supposed to wait for her,' Missy concluded astutely.

More brown hair fell forward as the boy shamefacedly tucked his chin into his neck and answered a very small 'yes.'

'Give me your hand,' Missy instructed quietly, 'and we'll go and see if we can find her.'

'Missy!' Colter's voice rang out sharper than he intended as his hand closed over her shoulder. He lowered his voice quickly to a firmer, less abrasive tone. 'We are not going to search this crowd for the boy's mother,' he said emphatically.

There was the hurt look of a wounded animal in her accusing eyes. 'We can't just leave him. He's only a little boy, Daddy,' she argued anxiously.

'I'm not so little,' Ricky inserted proudly. 'I'll soon be six.'

Colter flashed him a silencing look of ice blue, then turned back to his daughter. She had withdrawn again into her shell, a remote resentment clouding her more calm blue eyes.

'Look,' he sighed, his lips thinning with impatience at being backed into a corner. 'We'll take the boy to that policeman over there. His mother has probably already discovered he's lost and will have notified them.'

'Couldn't we take a few minutes to look first?' Missy suggested, glancing hesitantly at him through upcurving lashes.

'It isn't any of our business and we're not going to get involved,' Colter snapped harshly.

His jaw tightened as Missy flinched from his tone. Fleetingly, he had to acknowledge that Flo was right when she said he hurt people without meaning to do it. Tact had never been one of his virtues. He abruptly released her shoulder and turned to the boy.

'Come on,' he ordered crisply. 'We'll take you to the policeman. He'll help you find your mother.'

But Ricky held back. 'They don't know where Nonnie is.' His lower lip jutted out in a mutinous pout.

Colter stared at him for an instant, then reached down and swung the boy into his arms. Bright brown eyes curiously studied the face now at eye level. Unlike Missy, Ricky was not intimidated by the forbidding set of his jaw.

Nothing was revealed in Colter's expression, yet inwardly he admired the impertinent look. The discovery had barely registered before the hint of green in his eyes returned to the cold, harsh blue. The child meant nothing to him. He pivoted sharply towards the distant man in police uniform, aware that Missy's feet were dragging as she followed him. As far as he was cornerned it was enough that he had brought her to the Fiesta. It was ungrateful to involve him with this lost stray.

A small hand balanced itself on Colter's shoulder while Ricky took in his improved view of the crowd and the parade. Fingers tightened for a biting instant.

'Wait,' Ricky ordered imperiously. His forefinger pointed to Colter's left. 'There's Nonnie!'

Colter turned in the direction Ricky indicated, his alert gaze immediately picking out the woman frantically searching the crowd. As she drew nearer, a brow rose thoughtfully. Ricky's mother was hardly a woman. If Colter was any judge, she was barely out of her teens, and Ricky himself had asserted that he was almost six.

The girl was attractive, Colter decided, above average, despite the signs of exhaustion and strain etched in her features. The harried look had not occurred tonight but had accumulated over a period of months.

Then the hazel eyes, almond-shaped and slanted upwards at the corners, unusually attractive with their gold flecks, spied Ricky in Colter's arms. A wide smile of relief spread across her sensuously full lips as she hurried towards them. There was a vaguely untouched look about her that kindled a fleeting fire of desire in his loins until he remembered the boy in his arms. Women were available to him in abundance. He didn't need the entanglement of a small boy.

The crowds were so thick that Natalie was more terrified than she cared to acknowledge when she discovered Ricky was not where she had left him. He usually did exactly what he was told, although he might question the order. The excitement of the parade must have been too much for his adventurous nature to ignore.

Somehow she had known he wouldn't stray out of sight of the footbridge. Her fear had been that she would walk by him in the crowd and not see him. Only by the merest chance had she seen Ricky in the stranger's arms out of the corner of her eye.

'Oh, Ricky!' she exclaimed with a laughing cry as the stranger handed him to her, 'I thought I told you to stay by the bridge.'

Her relief at finding him unharmed was too great for Natalie to be as angry as she should have been with him. Tears filled her eyes, tears of relief and wretched tiredness. She brushed them away and proudly raised her head to thank the stranger.

Her breath caught in her throat, her body automatically stiffening at his bold appraisal of her slender form and the suggestion of jeering contempt. His aura of self-assurance bordered on arrogance. Natalie's initial impression had been that the man was handsome, but the unrelenting hardness of his face negated its effect.

The strange blue-green eyes seemed to strip away

her pride. The expensive leisure suit of brown stitched with tan spoke of money and his gaze was too discerning not to recognise her clothes as bargain store purchases.

'I want to thank you for finding Ricky.' Her expression of gratitude lacked sincerity, the result of his derisive look.

'You're holding me too tight,' Ricky whispered loudly in her ear.

It was his way of saying that he was too big to be held like a baby in her arms. Reluctantly Natalie let him slide to the ground, keeping a firm hold of one small hand. Her shaking fingers clutched a paper cup in the other hand.

'He was no trouble.' The low-pitched masculine voice drawled lazily, a contradiction to the alertness of his gaze. 'We were taking him to the policeman on the corner.'

Yes, Natalie thought with a kind of grim resentment, this arrogant stranger wasn't the type to involve himself more than superficially with the problem of a lost child, certainly not to the extent of participating in a search for her.

Ricky tugged at her hand. 'They threw candy from the floats. I found a piece and Missy let me keep it. Was that all right? I've already eaten it,' he added as an afterthought.

'Missy?' Natalie repeated blankly.

She followed his pointing finger, for the first time seeing the young girl standing beside the stranger.

'That's Missy,' Ricky explained, 'and that's her father.'

Compassion touched Natalie's heart. If the girl's father was as arrogant and callous as he looked, it was no wonder Missy seemed so sensitive and withdrawn. The girl was just reaching that awkward age when she needed the reassurance that somebody cared. Natalie remembered those heartbreaking years. If it hadn't been for her brother—But she had had her brother, and Natalie could only hope that the girl's mother was a vast improvement over her father.

'May I have my drink?' Ricky demanded.

'There isn't much left, I'm afraid,' Natalie answered as she handed him the paper cup half-filled with water. 'I spilled most of it looking for you.'

He drained it dry and handed the empty cup back to her, wiping his mouth with the back of his hand. At that instant, Natalie noticed the marked silence of the stranger and realised he was probably very anxious for her to take Ricky and leave. Squaring her shoulders, she turned to him.

'Thank you again,' she offered tautly. He nodded curtly in acknowledgement and Natalie tightened her hold on Ricky's hand. 'Come on. Let's go watch the parade.'

Her forced smile immediately changed into one of genuine loving at the sight of the bright brown eyes gazing back at her.

'Would you——' a hesitant voice began, stopping Natalie and Ricky as they began to turn away. 'Would you like to watch the parade with us?' Missy faltered.

Natalie saw the sharp look of reproach that the man gave to his daughter and knew he wanted to be rid of them. She had guessed correctly. Gold fires flared for an instant in her eyes before she quickly banked them to meet the girl's wavering gaze.

'Thank you, but I don't think so,' Natalie refused.

At the sideways look the girl gave her father, Natalie was aware that Missy had guessed the reason she had refused. There was a rebellious urge to stay just to spite the man, but Natalie knew she would be uncomfortable in his presence.

With more haste than was necessary she led Ricky through the crowds to the footbridge. Their previous vantage point near the river was occupied, much to Ricky's dismay. Natalie succeeded in finding a spot along the short, guarded rock wall where she could sit with Ricky perched on her lap. The minute she relaxed that aching tiredness swept over her, throbbing through every muscle and nerve.

The parade had started out as a treat for Ricky and a brief respite from her problems. It had barely begun when Ricky had become lost. What little energy she possessed had been expended in the search for him. She knew the stranger had silently condemned her for leaving the boy in the first place. Natalie acknowledged that he was partially right. But their vantage point for the parade had been such a good one and she had always been able to count on Ricky doing as he was told, so she hadn't dreamed he would stray from the spot. But what had gone right for her lately?

His small brown head leaned against her shoulder

and Natalie rested her cheek against his silky fine hair. Her lashes fluttered tiredly down. If only she had someone to lean on, she sighed heavily. Her exhaustion was mental as well as physical. Sinking her teeth into the bottom of her lip, she tried to hold back the waves of despair.

That terrible weekend three years ago when her brother Ned and his wife had been killed outright in an automobile accident, then it had seemed so logical and natural for Natalie to take her little nephew Ricky to raise. It was either that or make him a ward of the courts to be placed in a foster home. At the time she had thought she had a good job. She couldn't have guessed that the firm would go out of business within a few months, nor did she realise the constant expense of a small child.

As the clothes, medical, and baby-sitter costs mounted, Natalie was forced to take nearly any kind of work to try to make ends meet. The last job she had worked through an agency that provided daily help to homes in the area. On Friday they had fired her when she was falsely accused of stealing from one of the homes. Her weekly pay check, no matter how frugally she spent it, had never succeeded in lasting till the next one. The few groceries in their tiny apartment would last out the week and no longer. She simply had to find another job soon.

The weight of the small boy on her lap seemed to increase, numbing her legs into leaden sticks. When the last float emerged from under the footbridge, Natalie realised that Ricky had fallen asleep. As she smoothed the straight brown hair from his forehead, she knew all her efforts had been worth it, and all the future ones, too. Ricky was strong and healthy, intelligent and happy, trusting and loving, and supremely confident that she loved him. There was no hint of the shyness, unhappiness, or uncertainty in Ricky that she had seen in Missy.

Gently Natalie turned Ricky into her arms, his hands automatically circling her neck in sleep and hugging her tightly. There was a warm sensation of love in the way the small body clung to her. Rising to her feet and carrying the heavy burden of the sleeping child that strangely felt lighter, Natalie followed the milling crowd that had begun to leave the riverwalk area.

The street leading to their apartment was much travelled and well lighted, one of the main thoroughfares to downtown San Antonio. As Natalie walked past the parking lot congested with cars attempting to leave, she wished she could spare the money to take the bus. It was going to be a long walk home.

A white El Dorado pulled out of the parking lot, accelerating by Natalie. She had a fleeting glimpse of a thin, sensitive face pressed against the window and staring at her before the street lights reduced the two occupants of the car to silhouettes, one large and one small. Red lights from the rear of the car flashed a secret danger signal as the car braked and turned into the sidewalk curb ahead of Natalie. She shifted Ricky in her arms, her heart pounding with fear or pride.

The driver's door was opened and violently

slammed shut. As Natalie drew nearer to where the car was parked, she saw the arrogant stranger's long impatient strides eating up the distance that separated them. She could only guess that his daughter had insisted they stop when she recognised Natalie and the sleeping Ricky.

For all the seething fury she had sensed in his movements, the chiselled features that looked at her were remarkably cool and aloof. He stopped directly in her path, forcing her to halt and acknowledge him.

'May we give you a ride to your home?'

The offer was blandly made. Natalie decided that it had been a long time since this man had revealed his true thoughts in his facial expression.

'No, thank you.' She spoke concisely and with no hesitation.

She didn't want him to believe for an instant that she might be impressed by his obvious wealth or attention.

'With your son and my daughter as chaperones, I'm hardly likely to do you any harm,' he said briskly.

Natalie started to correct him by explaining that Ricky was her nephew, then changed her mind. Let him think what he liked. He probably wouldn't believe her if she told him the truth.

'My daughter is most anxious that you arrive at your home safely.' An undercurrent or sarcasm in his voice.

'It was her idea and not yours to stop, too, wasn't it?' Natalie flashed.

'Of course,' he agreed, letting her know that the

thought would never have occurred to him, just as she had guessed. 'And I don't look forward to the prospect of sitting up half the night trying to convince her that you and the boy had come to no harm.'

Natalie glanced at the car. The street light illuminated the apprehensive expression of the young face that watched them. It was conceivable that a sensitive young person might be so much concerned.

'We'll accept your offer,' Natalie submitted ungraciously.

The slight twist of his mouth informed her that he had expected no other decision. He didn't wait for her as he walked to the car and opened the passenger door. There was a darting smile of gratitude from Missy to him as she scrambled into the back seat, leaving the front seat vacant for Natalie.

The cheap cotton of Natalie's dress slid nearly up to her thigh as she tried to negotiate getting in without disturbing Ricky. Tugging her skirt into a more respectable place, she felt her cheeks stinging with embarrassment, conscious of those cold, watchful eyes that observed everything. Then her door was closed and he was around to the driver's side, sliding behind the wheel.

'Is he asleep?' Missy leaned forward on to the leather armrest in the middle of the front seats.

Natalie pushed back her hostility to answer quietly, 'Yes, it's past his bedtime.'

The car was in motion, the aristocratic profile concentrating on the traffic and ignoring Natalie completely.

'The parade was nice, wasn't it?' the girl suggested hesitantly as if she wasn't sure of her own opinion.

'Yes,' Natalie agreed. 'Ricky enjoyed it. It's the first time he's ever seen one.'

'Me, too. Except on television,' Missy qualified.

'Where do you live?'

Natalie was brought up sharply by the masculine voice, hating herself for forgetting to tell him her address, a situation she quickly corrected.

'Do you know where that is?' she inquired as an afterthought.

'I've lived near San Antonio all my life. There are few places I don't know,' he replied evenly.

And yet it was the first time his daughter had been to a Fiesta parade, Natalie added to herself. Her arm brushed the expensive leather upholstery. The failure couldn't have been due to a lack of money, of that she was certain.

'Have you lived here long?' the girl whispered— Natalie had the impression that it was because of her father and not the sleeping child.

'For the last few years,' Natalie admitted in an equally quiet voice.

'It's nice. I like San Antonio.'

Then Natalie remembered the slight qualification when the man had said that he lived 'near' San Antonio. 'Ricky said your name was Missy, is that right?'

'Missy Langston, short for Melissa,' she explained. Her hand made a slight, hesitant movement in her father's direction. 'Th-This is my father, Colter Langston.'

The name registered vaguely in Natalie's memory as belonging to someone of importance. She glanced briefly in his direction and found lazy green-blue eyes returning her look. The knowing glitter forced her to look away. He had seen the faint glimmer of recognition cross her face.

'My name is Natalie Crane, she identified herself for no other reason than to fill the suffocating silence.

'Ricky calls you Nonnie, doesn't he?' Missy replied.

A small smile pulled up the corners of her mouth as her fingers touched the head of the boy sleeping against her shoulder.

'When he was smaller, he couldn't say Natalie. That was the closest he could come to it.'

'Which of these places is your home?' Colter Langston had made the turn off the main thoroughfare on to the side-street where she and Ricky lived.

'The third house on the right,' Natalie answered.

The windows of the large structure were dark except for one small light in the rear. Natalie was glad. Lights would only make the old monstrosity of a house, the upper floors remodelled into apartments, look as shabby and neglected as the darkness hinted. She wished now she had asked to be let out on the corner. She had caught the faint note of derision in his question.

The car stopped next to the curb. Natalie was fumbling for the door handles as the headlights and motor were switched off. Her startled gaze watched Colter Langston get out of the car and walk round to her side. As she realized that this show of courtesy was for his daughter's benefit, her mouth tightened grimly. When her door was opened, she swung her legs around to step out.

'Give me the boy,' Colter Langston ordered, his strong hands reaching for Ricky's small waist.

'I can carry him,' she asserted firmly, drawing back from the outstretched hands.

'And get your key out of your purse and fumble with the door,' he mocked, drawing the boy away from her. 'I sincerely doubt that you want me rummaging through your purse for the key.'

Without being encumbered with Ricky, Natalie was quickly out of the car, glaring resentfully at the man so casually holding her sleeping nephew. She walked swiftly and familiarly over the broken concrete walk to the door, long, catlike strides keeping pace behind her. For once the key didn't stick in the lock, but turned instantly, opening the front door. A step inside, Natalie turned to take Ricky.

'He's fine,' Colter stated, 'Just point out your apartment.'

'It's upstairs,' she sighed, wondering if it gave him some sensation of superiority to see how humble her home was. She was simply too tired to care.

As she started toward the stairs, a door into the hallway opened and the iron-grey eyes of her landlady peered out. A brow arched upwards as she spotted the man with Natalie.

'I have told you repeatedly, Miss Crane, that I will not allow you to entertain men in your apartment.'

This is a respectable house!' Her landlady's voice rang out harshly.

Through sheer force of will, Natalie held her temper. The first of the month was coming shortly. If she hoped to gain a couple of days' grace to raise the rent money, she couldn't afford to become angry.

'He's only carrying Ricky to my room. He'll be leaving immediately, Mrs Thomas,' Natalie answered, her gaze flickering briefly to Colter Langston.

'Well, see that he does!' the woman snapped. and closed the door.

Natalie didn't want to guess what construction Colter Langston had put on the exchange that he had so aloofly observed. If she knew, she would almost certainly tell him just what she thought of his lordly ways.

At the top of the stairs, she unlocked the door to her one-room flat and reached for Ricky. Colter handed him to her without protest.

'Thank you for the ride,' she offered grudgingly.

'I'll pass it on to Missy. It was her idea.' A subtle reminder that she truly hadn't needed, and he was going back down the steps.

CHAPTER TWO

'You sit here quietly, Ricky, and eat your sandwich,' Natalie instructed. 'And don't bother anybody.'

'I won't,' his bright voice promised as he crawled on to the long bench, his chin barely above the wooden counter. 'Aren't you going to eat with me, Nonnie?'

'No, honey, I have to work.' Honey-brown hair was curling about her face and neck from the heat of the grill. She tried pushing it away from her face, but it was too thick and full to stay there.

Under the influence of her encouraging smile, Ricky picked up the sandwich, cut into sections for his small fingers to handle, and began eating with his usual gusto. The smile faded as Natalie turned away. Her temples throbbed from the heat and excessive noise. The air was stiflingly still with little promise of coolness from the setting sun.

A country-western band was playing a rousing tune in the main square of La Villita. The music was loud to be heard over the steady din of voices and laughter of the milling crowd. 'A Night in Old San Antonio', part of the Fiesta week activities, transformed La Villita, a re-creation of the small settlement that once existed there, into four nights of perpetual chaos. Every available inch of space was used for booths to sell ethnic food, drink and gifts native to the various immigrant people who had settled the land.

It was in a stand located in the Frontier section that Natalie had at last found work. Temporary, only for the four nights, but it would be an income, however small. The owner-operator of the stand had raised no objections when Natalie had asked to bring Ricky with her as long as he stayed out of the way. It had saved the considerable expense of a babysitter even if it did mean keeping Ricky up much later than she liked. It was only going to be for four nights and he could always curl up on the bales of hay behind the stand if he became too tired.

Turning another ranch steak on the grill, Natalie wearily wiped the perspiration from her forehead. She had a sinking feeling that all her efforts were in vain. In the last year, everything had seemed to go from bad to worse.

She had grown to love Ricky tremendously and she refused to grumble at the awesome responsibility her love brought. If only she could have an hour's rest from the pressure of her problems, she thought wistfully. If only she didn't feel so unbearably tired and worn out all the time, maybe she could think of a solution. What fun it would be to join in the merriment of the hundreds of people roaming through La Villita, seemingly without a care.

Dully Natalie glanced over her shoulder to be sure that Ricky was still sitting at the counter. At the reassuring sight of the silky brown head, she started to turn back, only to freeze into stillness as her gaze became locked by a pair of aloof green-blue eyes. A wildfire of dislike raced through her veins, amber flames brightening her hazel eyes.

His indifferent study of her was disturbing and Natalie found it impossible to meet it any longer. She let her gaze swing from Colter Langston to his daughter Missy, who was sitting on the bench next to Ricky, smiling shyly and talking to him in a low voice.

Averting her head with a jerky movement, Natalie concentrated her attention on the small steaks on the grill. What bitter irony to see him again! The feeling was mutual, Natalie was sure, that is if the man possessed any feelings. His handsome face was chiselled into cold, ruthless lines, the deep tan of his complexion offsetting the glacial shade of his eyes and the streaks of sun-gold in his hair. Lean and supple, he had the sinewy build of an athlete, or more figuratively, the latent muscular power of a cougar.

Yes, Natalie decided grimly, there was a great deal about him that reminded her of a predatory cat. The nobly proud and withdrawn look in his impassive expression, the air of supreme independence, the strength that was held in check until it was needed, then to be unleashed with lightning swiftness, the dangerous claws that seemed to be sheathed for the time being, the indifference to others' wishes unless it pleased him to indulge them, and, most of all, there was that hint of a primitive animal, undomesticated and disdainful of civilisation. Yet, in spite of it all, Colter Langston possessed a magnetic, almost hypnotic fascination, a kind of frightening lure of danger.

Natalie shook her head firmly to halt the fanciful

imaginings of her mind. It was sheer chance that she had seen him again, chance and his daughter's acquaintance with Ricky, and the Fiesta. Her mouth twisted wryly as she realized that for a few moments her money worries had been set aside.

'Nonnie?' Ricky's voice rang clear and sharp, only vaguely apologetic for interrupting her.

After dishing up two more plates, Natalie self-consciously wiped her hands on the gingham checked apron and walked to the counter where Ricky was seated, deliberately ignoring the man standing behind him.

'Hello, Missy,' she greeted the girl quietly, and received a hesitant nod in return.

'I ate all my dinner.' Ricky pushed the clean plate forward for her inspection. Before Natalie could comment, he rushed on, 'Missy said she would take me around and show me everything.'

'I'll keep hold of his hand all the time so he won't get lost,' Missy inserted anxiously.

'I'm sure you would be very careful, Missy, but——' Natalie began her denial. She glanced unwillingly at the emotionless, masculine face above the two children seated at the counter. 'I think Ricky should stay here with me. It's very crowded tonight.'

'Oh, Daddy!' Missy turned her anxious pleading face to Colter Langston, who viewed it without a flicker of interest. 'Please make Mrs Crane understand that we would take care of him.'

Natalie squirmed inwardly, knowing what a difficult position Missy was placing both of them in. She didn't have to hear him speak to know that the last thing Colter Langston wanted to do was squire her nephew around. His aloof gaze swung to her and Natalie steeled herself to meet it.

'The boy will be quite safe with us. We'll bring him directly back here once we've made the tour, Mrs Crane,' he stated with a trace of mocking inflection on the word 'Mrs'.

'It's *Miss* Crane. Ricky is my nephew.' The brief arching of his brow made Natalie regret that she had corrected him. 'Now, if you'll excuse me, I have to get back to work.'

'We'll bring Ricky back in an hour,' Colter responded smoothly.

'I didn't say he could go!' Natalie turned back in astonishment.

'The child has little else to do while you're working. What's the harm?' he challenged.

Resentment flared unchecked in her gaze, but it made little impression on him. She couldn't stand there and argue the point, especially in front of the two children watching the exchange so closely. Indecision hovered in her mind until she met the pair of pleading brown eyes, so loving and full of mischief. It would serve Colter Langston right to take Ricky.

'All right,' she sighed agreement. 'I'll expect Ricky back in an hour.'

Afterwards she wondered if she had been insane to agree. Colter Langston and his daughter were virtual strangers, regardless of how respectable they appeared on the surface. 'Respectable'—it was hardly an adjective that could be applied to him, not with any degree of certainty.

Yet there was the unshakeable impression that Colter Langston had been selfishly indulging the whim of his daughter, using Ricky to entertain her so he wouldn't have to. The more Natalie thought about that the more positive she became that it had been his only motive.

As the hour neared its end, Natalie kept searching the crowd, now grown to such proportions that they were elbow to elbow as they jostled their way to the various ethnic booths. The sky had darkened to a purpling black and La Villita was illuminated by strings of brightly coloured lights strung across squares and alleys and atop the booths. The time for her fifteen-minute break was approaching, precious minutes that she wanted to devote to Ricky.

Then, through the mob of people young and old, Natalie saw him perched again on Colter's arm as the three wound their way to the stand. Colter's hand firmly kept Missy directly in front of him. Ricky's brown eyes were round and wondering at all the things he had seen. She knew he would talk non-stop for an hour to share his tour with her. Even Missy's face was unusually animated and happy.

Ricky almost leaped into her outstretched arms. 'Did you have a good time?' Natalie smiled.

'Terrific!' he breathed, and would have launched into a full account then and there, but Missy broke in.

'We brought him back safely,' she offered earnestly.

'Yes, you did.' Her gaze flickered automatically from the girl to her father, her smile turning a little more reserved under his lazy, yet piercing look. 'Thank you.'

Natalie stood Ricky up on an empty corner of the counter bench, tucking his shirt tail back into his trousers. 'You should have seen the pretty eggs,' he told her excitedly.

' "Cascarones",' Missy added, more fully identifying the confetti-filled eggshells for Natalie's benefit.

'You break them over people's heads!' His dark, bright eyes rounded still more as Ricky passed on that startling discovery to Natalie. She couldn't help laughing at his amazed expression, the laughter erasing the lines of concern.

Missy reached into the small straw purse she was carrying and took out a red and a blue 'cascarone'. 'You can take these home with you, if you like, Ricky,' she offered.

Natalie's hand was resting lightly on Ricky's back. She felt him stiffen slightly, drawing himself more erect. She glanced curiously at his solemn expression as he stared at the brightly coloured eggshells in Missy's hand.

'Nonnie and me, we don't accept charity.'

A warm flush of embarrassment crept up her cheeks at the almost physical touch of the mocking gaze that was directed at her. It was so obvious that Ricky was repeating an admonition he had heard her say many times. She felt even worse when she saw the hurt look steal over Missy's face, the sparkle leaving her blue eyes.

'It's not charity.' Colter's low voice, calm and unruffled, drew Ricky's gaze. 'It's a Fiesta gift, just like at Christmas time.'

Barely moving his head, he turned to Natalie for confirmation of Colter's words. When it had been a simple, inexpensive gift from Missy, Natalie had not minded Ricky accepting the 'cascarones'. Now that her father had involved himself, she wanted to refuse. Her denial would not affect Colter Langston who was only backing up his daughter as she would have done in his place, but it would be one more simple treat that she couldn't give Ricky. She wished the innocent children did not have to suffer from the actions of an adult.

'That's right, Ricky,' Natalie agreed grudgingly. 'Why don't you go get your truck and show it to Missy?'

Carefully cradling the 'cascarones' in his hand, the little boy took off like a shot for the toy truck placed for safe keeping behind the counter. Apart from that one comment, Colter Langston did not take part again in the three-way conversation of Natalie, Missy and Ricky, but Natalie never lost her awareness of him, her nerve ends tingling whenever she felt his dispassionate gaze directed at her.

Her break was over and she was back working at the grill when Missy said goodbye to Ricky. Natalie doubted that Colter Langston had joined in the farewell. She was certain any courtesy had been extended by Misy.

As she had suspected, Ricky curled up very willingly on the bale of straw to the back of the stand—to watch the people, he said. Shortly after ten o'clock, she saw his head drooping in sleep. A few minutes later, he had shifted into a horizontal position; sleeping away completely unmindful of the din that hadn't let up since the gates of La Villita had opened up at five-thirty that afternoon.

Officially, the celebration of 'A Night in Old San Antonio' ended at ten-thirty each night, but it was closer to eleven-thirty before the grill was cleaned and Natalie was able to leave. The last three days she had spent in an exhaustive search for a new job. That combined with almost six straight hours on her feet over the sapping heat of the grill made her feel too weary to take another step. Time enough to collapse when she reached home, Natalie told herself firmly, and picked up Ricky and his truck and her purse to trudge to the gates of the Alamo Street entrance.

Just as she stepped through them, a tall figure pushed itself away from the stone walls of La Villita. Her tired brain identified Colter Langston a second before he lifted the sleeping child from her unprotesting arms.

'My car is across the street.'

'You don't have to——' Natalie began feebly.

His head was drawn back slightly, heightening the effect that he was looking down at her. 'Would you like a ride home or not? A simple "yes" or "no" will do.' The pitch of his low voice didn't change, yet there was an underlying harshness to it.

The prospect of the long walk to her apartment looked more daunting than a short ride with Colter Langston. Besides, in her weakened state, she found his strength and vitality intimidated her. Natalie held his cold, expressionless gaze for an instant.

'Missy's idea, I suppose,' she sighed, unable to acquiesce completely, and he didn't deny her observation. Wearily she pushed the hair away from her face. 'Yes, we will accept your offer.'

'My car is across the street,' Colter repeated.

Natalie had no trouble finding the white El Dorado in the half-empty parking lot. Once she was in the passenger seat, he handed the sleeping Ricky to her and walked around to the driver's side. As Natalie tried to shift Ricky into a more comfortable position on her lap, his eyes blinked open.

Craning his head around, he looked into the back seat, then at Colter. 'Where's Missy?'

'She's in bed, asleep.' Colter answered the question as if it had been asked by an adult.

'I'm tired, too,' Ricky agreed, and settled his head against Natalie's shoulder, dropping off almost instantly to sleep.

Natalie leaned her own head against the rich leather cushions, half-closing her eyes as the powerful car accelerated into the street. The darkness and quietness outside closed around her like a warm cocoon.

'I never realised silence could be so beautiful,' she murmured aloud, 'or so peaceful.'

The unceasing din of the crowds took on the aspects of a nightmare that was only barely remembered. Out of the corner of her eye, she studied his profile. The softly firm cushion of seat relaxed her tired muscles, lessening their ache, and Natalie felt a twinge of conscience that she hadn't expressed her gratitude for the ride more graciously.

'I do appreciate your taking Ricky and me home, Mr Langston. I hope your wife doesn't object.'

The last remark, incuriously offered, twisted the hard line of his mouth into a mirthless smile as he ran an eye over her face. 'I doubt it. She's dead.'

The callous announcement astounded Natalie. 'I— I'm sorry,' she said, for want of any other response.

'Are you?' His gaze never left the street. 'Why? Because she's dead or because I can't pretend to feel any grief over something that happened more than ten years ago?' Colter asked with asperity.

There was no answer Natalie could give to the frank question, so she subsided into an uneasy silence, a silence the taciturn man appeared to endorse. She didn't need to have a picture drawn to realise that Colter Langston did not indulge in idle conversation. He was brutally frank and straight to the point. Her unconscious probe into his personal life had been reversed as dexterously as an expert swordsman parries the thrust of an amateur.

When they arrived at the house where she lived, again Colter took Ricky from her while she retrieved her key from the scant contents of her purse. The landlady's hallway door opened a crack for her stern face to peer out, but mercifully she said nothing, letting her presence serve as a reminder of her admonition the night before.

As Natalie hurried up the stairs to her apartment, her tired legs stumbled over a step near the top. Instantly a firm hand was under her elbow, righting her. The hard strength and warm support that it represented was so overwhelming that Natalie wished she could lean against it if only for a moment. She pushed away the impulse and the hand was withdrawn almost immediately.

The door of her apartment opened wider than she intended, allowing an unobstructed view of the sparsely furnished but clean room. In the short time it took to transfer the sleeping child from his arms to hers, Natalie had the feeling that the entire room had been memorised by Colter's discerning gaze. Her thanks were self-consciously offered and summarily shrugged aside as he turned back down the stairs before she had closed the door.

Each succeeding night of 'A Night in Old San Antonio' was a repeat of the first. Colter and Missy arrived at about the same time and Missy spent most of the evening entertaining Ricky while Colter looked on. At closing, he was waiting outside the gates alone to give Natalie a lift home.

Her one offer to pay had been rejected with a derisive glance. After the third night, Natalie had ceased conjecturing that his motive might be more than a way to ease his sensitive daughter's imagination. Working nights, searching without success for a permanent job during the day, and caring for Ricky did not leave many moments for idle thought.

It was approaching midnight when Colter brought her home on Friday, the last night of the festivities at La Villita and the last night of her job. There was a fleeting thought as she took Ricky from his arms that there was little likelihood that she and Ricky would see Colter or Missy again. Before Natalie could utter any final goodbye, he was reaching around her for the doorknob and she realised that he couldn't care less that he wouldn't see her again. That was fine. Neither did she. She had only been thinking that Ricky might miss his daughter. She murmured a sharp 'Good night' and stepped into the apartment, adding the weight of her hand to the back of the door he was already pulling shut.

Weak and exhausted, wanting nothing more than to crawl between the covers of the daybed she shared with Ricky, Natalie instead walked to the tiny kitchen alcove and put a kettle of water on the stove to boil. As it heated, she spooned instant coffee into a cup, gathered pencil and paper and the pay envelope from her purse and set them all on the small table. She knew she wouldn't be able to sleep until she knew the true state of their finances.

Sipping the deliberately strong coffee later, Natalie reworked the figures. It didn't seem to matter how many things she eliminated as non-essential, there was simply not enough money to carry them through the next week. In the three years Ricky had been with her, the future had never looked as bleak and hopeless as it did at that moment. Burying her face in her hands, she began to cry softly, tired sobs and acid tears that couldn't ease the pain of despair.

The click of the doorknob turning brought her head up sharply in frightened disbelief. The lean masculine form of Colter Langston was framed in the doorway. His keen eyes missed nothing, not the ravages of tears on her face, the small stack of money meticulously counted out, the scribbled figures on the paper, nor the air of defeat in her sagging shoulders.

'What are you doing here?' she breathed.

'You forgot to take the key out of the lock.'

There was the jangle of metal as he tossed her key on to the table. When her stunned gaze turned to it, he took the few steps necessary to reach the table and placed a paper package in the middle.

'W-what's that?'

'A sandwich.'

'For me?' Natalie stared at the impassive, unyielding face towering above her.

'I had dinner this evening. Did you?' A brow arched inquiringly. 'Or did Ricky receive the meal you were entitled to for working at the stand?' Her sharply averted head was the only answer he needed. 'I thought as much.'

The derisive tone brought an immediate surge of pride. 'I'm not hungry,' Natalie asserted, trying to ignore the tantalizing aroma that set her stomach gnawing at her backbone.

There was a short exhalation of his breath that bespoke Colter's contempt of her refusal. 'Please spare me your little speech about charity. From the boy it was cute. From you, it would be ridiculous!'

Tanned fingers tore open the paper to reveal the two sliced halves of French bread mounded in the middle with barbecued beef. He slid it in front of her, disregarding the neat stacks of money he toppled.

'Eat it,' commanded Colter.

The glittering harshness of his gaze told her that he would shove it down her throat if she refused again. Torn between the desire to throw it in his face before he had a chance and to appease the hunger sapping her strength, Natalie stared into the bronze mask.

'What do I owe for your generosity?' she demanded.

An uncomfortable heat warmed her blood as his gaze travelled suggestively over her, insolently noting the feminine curves that her recent loss of weight had only accented. The corners of his hard mouth quirked with dry cynicism at the corners when his gaze returned to her face. Her cheeks still glistened from the tears she had shed, but gold sparks were flashing defiantly from her eyes.

'At least you've learned nothing is for free,' he commented. 'But all I want for the present is a few minutes to discuss something with you once you've eaten.'

'That's all?' Natalie challenged, wary of that vague qualification he had made.

'For the present,' Colter repeated, smiling coldly at the indignant flush that was appearing under his pinning gaze. 'The eventual outcome of our discussion will be strictly your decision. Does that satisfy you?'

Natalie flinched under his cutting mockery. 'Not really.' Her eyes unwillingly were drawn to the tempting sandwich.

'Eat. I have no intention of raping you.'

His bluntness stole some of her appetite but not a sufficient amount to lessen the hunger pangs. Strangely Natalie believed that he wouldn't attempt to molest her despite the vague feeling that she would be wiser not to hear what he wanted to discuss. At her first bite into the sandwich, Colter moved away from the table.

'What are you doing?' Natalie swallowed the bite quickly, turning in her chair as he walked behind her towards the kitchen alcove.

'Getting myself a cup of coffee.'

'I'll do that,' she said, quickly setting her sandwich down to push herself away from the table.

But his deceptively effortless strides had already taken him into the small cooking area. 'Why, Mother Hubbard? Because your cupboards are bare,' he answered drily. 'I'd already guessed that.'

As proof he opened the top door beside the sink to reveal the nearly empty shelves. Her pale complexion flamed as she watched him take a cup and spoon in the instant coffee. The kettle heated up again speedily and he poured the scalding water into the cup. As the sun-bleached head turned towards her, Natalie subsided quickly in her chair.

When he wandered back to the table, there was

only a faint hint of pink in her cheeks. She studiously avoided looking directly at him as he reclined his lean frame in the straight chair opposite her, relaxing with negligent ease. Eating under his perceptively watchful eye did not aid her digestive abilities.

Natalie started visibly when he leaned forward suddenly, his hand reaching to the side of her. Then she saw the object that had captured his attention, a framed photograph of her brother, his wife and Ricky that sat on the shelf beside the table.

'My brother Ned and his wife Susan taken on Ricky's second birthday,' Natalie explained defensively when his glance was turned sharply on her.

'Then he *is* your nephew.'

'Yes, he is.' Her chin tilted in proud defiance. 'They were killed in a car crash shortly after the picture was taken.'

'And Ricky had no other family?'

'Our parents are dead and Susan's mother was an invalid,' she responded, wondering why she was answering his probing questions at all.

'You must have been quite young yourself.' Colter continued his study of the photograph.

'Eighteen, if it's any of your business,' and she was rewarded for her sharpness with an immediate narrowing of his gaze.

But otherwise, his expression remained completely unruffled. 'That makes you twenty-one or twenty-two?'

'Twenty-one.'

This was not idle table conversation, but serving some purpose that Natalie couldn't begin to perceive.

She could only guess that it concerned something that he wanted to discuss with her.

'No boy-friends?'

'No,' she answered shortly.

She was unable or unwilling to explain that Ricky's advent into her life had brought a halt to nearly all her social activities, with male or female. A kind of loneliness, however reluctantly acknowledged, had become her constant companion.

'Few young men want the responsibility of another man's child,' Cólter observed drily, 'or the restrictions it places on a girl's social life.'

He had put his finger exactly on the problem, but his accurate perception didn't ease her wariness. Natalie refused to acknowledge the truth of his statement and remained silent.

'You're sacrificing quite a lot for the sake of the ɔoy.' He had replaced the photograph and was leaning back in the chair, tilting it on its back legs.

' "The boy" has a name. It's Ricky,' Natalie replied tautly, hating the way Colter Langston kept referring to him as if Ricky was an inanimate object. 'And I don't regard it as a sacrifice. It isn't Ricky's fault that his parents were killed.'

'Nor yours, although you seem determined to make up for it.'

'What would you suggest I do?' Natalie demanded angrily. 'Turn him over to the courts to be shuffled from one foster home to another without knowing the security of any family?'

'I don't imagine there was anything else you could

do under the circumstances.' Colter set the chair back on all four legs.

Despite his statement of agreement, Natalie sensed he didn't agree with her. She thrust the remains of the sandwich impatiently aside, losing her taste for any more of it.

CHAPTER THREE

'WOULD you mind telling me exactly what it is that you came to discuss?' Natalie challenged, tired of playing the game of being mouse to his cat.

Impassive and unrelenting, the bronze mask stared back at her. The only life to his expression was in the frosty glitter of his eyes. Even that was unreadable.

'This evening,' his hand moved the coffee cup away from the edge of the table, 'Missy told me that she wished her mother had not died giving birth to her. Hardly an unusual comment for a child to make, I'll admit, but her reason for the statement was that she would have liked to have had a little brother or sister. She's become very fond of your nephew.'

'I'm sorry if that has inconvenienced you,' Natalie retaliated.

Sympathy rose for Missy, who had probably been taught by her father not to expect too much affection from adults, especially parents.

His gaze narrowed. 'We live on a ranch. My aunt, who lives with us, takes care of Missy,' continued Colter. 'She's quite elderly. It's becoming increasingly difficult for her to do all the cooking and cleaning, etcetera, that's required. She has expressed a wish to retire, you might say.'

'I see,' Natalie murmured. The picture had begun

to form in her mind. He was seeking a replacement for his aunt, someone to take care of his house and his daughter. 'And that's what you want to talk to me about.'

'Exactly.' There was a faintly amused twist of his mouth. 'If you'll pardon the understatement, life hasn't been easy for you and the boy. And from the frantic scribbles on that paper, the future doesn't look very bright either.'

'If you mean, do I need a job? the answer is yes.'

'It isn't a job I'm offering you.'

It was difficult for Natalie to hold that level, ever-watchful gaze. She took a deep breath, feeling inexplicably tired of trying to match wits with someone who obviously was always one step ahead of her.

'Then what is all this leading to?' Natalie asked, wearily exhaling the breath she had just taken.

'I want you to marry me.' There was not the slightest change in his bland, unemotional tone, nor did his eyes waver from her face.

She blinked and frowned. 'Is that some kind of a joke?'

'I'm completely serious.' Now that the announcement had been made and her reaction studied, Colter Langston reached into his pocket for a cigarette and a lighter.

'But I don't love you, and you certainly don't love me,' Natalie returned in blank confusion.

'Hardly.' The idea that she might have thought he did struck a chord of perverted amusement, revealed in silent laughter.

Natalie couldn't see the funny side. 'I thought you said you needed a housekeeper and someone to look after Missy,' she reminded him with a trace of anger.

'I do.' Calmly he blew a cloud of grey smoke above the table. 'That's why I want to marry you.'

Her mouth felt dry and cottony. With a flash of irritation, she rose from the table, taking her cup and walking into the small alcove for more much-needed coffee.

'I'm afraid I don't see your reasoning,' she said shortly. 'You don't have to acquire a wife to obtain a housekeeper.'

'Don't I?' His low, drawling voice, cynically tinged with mockery, carried across the room. 'I want to be assured that whoever I get will be more or less permanent. Housekeepers tend to give notice. It's much easier to sever the strings of employment than it is the bonds of matrimony.'

'Marriage—that's rather a drastic measure just to keep a housekeeper, isn't it?' Natalie suggested drily as she poured water into the crystals of instant coffee.

'Not drastic, practical,' corrected Colter.

'I think the whole idea is ridiculous!' With an impatient sigh, she began stirring the brown liquid.

When Colter had mentioned that he needed a housekeeper, she had wanted the job, her heart leaping at the thought of Ricky living in the country and herself being there whenever he needed her. But this marriage was something else again.

'Why is it ridiculous? You need a job and I need a housekeeper. I've already seen that you work hard.'

His gaze swept over the small apartment. 'You're tidy and clean. You are obviously very fond of children and they return it—or at least your nephew does, and Missy is less silent with you than with most adults. I presume you can cook?'

'Yes, I can cook, but——' Leaning a hip against the counter, Natalie waved a hand in the air helplessly, 'but there must be half a dozen girls willing to marry you. Girls much more suitable than I am.'

'Not more suitable.' He rolled lazily to his feet, picking up his own empty coffee cup and walking to the alcove where Natalie stood. 'Better dressed, maybe, educated in better schools, from a different social sphere, and all of them could probably convince themselves that they're in love with me, or the Langston name and money. I don't want or need their love.'

There was such a decided sneer given to the last word that Natalie couldn't help adding coldly, 'Or anyone's?'

'Does that shock you?' His eyes glittered over her face. 'Nearly the entire world lives under that cloud of deceit.'

She had wondered before if he had any feelings. Now she knew he hadn't, not any of any depth at least. 'You don't want a wife. You want a slave,' she accused.

'It's illegal,' Colter returned without a lash flickering.

Natalie breathed in sharply with disgust. 'I can't believe you seriously expect me to agree to your proposal.'

'Why? It's not without compensations to you. You and the boy will not lack for material needs—food, clothing, shelter, instead of a hand-to-mouth existence. I can provide the financial means for him to have a higher education if he wants it. In other words, all your worries will be gone. You'll have nothing to concern yourself about except taking care of my home and Missy. Other than the times the boy is in school, he'll be with you constantly.'

It was a very tempting picture he painted and he knew its lure. What hope did she have to do as much for Ricky? What did the future hold for her but more nerve-racking days wondering how she was going to pay for some bill or put food on their table and a roof over their heads?

'What's the matter?' Colter asked drily. 'Are you still nourishing some childhood dream that Prince Charming will appear and carry you off into the sunset?' Natalie flashed him a resentful look. 'When was the last time you had a date?'

Despite the mutinous line of her mouth that longed to deny the arrogant certainty of his gaze, she averted her head.

'Over two years ago,' she admitted grudgingly. 'Doesn't it bother you that your friends would think it strange for you to marry someone like me?' she added, attempting to shift the subject from her social life, or lack of one.

'Why should they? You're an attractive girl. Tired and overworked, in need of rest and more meat on your bones and more attractive clothes to cover you.'

His hand closed over her chin, twisting her face around to see it better. 'In fact, you could be quite beautiful. The gold dust in your almond eyes and the sensual fullness of your lips would arouse any man's desire. Our marriage would probably be regarded as very romantic.'

His detached appraisal was disturbing, but not nearly so much as her rocketing pulse at his touch. In all the impressions Natalie had formed, she had forgotten or ignored his overpowering masculinity, the supreme dominating maleness. It was his virile attraction that held the element of danger she had sensed. And Natalie was susceptible—she could feel it in the sudden heightening of her senses. She was a female who had been too long without the attentions of a male.

Trying to fight back that discovery, she wrenched her head from his hold. 'Next you'll be examining my teeth like a horse!' she flared.

Colter leaned against the edge of the counter, disregarding her sarcasm. 'The marriage would be convenient for both of us. It wouldn't raise near as many eyebrows as hiring you strictly as a housekeeper would.'

'It's insane,' Natalie denied, staring at her cooling cup of coffee.

'It's logical. What's your answer?'

'I need time to think.' Although she wasn't sure what there was to think about, except that she was reluctant to say 'no'.

'I don't have time. Missy and I are leaving for the

ranch on Sunday morning. That only leaves to-morrow. There are certain arrangements that can't be postponed till the last minute,' Colter informed her, his arms folded in front of him.

'You can't expect me to give you an answer now,' Natalie responded, nervously running her fingers through her brown hair.

'I can and I do.' There was an underlying thread of impatience in his voice. 'What are your alternatives? You've had time enough tonight before I came back to assess what the future holds for you in the present circumstances.' He straightened from the counter, towering above her. 'I'm leaving, Natalie Crane, and I want your answer before I walk through the door.'

Her gaze flew to his face in disbelief, the cold, impassive face, the handsome lines etched with unrelenting firmness. He held her gaze for an instant, letting her see that he meant exactly what he said. Then his lithe, supple strides were carrying him towards the door without a backward glance.

At the click of the doorknob, Natalie's paralysis ended. 'Yes.'

Colter turned, his arrogant expression unchanged, not a trace of satisfaction or any other emotion.

'I'll pick you and the boy up at eight tomorrow morning.' His gaze made an all-encompassing sweep of the room. 'You won't be coming back here, so pack only what you need or want to keep. I wouldn't be concerned about clothes. You'll both be getting new wardrobes.'

Without giving Natalie a chance to reply or bidding

her goodnight, he was out of the door, his cat-soft footsteps sounding faintly on the stairs. She leaned weakly against the counter, her eyes turning towards the sleeping child.

'Have I done the right thing?' she murmured aloud, then turned her eyes towards the ceiling. 'Oh, God, have I done the right thing?' The only response to her whispered prayer was the sound of a powerful engine springing to life in the street below.

Natalie had expected to spend a restless night, plagued by doubts about her and Ricky's future, but she slept the sleep of the innocent. For the first time in recent memory, she awoke feeling refreshed and rested without that heavy weight of responsibility pushing her down. A marriage of convenience didn't sound quite as bad as it had last night.

Omitting their clothing and sparse household goods, there was little to pack. But the process wasn't speeded up by Ricky's unbounded excitement, generated not by Natalie's announcement that she was going to marry Missy's father, but by all the changes that were brought by it.

'Can I really have a pair of cowboy boots?' he asked for the hundredth time, Natalie was sure.

'Yes.' She smiled patiently, unable and unwilling to dampen his enthusiasm. 'As long as you're a good boy. Are you sure you have all your toys in the sack?'

'Yes,' Ricky sighed contentedly.

Apprehensions churned her stomach when Colter knocked on the door promptly at eight o'clock. Before the doubts could take hold, he had them and their few belongings stowed in the car, and the landlady cuttingly dealt with.

The entire day was a whirl of efficient organization, never allowing Natalie more than a passing opportunity to think about what she was doing. An entire wardrobe had been chosen by Colter, from the most intimate lingerie to accessories for an evening dress. While Natalie had her hair shampooed, styled and set, the same impersonal attention was given to Ricky's clothing needs, fortunately including a pair of cowboy boots.

She had barely caught her breath at lunch before Colter was whisking the four of them on to a chartered jet bound for Laredo and ultimately, by rented car, to Nuevo Laredo across the border in Mexico, where she and Colter were married. In the car and on the flight to and from Laredo, Missy and Ricky had kept up a steady stream of chatter in which Ricky always included Natalie but Colter was left out.

That evening the events of the day took on an unreal quality as if none of it had happened except in a dream. Breathing deeply of the warm night air, Natalie glanced at her dusty-coloured apricot pants suit, the elegant lines complementing her slender and curvaceous figure.

It had all happened. There was a heavy gold band on her finger to prove that she was Mrs Colter Langston. And there was Ricky standing in front of her beside Missy, staring down again at the pointed toes of his shiny new cowboy boots.

Her gold-flecked eyes were directed curiously at

Colter a foot or more to her right. As he had all day, he appeared aloof, detached from the group while in command of them. The casual suit that he wore with such negligent ease was cream-coloured, accenting the streaks of gold in his hair and pointing out the pale colour of his eyes against the dark tan of his skin. As if sensing her inspection, his eyes, hesitating closer to green than blue tonight, swung their gaze to Natalie from the precision drill teams entertaining the crowd.

'It's too late for second thoughts,' he told her quietly.

'Under his compelling gaze, Natalie couldn't look away. 'It's too soon to say whether I regret it,' she answered truthfully. She tilted her head to one side, her face softly illuminated by an overhead street light, her hair in its new flattering style glistening with a golden glow, the total effect feminine and unconsciously alluring. 'Do you?'

The mask of his expression didn't vary as his gaze raked her from head to toe. 'I never regret anything,' Colter replied.

'How wonderful it must be to be that confident,' she mused.

'The only time you regret something is when your emotions are involved.'

'And you don't have any emotions?' Natalie mocked the implacable mask.

'No, that curse wasn't put on me when I was born.'

Automatically her gaze shifted to Missy, protectively holding Ricky's hand. 'You don't feel anything?'

He guessed she was referring to his daughter. 'Responsibility.' Amusement flickered faintly around the corners of his mouth. 'That shocks you, too.'

'That's hard to comprehend.' A frown of concentration drew her finely arched brows together. 'Have you never cared deeply for anyone—your parents, your wife?'

Muscular shoulders moved in a careless shrug as he turned away, letting a sideways glance slide back to her face. 'I don't particularly care for myself. It's just as well you should discover that about me now, Natalie.' It still sounded strange to hear him say her name. It sounded as if he wasn't actually talking to her, a name that belonged to someone else. 'That way you won't expect very much from our marriage.'

If her subconscious had formulated any thought that something might grow between them, it died with his statement. There was a slight easing of her conscience at the same time. It wasn't a loveless marriage but a true marriage of convenience where each of them received what they wanted and expected no more.

'Look, Nonnie!' Ricky instructed excitedly. 'The parade is going to start.'

Obediently Natalie directed her gaze to the street and the university marching band that had assembled. Beyond them and the crowd lining the opposite side of the street was the spotlighted façade of the Alamo, the cradle and shrine of Texas liberty, the focal point of all the Fiesta activities celebrating Texas's independence from Mexico. The strategic Long Barrack stood watch to the side.

A drum roll from the band silenced the crowd as it anticipated the first notes of the song. In the hush of the Alamo, the strains of 'The Eyes of Texas Are Upon You' filled the air, inspiring and proud. As Natalie stood a little bit straighter, she was conscious of a pair of Texas eyes on her. She glanced at Colter, applause and cheers rippling through the crowd when the song ended. His vague air of boredom dampened her enthusiasm for the Fiesta Flambeau, the night parade marking the official end of the Fiesta.

This time Ricky stayed awake through the entire parade, although by the time they arrived at the hotel, his eyelids were beginning to droop. Hotel rooms during Fiesta had been booked months in advance, but Colter had used his money or influence to obtain a room with twin beds on in the floor below his.

This was not how Natalie had envisioned her wedding night—with her husband one floor above her, but then she had never expected to be left with Ricky to care for when she had indulged in her romantic imaginings. Nor had she expected to marry a man she didn't love. She didn't mind, she told herself as she slipped the expensively flimsy nightgown over her head and climbed into bed. Ricky was happy and that was all she had a right to ask for.

It was midmorning before she awoke. Natalie doubted if she would have then if Ricky hadn't hopped on to the bed, hungry and eager to be off to the ranch that Missy had told him about. Colter and

Missy were both in the lobby when she and Ricky hurried down.

'I'm sorry. I overslept,' Natalie apologised.

'You needed the rest.' Colter dismissed her apology in that offhand, indifferent way she was beginning to expect. 'If your lugage is packed, I'll send the bell-boy to the room. We'll leave as soon as you and Ricky have breakfasted.'

Natalie assured him that all was in readiness. There was a fluttering of nerves as she watched him walk way, realising that within a couple of hours she would be on his ranch, in charge of his home. And his daughter, she added.

Missy was already taking Ricky by the hand to lead him into the hotel restaurant. The marriage hadn't bothered her in the slightest. The only one Missy seemed interested in was Ricky. Natalie guessed it was because the young girl could lavish on the small boy all the love and attention that her father had rejected.

Colter joined them at the breakfast table for coffee. Natalie discovered, to her surprise, that she wasn't at all nervous with him. She had expected to be. They were married and they were strangers. For the next few years at least, they were going to share the same house and food, even if not the same bed. It was a marvel that she was taking the situation so calmly. Perhaps the shock had not worn off.

With all four of them sitting at the breakfast table, they looked like a complete family unit. Not boister-ously happy, as families are romantically depicted, because Missy had that shy withdrawn look she always wore in public places, and Colter, taciturn and implacable, held himself slightly aloof. Yet the naturalness of their image wouldn't leave Natalie.

As soon as the meal was finished, they left for the ranch. Some of Ricky's excitement over their soon-to-be-seen new home rubbed off on to Natalie. She longed to question Colter about it, but she decided against it. He might consider her questions more mercenary than curious.

Once the city of San Antonio was left behind the scenery claimed her attention. It had been so long since she had been in the country that the spacious expanse of blue sky stretching above rolling, timbered hills took her breath away. More spectacular were the limitless fields of spring wildflowers, sometimes dotting, sometimes filling entire valley meadows. Set off by the green of the grass, they were vividly bright, ranging from whites, oranges, yellows, pinks to the ever favourite sky-blue of the bluebonnet.

'How much farther?' Ricky piped up from the back seat, dodging the extra cases that wouldn't fit in the already full trunk.

'A few more miles,' Colter replied.

'How far is the ranch from San Antonio?' It hadn't seemed as though they had travelled very far from San Antonio and Natalie couldn't prevent herself from asking the question.

'Somewhere around sixty miles.' He was slowing the car and turning on to one of the lesser ranch roads that intersected the main highway.

'You could have easily driven back and forth to

the Fiesta,' she responded without thinking.

'I believe Missy thought she would miss something.' Colter glanced in the rear view mirror at his daughter who was listening patiently to Ricky. 'The only thing she might have missed was meeting the boy.'

The dryness of his tone forced Natalie to ask: 'Are you sorry?'

'No.' A brow arched briefly in her direction. 'Are you?'

'No,' she answered quietly, feeling strangely tranquil.

Within a few minutes, the car slowed again and turned on to a gravelled road, gliding dusty white beneath tall crossbars that heralded the entrance to the Langston Ranch. The road sloped gradually upwards leading towards a stand of tall trees. Through their branches, Natalie caught a glimpse of dark red and, as they drew closer, a smattering of ivory white. Guessing at Colter's wealth had not prepared her for the sight of the sprawling ranch house that lay beneath the towering trees.

Thoroughly modern, its style was traditionally Spanish with red-tiled roof and smooth stucco walls, scrolling wrought iron at the windows. Flowering brushes and shrubs abounded in exotic profusion, their vibrant flowers accented by the enormous white blossoms of a magnolia tree. The lane curved towards the house, then continued on through the stand of trees descending the slight slope they had climbed.

'We're home,' Missy announced unnecessarily.

As Colter braked the car to a halt in front of the

stone walkway leading to the house, a man came walking through the trees towards them—tall, broad-chested, wings of white mingled with otherwise dark hair beneath a western hat brim, older than Colter, perhaps in his late thirties.

'I see you're back, Colter,' the man said as Colter stepped from the car and walked to greet him. 'I was just coming up to the house to check.'

Missy and Ricky were faster getting out of the car than Natalie, who dawdled to get a longer look at the sprawling, elegant ranch house that was her new home. She missed hearing Colter's reply as she closed the car door.

'Did you enjoy the Fiesta, moppet?' The man tugged Missy's long braid as she walked by him to her father.

'Yes,' she answered politely, giving him a shy smile.

Ricky too had been taking in the sights and for once lagged behind Missy. His silky brown head was trying to turn simultaneously in all directions and still see where he was going, without success.

'Hello there,' the man greeted him when Ricky almost ran into him. 'And who are you?'

'My name is Ricky,' he announced unabashedly, taking his measure of the stranger. 'I think I'm going to live here.'

The man glanced curiously at Colter, then caught Natalie's approach out of the corner of his eye. The boy was forgotten as he studied her, and Natalie felt herself blossoming warmly under his admiring gaze. His brown eyes were telling her, respectfully, that he found her very attractive, but they didn't leave her with the feeling that she had been undressed. Instinctively Natalie knew she was going to like this man, whoever he was.

'Travis, I'd like you to meet my wife Natalie. Her nephew has already introduced himself, I believe,' Colter stated. 'Natalie, my foreman, Travis McCrea.'

If a thunderbolt had struck him, the attractive stranger couldn't have been more shocked. As self-conscious pink began to appear in Natalie's cheeks, he tried to hide his amazement.

'Forgive me,' he asked Natalie. 'I didn't realise Colter had any plans to marry again.'

'That's quite all right,' Natalie replied after Colter had failed to comment on his foreman's observation.

'Travis usually eats with us if he's around the house at mealtimes,' Colter informed her. 'You can file that away for future reference.'

'If you have any objections to that arrangement,' Travis McCrea interjected, 'I can make other plans.'

'None at all,' Natalie assured him with a genuine smile. 'I hope you'll continue the practice, Mr McCrea.'

'Travis,' he corrected, her smile immediately bringing an answering one of his tanned face. 'We aren't formal at the ranch.'

'Then call me Natalie.'

'Thank you, I will.' There was a curious glint in his dark eyes when he glanced briefly at Colter, but it was gone when he directed his warm brown gaze at Natalie. 'You'll be anxious to see your new home. I won't keep you, Colter.' He touched his hat with his finger and returned the way he had come.

'You liked him, didn't you?' Colter commented smoothly as they turned to follow the children to the house.

'Is there any reason why I shouldn't?' Natalie countered, wondering why she was on the defensive simply because she had immediately liked Travis McCrea.

'No.'

'Then why did you ask?'

'A lot of women find him attractive,' was the only reply she received.

'I would imagine so,' Natalie agreed, striving for a noncommittal tone.

His inscrutable gaze swung at her, frostily cool and aloof. 'Why do you feel guilty because you were attracted to him?'

'I don't feel guilty,' she denied, but his glittering look mocked her assertion.

'There's no need to be ashamed of feelings like that,' Colter said drily.

'How would you know? You don't have any feelings!' she shot back, unaccountably angered.

'Don't confuse feelings with emotions,' he answered in the same level voice as before, not reacting to Natalie's anger. 'I see, touch, hear, smell and taste as keenly as the next man. Sexual attraction between opposite sexes is a physical reaction. There is no emotion in desire.'

CHAPTER FOUR

A COLD finger ran down her spine, strangely chilled by Colter's detached implication that she might be attracted to Travis McCrea. The carved walnut entrance door stood open and Colter stepped aside for Natalie to precede him.

As she stepped across the threshold, she forced herself to remember that their marriage wasn't real, merely a convenient arrangement. It was clear that Colter had no intention of abiding by the traditions of a bride and groom; to do so would be a mockery. There had been no kiss after the wedding ceremony and now he was letting her walk into her new home instead of carrying her. Thank heaven, there was no need for pretence, she told herself.

Cool, white walls greeted her, accented by dark walnut wood. The floor was tiled in large squares of black and white. Natalie's glimpse of the living room extending out from the foyer promised that the interior of the house was as elegantly casual as the outside. But the main of her attention was focused on the stoutly built, older woman seated on the edge of a straight chair, her hand holding Missy's fingers. Her iron-grey head turned at the sound of their footsteps on the tiles, her blue eyes glinting curious and alert.

'So this is your bride, is it, Colter?' the woman said

in a no-nonsense tone as she rose to her feet.

There were few age lines on the woman's face, confined mainly around her eyes and mouth. Her features were stern but, unlike Colter's, her mouth gave the indication that it smiled frequently. It was a strong face and its beauty was in its strength rather than simple prettiness. This was a woman whose friendship was not lightly given.

'Yes, this is my wife Natalie,' Colter acknowledged, then introduced the woman to Natalie. 'My aunt, Flo Donaldsen.'

'How do you do,' Natalie smiled. Her hand was enclosed in the woman's firm grip.

'I hope you'll like it here, Mrs Langston.' The tone of Flo Donaldsen's voice said that she doubted it, as her piercing eyes flashed a speaking glance at Colter. 'Will you be wanting something to eat?' she asked Colter with distant politeness. 'I've already cleared the lunch food, so it wouldn't spoil. You said you would be back this morning.'

'That was my fault, Mrs Donaldsen. I overslept this morning,' Natalie spoke up.

'Cake or cookies and something cold will satisfy us until dinner,' Colter stated, subtly letting Natalie know there was no need to apologise. 'While you're fixing that, I'll show Natalie the bedrooms where she and Ricky will be sleeping. They are prepared?'

There was a silent challenge in his voice, almost daring his aunt to make a personal comment. The woman's mouth tightened fractionally before she replied that they were.

Walking down the corridor on the east wing of the house, Missy shyly pointed out her own bedroom to Natalie and Ricky, a feminine room of saffron yellow and ochre gold flowers. Ricky's room was next to hers, a single bed draped with a red, blue and white print with matching curtains and throw rugs, a distinctly boyish room. But it was the toy train set in the corner that caught his attention, and he impatiently waited while Missy showed him how to operate it.

'Was it yours?' Natalie asked after Colter had suggested they leave the children while he showed her where she would be sleeping.

'Many years ago.'

It was difficult for Natalie to picture him as a little boy. She guessed that he had been always older than his years and not at all the open, embracing child that Ricky was. As Colter opened the door across the hall from Ricky's, her idle musings were replaced by admiration. Beautifully crafted oak furniture dominated the room, its rich patina reflecting the sunny shade of the avocado and gold area rug. The gold shade was repeated in the drapes and sheer insets of the french windows leading out to the portico.

'W—was this your aunt's room?' Natalie breathed, unable to take her gaze away from the tasteful furnishings.

'No, she has always used the room off the kitchen, intended as the maid's or cook's quarters. I was never able to persuade her to take one of the bedrooms in the main section of the house once Missy was grown.

She insisted that she wanted her privacy,' Colter stated.

'Perhaps I should follow suit,' Natalie suggested hesitantly, wanting desperately to enjoy the luxury of this room while wondering at the same time whether she was asking too much. Essentially she was only the housekeeper.

'No, you are my wife. Your place is here in this room,' he returned smoothly. 'Besides, you'll want to be near the boy until he becomes accustomed to his new surroundings.'

'Yes, of course,' Natalie agreed, silently glad that his logic had vanquished her doubts.

'Missy will show you where the dining room is. Flo will have the refreshments out by now.' He turned towards the door, expecting Natalie to follow, which she did.

'Aren't you going to join us?'

'I want to check on a few things with Travis.'

Natalie hesitated in the hallway, watching Colter as he disappeared in the direction of the foyer. He had been away from the ranch almost an entire week, she reminded herself. Naturally he would be anxious to be brought up to date. She glanced at the other closed doors leading off the hall, wondering which one was his room. It would be austerely masculine like its occupant.

Then the sound of a toy train whistle drew her into Ricky's room. Joining them, she allowed Ricky a few minutes to show her how he could operate the train before she suggested that Missy take them to the dining room. The next item on her agenda after a sweet and a cool drink was to have Mrs Donaldsen explain the household routine.

At the walnut dining table, Natalie refused the pecan torte Flo Donaldsen offered, choosing to settle for the tall lime cooler. Missy was much less reserved in her great-aunt's company, eagerly responding to her questions about Fiesta, while Ricky began devouring his torte after the first tentative bite. When his plate was clean, he pushed it towards the elderly woman.

'May I have another?' he asked brightly.

'No, Ricky,' answered Natalie firmly before Flo Donaldsen had an opportunity to reply. 'One is enough.'

'Okay,' he agreed, not the least bit put out by her refusal as he took a big swallow of the lime drink. 'Are you ready, Missy?'

'I have to help Aunt Flo clear the dishes away first,' the young girl replied.

'If you don't mind,' Missy,' Natalie inserted gently, 'I'll help her and she can show me where things are in the kitchen. Maybe you could show Ricky around the house and yard?'

Missy hesitated for an instant, glancing at Flo Donaldsen for approval which was given with a slight nod. Excusing herself from the table, she took Ricky's hand and began leading him from the room.

The older woman didn't say a word as they stacked the few dishes and carried them through to the kitchen, a beautifully modern kitchen with every convenience a woman could want. On the counter of the walnut cabinets sat a colander full of squeezed lime halves next to a juicer.

'The limes were fresh?' Natalie murmured in surprise.

'Colter likes his fruits to be fresh.' The explanation was given tersely. 'He sends a truck to the Rio Grande valley once every two weeks for fruits and vegetables.'

'Couldn't he buy them locally?' she asked, blinking her gold-flecked eyes at the extravagance.

'He could,' Flo admitted, 'but he wants to be sure they're the best.'

'That must be expensive.' Natalie sat the dishes on the counter by the sink, the full extent of Colter's wealth slowly sinking in.

'He can afford it,' the older woman sniffed.

'Yes, I suppose so,' Natalie agreed hesitantly.

Youthful blue eyes studied her sharply from an ageing face before the subject was set aside and they stacked the plates and cutlery in the dishwasher. Flo switched it on and then briskly set about explaining the routine of the house.

Wiping the already immaculate dinette table that stood in the middle of the kitchen, Flo concluded, 'I've already had most of my things moved to the cottage after Colter telephoned me yesterday. I'll stay at the house tonight to help you with the evening meal and fix breakfast in the morning. After that you're on your own.'

Disapproval of their hasty marriage was visible in the rigid lines of the woman's slightly stooped shoulders as she walked to the stove to wipe the top off. Her thick fingers halted their circular movement and she turned to Natalie.

'I know why Colter married you,' Flo Donaldsen stated grimly. 'When it suits him, he can be very persuasive. I didn't see any love or pretence of love in your eyes when you looked at him. What did you marry him for? Was it his money?'

The blurted questions caught Natalie by surprise. She hadn't expected the older woman to speak so boldly what was on her mind. She stared at her fingers for a moment, studying the plain gold band while the other's sharp gaze watched her in awkward silence.

Tossing her head back proudly, Natalie met the look. 'It was a matter of convenience. He needed someone to look after his home and daughter, and Ricky and I needed a home. It wasn't his money nearly as much as it was the promise of some measure of security.'

Flo Donaldsen stared at her for more long moments before she breathed in deeply and turned away. 'I raised him from a boy. I blamed his father for always reminding him that he was a Langston and different from other people, but I think Colter was naturally born different. He's cold and heartless. You'll live to regret the day you married him.'

A chill raced over Natalie's skin as she apprehensively noted the lack of qualification in the woman's statement. There were no 'maybes' or 'mights'. It was a flatly spoken prophecy that held a ring of truth to make it doubly disquieting.

Small fingers tugged impatiently at her hand, demanding her attention. Thrusting aside the woman's pronouncement, Natalie glanced at the boy standing at her side. A smile appeared immediately at the face brimming with happiness.

Colter's approval or affection didn't matter to her. She would be his housekeeper and look after his daughter. Her reward would be in the shining contentment of knowing Ricky would have all the things she wanted to give him—a home, security and a future.

'What is it, Ricky?' Natalie asked patiently.

'Come and look at the swimming pool!' he exclaimed. 'There's one in the backyard!'

'I'll be there in a minute. I have to help Mrs Donaldsen first.'

'Run along,' the woman spoke up. 'I'll be starting dinner around five. You can come and help me then.'

'Please, you have to see it,' Ricky insisted.

'All right.' Natalie gave in laughingly, unable to deny the entreaty of those sparkling brown eyes.

The front of the house had only hinted at the beauty to be found in the rear gardens. Honeysuckle vines covered the rock walls, their sweet fragrance mingling with other heady scents. The scarlet pinks of oleander blossoms coated their bush home while the more delicate dusty pink of the mimosa tree dotted its branches. At the end of the walled enclosure was a swimming pool, its smooth waters reflecting the vivid blue of the sky.

A slatted bench swing was firmly suspended from

the thick branch of an oak. Natalie couldn't resist its lure and Ricky scrambled up to sit beside her, soon joined by Missy. Listening with half an ear to Ricky's chatter, Natalie drank in the tropical serenity of the garden, inwardly laughing at the thought of ever regretting the events that brought her here.

The relative inactivity of the swing soon palled for Ricky, and Missy obligingly produced a large beach ball for a lively game of catch while Natalie looked on. Relaxed, her worries gone, she didn't notice the increasing length of the shadows until she accidentally glanced at her watch and saw the hands pointing to half past four.

With a start of surprise at the quick flight of time, Natalie slipped out of the swing, calling to Missy and Ricky that she was going into the house to help Mrs Donaldsen prepare dinner. As she stepped through the french doors into the living room, she heard the sound of a car speeding into the driveway. Immediately there was the strident blare of the horn. Curiosity impelled Natalie across the room to the windows looking out to the front entrance.

Pushing the ivory sheer curtains aside, she saw Colter and Travis McCrea approaching the house through the trees. A dust cloud was just settling over the dark green foreign sports car that had ground to a halt in the drive. A woman with long, shimmering curls of red-gold emerged from the car, scantily clad in an emerald green midriff top and white slacks that rested on her hip-bones.

The thick walls of the house made her words of

greeting indistinguishable to Natalie, but she was left in little doubt as to whom they were meant for as the attractive, curvaceous redhead glided over the ground to Colter.

Natalie breathed in sharply in disgust when the woman didn't stop but continued her slow deliberate movements that first had her hands touch Colter's chest as her head tilted back to smile. But she didn't stop there. Her hands twined themselves about his neck while she suggestively and openly pressed her body against Colter's. His mouth was quirked derisively at the corners before it was pulled down to be claimed in an obviously passion-filled kiss.

Natalie's blood ran cold at the sight of Colter's hands resting lightly on the bare flesh of the woman's waist. His complete lack of resistance kindled a fiery rage that didn't ease when his head rose slowly from the woman's kiss. Not until she saw his gaze turn towards the house did Natalie let the curtain fall into place, suddenly aware that if Colter hadn't seen her at the window, Travis McCrea had.

She trembled with a frustrated kind of fury. If Colter had married her to stop the gossip that would have come if she had merely lived in his home as a housekeeper, then surely she was entitled to some respect from him as his wife.

Then she brought herself up sharply. That hadn't been his reason for marrying her. He had married her to be certain she wouldn't be free to leave whenever she chose. There had been no mention that there would be any pretence of a real marriage between them.

Her stomach lurched with sickening swiftness as Natalie realised that whatever women Colter knew, he would go on knowing. His very action at not attempting to forestall the woman's embrace with Travis looking on proved that he didn't care if Natalie became an object of ridicule.

It was a jolting discovery, a serpent in the garden of Eden. Her assumption that as his wife she was entitled to an outward show of his respect had been misplaced.

Her self-derisive thoughts were so loud Natalie didn't hear the car churning out of the gravelled drive. The opening and closing of the front door alerted her to the fact that she was still standing with her back to the window. Too late to move, she lifted her head in proud defiance, preparing to reject the pity that Travis's brown eyes would offer. But Colter walked into the living room alone, aloof, strikingly handsome, and arrogant, the adjectives that described him so accurately. His gaze flicked from Natalie to the window, then back to her face.

'Deirdre decided against staying.' His mouth moved into a humourless smile as he walked lithely into the room.

The smoothness with which he spoke the name of the girl he had just been kissing sent freezing ripples of anger through Natalie's veins. Yellow flames blazed in her eyes.

'Deirdre?' Her brow arched in haughty question,

determined to show him she was not a doormat to be walked on.

'Deirdre Collins, the daughter of one of the neighbouring ranchers,' Colter elucidated, stopping calmly in front of her.

Unwittingly Natalie's gaze was drawn to the hard line of his mouth, seeking traces of lipstick. 'More than a neighbour's daughter, surely,' she mocked.

Her cutting barb seemed only to amuse him. 'I believe she considered herself to be,' he agreed.

Again she was sharply reminded of his coldness, his lack of compassion for another human's feelings. She averted her gaze from the glittering mockery of his.

'Where's Travis? I thought he was with you,' she said coldly.

'I believe he was under the impression that you might be embarrassed.' Derisive laughter edged his voice.

'Because I saw you kissing that woman?' Her shoulders moved in an uncaring shrug, as if the scene hadn't concerned her in the least.

'Actually I was being kissed rather than the other way around,' corrected Colter with infuriating evenness.

'You were hardly protesting!' Natalie snapped, and immediately turned away, trembling with rage.

'Does that bother you?'

'Of course not!' she denied, trying to ignore the eyes boring into her rigid shoulders.

'Then why are you angry?'

Natalie was tempted to tell him that she wasn't, but she had already made the contrary clear. Tightening her fingers into impotent fists at her side, she turned back to him, subduing her temper to reply in an unruffled tone.

'I hadn't realised that you intended to broadcast the fact that I was nothing more than a glorified housekeeper and babysitter, undeserving of any degree of respect from you as your wife.'

'Do you mean you want us to pretend that we care for each other?' he jeered, revealing his contempt for the idea. 'To display affection for each other to outside eyes?'

'No, I don't mean that at all!' Natalie denied vigorously. 'I simply don't want to be held up to ridicule in the community where Ricky has to grow up.'

'Legally bearing my name will bring you a great deal of respect,' Colter stated.

Her mouth tightened into a mutinous line. 'And make me the subject of a lot of gossip,' she added.

'Do you care what people say?'

'Only if it hurts Ricky.'

'Do you feel neglected and insulted because I haven't kissed you yet, though I remarked once that you were desirable?' Colter inquired, a disquieting glitter in the eyes that roamed her face.

'I've already told you what I expect, and that's respect. Nothing more.' Her nerves suddenly vibrated at how very close he was standing to her, so virilely masculine, so sinuously strong.

'Do you mean you didn't expect to be the first woman I kissed after we were married?' His mocking amusement was unmistakable.

His finger touched the heightened colour in her cheek when Natalie flushed at the remembrance that she had expected a duty kiss after the wedding ceremony, a meaningless kiss to keep up appearances. She pressed her lips tightly shut rather than admit that. Glaring at his coldly remote blue-green eyes, she remained immobile under the caressing touch of his finger along her cheek and jaw, determined to show her complete indifference to him, an indifference that was equal to his.

'Perhaps I should correct that deficiency.'

The words were barely spoken and his hand was closing firmly over her chin. Her eyes widened in surprise as her hands came up to his chest to push him away. But the attempt was wasted motion as his arm swept around her to check the movement away from him.

The swiftness of his action was only implied and Natalie was aware of the slow deliberation that controlled Colter. When the hard line of his mouth began its descent to hers, she didn't attempt to struggle. Impassive submission was the best deterrent for an unwanted kiss.

The touch of his mouth drew an involuntary and tiny gasp of surprise. His coldness, remoteness, his lack of emotion had not prepared her for the warm, mobile pressure of his kiss. Natalie had expected his lovemaking to be forceful, even cruel, but certainly not this seductive mastery that coerced response. An enveloping warmth swept through her body as his hand slipped from her chin to the vulnerable curve of her throat.

His expertise was beyond her experience and she reeled from the shock of it when his head rose from hers. Had she kissed him in return? she wondered dazedly as she blinked at the unchanging mask of his aristocratic face. The betraying shudders within said that she had, although Natalie had no recollection of doing so. The predominantly green light in his eyes seemed to indicate an arrogant satisfaction as Colter examined the parted fullness of her lips, still trembling from the firm imprint of his mouth. The light didn't vary when it slid to hold her gaze.

'It's been a long time since you have been kissed, hasn't it?' he inquired, relaxing his hold on her throat and back so she could move away.

'Yes.'

From somewhere she dredged up the strength to reply, seizing on the thought as the reason that his kiss had inexplicably moved her. She had never been a prude. A man's kiss had always been pleasurable if not exciting.

'That's a pity,' Colter drawled lazily. Indifference was again drawn in his starkly handsome face, like a mountain cat tired of its prey after the first taste of blood. 'You might be quite good with a little more experience.'

Natalie sputtered indignantly before realising that her temper was wasted on Colter. He had already released her and stepped away, a lit cigarette between the lips that had just awoken her senses to his masculinity.

Spinning abruptly on her heel, she started for the kitchen, tossing over her shoulder, 'I'm going to help Mrs Donaldsen fix dinner.'

'Where's Missy and the boy?'

'Ricky,' her teeth grated in anger as Natalie emphasised her nephew's name, 'and Missy are playing ball in the back.'

Flo Donaldsen was all briskness and efficiency when Natalie arrived in the kitchen, instructing her first in the arrangement of items in the well-stocked cupboards. While Natalie prepared a fresh pineapple, the older woman started cutting thick portions of ham to be broiled as steaks with the pineapple rings.

If she noticed the glow that was still in Natalie's cheeks, she didn't refer to it, her comments on the advisability of their marriage already made. And Natalie was too eager to show Colter's aunt that she was not a novice in the kitchen to allow her mind to wander back to the disturbing kiss.

As Natalie began collecting the plates and glasses to set the dining room table, Flo Donaldsen said, 'I had Juan—he's the handyman and gardener—take your suitcases up to your rooms. I would have unpacked them for you, but I thought you'd rather do that yourself later tonight.'

'Thank you,' Natalie responded, silently wondering if the woman wasn't insinuating that she and Ricky would be better off to leave them packed. Shaking away that impression, she chose to add a less personal comment. 'The gardens and the house are very beautifully kept.'

'Hummph,' Flo sniffed, lifting the lid of one of the pans on the stove to check the vegetables being steamed. ' "Stone walls do not a prison make".'

Glancing at the older woman apprehensively, Natalie decided to ignore the remark. She could hardly regard herself as a prisoner in this house. Her presence here was the result of her own free will, the decision made with a full understanding of the relative permanency of her position in the home, at least until Ricky was grown.

The first meal in her new home was a successful one, successful from the standpoint that the food was deliciously prepared and the company was pleasant. Travis McCrea dominated the conversation with his easy confident charm, not at all obtrusive, with Ricky occasionally competing for control of the subject matter.

For the most part, Travis kept the conversation channelled to the events of Fiesta week in San Antonio, drawing out Missy's shy observations on the activities and chuckling at Ricky's bolder statements. Travis kept the talk away from personal inquiries into Natalie's life or the way she had met Colter.

Colter did not remain totally silent, but mostly he observed, his comments generally restricted to Ricky's questions about the ranch. He seemed to be prepared for Ricky's interest, and Natalie silently wondered how long his apparent patience would last under Ricky's insatiable curiosity.

When the dinner dishes were cleared and the strawberry dessert placed on the table, Ricky leaned forward to look past Natalie at Colter seated at the head of the table.

'Will you take me to see the cows and horses tomorrow?' he asked, but it was closer to a demand. 'Missy wouldn't take me to see them today. She said we weren't allowed down there.'

'Ricky!' Natalie said in a shushing tone, certain this time that he had trespassed too far by asking Colter to give him a tour of the ranch. 'Mr——' A sideways glance at the light brown head saw eyebrow-arching mockery at her almost formal reference to the man who was her husband. 'Colter,' she corrected quickly, feeling the warmth climbing up her neck, 'will be too busy tomorrow to show you around.'

'Will you?' Ricky asked, wanting to hear it from Colter's lips, ignoring Natalie's frown to be silent.

'I probably will tomorrow,' Colter agreed, 'but maybe the day after. We'll see.'

'Can I ride a horse?' Satisfied with his half-promise, Ricky pursued another tangent.

There was a trace of exasperation in Natalie's sigh that brought an amused glance from Travis McCrea's rugged face seated across the table from her.

'Have you ever ridden a horse before?' Colter asked him, not missing the smiling exchange between his wife and his foreman yet totally unconcerned by it.

'No,' Ricky admitted as if it was of little consequence to his request.

'Have you?' The compelling blue-green gaze was turned to Natalie.

'Some years ago, but I'm hardly experienced,' she replied.

'Pick out some suitable mounts for them,' he instructed Travis.

'I think I know just the pair,' the dark-haired man nodded, winking at Ricky, who was beside himself with glee.

'Do you ride, Missy?' Natalie asked, trying to include the young girl so she wouldn't feel left out of the activities.

A nervous glance was darted at her father, who responded for her. 'She used to ride. She was thrown from a horse two years ago and dislocated her hip. She hasn't been on a horse since then.'

Missy crimsoned at the detached criticism in Colter's reply. Natalie felt her heart reaching out to the young girl in sympathy. Fear was an awesome thing. Missy was not naturally adventurous, which only increased fear's hold.

CHAPTER FIVE

COFFEE followed dessert for the adults while Ricky and Missy excused themselves from the table to enjoy the last of the sunlight outdoors.

A scarlet-orange disc was hovering over the treetops when Natalie finished helping Mrs Donaldsen with the last of the dinner dishes and went in search of Ricky. There was a halfhearted assertion that he wasn't tired, but a yawn accompanied his statement and Ricky followed Natalie to his bedroom.

There was a bathroom situated in the hallway between his room and Missy's. While Ricky bathed, Natalie unpacked his cases, barely filling the empty drawers of the dressing-table and the roomy closet. She was just turning back the covers of his bed when he padded into the room.

'Will you read me a story? I washed real good.' He held out his small hands for her inspection.

Long, curling lashes fluttered down to conceal bright brown eyes long before the Three Bears discovered Goldilocks in their home. Natalie tucked the bedcovers tightly about him, brushed a kiss to the forehead covered with silky brown hair and tiptoed out of his room, leaving the door slightly ajar in case he called for her in the night.

Before Natalie returned to her own room, she

looked in on Missy. She was sitting in bed with a book propped on her knees. Her nondescript brown hair was free of its braid, flowing down her shoulders to her waist in crisp waves. Its length made the young girl's face look longer and thinner. Natalie silently resolved to persuade Missy to have her hair cut into a shorter style some future time when they were better acquainted.

'I stopped in to wish you a good night,' Natalie smiled.

'Is Ricky in bed?' Missy asked.

'In bed and already sound asleep, and he wasn't tired,' she laughed softly, and received an answering smile of understanding at Ricky's initial reluctance to go to bed.

Then the smile faded from Missy's face as she darted a shy look at Natalie. 'I'm ... I'm glad you and Ricky came to live with us,' she offered hesitatingly.

'So am I,' Natalie nodded calmly, knowing this was not the time to grasp too firmly at Missy's tentative hand of friendship. 'Good night, Missy, and have a nice night.'

'Good night—Natalie.'

As Natalie opened the door to her room, there was a satisfied gleam in her eyes. Ricky was adapting easily, as only a child can, to his new life, and Missy was on the verge of accepting them both completely and without reservation. The future seemed to hold a very rosy glow.

Her suitcases stood at the foot of the bed. As she approached them to begin her own unpacking, she spied the door, to what she had thought was a closet, standing ajar. The glimpse of lush carpet and shining porcelain revealed that it was not a closet.

Curious, Natalie stepped through the open doorway, gazing with pleasure at the spacious private bath. Contrasting the three white walls, the fourth was covered with a mural of a green landscape. But the most striking feature of the bathroom was the sunken tub, luxuriously deep and large.

Thick bath towels hung on a gold rack. A glass shelf near the tub held a dish of yellow-gold soap in the shape of rosebuds. Beside it was an unopened container of lavender-scented bath salts, no doubt a peace offering from Mrs Donaldsen.

The prospect of lazing in the sunken tub filled with fragrant bubbles was infinitely more inviting than unpacking the suitcases in the adjoining room. And, Natalie told herself, she could always unpack after a relaxing bath.

Thus convinced, she turned on the gold taps and adjusted the water temperature, liberally adding the lavender-scented salts. In her bedroom, she shook out the gold lounging robe from the smaller of the two suitcases and carried it and the cosmetic case into the bathroom.

Nearly three-quarters of an hour later, Natalie stood in front of the vanity mirror above the gleaming porcelain sink, feeling clean and refreshed and blissfully feminine. Fluffing the ends of her shining honey-brown hair with a comb, she tried to recall the last time she had felt free to spend so much time on herself. It seemed very long ago.

The cowled neckline of her robe curled in a wide circle about her neck, revealing the delicate hollows of her collarbones and the graceful curve of her throat. The muted gold shade intensified the sparkling amber lights in her hazel eyes. Her features were no longer etched with worry and tension, but soft and alluringly beautiful with her new-found security. With the pinched look of strain gone, Natalie didn't look nearly so thin.

With a satisfied smile turning up the corners of her mouth, she switched off the bathroom light and walked back into her bedroom.

Her expression froze at the sight of Colter standing near the bed in the act of tossing his shirt on the chair.

'What are you doing in here?' Natalie demanded in a less than commanding tone as she stared in disbelief at the leanly muscular and naked chest.

He spared her a sliding glance of unconcern as he unbuckled his belt and slipped it from the waistband of his trousers. 'Getting ready for bed.'

'But ... but this is my room,' she faltered, her heart beating wildly.

'Yes, it's your room, too,' Colter agreed, emptying his pockets on to the dressing-table top.

'Too?' she echoed weakly, still in the grip of surprise. 'But I thought——'

Colter turned slowly, his dispassionate face examining her startled expression. 'What exactly did you think?'

Natalie whirled away from his compelling gaze, her hand clutching the zippered front of her robe. Striving to achieve a calmness she was far from feeling, she breathed in deeply. The short burst of derisive laughter that followed her movement nearly brought back the sense of panic.

'You didn't honestly believe this was going to be one of those "in-name-only" marriages, did you?' Colter jeered.

Her temper flared instantly at his cynical tone. 'Last night——' she began indignantly.

But he interrupted with cutting swiftness. 'Last night accommodation with suitable privacy couldn't be arranged.'

'You may as well know now that I have no intention of going to bed with you.' Natalie tilted her head to a defiant angle. 'We may have gone through the formalities of a marriage ceremony, but we are not truly man and wife.'

'Not yet,' qualified Colter, his hands resting complacently on his hips.

'Not ever!' she flashed, spinning away from the unmistakably masculine figure to seek some place of safety.

With the swiftness of the cougar she had likened him to, Colter had a steel grip on her arm and was jerking her rigid body around to face him. His narrowed gaze raked her face with its look of outrage.

'Did you honestly expect to live in this house the dozen or so years before Ricky is grown without ever once having me touch you?' His other hand closed suggestively over her hip bone and pulled her against the taut muscles of his thighs. 'I'm a man, Natalie. The urge to possess a desirable and attractive woman like you is natural and I have no intention of denying it.'

Natalie had no idea what she had thought, if she had even given it a thought. She stiffly maintained the pressure against his hold, glaring at him coldly.

'I'm not a slave to be taken whenever the mood strikes you,' she stated sharply. 'You may have provided me and Ricky with a home and security. I'm grateful for that, but not even gratitude will make me submit to you. No one has ever touched me, and if you try, I'll scream.'

'And who will hear you?' Colter whispered softly, but with an undercurrent of derision. 'Flo is on the other side of the house, no doubt fast asleep, and her hearing isn't as keen as it once was. Your voice wouldn't carry to the quarters of the ranch hands. The only ones that would hear your cries would be Ricky and Missy.'

Natalie paled at the undeniable truth of his words. Fear took the edge from her anger as she frantically examined his aloof expression for some sign of compassion or mercy. Nothing. The only thing that gave her hope was the lack of desire burning in his eyes. She had seen the look that came into men's eyes when they wanted to make love to a girl, and it was noticeably absent in Colter's.

'You don't want me,' she asserted breathlessly.

His hold on her arm and hip didn't slacken. 'It's just as well that I'm not ruled by passion,' the hard line of his mouth moved into a mirthless smile, 'if, as you say, no man has ever touched you before.'

She gasped sharply as waves of panic assailed her. With her free hand, she tried to push herself away from his chest, to struggle free, but his strength was far superior to hers. He crushed her against him, almost denying her breath.

'If you fight me, I'll have to be rough,' he growled near her ear. 'If you'll let me, I'll be gentle.'

The roar of blood in her ears seemed to deprive the rest of her body of its strength. With the iron band of his arms pressing her against him, Natalie felt the nakedness of his skin burning through her robe, singeing her nerve ends until she felt nothing but him. She bent her head back, as far away from the hard chest as his hold would permit.

Fear and loathing glittered in her eyes that stared into his darkly tanned and impassive face, ruthlessly set with the implacability of his intent. Breath came in tiny gasps for air through parted lips.

'How can you do this when you know I'm not willing?' Natalie demanded, knowing her protest was useless, but refusing to submit like some passive slave.

Frosty blue-green eyes travelled lazily over her upturned face. 'I mean this marriage to begin as I intend it to go on.'

As she twisted her head away, Colter shifted his hold, pinning both arms behind her back in the grip of one hand. His free hand moved to her throat, the touch against her skin sending convulsive shudders quivering through her. Foolishly Natalie didn't guess his intention until she felt the zipper of her robe opening against her skin.

'No!' The word was torn from her throat in breathless panic.

She struggled desperately to impede the zipper's progress, succeeding only to a limited extent. With her bare foot she kicked at his shins. A wince of pain flashed across his face, but Colter didn't lessen his hold. Instead he swung her off her feet into his arms and carried her to the bed, dumping her on to the exposed sheets like a sack of potatoes.

Before Natalie could recover and slide off the opposite side, the overhead light was switched off and the weight of his body was on the mattress beside her, his hands instinctively finding her in the dark.

With all the power at her command, she fought him off, kicking and clawing at him like a wild thing. Occasionally she felt the warm wetness of blood where her nails had made their mark on his shoulders and back. Her frantic violence only sapped her energy, leaving her exhausted and weak on the bed, her arms stretched above her head by Colter's hands, her robe tossed somewhere on the floor.

A moment to catch her breath, that was all she needed, she told herself, and stiffened as she felt the warmth of his mouth on the cord of her neck. During all her struggles, he had not touched her, only warding off her flailing arms and legs and keeping her on the bed beside him. Her robe had been stripped from her, but the hands that did it had not been interested in the bareness beneath it.

Weakly Natalie tried to pull her wrists from his hands and twist her body free of the pinning weight of his chest. Her attempts were pathetic and she knew it.

'Stop fighting,' Colter ordered quietly. 'You'll only hurt yourself.'

'And you won't?' she hissed bitterly.

Her mistake was in turning her head to glare at him. Immediately his mouth took possession of hers, branding his ownership with burning thoroughness. At some point in the provocative mastery of his kisses, a whirling void opened up and Natalie was pulled into the burning blackness.

It was much later before Colter rolled away from her, not leaving until he had drawn an involuntary gasp of pleasure from her lips. For interminable seconds, Natalie lay weak and spent where he had left her, struggling to surface from the fiery sensations that swamped her consciousness.

In one part of her mind there was nothing but loathing for the man who had truly become her husband. The rest was still reeling from the sensual shock of his lovemaking, its aftermath not as unpleasant as she wanted it to be.

Rolling on to her side, she was filled with self-disgust at the admission, despising herself as much as she loathed Colter. If tears could have erased the memory, she would have cried. Instead she curled into a tight ball of misery.

The moon had risen above the treetops. Its light was streaming through the sheer curtains at the window, laying a silvery path across the bed. The droning song of the cicadas sounded in the distance, punctuated by the call of the bullfrogs, and a night bird trilled to the stars. The world should have stopped, but it hadn't.

'You'll live to regret the day you married him,' Flo Donaldsen's words came flying to her mind.

Fiesta. Natalie had married Colter on the last day of Fiesta San Antonio, a celebration of independence. Imprudently she had not guessed he intended to use her to satisfy all his needs. The gold band on her finger was a symbol of ownership and Natalie didn't intend to be a slave. If she and Ricky had to walk all the way back to San Antonio, she would not stay in this house another night.

'Natalie.'

Colter's fingers closed over her arm as he spoke. His tone was detached and impersonal, disregarding the complete intimacy they had shared only moments ago.

A shiver of sensual awareness danced over her skin, igniting an answering spark within her. The involuntary response of her body angered Natalie and she wrenched her arm free of his touch.

'Leave me alone,' she demanded tautly.

His reply was a punishing grip on her shoulder that pushed it back on to the sheet and held her flat. There was no more reason to fight, so Natalie lay in rigid unresistance, keeping her head turned away from him.

'Look at me,' he commanded. When she didn't comply, Colter took hold of her chin and twisted her face to his. 'I said look at me,' he repeated in a firmly relentless voice as she kept her gaze averted.

Resentment flamed brightly when Natalie focused her gaze on his face, moonlight shimmering white-gold on the sun-bleached hair falling across the smooth forehead. Metallic chips of blue steel looked back at her, immune to the loathing in her eyes.

'Don't touch me,' Natalie ordered contemptuously.

A brow flicked upward in cynical mockery while his other hand slid over her silken skin to the swell of her breast, effectively reminding her that she was not the one to give orders. Natalie breathed in sharply, but didn't draw away. It would have been useless.

'I know what you're thinking,' Colter stated evenly.

'Do you?' she jeered.

'You're thinking about running away,' he answered. Her brown lashes fluttered slightly in surprise, but there was no other admission in her expression that his guess was anywhere near accurate. 'Where would you go? You can't go back to your apartment because you know I'll follow. You don't have any money to get a new one. Without a job, how do you intend to support yourself and Ricky? Or were you planning to leave Ricky here?'

'Of course not,' Natalie retorted. Her teeth sank into her lower lip, too late to bite back her words of admission.

'What would you accomplish by running?' Natalie refused to reply to the quiet mockery of his question. 'Would it change what happened tonight? Would you be able to forget that it ever happened?'

He knew the answers to his questions before he asked them and she closed her eyes tightly to avoid seeing the truth he was trying to force her to admit.

'Little has changed,' continued Colter. 'You still have the security you wanted for you and the boy, the freedom from want, a decent home and clothing.'

'But look at the price I had to pay.' This time her voice was choked with emotion, her eyes still closed to shut out the image of his handsome face—only to have her mind's eye visualise it.

'Women of your age are rarely virgins,' he mocked. 'It isn't my fault that you were. And it was something I couldn't know until tonight.'

'It's your fault that I'm not now!' Natalie flared.

'Did you intend to remain inviolate the rest of your life?' The mouth that had aroused her desire curled into a derisive smile. 'Or did you think to take a lover at a future time while you denied your husband his marriage bed?'

'I didn't think about it at all.' Her reply was truthful.

She had been too relieved at having Ricky's future secured and the responsibility lightened on herself to consider her own personal future. Colter's own indifference had lulled her into believing the physical aspect of their marriage was not important.

'We're married. That's a fact you can't ignore,' Colter reminded her.

'And you don't intend to let me forget it,' Natalie responded bitterly.

'No, I don't,' he agreed. His pinning grip relaxed.

'So stop forcing a hysterical reaction that you don't feel. We both know it wasn't an experience totally without pleasure for you. There's no reason to pretend that it was. Leaving here would accomplish nothing and change nothing. Go to sleep, Natalie, and let someone who's a more convincing actress play the role of the outraged female.'

In the next instant she was free of his hold and his touch, trembling with an urge to strike out at him as he lay beside her. She suppressed it, knowing that Colter would not think twice about retaliating. She rolled on to her side away from his long length, curling her arms about the pillow and hugging it tightly to her.

Sleep was nearly immediate, denying Natalie the opportunity to consider what her alternatives were. There was not another conscious thought until morning when she became aware of the sunlight trying to shine through her closed eyes and the sensation that someone else was in the room with her.

The events of the night before came racing back and her eyelids sprang open, her gaze focusing on the empty pillow beside her.

'So you're finally awake,' but it was a woman's voice that spoke from the side of the room and not Colter's as Natalie had anticipated.

At the sight of Flo Donaldsen, Natalie pushed herself into a nearly upright position in the bed, dragging the covers with her. A telltale warmth invaded her face and she raised a hand to brush the hair away from her face to conceal her self-consciousness for a moment from the woman's sharp gaze.

'What time is it?' asked Natalie.

'Nearly ten. Colter left orders to let you sleep this morning,' Flo added in explanation. 'But I thought you'd want a chance to shower and dress before lunchtime. I'll be staying on to fix it, so you needn't worry about that.'

'Thank you,' Natalie murmured as her gaze slid away from the woman's discerning face only to rush back a second later. 'Where's Ricky?'

'Colter took him along this morning. Would you be wanting anything for breakfast?'

'No, just coffee.'

Flo Donaldsen nodded and left the room. There was a slight protest of her muscles as Natalie slipped from the bed and hurried into the bathroom, needing the cleansing waters of a bath in order to face the day ahead of her.

Her mouth had tightened into a grim line at Flo's pronouncement that Ricky was with Colter. Though she did not yet know Colter thoroughly, she knew consideration was not the motive for his action. He had known she wouldn't leave without Ricky.

He always seemed to be one step ahead of her. Even letting her sleep late had been a means of ensuring that his aunt was aware they had slept together.

After bathing and dressing, Natalie stripped the sheets from the bed, put on fresh ones from the linen closet in the hallway that Missy had pointed out the previous day. Then she made her way to the kitchen where Flo Donaldsen was fixing lunch. Natalie was setting the dining table when Ricky came bursting through the front door.

'Nonnie! Nonnie!' he cried excitedly as he rushed towards her.

Automatically she knelt to receive his quick hug and remained in the same position to be nearer to his level. Her loving smile was automatic and genuine as she looked into his snapping brown eyes, sparkling with immeasurable happiness.

'Oh, Nonnie! You should have been with us!' he exclaimed: 'I got to see the horses and barns and pet a dog and everything! And C-Colter,' he glanced over his shoulder as he struggled momentarily with the name, 'is going to take me out to see the cows and their babies this afternoon,' Ricky concluded gleefully.

Natalie's gaze swept past Ricky to the man standing in the archway of the dining room, blue-green eyes holding her gaze. Colter's lazy yet alert study of her sent the blood pounding through her veins, anger seething at the selfish way he was using Ricky to ensure that the boy would be against any suggestion that they leave the ranch.

'The boy can come,' Colter qualified amicably as he stepped farther into the room, 'providing you don't have any objections.'

'I can, can't I?' Ricky pleaded.

Natalie glared at Colter. 'Would my objections matter?' she taunted.

His gaze narrowed, the colour of his eyes shifting to a harsher shade of blue, frosty and cold. 'If you've made other plans, then say so.'

Deliberately Natalie ignored his challenge as she flashed a tense smile at the small boy standing in front of her. 'Go and wash your hands, Ricky. We'll talk about it after lunch.'

He hesitated as if to argue for immediate permission, then scampered away. Natalie straightened stiffly, her head drawn back to a defiant angle.

'You don't play fair,' she accused in an ominous undertone.

'I don't "play" at anything,' Colter returned.

Involuntarily her voice rose. 'You know very well what I mean! Every little boy dreams of being a cowboy, and you're deliberately making sure that Ricky realises that his dream can come true if we stay here.'

'Is there some question that you will?' There was an arrogant lift of his eyebrow.

A stabbing pain jabbed at her chest as Natalie realised that she inwardly had accepted the situation. It was a disturbing discovery to acknowledge that all her protests were only bold talk that she had no intention of backing up with action. She was ashamed of her helplessness, the lack of strength that had prompted her to accept his offer of marriage without giving any thought to the consequences.

Despite Colter's insensitivity, he was strong. In the short time she had known him, Natalie had learned what it was like to have a man to rely on, to make the decisions. So while she cursed her weakness, she resolved not to reveal it to Colter. Let him think that some day she might leave, she told herself, and some day she would find the strength to do it.

He was still waiting for her answer, his alertness more pronounced than ever at her silence. There was satisfaction in realising he was not entirely certain of her reaction. Gold dust sparkled in her almond eyes as she met his searching look. Without replying Natalie turned away, a mysterious smile flitting over her mouth.

'I want an answer,' Colter stated.

When Natalie failed to answer and started to walk away, his fingers closed over her arm and spun her around.

The hard pressure of his hand was like a catalyst, suddenly causing a rush of vivid memories, recalling the way he had caressed her so intimately the night before and her own instinctive reaction to his touch.

Immediately she tried to pull free of his hold, hissing angrily, 'Don't touch me!'

When she failed to pull free, her other hand raised to strike a lean cheek and the taunting curve of his mouth. But its movement was halted in mid-swing by the vice-like grip of his hand and Natalie was twisted against his muscular length, her breath stolen by the sudden contact.

'You're a disgusting animal!' she spat softly, and drew a short derisive laugh from Colter.

'And you're a wildcat.' His eyes mockingly inspected her face. 'I enjoyed taming you last night.'

The instant of immobility at the hard pressure of his body against her was gone, chased away by his jeering comment. Although knowing it was futile, Natalie struggled against his hold anyway.

'Let me go!' she demanded hoarsely. 'I despise you. I don't want you to touch me!'

The last vibrated in the air. There was a movement behind Colter and for a frightened second Natalie thought it was Ricky witnessing their argument. Then her face flamed in embarrassment when she saw Travis McCrea, his brows drawn together in a concerned frown. She sensed his indecision, uncertain whether to step forward and interfere or to leave before his presence was noticed.

Colter turned his head to see the reason for her disconcerted expression. Natalie glanced tensely at his almost impassive face, noting the narrowing of his gaze as Colter dared Travis to intervene. Then her look slid back to Travis, the frown gone, a humourless smile curving the mouth that had been grim.

'Your first argument, huh?' Travis inserted casually as he walked into the dining room. 'I've heard that's always the first sign that the honeymoon is over.'

Accepting Travis's observation, Colter studied Natalie's averted face, its colour only just beginning to return to normal.

'Do you wish you could run home to Mama?' he jeered, lowering his voice to a pitch that wouldn't carry his words to Travis's hearing.

There was no sign that the dark, rugged foreman had heard his question. As Colter's hold on her arms slackened, Natalie pulled away, ignoring his jibe and murmuring self-consciously, 'I have to help Mrs Donaldsen.' A faltering excuse, but the only one she had.

CHAPTER SIX

STRANGELY life fell into a comfortable pattern for Natalie. Although her pride demanded that she pretend otherwise, the undemanding routine of cleaning house, taking care of Missy and Ricky, and preparing meals was truly enjoyable. She had never been career-minded, always desiring a home and family. Now that she had both, there was a sense of fulfilment that more ambitious members of her sex would never understand.

Not that everything had gone smoothly. Initially there had been confusion when Flo Donaldsen had departed for her cottage, but Natalie had soon found her way around. And there had been the task of enrolling Ricky in the afternoon kindergarten class at the local school for the rest of the term.

Colter gave her almost free rein, providing her with keys to the El Dorado, giving her a list of the stores he had accounts with, and generally letting her do as she pleased as long as she maintained their bargain.

During the day, Natalie never had to suffer his company alone, since he only appeared at mealtimes and then in the company of Travis McCrea. In the evenings he was in the house most of the time, but those were the hours she spent with Ricky and Missy. Colter never requested her company nor indicated a desire to establish a more companionable relationship between them.

When they were alone, Natalie didn't hesitate to let her distaste of him show, but the sensuous warmth of his kisses always produced a reaction that was purely physical and out of the bounds of her control.

Natalie had just returned the vacuum cleaner to the utility closet when she heard the front door open and close. She glanced swiftly at her wristwatch, wondering if she had lost track of time and Missy and Ricky were home from school.

But it wasn't nearly time for them, so she moved curiously to the living room. Her steps halted abruptly at the sight of the vivacious redhead wandering familiarly about the room. It was the woman Colter had identified as Deirdre Collins who had thrown herself into his arms the first day Natalie had arrived at the ranch.

'May I help you?' Natalie inquired, knowing her face and voice were stiff and cold, and not caring.

The redhead turned, a haughty look to her green eyes as she openly surveyed Natalie. Poise, sophistication and wealth were stamped in the clothes and hairstyle that the strikingly beautiful woman wore. In spite of herself, Natalie thrust her chin to a slightly more defiant angle. The action drew an immediate smile of satisfaction to the perfect copper lips.

'You're the new Mrs Langston, of course,' the redhead murmured with brittle friendliness. 'I'm Deirdre Collins. I wanted to meet you and offer my congratulations. I hope you don't mind me barging in this way.'

A manicured hand waved the air in apology. 'I'm used to coming and going as I please. It never occurred to me until just now that Colter might not have mentioned me.'

'Yes, he has. Your parents are our neighbours, aren't they?' said Natalie. Her temper was slowly reaching the boiling point, increased by Deirdre Collin's patronising attitude. 'As a matter of fact,' she added boldly, 'I believe you were here the first day Colter and I returned after we were married. I'm sorry I didn't get to meet you then.'

The woman's gaze narrowed slightly as she met the flashing amber caution lights in Natalie's eyes. 'I hope,' Deirdre hesitated, obviously choosing her words carefully, 'my appearance that day didn't upset you.'

'Not in the least. After all, you weren't aware that Colter was married,' she returned with the same caustic edge to her voice.

Deirdre stared at Natalie for a long moment before swinging her emerald gaze around the room. 'Colter has a beautiful home, doesn't he? Are you the domesticated type?' The sarcasm gleamed out through a see-through veil.

'Yes, I am,' Natalie admitted without any apology.

'I loathe the routine of a house myself. I would make a lousy wife.' Again a smile curved the copper mouth. 'Besides, a wife always gets taken for granted. I'd rather have a man waiting on me, seeking my favours, rather than the other way around. No man should see a woman when she first gets up in the morning. It destroys his illusions.'

Natalie knew exactly what Deirdre was hinting at and she realised that she had unconsciously known all along that Deirdre had probably been Colter's mistress. But was she insinuating something more? That she still was?

Colter could have a dozen mistresses for all Natalie cared, but if he thought she was going to welcome them into her home—and it was her home—then he was in for a rude awakening.

'I'm sorry Colter isn't here, Miss Collins. I know he'll regret missing your visit.' As tactfully as possible Natalie was suggesting that Deirdre leave. Under no circumstances was she going to offer the redhead any refreshments.

Deirdre laughed throatily. 'I know Colter will be sorry he wasn't here. With his callous sense of humour, he would have found our meeting very amusing.'

'Would he?' Natalie challenged coolly, fighting for the self-respect that Colter seemed intent on denying her, directly or indirectly.

The question was ignored as Deirdre smiled sweetly, silent laughter in the green eyes at Natalie's bristling stance.

'I realize that slaving around the house the way you do, there must be a thousand things that need to be done, so I won't keep you, Mrs Langston.'

'Slaving' had been a poor choice. Involuntarily Natalie jerked her head when it was used. She had the fleeting impression of a cat cleaning its whiskers in satisfaction as Deirdre started towards the front door.

'Give Colter,' deliberately the redhead hesitated as she glanced over her shoulder at Natalie with a knowing smile, 'my love, will you? I'll see him another time.'

Natalie was rooted to the floor, frozen by her anger, an anger divided in equal shares among Colter, Deirdre and herself. When the door clicked shut, it took her a full second to realise that Travis McCrea had walked in as Deirdre walked out. Velvet brown eyes searched her rigidly held expression of unconcern behind which Natalie's anger smouldered.

'Are you all right, Natalie?' Travis asked quietly.

'Of course.' But there was a brittle edge to her airy reply.

The immediate grim line that tightened his mouth made Natalie realise that she had betrayed herself. She quickly averted her face and walked over to needlessly plump a cushion on the couch. Natalie had never been one to give way to hysteria, but she was possessed by a frightening urge to throw herself on to the couch and sob out her humiliation.

'Was there something you needed, Travis?' She tried to ask brightly, but it was forced and it showed.

He remained in the open hallway, watching her through the carved walnut poles. 'No,' Travis responded. 'I noticed Deirdre's car in the drive.'

Natalie met his warm brown gaze, her own swinging over the strong, broad face, the thick brows and the silver wings in his jet black hair. Not for the first time in the last two weeks, she silently wished that if she had been determined to make a loveless marriage for Ricky's benefit, she could have married this strong, quiet man instead of Colter. But hindsight never changed anything.

Shrugging self-consciously, she said, 'Deirdre stopped over to offer her congratulations.'

'I'll bet,' Travis mocked drily. 'What she really wanted was to meet the woman who snared Colter when she'd failed.'

'Snared? That's a joke,' Natalie laughed bitterly. 'I'm the one who's trapped.' Immediately after the slip was made, she regretted it. She sank dejectedly in the nearest chair, wearily pressing a hand to her suddenly throbbing temples. 'I'm sorry, I shouldn't have said that. It's not true.'

'You can't pretend in front of everyone, Natalie.' Although he was still standing in the hallway, his voice seemed to reach out to touch her in reassurance. 'Taking my meals at the house as regularly as I do, I haven't needed much insight to see that you and Colter don't act like newlyweds.'

'Please.' Her head moved in a negative shake. 'The way I feel right now, if you say another kind word, I'll break into tears.' As quickly as she slumped into the chair, she pushed herself out of it, determinedly squaring her shoulders. 'I have what I wanted and I'm not going to start complaining simply because my loaf of soft bread has a hard crust.'

Travis nodded an understanding, a glint of admiration in his eyes His head turned slightly towards the door just as it opened and Colter walked in. His blue-green gaze swung from Travis to Natalie and back to his foreman with aloof detachment.

'Is something wrong?' Colter inquired, pulling off his leather gloves and tossing them on the small table.

'No, I was just leaving,' Travis replied, and set his wide-brimmed hat on his dark head. 'I'll see you to-night, Natalie,' he offered in goodbye as he opened the door.

When the door closed seconds later, Colter stared at it in a thoughtful silence that scraped at Natalie's raw nerves. She stiffened instinctively as his gaze flicked derisively to her.

'Travis doesn't usually come to the house during the day,' she stated defensively.

'Neither do I,' he reminded her. 'But today I want to shower and change before I drive into San Antonio.'

He turned from her and started down the hallway to their bedroom, his fingers making short work of the buttons on his shirt. Anger raged within Natalie that he should casually ignore her. She was in no mood to be brushed aside so easily, and she followed him down the hall.

'Are you going with Deirdre?' Natalie asked with deliberate softness, as she stopped just inside the door of their bedroom.

Colter laughed softly. 'I wondered how long it would take before you got around to her.'

'She was here earlier.'

'I know.' He unbuttoned the cuffs of his shirt and

sat on the bed to remove his boots. 'I was just leaving Flo's cottage when Deirdre stopped by to see her. Was that why Travis was here? To rescue you from her clutches?' he mocked, rising to his feet and stripping the shirt from his back. The marks left by her finger-nails were clearly visible on his naked shoulders. 'Perhaps he doesn't know you can defend yourself.'

'He's more of a gentleman than you are,' Natalie retorted.

Colter's ever alert gaze studied her with amused indifference from his handsome but otherwise impassive face. He tossed his shirt to her.

'Throw that in the dirty clothes basket,' he ordered.

Fuming silently, Natalie wadded the shirt in her hands, toying with the idea of throwing it back at him, only to dismiss it. In the end, she would pick it up and put it in the hamper anyway. He was watching her face, seeing the silent argument flitting across her features, and his mouth quirked in satisfaction as she walked to the hamper.

At his mockery, Natalie threw caution to the wind, hurling the shirt back to land at his feet. 'Throw your own dirty clothes away!' she flared. 'I'm not your maid!'

'Deirdre said you might be upset,' Colter said lazily.

Fury carried Natalie across the room, halting her a couple of feet in front of him. Before the rubbery sensation that was attacking her legs could take hold in the rest of her, she struck out at him. The paralysing sting of her palm felt oddly pleasant as she glared

her dislike. The lean hard cheek bore the pale imprint
of her hand that he hadn't attempted to stop, the
colour slowly changing to red while his eyes glittered
with cold blue fires.

'I don't want that woman in my house!' Natalie
raged.

'Your house?' The searing softness of his voice was
like a rapier thrust through velvet.

'Yes, my house,' she repeated, her wrath too fully
aroused to notice Colter's. 'I legally sleep with you,
which makes it as much my house as yours—if not
more, since I take care of it. And I don't want that
woman to set foot in it again!'

'If she so desires, Deirdre will continue to come here
whenever she likes,' Colter stated. His mouth thinned
into a forbidding line.

'No! I don't care how many mistresses you have,
but I will not tolerate the humiliation of having them
paraded beneath my nose!' she insisted vigorously.

'The only things you tolerate are my money and my
home.' His sarcasm lashed out at her.

'And your touch,' Natalie jeered.

Colter's lip curled derisively. 'What makes you pretend that you don't like my caresses?' he demanded
contemptuously. 'Is there some virtuous part of you
that denies physical desire exists?'

'You egotistical beast! What makes you think
you're so irresistible?' She tilted her head back to
look full into his face with haughty disdain.

Blue diamond chips raked her length with suggestive thoroughness and Natalie's blood started to race like fire through her veins.

'Shall I show you?' he asked with a growling purr.

The blazing topaz flames in her eyes sputtered and died, her bravado rapidly fading. Her senses churned with quivering awareness, traitors to her pride. The cutting edge of his diamond gaze slashed away the attempt of her lips to form a protest.

Mutely Natalie spun away. A retreat, however cowardly, was more strategic than the unconditional surrender Colter had planned. But her move was anticipated as his fingers closed over the soft flesh of her arm and pulled her back. With her free hand, she tried to push herself away from his naked chest, a futile attempt that failed when he applied pressure to the small of her back, moulding her to his muscular thighs.

There was no mercy in his slow, torturing embrace. His strength was superior. Even when she gained the use of her other hand after he had released her arm, Natalie could not ward him off.

Arched away from him, her face twisted to the side to elude his kiss, she felt the scorching touch of his mouth against the slender curve of her throat. Unhurried, Colter explored the pulsing vein of her neck, the hollow of her throat, and, pushing aside the collar of her blouse, sought out the sensitive areas of her shoulder.

The unending assault retracted its leisurely trail to her neck where Colter nibbled sensuously at her earlobe, sending waves of unwilling ecstasy shuddering through her body. That insidious, primitive desire was growing inside her. It was only a matter of time until he claimed her lips and she would be lost.

'Damn you!' Her whispering curse sounded more like a sob. 'Let me go!'

His mouth moved along her cheek and she felt it curve into a smile as Colter rubbed his jaw against her smooth skin.

'Not yet.' The seductive pitch of his voice was riddled with mocking laughter.

Her fingers closed over his jaw and chin and tried to push away the mouth that was roaming at will over her eyes, cheeks and forehead.

'Please, stop,' Natalie gasped, unwillingly begging for her release, her pride cast aside to be regained, she hoped, when she was free of his touch. 'Deirdre can come any time,' she promised. The corner of her mouth was being teased by his warm lips. 'You can start a harem in the house. I don't care! But let me go!'

'Would you have me ignore my wife for a harem?' Colter mocked huskily.

'You have to go to San Antonio,' she protested as his mouth slowly began moving over hers. His hand was cupped under her chin, preventing her from moving away.

'Kiss me,' he commanded against her mouth.

He was being deliberately provocative, tantalising her lips with the nearness of his without kissing her. There was a building hunger to know the elemental mastery she had experienced before.

'No,' Natalie refused, fighting with every stubborn fibre of the resistance she possessed.

The arm around her back tightened with crushing force. 'Kiss me,' Colter repeated with ominous softness, 'or we'll still be here when Missy and Ricky come home.'

A helpless moan escaped her trembling lips. Instantly the tense muscles around her mouth relaxed. Instinct and experience gained from Colter guided the tentative movement of her lips against his. At first he remained passive under her touch, letting Natalie find out for herself the fine art of initiative rather than response as she began an intimate and mobile exploration of his lips, growing bolder until she felt the answering warmth of his.

Not another action was directed by conscious thought. For Natalie it was like almost drowning, then bursting to the surface and feeling more alive than ever in her life. His bruising ardour was matched by the urgency of her lips. Shock wave after shock wave quaked with primitive tremors through her body.

When Colter gradually eased his mouth from its possessive claim of hers, Natalie was incapable of the slightest movement. Shaking hands rested on his naked shoulders while her head remained tilted back. Behind her closed lashes, she could feel his gaze inspecting the passion still written on her lips.

'Tell me again,' Colter jeered softly, totally in control, not reeling from the physical impact of their embrace as Natalie was, 'that you only "tolerate" my touch.'

Tears of hurt anger shimmered in her eyes, stinging and smarting like salt on a wound. 'I did what you ordered,' Natalie said in a choked, trembling voice. 'Now will you let me go?'

The expressive lift of his shoulders mocked the stubborn hold on her pride in the instant before he released her completely. Yet the distance between them didn't erase the memory of his hard body pressed against hers, nor the exciting fire that had consumed her. She couldn't meet his eyes that glittered now with a greenish hue. She walked slowly to the hallway door, pausing in its frame.

Without turning around, Natalie said, 'I hate you, Colter. Or is hate another emotion that you don't recognise?'

His only reply to that question was an abrupt laugh. 'I shall be home for dinner tonight, my loving wife,' he mocked sardonically. 'So, please, no poisonous mushrooms or arsenic, or I shall be forced to make you eat it so you can die with me.'

'And I was planning to spend the rest of the afternoon looking for some deliciously deadly mushrooms,' Natalie quipped sarcastically, and hurried into the hall, knowing her barbs were ineffectual but needing them just the same.

The next week Natalie threw herself into a frenzy of activity, inventing cleaning where it wasn't needed, outdoing herself in the cooking of their meals, taking part in excursions with Missy and Ricky, working until all hours of the night to avoid the bedroom. She was never entirely certain that Colter was asleep when she did slip between the covers. He never said a word, viewing her devotion to the house and children with derisive amusement.

Her weight loss was becoming apparent again and the weary circles of exhaustion were faintly making their presence known. Natalie had not thought the telltale signs were visible to anyone but herself.

As she glanced into the oval mirror in the dining room, she pinched her cheeks in an old-fashioned effort to bring colour to her face before entering the living room to let Colter and Travis know that dinner was ready. As had become her habit of late, Natalie addressed her announcement to Travis, her tired spirits brightening a little under the warm glow of his regard.

'Ricky and Missy are at the table, so dinner is ready whenever you are,' she said.

'How about giving me five minutes to finish this beer?' Travis asked, holding up his half-empty frosty glass of beer. 'I've been dreaming about a tall, cold one all day and I hate to rush it down.'

'It was warm today,' Natalie agreed, not looking directly at Colter but supremely conscious of his sinewy length stretched out in the chair.

'Warm?' A black brow was raised by Travis at her understatement. 'It was practically a furnace out at the pens,' he corrected quietly. 'A case of cold beer would have been as refreshing as a blue norther sweeping in

from the Plains for the hands out there today. I hate
to think about tomorrow.'

Natalie remembered how gritty Colter had looked
an hour ago when he came in from the spring round-
up. His shirt had been stained with perspiration and
dirt. The bleached brown of his hair had been a dusty
shade even with the shield of his wide-brimmed hat.
At the time he had looked hot and tired, not the
vitally fresh and masculine man that was visible in
her side vision now.

'Why don't you ask Natalie to bring out a case of
beer tomorrow afternoon, Travis?' Colter suggested
lazily, studying the film of foam coating his empty
glass when she glanced at him in surprise.

Travis gave him a long look before draining his
glass. 'Natalie has plenty to do without running out
to the pens.'

'Oh, she won't mind.' The hard line of his mouth
turned upward at the ends in a mirthless smile as
Colter directed a darkly sardonic glance at Natalie.
'My wife,' he said with sarcastic emphasis, 'enjoys
filling every waking hour of the day with an endless
assortment of tasks.'

Her gaze fell away under his abrasive thrust, catching for a split second the questioning and concerned
glance that Travis gave her. The blood mounted
briefly in her face, Colter's subtle jibe finding its mark.

Fixing a bright smile on her mouth, she turned to
Travis. 'Of course, I'll bring out some beer tomorrow.
It won't be any trouble. Now, if you will excuse me, I'll
go and dish up the soup.'

'We'll be right there,' Travis answered.

No other mention was made of the way Natalie was working. During the meal Travis kept the conversation centred on the children and their activities. After they were finished, Travis stayed only for coffee, then left. Natalie had no idea where Colter disappeared to after the table was cleared. She didn't think she had heard the car leave, but she wasn't going to check.

With the same determination that had got her through the week, she spent the biggest share of the evening with the children. At eleven o'clock she was still in the kitchen, cleaning the overhead hanging lamp. The night air was still and uncomfortably warm.

Standing on the table top, Natalie wiped the perspiration from her brow with the back of her hand. The downward movement of her head brought a figure into focus standing in the doorway. She turned with a jerk, nearly upsetting the soapy pan of water at her feet. Water sloshed over the side as she recognised Colter leaning against the door jamb. She turned quickly back to her work.

'Did you want something?' she asked icily.

'I thought I would show you the way to get to the cattle pens tomorrow,' he answered coolly.

'You're going to show me tonight?' Natalie laughed scornfully. 'It's dark outside.'

'I meant on the map,' responded Colter drily.

Reaching up to wipe the chain with which the lamp was suspended from the ceiling, Natalie hoped she concealed the guilty flush at her own ignorance.

'I'll be finished here in a minute,' she said, striving for the coolness of a moment ago.

'No hurry,' Colter drawled.

She had been taking her time, but under his watchful eye, she hurried to finish the task. The exertion of stretching to cover every inch and the layers of heat that clung to the ceiling brought a sudden wave of suffocation. The first one Natalie fought off, but the second one had her reeling with a strange giddiness. In the next instant, a pair of hands had closed around her waist and were lifting her on to the floor.

'I'm all right,' Natalie protested weakly.

Colter let her lean against the table, removing the hands that disturbed her equilibrium as much as the heat. 'Of course you are,' he mocked harshly.

'I am. It was just the heat,' she insisted.

'I don't particularly care.' A thin thread of impatience was in his voice. 'You can work yourself into an early grave or simply collapse from exhaustion. Either way, I'm not the one who's suffering the consequences. You are. You can stay here and work for another three hours, but I would like to go to bed. So if you don't mind I'll show you the map now.'

If Natalie had thought to gain his sympathy, he had cruelly informed her how misguided her attempt had been. His indifference to her as a woman, a human being, was just as cutting. Suddenly she felt hopelessly defeated.

Silently she followed him as he walked from the kitchen to the small study–ranch office that she never entered except to clean. Her mind had a difficult time concentrating on the pencil tip moving over the large map of the ranch. Natalie could only hope that she remembered the way in the morning. It didn't seem too complicated.

'Can you find it?' Colter asked crisply.

'Yes,' she answered dully, resolving to return to the study in the morning after Colter had left to examine the map again.

'Never mind,' he sighed in disgust. His eyes had narrowed into blue-green slits as he minutely inspected her face. 'You're too tired to even know your own name. I'll show you in the morning.'

With that, he turned off the desk lamp, threw Natalie a curt goodnight and walked from the room. Dazed by his complete lack of interest, more hurt than she cared to admit that he couldn't even pretend concern and suggest that she go to bed, too, Natalie stared after him in silence.

He had been right. She was the only one who was suffering. And she had Ricky to think about. What had she hoped to prove? That because Colter was treating her like a slave, she was going to work like a slave from sun-up to sundown?

Colter was in bed when she entered the room. He glanced at her uninterestedly and turned on his side. She continued through to the adjoining bathroom, bathed and changed into her nightclothes. Colter didn't stir when she crawled into bed beside him. A tear slipped from her lashes for no reason that Natalie could think of and she drifted into a tired, troubled sleep.

The house was nearly immaculate from her earlier efforts so the next day Natalie made no attempt to find herself work. As he had stated the night before, Colter showed her the route to the cattle pens. It was remarkably easy and she wondered why she hadn't grasped the directions last night.

Ricky was home in the morning and they spent most of it outdoors before the sun had reached its zenith. He had always been content playing by himself. This morning Natalie sat idly on a lounge chair and watched.

Lunch was not the extensive meal she usually prepared, but just as filling for all its simplicity. She had learned her lesson. She was not going to prove anything else to Colter Langston. Although Natalie still wasn't certain what she had set out to prove in the first place.

The ice chest was filled with cold beer already cooled in the refrigerator, packed with ice cubes to maintain the frigid temperature inside the cans. It was a struggle loading it in the back seat of the car, but Natalie got it in and started for the cattle pens.

It was almost mid-afternoon and it was hot. To hurry would kick up dust on the dirt roads that laced the various sections of the ranch together. Natalie was content to keep a leisurely pace.

Again wildflowers dotted the route, pointing up the greenness of the spring grass and the darker green shade of foliage of the oaks and cedars. She recognised wine cups, bluebonnets, Indian blankets, Mexican hats, and white prickle poppies among the others she couldn't identify. The air was fragrant with their perfumes.

Butterflies and moths flitted from blossom to blossom with the bees while birds encouraged their efforts in song. A silver ribbon twisted through the meadow, and as Natalie turned on to the road that would lead her to the pens, she heard the stream chuckling over the rocks in its bed.

The sound died away and the bawl of cattle began to grow increasingly louder, reaching its fever pitch of intensity as Natalie slowed the car to a stop near the dusty haze that hung over the large pens. As she climbed out of the car, the combined heat of man, beast and sun closed over her with a suffocating hand. The stench of sweat, burning hair, animal discharge and some medicinal odour filled her nose with almost sickening results.

There was activity and movement everywhere as Natalie approached the board pens. Dipping, branding and ear-tagging were carried out with steady efficiency by horse and rider or the man on foot. The rope-swinging, leg-slapping and fast riding so often depicted in western movies was not in evidence. Despite the acrid smells and the unceasing din, Natalie watched it all in helpless fascination.

Shielding her eyes from the incredible glare of the sun, she studied the human occupants of the pen. A few of the men noticed her standing on the roadside, but she was soon forgotten in the unending demand of their work. All of them were dressed nearly the same, dark blue levis, the colour of their shirts and hats almost indistinguishable now due to the dust that coated everything.

Yet Natalie had no difficulty at all in picking out Colter from the others. Work-stained like all of them, there was an invisible cloak that set him apart. He sat easily in the saddle of a muscular chestnut horse. Natalie knew he was aware of everything going on around him.

Her concentration was centred on Colter. She didn't notice the horse and rider quietly approaching until the buckskin's head blocked her view. Her startled glance was caught by the gentle caress of Travis's eyes before he swung their attention to the pen.

'What do you think of the exciting, action-packed life of a cowboy?' he asked drily. 'Heat, stench, noise and ill-tempered cows. Who do you suppose we can appeal to for better working conditions?'

'I suppose the Man Upstairs,' Natalie smiled, tilting her head back to look up to the broad-shouldered man in the saddle, squinting her eyes when her hand could no longer shield them from the sun's glare.

'You should have a hat if you're going to be out in this sun,' Travis commented with a vague note of genuine concern.

Natalie thought of her wide-brimmed straw hat with its bright artificial flowers. It was strictly the garden and pool-side kind, a ludicrous sight out here.

'So I've discovered,' was her reply. 'I'm a true greenhorn,' she sighed. 'I didn't realise there were so many things involved in a round-up.'

Travis smiled broadly. 'It's more than rounding them up and branding the calves. They all have to be run through chutes and dipped for disease. The sick and crippled have to be separated and doctored. The calves are branded and ear-tagged with the bull calves being castrated to be sold later as feeding steers. None of it's romantic or fun.'

Natalie coughed as a cloud of dust swirled around her, kicked up by a cow trying to elude a snaking rope. 'I agree,' she said in a voice still choked by the dust. 'The beer is in the back of the car. Do you want me to get it?'

Travis's gaze shifted out to the pens in quick assessment. Colter was quietly walking his horse around the small herd in a route that brought him to the fence rail where they were.

'What do you think, Colter?' Travis asked. 'Break now or finish the rest of this herd?'

Colter's reply was unhesitating and Natalie guessed the decision had been made before he had ridden over. 'We'll finish this group and run the last herd in. They can be settling down while the men are resting.'

He hadn't even glanced at her. She couldn't stop the rigid tensing of her jaw. 'How long will that be?' she asked.

There was a brief sliding glance over her face before Colter dismissed her from his attention. 'Half an hour or more.'

'Am I supposed to stay?' Her voice was taut and

weary-sounding as Natalie tried to hide her growing resentment at Colter's impersonal attitude. 'I still have to fix the roast for dinner, and Missy and Ricky will be coming home soon.'

She was pinned by the sharp edge of his steel-blue gaze, his chiselled features dispassionate and aloof. 'You can go or stay, whichever you want, but don't come crying to me about how much you have to do. If you want a shoulder to cry on,' he glanced with mocking scorn at the tall, rugged man astride the buckskin, 'I'm sure Travis would be more than happy to offer his.' A dark, angry flush crept into Travis's tanned cheeks, drawing a curling smile on Colter's ruthless mouth. 'As a matter of fact, Travis, why don't you ride to the house with Natalie and bring the pick-up back for the ice chest? You'd like that, wouldn't you?'

With a contemptuous light still in his eyes, Colter reined his horse back to the centre of the pens. Self-consciously Natalie looked away from Travis. She had guessed that he liked her, but Colter had deliberately implied that his affection was deeper. What was more humiliating, Colter didn't care.

'That man is too damned observant,' Travis muttered savagely beneath his breath. 'He notices things that are none of his business.'

Natalie studied him through her lashes, although Travis never looked at her as he dismounted and waved to one of the men to take his horse. Angry resentment was in every severely controlled move as he vaulted the fence and walked to the car with Natalie trailing in sympathetic embarrassment behind him. In brooding silence, he took the ice chest from the car and carried it easily to a spot of shade under an oak. A jerky movement of his large hand signalled that she should drive.

When they were back on the road to the ranch house, Natalie glanced hesitantly at the darkly handsome man in the passenger seat, his arm resting on the opened window, a tightly clenched fist pressed to his lips, as he stared unseeingly out of the window.

'Travis, I'm—sorry.' Her fingers nervously clutched the wheel. 'Colter shouldn't have said that.'

'Why? It's true.' A muscle in his jaw jerked as he spoke. 'I should have handed in my notice that first week you came when I realised the way I felt,' he said with calm acceptance.

There was little Natalie could say. She couldn't offer him any encouragement, especially when her feelings towards him were limited to friendship and admiration. Yet the thought of being deprived of his steadying companionship, of facing all those meals alone with Colter's indifference, struck cold chills in her heart.

They both were silent the rest of the way to the ranch. Natalie realised that Travis had not wanted her to speak. For her to say that she was only fond of him would have been just as cruel as giving him false hope. He was not the type of man to read what he wanted into her silence. At the same time, there was a sense of assurance that he would be there if she ever needed him, with no questions asked and no strings attached.

Her mind kept asking if things would have been different if she had met Travis and Colter together at Fiesta San Antonio. The answer should have been easy. But there was the uncomfortable discovery that it was not. Another question loomed to the front. Why would she have chosen Colter over Travis? That answer eluded her as well.

CHAPTER SEVEN

THE start of Ricky's riding lessons had been postponed until after the spring round-up was over. Natalie had decided to wait and refresh her own skills while Ricky learned. On the day of the promised event, Ricky had awakened when the eastern sky was a lemon dawn. It had required nearly all of Natalie's ingenuity and patience to keep him occupied at the house until the appointed hour they were to meet Colter at the barns.

Ricky had persuaded Missy to come and watch and she was now trailing after Natalie while Ricky impatiently blazed the way, hopping from one foot to the other at Natalie's slower pace. Colter was just walking out of the corral gate when they arrived. Ricky darted past Colter through the open gate, intent on the horses tied to the rails inside.

'Which one is mine?' he asked excitedly, never taking his rounded dark eyes from the two horses.

'The bay on the left,' Colter answered.

'What's his name?' Ricky breathed. Now that his horse was in view the need to hurry seemed to have fled.

Colter shrugged. 'Joe.'

'Joe?' Dislike for the name was evident in the boy's tone and his wrinkled nose. 'That's not a good name.

I'll call him Lightning,' Ricky decided.

Natalie had studied the two horses in silence. The stocky bay that Colter had identified as Ricky's was the same size as the sorrel standing beside it, perhaps even more muscular. She had anticipated that Ricky's mount would be a pony if not a small horse.

A frown of concern creased her forehead as she glanced to Colter's impassive face. 'Ricky's too small to ride a full-grown horse.'

'A small pony can be just as hard to control as a big horse,' Colter replied firmly. 'There isn't a better horse around than Joe. You could set off a stick of dynamite beside him and he wouldn't bat an ear.'

'His name is Lightning,' Ricky corrected. 'Can I ride him now?'

'Walk over and untie his reins and bring him here,' Colter ordered. 'Be sure to come up on his side so he can see you.'

Ricky was off like a shot. Involuntarily Natalie stepped forward, her mouth opening to add her own words of caution to Colter' clipped commands. Steel fingers closed over her wrist.

'Let him be.' A thread of steel also ran through Colter's quietly-spoken words. 'You can't do everything for him.'

'He's so small,' Natalie gulped. Her gaze skittered away from the blue-green shimmer of his eyes and the tawny gold of his hair. She wished for the steadying influence of Travis instead of Colter's unsettling presence.

'If you're going to become hysterical, go back to the house,' was his callous response.

Pressing her lips tightly together, Natalie resolved not to voice any more of her inner apprehensions and suffer Colter's ridicule. She watched in controlled silence as Ricky was swung into the tiny saddle on the horse's broad back.

All of Colter's instructions during the first lesson were crisply worded in a no-nonsense tone. Several times Natalie wanted to explain what Colter said in simpler terms that Ricky could understand, but held her silence, discovering minutes later that Ricky seemed to understand the adult level of Colter's orders. Not until the lesson was over, one that was much too brief as far as Ricky was concerned, did Colter indicate that Natalie should try her horse.

After she had awkwardly circled the corral the first few times, most of her forgotten skill returned. But under Colter's critically appraising eye, Natalie felt less than adequate. Only once did she feel a glow of satisfaction, and it wasn't due to her efforts.

Missy, who had been painfully silent all the while she had sat on the top rail of the corral, watching first Ricky then Natalie, had finally made a comment. 'Natalie should keep her heels down, Daddy,' she said.

Natalie had seen the swift glance Colter had given his daughter, but he had merely called out to Natalie to confirm Missy's observation. Two thoughts had occurred to Natalie simultaneously. The first was that Missy wasn't quite as reluctant to ride as she said and the second that Colter wasn't as indifferent to his daughter as he seemed.

When the lessons were over and the horses were cooled off, unsaddled and turned out to graze, the four of them walked back to the house. While Ricky was bragging to Missy about his prowess in the saddle, Natalie tried to thank Colter for giving the lessons, which she knew were the first of many. Somehow, in her wording, she managed to convey the wrong impression and received a cynical look from Colter.

'Are you trying to say that you appreciate my time but you would prefer Travis?' he mocked.

Her eyes widened. 'No,' she protested quickly. 'I only meant that I appreciated you keeping your word with Ricky and teaching him to ride.'

'Did you think I wouldn't?' Again his blue gaze slashed at her.

'No, I did think you would——' Natalie began defensively.

'But you thought I would have someone else teach you, is that it?' Colter interrupted with a humourless smile.

'If you're trying to say that I was looking forward to spending time alone with Travis, then you're quite mistaken.' Her voice trembled as indignant anger took hold.

'I didn't say that at all. You did,' he responded complacently.

'But you were thinking it,' she retorted.

In a series of fluid movements, Colter halted her steps with a hand on her wrist, turned her to face him, and cupped her face in the firm grip of his fingers. There was a mercurial rise of her pulse as she stared into the enigmatic depths of his green-turquoise eyes. Their attention was centred on her parted lips.

'Do you know what I'm thinking now?' he asked with receptive softness.

Her legs were suddenly rubbery and her hands touched his waist for support. A jolting current was transmitted to Natalie, almost rocking her back on her heels.

'The children,' she whispered in protest at the slow descent of his head.

His hand had moved from her arm to the soft pliant flesh of her back, obedient to his every command. She felt the warm breath of his silent laughter an instant before his mouth closed over hers. She shuddered once in resistance before yielding to the exquisite presure of his kiss.

Almost before it had begun, Colter moved away. Natalie swayed slightly towards him. His hand slid iightly from her throat to her shoulder, stopping her. This totally physical reaction she had to his touch drew a sigh of dismay from her throat. Would this betrayal of her pride never stop? she demanded silently. She loathed him. Her lashes fluttered upwards, but she saw he wasn't lookir g at her.

'What is it, Ricky?' Colter asked calmly.

With panic-stricken swiftness, Natalie turned her head to the small boy standing in front of them, Colter's hands still holding her prisoner. A thoughtful frown creased Ricky's forehead as he stared at Colter.

'Do you like all that kissing stuff?' he asked, screwing his face up in dislike.

'It's like spinach,' Colter answered in an amused tone. 'You begin to like it when you get older.'

'Oh,' Ricky nodded, the subject no longer of interest to him. 'Come on, Nonnie. You said we could have some cookies and milk.'

'I'm coming,' Natalie murmured, slipping free of Colter's unprotesting hold.

Keeping her eyes downcast, she followed Ricky to the house, vividly aware of Colter's catlike footsteps behind her.

Her and Ricky's riding lessons continued for a week, held in the cool hours of the morning under Colter's supervision. Ricky's sturdy, tractable bay was anything but Lightning, although he obeyed the slightest command—right or wrong—that the reins in Ricky's small hand gave. The commands were more often wrong than right. The uncanny way the horse sensed each time Ricky lost his balance and slowed to a walk or a stop to allow him to regain his seat endeared it to Natalie's heart.

Her own efforts were much more successful. And she found that under Colter's tutelage, she learned more about riding a horse than just staying in the saddle. There was a glow of accomplishment on her face when she circled the corral at a walk, a trot, and a canter, executed a series of figure eights and received not one criticism from Colter.

'We'll go out after lunch,' he said as Natalie dismounted, 'and see how you do in the open country.'

She darted him a look of suppressed excitement, wanting to express her joy and knowing he would regard it with mocking amusement. So she simply nodded a silent agreement and walked away to cool her sorrel, keeping the sensation of triumph locked inside.

After the lunch dishes were cleared and Ricky was safely on the schood bus for his afternoon session, it was a different story. Natalie paused on her way to the barns to stand beneath an oak tree and gaze at the verdant meadow stretching out below her. Her mind's eye pictured the image of herself cantering the sorrel over the meadow, a slight breeze blowing her hair. It was an idyllic image that soon was to come true.

She hurried her steps along the path through the trees, breaking into the sunshine a hundred feet from the corral. There she stopped short, the colour draining from her face. Her sorrel was hitched to the outside rail of the corral with Colter's blaze-faced chestnut beside it. Colter was tightening the saddle cinch.

But it was the flashy black and white pinto impatiently stamping the ground and tossing its arched neck only a couple of feet away from Colter that Natalie was staring at, her happiness departing with the speed of a supersonic plane.

Astride the spirited pinto was Deirdre Collins, sophisticated and chic in her split riding skirt of rust brown with a matching vest over a white blouse. A flat-crowned, wide-brimmed hat of the same shade of brown accented the fiery lights of her long hair caught at the back of her neck. There was smug satisfaction in the emerald green eyes as she studied Natalie's look of stunned dismay.

'There you are, Natalie,' Deirdre called out gaily, directing Colter's unreadable glance in her direction. 'Colter and I have been waiting for you.'

Natalie unconsciously bristled at the familiar way Deirdre coupled her name with Colter's. Her chin lifted with rigid pride as she forced her feet to carry her to the pair.

'I didn't know you were here, Miss Collins, or I would have been here sooner,' she replied curtly.

That remark drew a melodious laugh from the redhead which angered Natalie further. She cast an accusing glance at Colter's lazily watchful eye. The mocking light in his blue-green eyes subtly reminded her of her rash statement after Deirdre's last visit to the ranch, the time she had tried to elude his embrace by promising that Deirdre could come any time. And Natalie flushed in silent outrage.

'Daddy was checking some cattle not too far from here,' Deirdre was saying. 'I decided at the last minute to go with him and ride over for a visit. When Colter told me he was taking you for your first cross-country trip on horseback, I invited myself along. I hope you don't mind.'

'Of course not,' Natalie replied stiffly.

'I can't imagine what it's like learning to ride,' Deirdre added in a patronising tone. Her gaze shifted from Natalie to Colter, an intimate expression in their green depths. 'Colter and I were practically born in the saddle.'

A chill vibrated Natalie's nerve ends. Her riding ability was no match for theirs. She could feel her confidence already dissolving. Her stomach churned sickeningly as she saw herself forgetting everything that Colter had taught her. There was a terrifying urge to flee before she was humiliated by their superior skill and became the object of silent ridicule.

Colter untied their horses, walking to Natalie and passing her the reins of the sorrel. His perceptive gaze swept her face with mocking thoroughness. His whipcord length blocked Deirdre's view of Natalie's trembling hands as she took the reins, but he had noticed them.

'You forgot your hat,' he said drily.

'My hat?' Natalie echoed blankly. 'I don't wear a hat.'

'There hasn't been any need for one in the mornings, but you certainly can't ride in this midday sun without one,' Colter stated firmly.

The reins were clutched tightly in her hands while the humiliating image of herself in that wretched sunhat with its ludicrous flowers flashed through her mind. Mutinously she averted her head.

'I don't need one,' she answered tautly, placing a hand on the saddle horn to mount.

But Colter's fingers dug into the sleeve of her blouse. 'I said go to the house and get your hat.'

Poisonous gold flecks sprang into her eyes as she met his unrelenting gaze. Then her gaze flickered past him to Deirdre, who was watching their silent battle of wills with obvious pleasure. Without a word,

Natalie wrenched her arm free of his hold and angrily tossed the reins at him. Then she spun around and stalked towards the house, resentment blazing in every rigid muscle.

How long would they wait for her to return? she wondered with trembling rage. Because she had no intention of riding with them, certainly not with that stupid hat on top of her head. With impotent fury, she slammed the front door behind her and didn't slow her strides until she reached the kitchen. She stood by the table, needing a release for the rage that consumed her.

Yanking a bucket and brush from a closet, Natalie shoved the bucket beneath the taps in the sink, poured a generous amount of ammonia in the bottom and filled it with hot water. Seconds later she was on her hands and knees on the floor, stripping the wax from the surface with savage scrubbing motions of the brush. The floor was half-done when she heard the front door open and the commanding summons by Colter for her. Her mouth tightened grimly, but she didn't answer.

Nor did Natalie glance up when his footsteps stopped in the doorway of the kitchen. 'I thought I told you to get a hat,' he said with ominous softness.

'I'm busy,' she snapped, dipping the brush in the soapy water and sloshing it over the floor.

'You are going riding.' Each word was concisely and emphatically spoken.

'You and Deirdre will find the ride infinitely more

satisfying alone, I'm sure,' Natalie responded sarcastically.

She rose to her feet, setting the pail of water on the table while she began to move the kitchen chairs out of the way, aware of the steel gaze that followed her every movement and uncaring for its harshness.

'Are we going to go through this again?' Colter demanded. Natalie didn't reply, but mutinously kept moving the chairs. 'Are you going to get your hat or am I?'

'Go and get it if you want,' Natalie shrugged indifferently, 'but I am not going riding.'

'Because of Deirdre?' he jeered harshly.

In a fit of temper, she stamped her foot on the floor, turning to face him in a trembling rage. 'I am not going to have that woman making fun of me! I don't care what you do to me, but I am not going to wear that ridiculous hat!'

There was a slight tilting of his head to the side in curious amusement. 'Ridiculous?' Colter repeated.

'Yes, ridiculous!' she flashed. 'You know very well that the only hat I own is that straw one with the flowers!'

Laughter rumbled from his throat, taunting in its mockery.

'It is not funny!' Natalie declared in a voice that quivered with uncontrollable anger.

But the low sound continued. Before she took the time to consider her actions, Natalie was reaching for the bucket of soapy water and emptying it in his direction. Only a few scattering drops fell on him as he side-stepped the bulk of it with ease. Silence splintered the room. Then the glint of reprisal was focused on Natalie through narrowed eyes.

Intimidated in spite of her own anger, she took a hasty step backwards as Colter moved forward. She forced herself to stand still, fighting the cowardly inclination to run while her heart pounded in her throat. She succeeded until he towered in front of her. Too late Natalie tried to pivot away.

Her shoulders were seized in a punishing grip and her back was pulled roughly against his chest. The outline of his masculine form was impressed on to hers. Quicksilver shivers raced up her spine as Colter buried his mouth on the taut curve of her neck. His hands glided smoothly down her arms, sliding on to her stomach, their erotic touch igniting the kindled desires of her flesh.

'You made me do it, Colter. You shouldn't have laughed.' The words vibrated huskily from the emotion-charged tenseness of her throat.

Under the drugging influence of his touch, she hadn't the will to resist when he turned her into his arms. His warm bruising mouth moved sensuously over her lips as he easily lifted her off her feet and cradled her in his arms.

'Fire should be fought with fire,' Colter murmured mysteriously, his head moving a tantalising inch from hers.

Her arms had instinctively circled his neck for support. As he burned her mouth with a fiery kiss, his statement wasn't nearly as mysterious as it had seemed a moment ago. Natalie was distantly aware of the smooth strides he was taking. There was even a fleeting sensation of satisfaction at the thought of Deirdre walking into the house and the livid greenness of her eyes if the redhead saw the way Colter was kissing her.

A blithe, melodious song seemed to fill her hearing like the trill of a bird, and Natalie closed her eyes tighter to savour the joyful sound. His ardent touch was truly embracing her with a buoyant feeling that she was floating on a cloud. Unwillingly she moaned softly when he took his lips away from hers. Blinking her eyes weakly, she could look at nothing but the provocative curve of his mouth.

'So you wanted to get me wet, did you?' Colter mocked softly.

There was a split second of dazed shock at his taunt before she felt him lifting her away from his chest, then she was falling. Her mouth opened to call out and water closed around her, drowning her efforts as she gulped in the chlorinated water of the swimming pool.

The lethargy his kiss had induced was immediately gone, her arms flailing the water to fight for the surface. Coughing and spluttering, she reached the concrete edge, pulling herself on to the deck, feeling like a half-drowned cat.

Pushing the straggling, wet locks of hair from her eyes, Natalie turned to glare angrily at Colter. A wide smile split his usually impassive face, the white flash of his teeth laughing at her predicament. Yet

Natalie was mesmerised by the smile, the genuine grin. She had never seen Colter smile and its effect was dazzling.

'I'll convey your apologies to Deirdre,' he chuckled.

Not until he had disappeared around the side of the house did Natalie move, suddenly shivering from the clinging wetness of her clothes.

Colter didn't return to the house again that afternoon. But he unexpectedly appeared in the kitchen as she was adding the dressing to the spinach salad she had made for the evening meal. He unceremoniously dumped the boxes in his arms on to the table. Nervously Natalie turned, self-consciously wiping her hands on her apron.

'You have no more excuses for not riding,' Colter stated, his impersonal gaze sweeping her face and hair.

There was a rush of pleasure as she recognised a hat box. But she forced herself not to hurry as she opened it and removed an ivory felt stetson hat with a wide brim. The other box contained denim slacks with a matching jacket. She raised her gaze from the clothes to sincerely offer her thanks, wondering silently if his gifts had been motivated by a thoughtfulness for her feelings or by simple practicality.

But Colter spoke before she had a chance. 'By the way,' he said smoothly, 'we're going to have a house guest this weekend. I thought I'd better tell you now so you'd have plenty of time to get the spare room ready.'

'One guest?' Ice froze the blood in her veins, almost stopping the beat of her heart. Her temper would never allow her to endure Deirdre's company for an entire weekend.

'Yes, only one.' Colter studied the betraying quiver of her chin. 'Why?'

'No reason,' Natalie shrugged, carefully folding the clothes back into their box. She closed her eyes tightly at the pain in her chest and shoved the slacks on top of the jacket. Her fingers curled tenaciously over the edge of the table. 'Did you have to invite her here, Colter?' she demanded suddenly in desperate protest.

'Her?' A light brown brow rose arrogantly. 'I never said the guest was a female.'

'Oh, stop playing games!' she sighed angrily. 'I know you invited Deirdre to pay me back for this afternoon. It's that sadistically cruel streak in you that wants to be certain I'm sufficiently humiliated to remember my place.'

'When have I ever been cruel to you?' His metallic gaze locked with hers.

There was a slight shifting of his stance so that she was cornered by the table and a chair, her escape blocked by his lean form.

'With your coldness, your indifference, the aloof, cynical way you mock life,' Natalie answered in a quiet but firm voice. 'A newborn baby needs more than food and warmth. He has to have affection and attention or he simply dies. Adults aren't any different.' She searched his carved mask. 'Colter, don't you truly care about anyone? Isn't there someone's happiness that is important to you?'

'Are you trying to save my soul, Natalie?' There was a wry twist to his mouth.

'I guess I'm trying to find out if you have one—if there's anything you would sacrifice for the benefit of someone else,' she answered softly, an unexplainable aching throb in her throat.

A surge of restlessness visibly rippled over him. 'No.' The slicing edge of his clipped answer made Natalie wince. Long, lithe strides carried him to the door where he paused to study her with deliberately arrogant detachment. 'Nor do I have any desire to punish or humiliate you,' Colter stated. 'Our guest this weekend is Cord Harris. A man.'

But Natalie found little comfort in his announcement.

On Friday afternoon, the drone of a small plane sounded above the house. Colter had made no further mention of their weekend guest, not even explaining whether he was a friend or a business acquaintance. Natalie glanced through the window, seeing the red plane descending towards the ranch before she lost sight of it in the trees. Was this Cord Harris? she wondered. Colter had not said how he was arriving, although she knew there was a dirt airstrip beyond the barns.

In case it was their guest, Natalie set two beer glasses in the freezer section of the refrigerator to frost. Twenty minutes later she heard the front door open and the sound of Colter's voice and that of another man. Smoothing the skirt of her yellow-flowered dress, she walked through the dining room into the living room.

Hesitating near the middle of the room, she studied the stranger while waiting apprehensively for the two men to notice her. Taller than Colter, the man had raven-dark hair and nearly black-brown eyes. High cheekbones emphasised the patrician look of his features. The suggestion of arrogance was there, too, not so blatantly forceful as Colter's because the stranger's was tempered by a ready smile.

'Where's Flo?' the man asked in a richly resonant voice. 'I expected her to meet us at the door.'

At that instant the man's dark gaze swung to the living room, but Natalie had already braced herself for the startled, curious look that sprang into his eyes. The very fact that he had expected Colter's aunt indicated he was unaware of Natalie's existence.

'Hello.' There was a faint quiver of anger in her voice, her smile taut with the discovery that Colter had not mentioned her.

'Didn't I tell you when you called that Flo had retired?' Colter asked with infuriating calmness. 'More or less, anyway. With her church and charity work, she's hardly ever at home.'

'No, you didn't tell me.' A narrowed look of hard appraisal was turned on Colter by their guest.

'Then I probably forgot to mention my wife,' Colter went on, impervious to the suggestion of censure as he directed the tall, dark-haired man's attention to her. 'This is my wife, Natalie. Cord Harris,' he introduced with an off-hand gesture.

A rueful smile accompanied the hand Cord Harris extended to her. 'I feel I must apologise for my ignorance,' he murmured.

'Don't, please,' Natalie refused, her chin lifting in proud defiance. 'It was a very quiet and quickly arranged ceremony.'

Colter's level gaze was locked on to her face. 'What she means is that we met at the Fiesta and slipped across the border to get married.'

His detached explanation left no room for any romantic construction to be placed on their hasty wedding. That goaded Natalie into discarding any pretence that their marriage was based on love.

Amber lights were still flashing in her eyes as she swung her gaze to the man at Colter's side. 'You see, Mr Harris, I met all his requirements. I could cook, keep house, and liked children.' Before either of them had a chance to respond, she rushed on. 'Would you two like a beer?'

'Yes,' Colter said drily. 'That's a good idea.'

With the slight inclination of Cord's head in agreement, Natalie walked swiftly from the room, her hold on her temper almost snapping completely. In the dining room, she was halted by the accusing demand she heard Cord Harris issue to Colter.

'What kind of marriage is this, Colter?'

'It suits us,' was the shrugging reply. 'At least I'm not twisted around a woman's finger the way you are.'

'Some day you're going to get brought to your knees,' Cord stated grimly, 'and you're going to find that it's a position that's not so much humbling as it's enlightening.'

Silently Natalie wished those words were prophetic and not wishful thinking. She would like to see Colter grovelling for a woman's affection. She brought them their frosty glasses of cold beer and would have retreated to the kitchen had not Missy and Ricky arrived home from school at that particular moment. After a shyly affectionate greeting, Missy dutifully introduced Ricky, who was as usual not the least bit bashful in front of the stranger.

'Didn't Aunt Stacy and Josh come with you?' Missy asked.

'Not this time,' Cord answered with the patient attention of a man who genuinely likes children. He glanced at Natalie to explain. 'Stacy is my wife. She and our little boy usually come with me any time I'm on a horse-buying trip. But our own annual registered quarter horse sale is only a couple of weeks away. Colter was best man at our wedding. I know Stacy will regret missing this opportunity to meet you.'

'I would like to meet her, too,' acknowledged Natalie.

There was a funny ache in her heart at the way he so caressingly spoke his wife's name and the special light that appeared in his dark eyes whenever he mentioned her.

'How old is your little boy?' Ricky piped up.

'Nearly three,' Cord answered.

'He's too young to ride a horse,' Ricky told him sadly.

'A bit.' A barely suppressed smile edged the corners of Cord's mouth. 'Although sometimes he rides with his mother or me.'

'I've learned how to ride by myself,' Ricky announced importantly. Then he darted a cautious glance at Colter. 'Almost,' he qualified.

'That's enough visiting for now,' Natalie said quietly, knowing Ricky would continue without pause if he had a willing participant. 'Go change out of your school clothes. And don't forget to change your shoes.'

'I'll make sure he does, Natalie,' Missy offered tentatively.

Natalie smiled her thanks.

'Missy doesn't seem quite as reticent as she did before,' Cord Harris observed after the two children had left the room.

Colter's glance slid thoughtfully to the taller man. 'She's become attached to the boy. She's very fond of him.'

Cord fixed his attention on the light reflecting through the amber liquid in his glass. 'That's understandable. She had a lot of love to give and no one who seemed to need it.'

'We've known each other a long time, Cord.' There seemed to be a hidden warning in Colter's statement and the two men exchanged measured looks.

Natalie felt the sudden tension, the clang of hard steel when two forces of equal strength meet. It was almost with relief that she heard the front door open and Travis walked through. There was a veiled look to his brown eyes when he glanced at her, but they still managed to convey a silent greeting before he turned to the other men.

'Karl looked at the plane's engine and carburettor, Mr Harris,' he said. 'He couldn't find anything wrong, but he suggested that you should call in an airplane mechanic to be safe.'

'Is something wrong with the plane?' Natalie frowned.

'It cut out on me twice on the way here, but I didn't have any trouble after the first hour of flight,' Cord explained. 'The annual inspection on it was just a week ago. I'm sure it's all right,' he smiled thoughtfully at Travis. 'Thank Karl for checking it out, will you?'

'I will,' Travis nodded, and left.

With Travis's departure the two men began discussing the merits of the brood mares Cord Harris had come to see with the thought of purchasing one or more of them. That brief friction that had occurred only minutes before was ignored or deliberately forgotten.

CHAPTER EIGHT

'CAN I have a ride in your airplane, Mr Harris?' Ricky requested.

'Ricky!'

Natalie's sharp reproval failed to silence him as he glanced up, a serious frown drawing his brows together as he met her quelling look.

'But I've never been in a plane yet,' he reasoned.

'Not this time, I can't take you up,' Cord Harris apologised. 'Maybe the next time I come I'll have more time, but now I have to go home. My little boy is waiting for me.' He turned to Natalie and offered his hand. 'Thank you for having me here.'

'There's no need for thanks. You're welcome any time,' she insisted.

The dark-haired man bent to Missy, brushing her cheek with a light kiss. 'I'll bring Josh when I come again,' he promised with a wink, and she smiled in return.

Then Colter was walking with him to the plane, a red Cessna parked on the edge of the airstrip. Over the weekend, Natalie had observed the unusual regard Colter held for Cord Harris. Of course, Cord Harris was a man whom nearly everyone would respect and admire whether they hated him or liked him. The unusual part was that Colter did.

A small sigh quivered from her throat as Colter rejoined her and Ricky and Missy. She studied him surreptitiously from the corner of her eye. This man standing beside her, her husband, a bronzed sun-god, she wondered if she would ever understand him. She knew him intimately and didn't know him at all.

Natalie wondered if she would ever solve the enigma of her own ambivalent emotions towards him. On the one hand, she despised him for the way he used her. On the other she kept being drawn to a fiery inner core that she seemed to catch glimpses of without ever being certain it was there.

The scarlet and white plane taxied to the near end of the dirt runway. The rudders and ailerons were checked. Brakes were set and the motor revved. Then the flaps were partially lowered. Cord saluted them in a final goodbye as he gently rolled the plane on to the strip, quickly gaining momentum.

As Natalie watched the wheels lifting from the surface as the plane became airborne, she wondered if Cord Harris understood her husband—if he could explain the coldness that permanently encased Colter. In Natalie's rare visits to Flo Donaldsen's cottage, not even Colter's aunt had been able to say why he had been deprived of the capacity to care.

Lost in the labryinth of her thoughts, Natalie had been watching the plane without seeing it, deaf to the sputtering sound coming from its engine. Ricky's fingers tugged her arm.

'What's wrong with the plane, Nonnie?' he asked.

By then the engine had died completely and the

red plane was sliding quickly towards the ground, past the end of the runway and with insufficient altitude to glide safely back to the clearing. A few scattered trees stood in its path.

The white El Dorado in which they had all ridden to the grassfield was suddenly in her vision. She glanced in startled surprise to her side only to discover that Colter was no longer standing next to her. While she had been paralysed by what was happening, he had been reacting.

'Missy!' Natalie grabbed the young girl by the shoulder, the thin face as white and frightened as her own. 'Run to the barns and get help! As fast as you can!'

Without a word Missy turned and ran with Ricky following. Now Natalie ran, not in the direction of the barns where the children were going, but towards the beckoning white rear of the car and the disappearing airplane. The crunching crash of metal on to ground and trees came next, seeming to go on for ever yet lasting only fleeting seconds.

As she raced by the end of the runway through the trees, the sound of a pick-up truck came from behind her. Catching her breath against a tree-trunk, Natalie glanced over her shoulder, wanting to wait for the help that was arriving and knowing every precious second might count. Resolutely she pushed herself away from the tree and stumbled on.

As she arrived at the crash site, her stomach turned sickeningly at the sight of the twisted wreckage of the red and white plane. Terror filled her heart, and she felt sure no one could survive that mess of tangled steel. Then a movement claimed her attention. It was Colter straining to open the caved-in door. Sobs tore at her throat at his supreme effort that was doomed to futility.

The pick-up truck squealed to a halt behind her. With rounded, pain-filled eyes, Natalie looked over her shoulder at the men vaulting from the truck, focusing her gaze on the broad form of Travis McCrea. The shattering of glass sounded from the wreckage and she turned to see Colter tearing the broken fragments from the windshield of the plane.

Then her vision was blurred. At first, she thought, from tears. Her lungs expanded slowly in building fear as she recognised the cause of the shimmering haze. In confirmation, there came the crackling of flames. The air was expelled from her lungs in a heart-ripping scream.

'Colter!' This time Natalie screamed a name, her heart filled with terror that he would die along with Cord. 'Colter! No!'

Now the fire was visible, hungry flames eating their way from the snarled tail section towards the wings and the ruptured fuel tanks. In that freezing second of utter danger, Natalie knew she didn't want Colter to die as she had so often thought. She loved him! She wanted him to live!

With a smothered cry, she started running towards the plane. Fear impeded the co-ordination of her movements. Grey-white smoke was beginning to change into grey-black smoke, hiding him from her sight. Then her shoulders were caught in a fierce grip. She struggled uselessly against it, sobbing Colter's name with every breath she drew.

'You'll get yourself killed!' Travis's voice implored angrily.

'I don't care!' Natalie cried. 'I've got to reach him. Colter——' Tears gushed from her eyes as Travis failed to listen to her pleas.

Then she heard his whispered, 'My God!'

Twisting her head around, Natalie saw a figure emerging from the smoke. With a sharp stab of relief, she recognised Colter's lanky form and the bulk of Cord Harris's tall, heavy body in his arms. Then the flames reached the fuel tanks. The force of the explosion knocked Natalie off her feet, catapulting her to the ground with Travis's protective weight shielding her from the bits of debris.

Flames and black smoke billowed into the air. Suffocating, searing heat tore at her lungs before she was pulled to her feet by Travis and pushed away from the inferno. The green leaves of the surrounding trees were transformed into curled ashes floating aimlessly through the air, suspended by the torrid currents from the fire.

The impetus of Travis's hand pushed her several feet away. But Natalie had no thought to save herself. Turning back, she wanted only to reach Colter. The other ranch hands were of the same mind as she saw them racing to his prone figure, spreadeagled over Cord Harris in an instinctive effort to protect him from the exploding flames.

Two of the men pulled Colter to his feet. Semi-conscious and dazed, he was led and half-carried a safe distance from the burning wreck. The other men, Travis amongst them, were making a human stretcher of their arms and carried the inert body of Cord Harris to safety.

The screaming wail of sirens was in the distance as Natalie's quivering legs carried her to Colter's side. There was the crimson of blood staining his chest, arms, and hands. His hair had been singed by the flames.

'Colter, are you all right? Are you hurt?' Tiny sobs shook her voice.

'Don't worry about me.' Despite the growling force of his words, there was a glazed look to his eyes as he pushed her away. She had obstructed his view of the two men bending over Cord Harris. 'We've got to get him to the hospital.'

'The ambulance and rural fire trucks are here now.' Travis was beside them, a restraining arm across Colter's chest. 'But I'm afraid it's too late.'

The words wiped the glazed look from Colter's face. With a lightning movement, he pushed Travis's arm away, swinging his hand up in a vicious backhand slap that staggered Travis.

'No!' Colter shouted. Cold fury twisted his handsome features. 'Damn it! He's not dead! He was alive when I pulled him from that plane!'

'Oh, Colter, don't,' Natalie sobbed, trying to stop him as he made his way towards the limp form on the ground.

The only hands he respected were those of the white-coated ambulance attendants arriving on the scene. The look in those green-blue eyes terrified Natalie as he stared at the blood-marked face on the ground. It was as if he was willing Cord back from the dead.

'He must be bleeding badly inside,' Natalie heard one of the attendants mutter.

'I feel a pulse,' the other one whispered as though he was afraid he would frighten it away. 'Weak, but it's there.'

With practised skill, the body was slipped on to the stretcher and carried to the ambulance. Colter followed, linked by some invisible wire to the unconscious but living Cord Harris. As the doors swung shut, Natalie turned to Travis.

'Get Flo to watch the children,' she ordered.

Without giving him time to acknowledge, she raced for the white El Dorado, sliding behind the wheel and reversing the car almost before the motor had turned over a second time. The ambulance siren screamed for her to follow and she did, its wavering shriek so like the ebb and flow of life.

At the hospital, the admitting nurse directed Natalie to the surgical wing. There she found Colter sitting on a couch in a small alcove off the corridor. He was leaning forward, elbows on his knees, his hands clasped in front of him, staring at the closed doors marked 'Surgery'. His gaze flicked to her in impersonal identification as she sat down beside him. Except for the hand she placed on his thigh, she made no gesture, uttered no words of reassurance. At the moment, all of them seemed without meaning.

The minutes dragged with immeasurable slowness and they waited in mindless silence. Colter was like a statue carved from stone, tensely rigid and unmoving except for his eyes that followed every person who left or entered the surgery doors.

With no conception of how much time had passed, Natalie saw his gaze narrow as a short, ageing man stepped through the surgery doors. He was not gowned in the familiar green of surgery. A white coat flapped about his legs as he walked purposefully towards them, his face permanently drawn in lines of gruffness.

'I thought I told you to get those hands taken care of,' he snapped at Colter.

'They're only scratched,' Colter growled.

'Scratched?' the man scoffed. 'Filled with dirt and glass, too. There's nothing you can do here except pray. He'll either be in there for hours while they try to put all the pieces back together or it'll be over in minutes.'

'Cord is going to live,' Colter stated, his eyes vividly blue in challenge.

'Are you asking me or telling me?' the man mocked. 'Because if you're asking me, the only one who can answer that question is God Almighty. All that can be humanly done is being done. The authorities have notified his family.'

'His wife——' Natalie began.

'She's flying in, although I don't know how she has the guts after what happened to her husband.' The man reached down, taking a firm grip of Colter's arm. 'Come on. We'll get those hands and arms cleaned up.'

There was an instant of stiff resistance. Then Colter rolled to his feet, an impatient cougar-like spring to his steps as he followed the man down the corridor. Natalie went along. Her tawny hazel eyes closed tightly at the sight of the slashes on his hands and arms from the broken windshield of the plane. The depth of her love for Colter made her feel the pain he seemed impervious to.

Then his blood-stained and torn shirt was put back on, covering the majority of the bandages except those on his hands. Their silent watch was resumed outside the surgery doors. A nurse brought them coffee which Natalie sipped sporadically and Colter ignored.

More time inched by. Light hurried footsteps sounded in the hall, accompanied by long, masculine strides. Colter was on his feet as Travis appeared with an attractive brunette at his side. She walked straight to Colter, her hands reaching out for his while she mutely smiled a tremulous greeting.

'Are you all right?' Travis asked Natalie quietly.

'Yes,' she whispered tautly.

'Dr Matthews called and suggested I meet Cord's wife at the airport,' he explained.

Her gaze turned to the slim brunette, and she was barely aware of the comforting hand Travis placed on the back of her waist. She marvelled at the control in Stacy Harris's voice when she spoke.

'Travis told me the way you risked your life to

save Cord.' The brunette's words of thanks were softly spoken but without the tremor that blocked Natalie's speech. 'There aren't any words to thank you, Colter.'

'Cord's thanks will be enough.' A muscle twitched in Colter's jaw.

Stacy Harris glanced over her shoulder as if following Colter's gaze to the surgery doors. 'He's still in there, isn't he?' A shudder trembled through her and she hugged her arms about her as if to ward off the cold.

'They said it would be some time yet before he's out,' Natalie offered in a weak voice.

It was more than two hours before a tall, heavy-set man emerged from the surgery doors, weary and grim, a mask hanging about the neck of his green gown. In a tired voice, the surgeon told them that Cord had survived the surgery, implying that he considered it a miracle. His injuries were extensive and serious, ranging from a severe concussion and broken bones to internal injuries.

'When may I see him?' Stacy Harris asked quietly.

'They'll be taking him from the recovery room later to intensive care. It'll be some time yet,' the doctor replied. 'He's fighting every inch of the way, Mrs Harris, and that's about all I can tell you.'

'Thank you.' A solitary tear slipped from Stacy's curling lashes, the first one Natalie had seen.

A quaking sigh of relief came from Natalie. Travis's gaze flew down to her face in concern and understanding. When the doctor left, he took the edgy silence with him. Colter walked to the window looking out to the west and stared at the sky shot with crimson arrows. Natalie couldn't stop herself from following.

Without glancing at her, he asked, 'Is Flo watching the children?'

'Yes.'

'He's going to make it,' Colter stated.

'Yes,' Natalie agreed.

'I'm sending Travis back to the ranch.' His gaze flicked from the window to her face. 'I know you want to go with him, but you're staying here with Stacy.'

Natalie's head jerked away as if he had physically struck her. 'I planned to stay anyway,' she said through the tight lump of pain in her throat. It felt like her heart. 'You are in no condition to drive home with those hands.'

He glanced at the bandages as though he had forgotten them entirely. Offering no acknowledgement, Colter turned away and walked back to the small alcove where Stacy waited. He had always had the power to hurt her. Now, with the new-found love Natalie felt, he had even more.

At midnight, Stacy was allowed to see Cord. She returned to the waiting area pale and shaken, but still in remarkable control of her poise. His condition hadn't worsened nor had it improved.

The doctor who had cleaned and bandaged Colter's arms came bustling down the hospital corridor at two in the morning. At the sight of him, Colter stiffened, his head thrown back and a taut line to his mouth.

'What happened, Matthews?' Colter demanded.

'Are you still here, Langston?' the doctor snapped.

'What happened?' he repeated.

'Your friend isn't the only patient in this hospital. You're going to be next if you don't go home and get some rest.' The man's scowling face was turned to Natalie. 'Take your husband home. The next few days are going to be rough going. He might as well get some sleep while he has a chance. I've already made arrangements for Mrs Harris to sleep here at the hospital. The nurses will see that she's as well cared for as her husband.'

'I don't need any sleep,' Colter denied in an expressionless tone.

'Get out of his hospital or I'll have you thrown out.' But the doctor's threat made little impression on Colter. A heavy sigh broke from the older man's lips and his expression grew serious. 'I'll notify you personally if there's the slightest change either way, Colter, but go home.'

'Please, Colter,' Stacy added softly. 'You and Natalie have done so much already. If the doctor doesn't phone you, I will.'

Natalie would have added her own pleas to theirs except she knew Colter wouldn't listen to hers. For once, Colter obeyed someone else's orders. Within a few minutes, she and he were in the car and bound for the ranch. Not one word was spoken between them until Natalie halted the car in the driveway.

'Would you like me to help you wash?' she asked.

'I can manage,' he rejected her offer curtly.

When they entered the house, Flo appeared in the

living room wearing a long jersey robe to cover her
nightgown. Colter didn't even glance at his aunt, but
strode purposefully down the hall to their bedroom.
It was left to Natalie to bring Flo Donaldsen up to
date.

'Travis told me it was a miracle Cord was still alive
at all,' the woman murmured with a weary shake of
her head when Natalie had told her all she knew.

A wave of nausea swept over Natalie as she remembered the terror that had gripped her. 'I still
don't know how Colter got him out of that plane before it exploded.'

The grey-haired woman was staring sightlessly beyond Natalie. 'I once accused Colter of not possessing
any emotion. I was so wrong. So very wrong.'

The amber flecks in Natalie's eyes glowed with
sudden brilliance. Colter's reactions had been totally
emotional, not just by rescuing Cord, but afterwards
when he refused to consider him dead and later again
at the hospital. He was capable of very deep-seated
emotions. That cold hard shell was only an outer
covering that had not been pierced until today. There
was a tumultuous leap of her heart.

'You must be tired,' Flo Donaldsen announced. 'The
children are sleeping soundly in their beds and it's
time that you did the same.'

'Yes, I am tired,' Natalie said, but she actually felt
marvellously awake.

'I'll take care of breakfast in the morning for the
children,' the woman offered.

Please wake us if there are any telephone calls from

the hospital,' Natalie asked as she started down the hall after Colter.

'I will,' Flo smiled. 'No matter what the news is.'

The bedroom light was on. She found his bloody, torn shirt in the bathroom and the evidence that Colter had washed. But he wasn't there. Natalie tiptoed into Missy's room and then Ricky's room, thinking he might have been prompted to check on them. He was in neither. Surely he wouldn't have gone back to the hospital, she thought wildly.

Hurrying through the other rooms in the house, she saw from the living room window that the car was still parked in the driveway. A light was on in his study. When Natalie re-entered the living room, she felt a breeze of night air blow on her face. The french door to the back patio stood open.

Stepping into the darkness, Natalie saw Colter almost instantly. He was sitting in one of the chairs, his legs stretched out in front of him, his head tilted back to stare blankly at the sickle moon. She started to speak, then she noticed the can of beer in his bandaged hand, the metal catching the faint glow of the moonlight. As she watched, his fingers moved, slowly tightening around the can, unconsciously crushing the aluminium container without his even noticing the liquid that spilled down his hand.

'You're supposed to drink the beer,' she murmured softly, walking over to remove the can from his hand, 'not spill it all over the patio.'

Colter sighed, but didn't reply, although she felt his gaze move to her face.

'It's going on four o'clock,' Natalie smiled at him gently, loving him so very much that it was almost a physical pain. 'Won't you come to bed?'

In a slow, reluctant motion, he rose to his feet, but made no move to enter the house. She wanted desperately to tell him that she understood the silent anguish he was going through. Fear held her words in check, fear that he would reject her sympathy. She stood uncertainly at his side, wondering if she should repeat her question or simply leave him.

'Colter.' She said his name with an aching throb in her voice. 'You need to rest.'

'Do I?' His voice, husky and warm, vibrated around her, physically touching her with his evocative tone.

'Yes, you do,' she whispered.

With a fluid turn, Colter faced her, his features hidden in the shadows, the moon trailing a silvery pale light over his light brown hair.

'How long has it been since I've touched you, wildcat?' Behind the soft caress of his words was the harshness of mockery that she knew so well. Her watery knees threatened to buckle.

'Please, Colter,' casting aside the surging need his question had aroused, 'I want you to rest.'

A soft chuckle came from the shadows of his face. 'But that's not what I want.' Hard decision laced his statement.

Her breath was drawn in sharply as his hands closed over her hips and she was pulled against his male hardness. Before she could control the sudden explosion of her senses, his mouth was covering hers with searing hunger. Her lips parted on contact, allowing him to take all the sustenance he desired. His appetite was ravenous as he demanded the full satisfaction of the melting softness of her body.

Then Colter broke free and an inaudible sigh broke from Natalie's lips to feel again the consuming fire of his kiss. Steel fingers closed over her wrist, biting into her flesh. Ignoring her involuntary cry of pain, he pulled her through the patio doors, the glass rattling in the panes as he slammed them shut. The momentum of her shaking legs carried her to his side. Using it, Colter swept her into his arms, the gauze of his bandages scraping the bare skin of her arm. For an instant it broke the seductive spell of his touch.

'Colter, your arms,' Natalie protested faintly. 'You're hurt!'

There was no reply until they reached the bedroom, where he let her feet swing to the floor. His arm still circled her waist, moulding her against his length while his other hand brushed the hair from her cheek.

'Then don't fight me tonight, Natalie,' he murmured.

The beat of her heart fluctuated wildly as the bedroom light illuminated his expression an instant before it was switched off. The forbidding set of his jaw was there and the unrelenting line of his mouth, but there was no remote indifference in his eyes. They had blazed with desire—for her!

CHAPTER NINE

Sunlight danced over her face, warming her skin with its golden kiss. Natalie snuggled deeper into the embrace of the strong arms that held her.

'I was beginning to think you were going to sleep until noon,' a low voice whispered into her hair.

Keeping her eyes tightly closed, Natalie smiled dreamily and slowly moved the top of her head against Colter's chin. The scent of his maleness was like a heady wine. She was afraid to speak, afraid to let all the sensations of love come spilling out.

'You're a bewildering creature, Natalie,' Colter murmured, shifting her into a more comfortable position and bringing her nearer to his face on the pillow.

'Why?'

The smile remained when her lips moved to ask the throaty question. Her lashes fluttered partially open to let her eyes drink their fill of his handsome face. There was a jade glitter to the eyes that were roaming lazily over her features.

With his usual arrogance, he ignored her question. 'I'm hungry. Get up and fix me some breakfast.' The order was softly given, closer to being a request than a command.

Reluctantly Natalie untangled herself from his arms, instantly missing the warmth of his bare flesh against hers. In the darkness of last night, it had been easy to conceal her love from him. The brilliant sunlight would undoubtedly reveal the love she wasn't ready to acknowledge.

There was a desire to keep it to herself a little while longer. Colter was much too observant for her to hide it from him for ever. Besides, she wanted him to know. But she wanted to tell him in a moment that was not heavy with the after-effects of passion.

Her gold robe was lying on the foot of the bed and Natalie reached for it as she slipped from beneath the covers. Quickly stepping into it, she zipped it to the top, then glanced at Colter. He had pushed himself into a half-sitting position with the pillows at his back. The white of his bandages stood out starkly against the tan of his face and chest. The half-closed look with which he gazed at her exhibited a lazy thoughtfulness.

'Bacon and eggs?' Natalie questioned, and he nodded. She started towards the door. 'It shouldn't take long. Would you like me to bring it on a tray?'

'I'm not an invalid,' he said drily, 'but if I'm not there when it's ready, I guess you could bring it here.'

The hands of the kitchen clock indicated that it was nearly midmorning. Missy was in school and from the window over the sink, Natalie could see Flo Donaldsen sitting in one of the patio chairs. She guessed accurately that Ricky was playing somewhere nearby.

As she began placing the bacon strips in the square skillet, the door in the kitchen leading outside opened.

With a happy smile, Natalie turned to greet Flo, but it was Travis who walked in. He stopped at the sight of her, the expression on his ruggedly handsome face freezing a little.

'Good morning, Travis.' Some of the happiness that bubbled from the eternal fountain of her love crept in to add an airy lilt to her voice.

His mouth moved into a smile that didn't reach his eyes as her greeting gave him back his mobility. 'Good morning, Natalie. I was just bringing in the mail,' he explained, tossing envelopes and magazines on the table.

'Is there anything important I should take to Colter?'

'Not that I noticed,' Travis answered slowly. 'Is that his breakfast you're cooking?'

'Yes, he's still in bed,' Natalie answered.

There was a husky undertone in her voice, placed there by the vivid memories of the ardent lovemaking they had exchanged in the pre-dawn hours.

'You look especially radiant this morning.' His dry observation veiled the sparkle in her eyes. The hand holding the fork paused above the bacon-filled skillet as Travis asked, 'Is there a reason?'

'Yes,' she answered, suddenly conscious of his feelings towards her.

His hands were resting on his hips in a vaguely challenging stance. 'The look of a woman in love, perhaps?'

She bent her head for an instant, wishing she didn't have to hurt him although she had never once thought that she might be in love with him. Then she slowly turned to him, giving him a faint look of apology but not regret.

'Surely you guessed earlier the way I felt,' Natalie prompted gently. Travis had been there at the crash site when she had discovered she loved Colter.

Dark lashes shut out the look of pain in his brown eyes, a momentary look that was gone when Travis opened his eyes. 'I guess I couldn't believe that it happened.'

'It did happen,' Natalie smiled faintly, 'and I wouldn't change the way I feel for all the money in the world.'

His long legs moved him towards her in slow deliberation, his brown gaze searching every corner of her face. 'I want you to be happy, Natalie,' he said with taut control. 'May I—kiss the happy bride?'

She hesitated for only a second before she turned her face up to his. With both hands, Travis framed her face as if memorising each feature. Tears shimmered in her amber eyes at his pain. He lowered his head towards her lips.

'For all the times I'll never hold you, Natalie,' he said in a husky, aching whisper.

Then he was kissing her, the pressure of severely checked passion trembling the mouth that claimed hers. But his possession was short, drawing away from her as he breathed in deeply. The twisting pain of lost love marred his rugged face in the instant before he spun away towards the door. Natalie wanted to call out to him, to say something that would ease his hurt.

She was the cause of his anguish, so there were no comforting words she could offer.

Robbed of a little of her joy, or more correctly sobered by the discovery of the harsh side of love, Natalie turned back to the breakfast she was preparing for Colter. Minutes later, she was sliding the eggs on to a warmed plate and adding the bacon. Juice, coffee and toast were already on the tray where she set the plate. Humming lightly to herself, Natalie picked up the tray and started for the door. It burst open before she reached it and Ricky came tumbling in.

'Morning, Nonnie,' he cried gaily.

'Good morning, Ricky. Good morning, Flo,' she added brightly to the older woman, who had followed Ricky at a more sedate pace.

'Are you just eating breakfast?' Ricky exclaimed in a scolding tone. 'I'm going to help Flo get my lunch.'

'I'll take this to Colter and come back to help you,' Natalie winked.

'Colter isn't here,' Flo frowned her surprise at Natalie's words. 'Ricky and I just talked to him in the driveway. He's on his way to the hospital.'

'But he asked me to get breakfast.' She stared in blank confusion at the older woman.

'All I know,' Flo shrugged in sympathy, 'is that he said he'd telephoned the hospital. He didn't sound satisfied with the information he received. I imagine he forgot all about eating.'

'He could have told me he was leaving,' Natalie said in a protesting murmur.

'Colter isn't in the habit of informing anyone about his plans,' Flo reminded her.

That was true, Natalie admitted. She had rarely known where he was during the day. Yet surely after last night—she shook that thought away. His thoughtlessness had been caused by his concern for Cord Harris. She could not fault him for that.

Colter didn't return for the evening meal, although Natalie postponed serving it for nearly an hour in hopes he would come. Nor was Travis there, sending word to the house in the afternoon that work would be taking him to the opposite end of the ranch. Flo had naturally returned to her cottage, which left only Missy, Ricky and Natalie sitting around the large dining room table.

It was after midnight when Natalie heard the crunch of the wheels in the gravelled drive. Uncurling her legs from the sofa, she closed the book in her hand, completely aware that she had been reading the same page for over an hour without grasping a word, and tossed it on the adjacent cushion. She opened the front door before Colter's hand could touch the knob.

'Hello.' Natalie smiled in accompaniment to her breathless greeting.

'I thought you'd be in bed.' His gaze flicked over her tiredly as he walked by.

'I waited for you,' she explained unnecessarily. 'I wasn't sure if you'd eaten and I wanted to know how Cord was.'

'He's still listed as critical, but his condition is improving, so the doctors say,' he sighed with bitter scorn. 'I'm not hungry. Deirdre and I ate at the hospital cafeteria.'

'Deirdre?' Natalie questioned hesitantly. 'You mean Stacy.'

'No, they sent her a tray so she could stay with Cord.'

Unconsciously she followed as he walked down the hallway to their bedroom, briskly removing his jacket as he went. She tried to ignore the sinking in her heart.

'What was Deirdre doing there?' Jealousy goaded her pride into asking the question.

'She heard about the accident. So she came to the hospital to see how he was and if there was anything she could do to help,' Colter answered sharply.

'Does she—know Cord and Stacy?'

'No,' he mocked sarcastically, 'Deirdre always offers her sympathy to complete strangers. Of course she knows them!' he snapped.

As he tugged at the sleeves of his shirt, Natalie saw him wince involuntarily when the material caught at the adhesive of his bandages.

'Let me help you,' she offered quickly, stepping forward to ease the material over the gauze.

'Save your mothering for the children.' Colter pulled away from her touch, giving her a look of savage irritation. 'I don't need it.'

Hurt pride lifted her chin to a defiant angle as Natalie turned away, leaving him to struggle on his own. With jerky movements, she began her own preparations for bed, trying to convince herself that

Colter was tired and worried. Slipping the nightgown over her head, she heard the bed accepting his weight.

'Flo said she would stay with the children tomorrow,' Natalie said stiffly.

'What for?' Colter asked uninterestedly.

Natalie glanced sharply over her shoulder, her gaze sliding away from the impersonal hardness of his. 'So I could be with Stacy,' she said, averting her face from his remote eyes.

'There isn't any need.'

'Why not?' Natalie challenged, the clinging nightgown whirling about her legs as she turned quickly around. 'You wanted me to last night.'

'That was because you were available.'

'And I suppose Deirdre will be at the hospital tomorrow,' she murmured cattily.

His gaze narrowed. 'Yes, she'll be there and so will I. You're a stranger to Stacy. Deirdre and I have known her since she married Cord. Besides, it's more convenient.'

'Why convenient?' Natalie demanded, jealousy tearing at her heart.

'Because Deirdre has an apartment in town. She can be at the hospital in minutes if Stacy needs her.'

There was a betraying quiver of her chin as she met his mocking eyes. 'Maybe you should stay there,' she suggested sarcastically as she walked stiffly towards the bed. 'It would be more convenient than driving back and forth.'

'I'll consider it,' Colter said levelly, and rolled on to his side.

The trembling of her chin started other quivers through her body. Her emotions, muddled and confused, touched off conflicting urges. She wanted to scream at Colter to go to Deirdre now, to throw things at him and arouse him out of his indifference if only to gain his anger. She wanted to bury her head in the pillow and cry with frustration and the futility of her love. Most of all, she wanted to touch him, to apologise, to make him understand that she didn't want to fight him—she wanted to love him.

In the end, Natalie did none of those, but switched off the light and slid beneath the covers to lie in rigid silence listening to his even breathing. Why had she thought anything had changed, she asked herself, simply because for a short time the night before Colter had desired her?

Natalie was awakened the next morning by the sound of closet doors opening and closing. Through the curtain of her lashes, she watched Colter shrug into a shirt of light blue print and tuck it into the waistband of his denim slacks. As if he sensed her eyes on him, his piercing gaze swung to her. Its discerning quality made feigning sleep impossible. Natalie forced her eyes to open slowly, moving her shoulders to pretend that she was just awakening.

'Don't bother to get breakfast for me,' Colter drawled, reaching for the matching jacket on the chair.

'Will you be home for dinner tonight?' she asked as though his presence was of supreme indifference to her.

'If I'm not here, eat without me,' was his clipped reply.

But the very fact that he had answered in that way forewarned Natalie that he wouldn't be home. The entire day and night she was tortured by fears that her spiteful words had driven him to Deirdre, although she silently realised that no one could make Colter do anything he hadn't already decided to do.

Refusing to humiliate herself by waiting up for him again, she went to bed shortly after Missy and Ricky did, tossing and turning until she fell into a troubled sleep. She didn't hear him return. The only evidence that he had consisted of the clothes he had worn lying on the chair and the rumpled pillow beside her own.

For two days, Natalie didn't see Colter, only signs that he had returned to the ranch. On the afternoon of the third day, she, Ricky and Missy were at the corrals where Ricky was resuming the riding lessons that had been interrupted. This time they were under Travis's supervision, since Ricky had appealed to him the night before.

Ricky was cantering the stocky bay around the enclosure. The horse's front hoof struck an outsized chunk of earth and he lurched forward before regaining his rhythmic stride. The slight stumble was all it took for Ricky to lose his balance and tumble to the ground. Travis reached him almost before the first wail broke from Ricky's lips. Natalie and Missy were only a step behind.

'Oh, Ricky darling, are you hurt?' Natalie reached

anxiously for the crying boy as Travis helped him from the ground. His little arms wrapped themselves tightly around her as Ricky buried his face in her neck and continued to sob uncontrollably.

'Put him back on the horse.' The snapped command came from behind them.

Natalie's arms tightened protectively around Ricky as she turned to glare at Colter, striding towards them in tight-lipped coldness.

'He's been hurt,' she protested, but Colter's hands were pulling the child away in spite of his efforts to cling to Natalie and hers to keep him there.

Ignoring Ricky's suddenly increasing cries, Colter carried him to the patiently standing bay and sat him in the saddle, picking up the loose reins and handing them to Ricky.

'Nonnie!' Ricky wailed, clutching the saddle horn tightly and ignoring the reins Colter was placing in his hands.

Natalie tried to rescue him, but Colter's arm swept her away. 'You cruel, horrible beast! Can't you see he's hurt?'

Sharp spears of blue steel turned threateningly to the crying boy. 'Are you hurt, Ricky?' Colter demanded, and received a tiny nod that he was. 'Where are you hurt?' When Ricky failed to answer, Colter taunted, 'You're afraid, aren't you?' Ricky's cries had reduced to gasping sobs as he stared wide-eyed at Colter's accusing face.

'Of course he's frightened,' Natalie defended. 'That's a long way for a little boy to fall.'

'He's going to fall off again if he doesn't take those reins,' Colter stated grimly, looping them around the horse's neck within Ricky's reach.

Before Natalie could guess what Colter planned, he slapped the horse on the rump, sending it trotting away. Her heart jumped into her throat. There was a terrified look on Ricky's face as he started to slide from the saddle again. Immediately the docile bay slowed to a shuffling walk and Ricky pulled himself upright in the saddle.

'Now pick up those reins,' Colter commanded. Without any directing hands on the reins, the bay stopped. Ricky's hands were frozen on the saddle horn. 'Pick them up or I'll hit the horse again.'

'Colter, for God's sake!' Travis exclaimed angrily.

Colter ignored the protest as he took a threatening step towards the horse. Ricky immediately took the reins in his hand, still shaking and wide-eyed, but the sobbing had stopped.

'Walk the horse around the corral.' The harshness was gone from Colter's voice, but the firmness remained. After a hesitant glance at Natalie, Ricky obeyed. At a walk and a trot, Colter made him circle the corral several times. 'Now, canter Joe around the corral once,' he ordered.

Natalie's mouth opened in instant, outraged protest, only to close in disbelief when she heard Ricky speak. 'His name is Lightning.' And it was Lightning he nudged into a canter.

'I did a good job, didn't I?' Ricky smiled from ear

to ear as he stopped the horse in front of Colter.

'Yes, you did,' he agreed, lifting Ricky out of the saddle on to the ground. Natalie started to step forward, but Colter was already instructing Ricky to cool the bay. Then he turned to Missy. 'Do you see how it's done?'

The young girl immediately buried her chin in her chest at his question, her thin face pale and drawn. Without a glance at either Travis or Natalie, Colter walked to his daughter and swung her slender length into his arms. There was mute appeal in the clouded blue gaze Missy directed at her father's impassive expression.

But Colter stepped through the corral gate and to Natalie's sorrel horse tied to an outside post. He set Missy in the saddle, untied the reins and climbed up behind her. His arms protectively circled her as he walked the horse away from the corral in the direction of the open meadow beyond the stand of trees.

It was two hours later that Missy came rushing into the house, her face flushed and excited, her eyes sparkling with pride. Her words ran into each other in her hurry to tell Natalie and Ricky of her accomplishment in conquering her fear of riding.

'Daddy said I wasn't to be ashamed that I was afraid. He said being afraid of horses was like being afraid of the dark and I had to learn there was nothing that would intentionally harm me. He rode with me for a long way just talking and making me relax and remember how much fun I used to have riding. Then he got off and I rode by myself for a while. And Daddy said I was almost as good as I used to be, and with practice, I would get better.'

Natalie's smile was mixed with astonishment at the animation on the young girl's face. She couldn't ever remember Missy being so confident or talkative. And she wasn't finished yet.

'We talked about a lot of other things on the way back,' Missy continued. 'Daddy said I wasn't a little girl any more, that I was becoming a young lady and maybe it was time I stopped wearing my hair in braids. Do you think I should get it cut, Natalie?'

'I can make an appointment with the hairdresser and we'll see what he suggests, but I think you would look very pretty with short hair,' Natalie suggested.

'Oh, do you think so? I told Daddy I was skinny and plain, but he said I was probably one of those girls that would bloom late in my teens and just knock everyone off their feet. Can you imagine that?' Missy breathed. 'Shall I change into a dress for dinner? Daddy said I would look good in blue because it matches my eyes.'

'I think that would be a good idea.'

'Come with me, Ricky,' who hadn't been able to get a word in edgewise. 'And you can help me brush my hair.'

As she watched the two of them dash from the dining room, Natalie decided it was amazing what a man's attention could do for a girl. She had always sensed that Colter could be overwhelmingly charming if he chose to be. In the face of Missy's transformation, it was difficult to keep nurturing her anger over the harshly callous way he had treated Ricky, particularly as it had proved correct.

CHAPTER TEN

COLTER didn't come to the house until it was exactly mealtime, his face a smooth mask that seemed to belie Missy's account of their afternoon ride. He pulled out the chair at the head of the dining room table and sat down.

'Aren't we going to wait for Travis?' Natalie asked.

'He won't be eating here.' The answer was clipped out with no explanation.

Natalie could only guess that Travis had made other plans rather than observe her with Colter, knowing the way she felt. She ladled the soup into the bowls.

'How is Cord?'

'He responded lucidly to the doctors today. They don't have any more reservations about his recovery.' Again that impersonal tone marked his words.

Apart from Natalie's expression of relief at that news, Colter's statement brought an end to the conversation. Without Travis's participation in the routine of after-dinner coffee and with the children excused from the table, Natalie found the continued silence scraping at her nerves.

'Are you going to the hospital tomorrow?' she inquired stiffly, taking a sip of the coffee that was still too hot to drink.

'No, I'll be needed at the ranch now.' One arm was draped over the back of his chair as Colter stared with brooding thoughtfulness at his china cup.

Natalie glanced at him quizzically. There had seemed to be a hidden meaning in his reply. His impassive gaze caught her look and the line of his mouth hardened.

'You might as well know,' he said with cold arrogance, 'I've fired Travis.' He glanced at his wristwatch. 'He should be packed and gone by now.'

'You fired him?' she repeated incredulously. 'But why? What did he do?'

'That's none of your business.'

'Surely he'll stop to say goodbye to Missy and Ricky,' Natalie persisted, unable to understand Travis's abrupt dismissal.

'Don't you want to say goodbye to him?' Colter mocked harshly.

'O—of course,' she stammered. 'Travis has—has been very kind to me.' The sound of disgust that Colter made roused her anger. 'And a gentleman,' she added sharply, 'regardless of what you think!'

'He's a man,' he jeered softly. 'I can't believe that there weren't a few stolen kisses.'

Uncontrollably Natalie flushed, remembering the innocent kiss she and Travis had exchanged the morning after the crash. Colter would never regard it as innocent.

'Where is Travis going?' she asked instead, striving for composure. 'Did he say what he was going to do?'

'Isn't it strange?' Colter chuckled without humour.

'You're more upset by his leaving than he is. When I told him he was through, he seemed relieved. I had the feeling contingency plans had been made between you.'

'What do you mean?' Her voice was unsteady, sickened by his implications.

'I hope you aren't thinking of running away with him. I can make life very miserable for you.'

Hurt anger trembled violently through her. 'More miserable than it is now?' Natalie taunted. 'I think that's impossible!'

The muscles along his jaw leaped savagely. 'We made an agreement and you're going to keep it!'

'And how are you going to make me do that?' she challenged. 'Lock me in every night? Post a guard at the door whenever you're gone? I'm not your slave, Colter Langston! I'm not chained to you!'

Her hands were on the tabletop next to her cup, clenched into impotent fists. With a lightning move, his fingers closed over one of her wrists with punishing fury as he leaned threateningly towards her.

'You will do as I say and like it!' he growled.

Her reaction to his imperious arrogance was instantaneous. Her free hand gripped the coffee cup and threw the scalding liquid into his face. Frightened by the cry of pain, Natalie bounded to her feet and raced to the front door, hearing the crash of china and chairs as the partially blinded Colter began his pursuit.

Through the door and into the moonless night, she ran. Fear for her own safety was replaced by prayer that she had not injured Colter. Yet she couldn't go back and endure any more of his insults. His cruel insistence that her wishes and feelings were of supreme indifference to him wounded her more than the falseness of his accusations.

Madly racing for the concealment of the oak trees, Natalie reached them as the front door slammed behind Colter. The black trees hid her from his sight, but the darkness also worked against her. She stumbled over tree roots, was slapped in the face by low-hanging branches, and only the light from the barns glittering through the leaves kept her going in the same direction. As she burst into the open, she heard Colter crashing through the trees.

Her feet were not directed to any particular destination. Her only aim was to escape, momentarily anyway, Colter's retribution. The yardlight flickered over a large metallic object. As Natalie drew nearer to it, she recognised its shape as a pick-up. Then a dark shape separated itself from the truck, rushing out to meet her. For a screaming second, she thought it was Colter.

'Natalie?' Travis's low voice was mixed with surprise and concern.

With a gasping sob for breath, she threw herself into his arms, clinging to the broad chest with what little energy remained. Holding her close, Travis brushed the tangled hair from her face.

'What's wrong? What has he done to you?' he demanded grimly.

'Nothing. Everything,' she whispered wildly. 'He told me——'

'Take your hands off my wife, McCrea!' Colter's harsh voice sliced off the rest of Natalie's explanation.

'I don't work for you any more, Colter,' was Travis's low reply. 'I don't take orders.'

As Colter walked closer, Travis set Natalie to the side and stepped in front of her, shielding her with his body.

'To get to her, you're going to have to go through me,' Travis said, in that same soft undertone that sent shivers of fear racing down Natalie's spine.

'Don't threaten me, McCrea,' Colter warned. 'I've whipped bigger and stronger men than you.'

'You're going to have to do it again. I've stood by and watched long enough while you walked on Natalie with your muddy boots. I'm not going to keep silent any more.'

'Travis, please!' Natalie clutched at his elbow to restrain him, the muscles flexed and ready in his arm.

'Keep silent?' Colter's lips curled into a jeer. 'Were you silent when you held her in your arms and kissed her?'

The tall, dark-haired man took a threatening step forward. Natalie eluded the arm that tried to keep her behind him and raced in front of Travis, spreading her fingers on his broad chest to stop him.

'Stop it! Both of you!' she cried in desperate anger. A hasty glance at the forbidding faces of the two men told her that her pleas had fallen on deaf ears.

'If Natalie wouldn't end up hating me,' Travis went on, 'I'd kill you for that remark.'

'Are you trying to deny it?' Colter laughed harshly.

'Natalie's already admitted you've kissed her.'

'He kissed me, yes! Once!' Natalie admitted shrilly, trying to stop the fight that neither man could win. 'But not the way you think!' Beneath her hand, she felt the sudden stillness take hold of Travis.

'Why should it matter to you, Colter, that another man finds your wife desirable?' There was an odd watchfulness about his brown eyes as Travis studied the man challenging him. 'It never bothered you when men made a play for your first wife. Not even when they succeeded. Why does it concern you that I want Natalie? Or is it that you're afraid that she wants me?'

'She's staying with me,' was the snarling reply. As Colter took a menacing step closer, the light illuminated his face, revealing the murderous thrust of his rapier gaze. 'All the plans you've made to run away together might as well be cancelled, because there's no place you can go that I won't find you!'

'What's one woman more or less to you?' Travis taunted.

'Get out of the way, Natalie,' Colter ordered in an ominously soft voice.

'No.' She refused weakly at first, then gathering strength, 'No!' Travis made no attempt to stop her as she raced to Colter, digging her fingers into the iron bands of his arms. 'I won't let you fight!'

With a casual, shrugging movement, Colter broke free of her grip. The harsh glitter of his eyes swept her face as he took her by the shoulders, mocking her puny attempt to stop him.

'It won't do you any good to try to protect him,' Colter told her coldly.

'You crazy, blind fool!' Travis laughed bitterly. 'It's not me she's protecting. It's you!'

A sound of disgust came from Colter as he flicked his gaze from Natalie's pleading eyes to challenge Travis. 'You don't expect me to believe that, do you?'

'You've finally joined the rest of us mortals, haven't you, Colter?' A heavy sigh broke from the other man's lips as the tension of battle left his muscles. 'You've left your mountain lair and now you know what it's like to love someone until it feels like your guts are being torn out.'

Natalie gasped sharply at Travis's sardonic declaration, unable to believe there was any truth in it. The hands gripping her shoulders increased their vicelike hold. Her doubting gaze swung to Colter's face. Unearthly pain flickered across the usually impassive and hard features as he stared beyond her at Travis.

'Is it true?' she whispered. Her hands touched his waist, her body swaying closer despite the punishing grip of his fingers. 'Oh, Colter, please? Is it true? Do you love me?'

The mask was gone. With aching hunger, his gaze swept her upturned face before he crushed her against his chest, holding her so tightly that she couldn't breathe. His chin and cheek rubbed the top and side of her hair, a rough, feline caress from a mountain cougar.

'Yes,' Colter groaned. 'Yes, I love you, Natalie.'

Quivering sobs of utter happiness shook her frame,

tears of joy streamed from her eyes. She hadn't believed it was possible. Drowning in the overflowing cup of her love, she was too choked to speak, savouring the punishing glory of his arms.

In the flicker of an eye, he was shoving her violently aside, striding from her into the shadow of the trees without a backward glance. Stunned by his unexpected action, Natalie could only stare after him for a paralysed moment.

'I never thought anyone could reach him.' She pivoted sharply towards Travis's quiet voice, having forgotten he was there. 'Without you he'll die, Natalie,' he murmured.

There was pain in the brown eyes that looked at her. 'And you,' she asked softly, compassion forcing her own happiness back for a moment, 'what will you do?'

'I'll live,' he smiled wryly. 'I only looked on you from afar. I won't have those memories of holding you in my arms in the middle of the night.'

'You don't have to leave,' she whispered.

'Yes, I do. You know that.' Travis breathed in deeply, seeming to shrug off the pain. 'I've saved some money. I think I'll get a place of my own.'

'I wish you all the happiness in the world.'

He turned towards the pick-up. 'Colter left so he wouldn't stand in the way of what you wanted. He's never before placed anyone's desires above his own. Don't torture him any longer, Natalie.'

Her feet began moving backwards. 'Goodbye, Travis,' she offered huskily before she turned and raced to the house.

But the impetus of her love made it feel more like floating. Flinging open the front door, she paused on the threshold, halted by the stark pain in Colter's eyes as he stood in the hallway.

'I knew you wouldn't leave without Ricky,' he muttered, turning his head from her. 'May God give me the strength to let you go again.'

There was the sound of the pick-up motor grinding to life and the crunch of wheels on the drive before it sped by the house.

'Travis is. leaving,' Natalie said softly. 'I'm not going with him and I'm not going to meet him. I never planned to.'

'What do you take me for? Some kind of blind fool?' Colter exploded. A savage fury broke around her as he swung a blazing look to her face. 'I came down that morning to have the breakfast I thought you were so lovingly preparing. I heard you tell Travis that you loved him and all the money in the world didn't matter to you! I saw the look in your eyes, all soft and warm, before he kissed you.'

'Oh, Colter, no!' She ran to him, her hands touching the muscles of his chest stiff with rage. 'I was telling Travis that I loved you! Whatever I said about money was to let him know that I didn't care if you were rich or poor. He asked if he could kiss the bride.'

Colter turned away from her in disgust, unable to believe her.

'I swear it's the truth, darling,' Natalie vowed in a throbbing voice. 'How could I go into another man's arms after what we shared that night? I love only you.' He stared at her, searching her face, wanting to believe. 'Don't you see?' she reasoned. 'That's why it hurt so tonight when you kept accusing me of having an affair with Travis. I love you, not Travis.'

'You said life was miserable with me,' he snapped.

Colter flinched when her fingers touched the muscle leaping so wildly in his jaw. 'Isn't life miserable when you think the one you love doesn't love you?' Natalie argued softly.

'It's hell!'

As the words were clipped out, he was sweeping her into his arms, burning his brand on to her mouth. She savoured the bruising caress of his hands, needing the reassurance of his love as much as he needed hers. For long moments they strained to break the bonds of physical restriction. Then Colter reluctantly pulled his mouth from hers, gently cupping her face with his hands, breathing raggedly as he rubbed her forehead with his in a surrendering gesture.

'After the way I've treated you, I have no right to your love,' he muttered in self-disgust. 'At this moment you should be hating me.'

Natalie pressed herself more tightly against his length. 'A thousand times I told myself that I did hate you. There were moments when I wished you were dead. When I saw the plane catch fire and knew you could be killed, I realised I didn't want to live without you. Suddenly I didn't care why you had married me or why you took me to your bed.'

A convulsive shudder trembled through him.

'I never thought I was capable of feeling more than

surface emotions. The sight of Cord trapped in that wreckage shattered that illusion,' Colter sighed, lifting his head to gaze into her face. 'And when you walked into the hospital and sat down beside me, not saying a word, just touching me to let me know you were there if I needed you, I felt—I felt like the lowest creature that ever walked the earth. I understood why Cord had mumbled his wife's name when I pulled him from the wreck. I had this terrible need to have you with me. And there you were.'

'Deirdre?' she questioned softly.

He looked deep into her glowing topaz eyes. 'I never saw her except when she was at the ranch the times you know about and at the hospital. I had no need to see her. I found too much pleasure in arousing my reluctant wife.'

Gently Natalie kissed his lips. 'I love you.'

There was an exceedingly humble light in his eyes, the proud arrogance gone, the aloof remoteness something belonging to the past.

'There's a lot you're going to teach me,' Colter smiled ruefully. 'I don't know anything about being a husband or a father. I'd like to get to know my daughter. It's my fault she's so shy and insecure. I now understand the agony of believing that the one you adore doesn't care for you.'

'It's simple, darling,' Natalie whispered. 'All we have to do is draw Missy into the circle of our love.'

'And Ricky,' Colter added softly, a wondrous smile curving his masculine lips so near to hers, 'and all the other children we're going to have.'

FOR BITTER
OR WORSE

For
Bitter
or
Worse

Was there no way Stacy could reach Cord? Bitter, still confined to a wheelchair, he lashed out at everyone, especially his wife. He believed her love was pity.

"It would have been better if I hadn't been pulled from the plane wreck," he told her. And Stacy despaired at her inability to help him.

Then Paula Hanson, a confident, blond physiotherapist, arrived. She taunted Cord into helping himself, restoring his interest in living. But Stacy couldn't help jealously wondering if Paula had also restored his interest in loving?

CHAPTER ONE

STACY PAUSED at the opened bedroom door. Her fingers nervously smoothed the side of her hair pulled sleekly back in a clasp at the nape of her neck. A faintly medicinal scent tinged the air as she gazed around the empty room, masculine in its decor.

The house was quiet in the early-morning stillness. Distantly Stacy heard the soft bustle of Maria preparing breakfast. Anxiously her brown eyes, moving swiftly to search the living room, swept the foyer. They stopped at the sight of a wheelchair sitting in front of the veranda doors.

An achingly familiar dark head was resting against the chair back. Black hair in waving disarray glistened in the soft light of full dawn. The man in the chair sat unmoving in front of the window.

A quivering sigh trembled through Stacy. It was barely morning and Cord was already staring silently out of the window. It promised to be another one of those days. There had been so many of them lately it was becoming difficult to remember the good days.

Thank goodness Josh was staying with Mary and her boys for a couple of days, Stacy thought with weary relief. Cord's black moods were beginning to take their toll on their son no matter how Stacy tried to shield Josh from them. Unbidden, the admission came that her own nerves were strained to the point of rawness.

Her brown eyes darkened with anguish at the sight of the once proud and vital man confined to a wheelchair. She felt the mental torture and pain almost as intensely as her husband did. Worst of all to bear was her inability to help him.

As if he sensed her presence, a large hand gripped a wheel and pivoted the chair around. Hurriedly Stacy fixed a bright smile on her lips before she was impaled on the rapier thrust of Cord's dark gaze.

"Good morning, darling," she murmured smoothly. "You're up and about early today."

"Yes," was Cord's harshly clipped response.

He propelled the chair forward at her approach. His clean-cut features were rigidly drawn in forbidding lines. As Stacy bent to kiss him, Cord averted his head slightly and her lips were scraped by the roughness of his lean cheek covered by a shadowy day's growth of beard. His continuous rejection of any display of affection from her cut to the quick, but Stacy tried to conceal it.

"You forgot to shave this morning," she chided laughingly, and stepped behind his chair to push him into the dining room.

"I didn't forget. I just didn't see the need," he replied tautly.

"You haven't kissed a sheet of sandpaper lately or you might change your mind about that." The forced attempt at light humor made her voice sound brittle.

"No one is making you do it, Stacy."

Cord sounded so cold and insensitive that she had to close her eyes to remember that he really loved her. It was only his bitterness talking. She couldn't blame him for being bitter.

"No one is making me," she agreed, keeping the tone of lightness, however artificial it was. "I do it strictly out of desire."

She pushed his chair to the head of the table, already set for breakfast. As she released his wheelchair handles and stepped to the seat at his right, she felt the slash of his gaze.

"Since when did my passionate wife become satisfied with a mere kiss on the cheek?" Cord jeered softly.

Stacy flinched inwardly. "It's enough for the time being." She reached for the juice pitcher sitting in the middle of the table. "It won't be forever."

His mouth quirked cynically, and something sharp stabbed Stacy's heart at the action. Maria's appearance with the coffee forestalled any caustic response Cord intended to make.

"Breakfast will be ready in a few minutes," Maria announced, filling the coffee mugs and setting the pot on the table.

"Fine," Stacy smiled, using the break to change the conversation as the plump Mexican woman left the room. "Travis will be in shortly," she told Cord. "We want to go over the yearling list with you to get your recommendations on the ones we should keep as breeding prospects."

"Spare me a token involvement." His lips thinned, hardening his expression. "You and Travis have very capably operated the ranch this past year without my help or advice. I don't need any magnanimous gestures implying I still have a hand in running things."

Stacy's control snapped, pain bursting through her chest. Pressing her lips tightly together, she tried to breath deeply. She couldn't endure another bitter argument.

"Cord, please. Let's not get into this again," she begged tautly.

"Then don't patronize me!" he snapped.

"We aren't," she protested.

"Aren't you?" Dark eyes flashed like burning coals. "Go over the list of yearlings," he mocked sarcastically. "The Circle H is your ranch. Do what you like!"

"It was your ranch. It became our ranch, but it was never mine," Stacy cried out in frustration. "All Travis and I have been trying to do is keep it going until—"

"—Until I was well again?" Cord interrupted, a sardonic dryness in his tone. A contemptuous sound came from his throat. "It's very likely that I'm as well as I'm going to get."

"No."

But it was a whispered word, half choked by an invisible stranglehold around her throat.

"Face the truth, Stacy," he demanded harshly. "It would have been better if Colter hadn't pulled me from the wreckage of the plane."

"How can you say that!" she breathed in sharply. Her hands were trembling. She stared at them, remembering the agony she had suffered nearly a year ago when she had thought Cord might not live. "I love you. How could you possibly think anything would be better if you were dead?"

"Look at me." When she didn't immediately obey his order, his fingers dug into the bones of her slender wrist and twisted it until her widened brown eyes met the chilling darkness of his. There was an arrogant flare of his nostrils in challenge.

"Look at me, Stacy, and tell me if it's love you feel or pity."

Stacy obeyed, slowly inspecting his masculine features. A year's convalescence had paled his sunbrowned skin to a golden hue. The chiseled lines were blunted by a weight loss that hadn't been completely regained. Yet the rugged leanness only seemed to increase his compelling looks. Marriage had not lessened the physical attraction Cord held for her, only heightened it.

There was nothing about his handsome face to pity, nor the wide shoulders and strong arms. But when her gaze slipped to his long, muscled legs that had once enabled him to tower above her, Stacy was forced to remember that Cord sat in a wheelchair.

Her heart cried at the injustice of it. It was like seeing a noble savage, proud and arrogant and chained against his will.

Yes, it tore at her heart, but it did so because she loved him.

"I love you, Cord," she answered at last, lifting her gaze to his face.

He sighed heavily and released her wrist. His hand closed around the juice glass. There was a suppressed violence about him, as if he wanted to hurl the glass and see it shatter into a thousand pieces.

Stacy laid a hand on his forearm and felt him stiffen at her touch. "Cord, you have to believe you'll walk again." She leaned toward him earnestly. "It isn't as if you're without hope. This last operation, you did regain some feeling in your legs. It's just a slow healing process until the doctors can test how extensive the recovery will be."

His hard gaze shifted to her with lazy cynicism. "Or how limited," he reminded her dryly. "Forgive me if I'd rather prepare for the worst," he mocked, shrugging his arm away from her touch.

He released the brake in the wheelchair and pushed it away from the table. "Tell Maria that I'm not hungry."

"Cord, you have to eat!" Stacy protested as he rolled toward the living room.

"I don't *have* to do anything," he replied without a backward glance.

Stacy started to follow him, then sat back in her chair. Their somewhat embittered discussion had stolen her appetite, too.

It revealed so much of the frustration they had known in the past year since the engine of Cord's plane had failed on takeoff from a friend's ranch and he had crashed.

Her own father had been killed in an air crash of a private plane, which Stacy had survived. The memory of that had been vivid when Stacy had flown to San Antonio, uncertain whether Cord would be dead or alive when she arrived. Even when she got there, it was days before the doctors felt confident about his recovery.

Their immediate concern had been stopping the internal bleeding and making the necessary repairs to keep him alive.

The operation to relieve the pressure on the main nerve trunk to his legs had been too delicate and complicated to attempt in his critical and weakened condition following the crash, so the decision had been made to wait until he had recovered his strength before attempting it.

At the time, Stacy had been too grateful to have him alive to risk losing him on the operating table, so she had agreed with the medical opinion.

Given a second chance, Stacy knew she would make the same decision. The operation to relieve the pressure had been performed only a short time ago.

It was successful to the point that he now had some feeling in his legs, although he hadn't regained the use of them.

That, the doctors felt, would depend on the body's healing process, which required time and hope. For Cord, hope was becoming threadbare from overuse. He could no longer hold on to it with any certainty that it would be fulfilled.

After being an invalid for nearly a year, his patience was gone. He had expected immediate results from the operation. Numbed legs instead of no feeling had not given him enough encouragement. After living a life that demanded physical exertion of all sorts, Cord faced the looming prospect of limited activity with growing bitterness. In this bitterness, he lashed out at everyone, and most especially Stacy.

If he was trying to break her tenacious hold on hope, she wondered how long she would be able to hold on to it under his attacks. The strain of the last months was wearing on her, too. Sighing, she reached for the coffee.

"Stacy?" A male voice questioningly called her name with quiet concern.

She sensed he must have spoken before, only she hadn't heard him. She glanced up and smiled at the dark-haired man standing beside the table. It was a haunted smile, a ghost of the animated warmth that it usually carried.

"Hello, Travis. I'm afraid I didn't hear you come in," Stacy apologized, gesturing toward a chair opposite hers. "Have some coffee."

"I saw Cord out on the veranda. Isn't he coming with us?"

Travis McCrea sat down, smoothing a silvered wing in his otherwise dark hair.

Maria walked in carrying the breakfast plates for Stacy and Cord, enabling Stacy to avoid Travis's question for the time being. Maria frowned at the empty space at the head of the table and glanced at Stacy.

"Where is Mister Cord?"

"He's out on the veranda. He said he wasn't hungry,

but why don't you take him a tray in case he changes his mind," Stacy suggested, knowing that Cord would probably leave the food to sit or feed it to Cajun, the German shepherd.

Maria agreed, clicking her tongue as she hurried back toward the kitchen. "He will never be strong again if he doesn't eat."

Stacy sighed, drawing Travis's brown gaze. Perceptively he noticed the slight droop to her shoulders. There were faint shadows beneath her eyes and a trembling line to her mouth.

"Has he let loose already this morning?" Travis inquired gently.

"Yes," she nodded with a wry twist of her mouth.

There was no point in lying or in pretending that she didn't know what Travis was talking about. He had known Cord much longer than she had. He had even been there when Cord was pulled from the plane wreckage.

At the time Travis had been the foreman for Colter Langston, Cord's best friend and best man at their wedding.

And Travis had been the one who had met Stacy at the San Antonio airport and driven her to the hospital where Cord had been taken.

A few days after the accident, he had stopped by the hospital. It was then that Travis had told her he had quit his job with Colter and was striking out for parts unknown.

Stacy had never delved into the precise reason that Travis had left after working so many years for Colter, although she had her suspicions. Aware that Cord's convalescence would be a long one, without being aware how long, Stacy had asked Travis if he would temporarily fill the post as foreman on the Circle H until Cord was able to take over again. Almost a year later, he was still here, temporarily filling in.

"I suppose I should be used to Cord's outbursts of frustration by now." Stacy rubbed a hand across her forehead, a gesture of mental tiredness.

"No one ever gets used to it," answered Travis.

"I suppose not," she sighed.

Maria walked through the dining room with an attractively set breakfast tray for Cord. The fluffy omelet on her own plate didn't arouse Stacy's appetite, but she began eating it anyway. There was too much to be done this morning to attempt to accomplish it on an empty stomach.

The sound of the sliding glass doors opening to the veranda was heard, and unconsciously Stacy tensed as Maria's shoes clattered onto the cobblestoned veranda.

The musical lilt of Maria's voice speaking in her slightly accented English was carried into the dining room, although her exact words were not distinguishable.

There wasn't any difficulty understanding Cord.

"Dammit! I told her I wasn't hungry!" His angrily shouted words were followed by a resounding crash as the breakfast tray was obviously hurled away. "Maria, I—" This time there was a faintly apologetic tone in his voice, but Cord didn't complete the sentence.

Tears burned the back of Stacy's brown eyes. Her gaze ricocheted away from the grim line of Travis's mouth. It was all she could do to keep from crying.

"He's in rare form this morning," Travis commented dryly, sipping at his coffee. "I hope he doesn't explode like that around the colts. They're high-spirited at the best of times."

"There's no need to worry. He isn't coming with us," Stacy said tightly, concentrating on the omelet on her plate.

"He's not?" A dark eyebrow flicked upward in a measuring look.

"No," she repeated.

"Did he give a reason?"

"Oh, yes," she nodded wryly. "He said he wasn't interested in a token involvement. He felt we were patronizing him by pretending he still made decisions about how the ranch was run."

"The entire breeding program for the quarter horses is his. Did you mention that?" Travis laughed without humor. "How are we supposed to know what he was trying to develop?"

"I don't think Cord cares anymore." There was a lump in her throat, large and painful. "He said we've run the ranch very capably without him and we can keep on doing it." Her eyes were clouded by inner distress as she glanced at the brawny man sitting opposite her. "He's convinced he isn't going to get any better."

"A man like Cord doesn't give up no matter what he says. Inside he keeps on fighting," Travis stated.

"Does he?" Stacy's chin quivered. "Today he said that he wished Colter hadn't pulled him out of the plane. I understand how he must feel, but—" she pressed a hand against her mouth to check the sob that rose in her throat "—he doesn't seem to care any-more about anything, not even the ranch." *Or me,* she could have added, but didn't.

"He denies that he cares because he cares too much."

"I wish I could believe that." Heaven knew that she tried. "It's my own fault that he feels the way he does about the ranch. Whenever there was a problem this past year, I wouldn't let you tell him about it until it was solved. I didn't want him worrying when it was so important that he rest. I let him think everything went smoothly. If I'd listened to you, Travis, Cord wouldn't think I was patronizing him now."

"Stacy, you can't tear yourself apart wondering if things would have been easier if you'd decided differently. What's done is done and we have to go on from here. Today we have a crop of yearlings to look at, so eat your breakfast." His voice was mockingly gruff but his smile was understandingly gentle.

Stacy returned the smile. "What you really mean is to get hold of myself." Her mouth curved in a self-deprecating line. "I don't know what I would have done if you hadn't been here to help this past year. And to listen."

"I hope I've been of use as a sounding board. You can't keep it bottled up inside without eventually breaking." He finished his coffee and set the mug on the table.

"What about you, Travis?" she probed softly, suddenly feeling guilty for burdening him with so many of her problems without a thought to his own hurt. "Haven't you needed a sounding board?"

Pain flicked briefly through his brown eyes. In his mind danced a haunting vision of a young woman with honey-brown hair and gold-flecked eyes—Natalie, the wife of his former boss, Colter Langston.

"Time." Travis breathed in deeply, chasing away the image. "Time has a way of healing things. Time and work."

Stacy left it at that, finishing the last mouthful of omelet.

"I want to speak to Cord before we get started with the work," she said.

"I'll come along if you don't mind." He rose from the chair, picking up his stained Western hat. "Maybe I can persuade him to come along with us."

Nodding agreement, she stepped away from the table.

She was skeptical of his chances of success, but at this point there was no harm in trying.

The broken glass and plates had been swept up. There was a darkened spot on the cobblestones where the liquid, either coffee or juice, hadn't completely dried.

Cord was sitting silently in his wheelchair as Stacy and Travis walked through the veranda doors. His hooded look never wavered from the distant hills, but Stacy knew he was aware of their approach.

"We're on our way to the stables," she said quietly.

"So?" Cord's voice seemed to come from a deep, dark place inside, a sarcastic inflection laced with disdain.

It was impossible to say that she wanted to be certain he was all right, and that he didn't need anything before she left. Cord was plainly revealing his scorn for any display of concern from her. She glanced hesitantly at Travis, wishing she hadn't felt the need to come out to the veranda.

Travis, with his usual unselfish perception, bridged the taut silence. "Cord, I'm a cattleman. You ask me about Herefords or Angus or Santa Gertrudis and I can discuss their merits with anyone. Ask me about a good cowhorse and I'd know about that. But breeding horses and bloodlines, that's not my field."

An aloof black gaze swept to Travis. High cheekbones accented the leanness of Cord's features, intensifying the patrician arrogance stamped in each chiseled line.

"Then you'd better learn." Indifference to the problem chilled Cord's reply.

"Cord!" Stacy breathed his name, frowning her protest to his continued withdrawn attitude.

But the raven-dark head had already turned away, terminating further discussion of the subject. "Take the dog with you when you leave," Cord dismissed them coldly.

Stacy's patience evaporated. "Cajun can stay here." Temper trembled on the soft edges of her voice. "After you've driven everyone else away, Cord, you might be grateful for the company of man's best friend."

The impassive profile dipped slightly toward the black and tan shepherd lying beside the right wheel of his chair.

"You may have a point, Stacy," Cord replied evenly with the same degree of detachment as before. Then his gaze slashed to her. "A dog never stays with someone out of pity."

Her lips parted to reiterate that she loved him, but the lack of faith Cord had in the depth of her love for him hurt.

"You have a one-track mind, haven't you?" she accused hoarsely. "I would never feel sorry for you, Cord. You're too filled with self-pity for there to be any room for mine."

Pivoting sharply, she walked stiffly from the veranda. Seconds later, Travis's long strides had him walking beside her to the stables. She cast him a sideways glance, temper giving way to chagrin.

"I don't suppose I should have said that," she sighed. "He's always been able to make me lose my temper."

"I don't know if you should have or not." The grooves around his strong mouth deepened. "But if Cord is going to dish it out, he might as well learn to take it."

That sounded all well and good. True, she had turned the other cheek for a long time, but it didn't make her feel better to retaliate in kind. All she knew was that she would feel miserable until she apologized. Cord needed understanding. She should have appealed to his reason, not fed his anger.

Hank was standing in front of the stables when they

approached. His leathered face, browned by the sun, hadn't aged at all in the nearly five years that Stacy had known him. He raised a hand in greeting, a glint of respect in the bright eyes when they focused on her.

From the stud pens, a sorrel stallion whickered to her, tossing his flaxen mane and stretching his neck over the rails. When Stacy failed to walk to him, Diablo whirled away from the board fence in a display of temper.

CHAPTER TWO

STACY SLID THE VERANDA DOORS open and stepped through. The setting sun was casting a golden hue on the whitewashed adobe walls of the house. The crimson flowers of a bougainvillea provided a brilliant contrast.

Colorful Mexican pots, suspended by decorative macrame hangings, were overflowing with thick green foliage.

The German shepherd's tail thumped the cobblestoned floor.

He rose lazily from his place by Cord's wheelchair to walk to his mistress, thrusting a wet nose against her hand in affectionate greeting.

Cord glanced over his shoulder, his gaze raking Stacy from head to toe. There was no admiration, no approval, not even interest in his look.

She could have been wearing sackcloth and ashes instead of the richly dark hostess gown in gold that did attractive things to the light tan of her skin and the highlights in her hair.

"I thought you were doing book work in the study," he commented.

Yet his meaning seemed to be that if he had thought

Stacy was going to come to the veranda, he wouldn't have been there.

"Not tonight." She moved nervously to one of the arched columns supporting the veranda roof. She thought she felt him watching her and turned, but Cord was studying the ripples of gold sunlight in the swimming pool.

"Paperwork has a way of piling up if not routinely handled," he said, then shrugged a shoulder. "But that's your affair."

His hands gripped the wheels of his chair, expertly spinning it around with a minimum of effort.

It was a full second before Stacy realized he was intending to reenter the house and leave her alone on the veranda.

"Cord, don't leave." She took a step toward him, then hesitated.

He stopped, turning his chair at an angle that would bring her into view.

The gold light of sunset bathed his features, changing them into a mask of pale bronze.

A dark eyebrow arched in arrogant question. "Why?"

"I want to talk to you."

Her voice broke slightly, driven to desperation by the way he had continually avoided her during the past two days.

"About what?"

His impassive expression didn't change. Not even an eyelash flickered.

"The things I said the other day—" nervously Stacy

ran her fingers through her hair "—about your feeling sorry for yourself. I shouldn't have said that. I'm sorry."

The desire to rush to him was strong. She wanted to sit at his feet and rest her head on his lap. She wanted to feel his hand caressing her hair. If he had smiled even faintly, she would have. But the bronze mask didn't crack and pride kept her standing near the pillar.

"Does that mean you've reconsidered and decided that I don't feel sorry for myself?" His mouth twisted sardonically. "Or that you're sorry you said it?"

Her chin lifted a fraction of an inch. "To be truthful, Cord, I don't know how you think or feel anymore. You've started shutting me out. Every time I try to get close to you, some invisible barrier goes up and I'm on the other side. I don't know how to reach you anymore."

"I'm not shutting you out," he replied evenly.

"Then what's happening?" Stacy lifted her hands palm upward in a beseeching gesture, asking to understand.

"Maybe you haven't adjusted to the fact that now you're married to a cripple. Things can't be the same as they were before the accident."

"Why not?" she protested.

"You can never bring back yesterday."

When Cord wheeled his chair through the veranda doors, Stacy didn't call him back. Her heart cried silently for the man who had once laughed and smiled and had swept her into his arms at the slightest provocation. Somewhere behind that barrier of bitterness that man still existed, but first Stacy had to find the key to unlock the barrier or else batter down the walls.

She doubted if she possessed the strength for the battering.

She didn't sleep well that night. She tossed and turned alone in her bed, haunted by the memories of the nights she had spent in Cord's arms and praying for their return.

The fear that Cord might be right and he would never walk again keep reasserting itself. Maybe she should face the possibility, but she refused to give up hope.

When she finally drifted into an exhausted sleep, she was determined not to let Cord give up hope, either.

Late the next day, she was in the study catching up on the paperwork she had let go the night before, when a car door slammed in the driveway, followed by the slamming of another door and the sound of young voices.

A quick smile lighted her face. The entry was never made in the ledger, as she rose from the desk and hurried into the foyer to the front door. She opened it at the same instant that a small black-haired boy with snapping dark eyes raced toward it.

"Mom!" he cried excitedly.

Her hands reached out, lifting him into her arms. "I've missed you, Josh!" she declared, kissing his tanned cheek and hugging him tightly.

He squirmed uncomfortably. He had informed her a month ago that he was getting too old for that mushy stuff, but habits die hard in mothers and Stacy was no exception.

However, with Jeff and Dougal Buchanan only a few steps behind Josh, she let him slide to the ground before she embarrassed him too severely.

"Did you have a good time?" she asked.

"You bet!" he nodded vigorously.

A string of details followed, ranging from Jeff riding him on the handlebars of his bicycle to the collection of rocks he had found. When he took time out for a breath, Stacy was certain he had only scratched the surface.

"Hold it!"

She held up a hand to stop the flow of words. "It sounds as if you could talk all night. But first I think you'd better help Mary bring your things to the house, don't you?"

Josh's dark eyes grew all round and innocent. "Bill is helping her, and he can carry a lot more than I can 'cause he's bigger than me."

"I bet there's something that is just your size you can carry," she said with a smile.

Stacy didn't doubt for an instant that those big dark eyes of her son had charmed his way out of a lot of things he hadn't wanted to do.

She took him by the shoulders and turned him back toward the big station wagon parked in the driveway.

"Go on."

She gave him a little shove toward the car and he moved reluctantly toward it.

A slight frown drew her brows together as Stacy glanced at the stocky man unloading Josh's tricycle. In order for Bill Buchanan to be free at this hour of the afternoon, he had to be combining a medical visit with a social call.

A quick mental calculation confirmed that Cord was just about due for another examination. A twinge of unease darted through her.

Her attention shifted to the red-haired woman walking toward her, Josh's small suitcase in her hand. "Hello, Mary," Stacy greeted. "You seem to have survived a week of Josh with no scars."

"With my two wild Indians, what's one more?" her friend laughed.

"He wasn't any trouble, was he?"

"None at all," Mary Buchanan assured her.

"I've got my rocks!" Josh came rushing toward the house again. This time he was proudly carrying a paper sack that bulged at the sides. "Where's daddy? I want to show him."

"I'm not sure. He's in the house somewhere," Stacy told him, and stepped to one side as Josh darted past without slowing up. The two older boys followed at a more sedate pace.

"How are you, Stacy?" Bill Buchanan joined his wife.

"Fine, just fine," she answered quickly, perhaps too quickly.

A decidedly clinical eye scanned her features.

"I would say the circles under your eyes have got a bit darker," the doctor observed. "Part of the plan to have Josh spend a week with us was for you to get some rest. You can't keep burning the candle at both ends."

"I meant to rest," Stacy laughed, but it sounded brittle and artificial. "But I keep trying to catch up with all the work. It seemed that the more I did, the more there was to do."

"It's always that way," Mary agreed.

Stacy ignored the look of professional concern in Bill's eyes. Her problem was more than overwork. Somehow she couldn't bring herself to confide the truth.

Her relationship with Cord was strained—Travis knew because he saw them together so often.

"Come in and have something to drink. I don't know where my manners went." Quickly she changed the subject. "I'm certain Maria has some tea or lemonade in the refrigerator. Unless you would rather have coffee?"

"Something cold, I think," Mary responded, walking into the house. "What about you, Bill?"

"Yes, a cold drink will be fine. Where's Cord?" He glanced around the living room. "While you're rustling up some refreshments, I might as well see him. How's he doing, by the way, Stacy?"

"The same," she answered noncommittally. "If the boys are with him, by the sound of their voices, he's on the veranda."

"Probably buried beneath the pile of Josh's rocks,"

Mary laughed softly. "Whoever said little boys were made of snails and puppy-dog tails forgot to include rocks!"

"And toads and lizards and worms," Stacy added. "You two go ahead. I'll go to the kitchen and let Maria know you're here."

"I'll be on the veranda with the boys," Mary replied.

A few minutes later Stacy carried a tray of lemonade and cookies to the veranda. Neither Cord nor Bill was there.

It was several minutes before the three boys were situated with their glasses and cookies. Stacy sank on to a chaise lounge near Mary's chair.

"From the looks of you, I should have kept Josh another week," the redhead commented. "Bill is genuinely concerned about you, you know," she added gently.

"If you had kept Josh another week, I would have started worrying about him," Stacy smiled, trying to make light of Mary's remark.

"Seriously—" Mary shook her head "—how long do you think you can keep up this pace? You're trying to run the ranch, your home, take care of Josh, be a practical nurse for Cord and probably a hundred other things I haven't mentioned."

"I have a lot of help," Stacy pointed out. "If I didn't have Maria and Travis, I would have collapsed a long time ago. But it really isn't so bad, just hectic."

"Well, you should take a break and get away—for a little while if nothing else," Mary concluded.

"Cord needs me." A bittersweet smile played with

the corners of Stacy's mouth. "If it was Bill, would you leave him?" She paused. "Even if it was for a little while?"

"No." There was a rueful grimace as Stacy made her point. "They would have to come and drag me away by force."

"Who would drag you where?" Bill pushed Cord's wheelchair through the opened veranda doors.

A warning glance from Stacy checked Mary's initial reply.

"If you didn't hear the first part of the conversation then I'm not going to tell you." The redhead switched her attention to the impassive man in the wheelchair. "Now that my husband is finished poking and pricking you all over, would you like something cold?"

"Yes, I would," Cord smiled, but Stacy noticed the brooding darkness in his eyes.

"I'll get it," she offered quickly when his gaze swung to her, piercing and searching.

"I'll do it," Mary insisted as Stacy started to rise from her chaise lounge. "There's no need to stand on ceremony with us. Sit down and relax—heaven knows you have little enough opportunity to do that."

"Okay," Stacy submitted, and leaned back.

When Cord asked in low mockery, "Feeling overworked?" she wished she hadn't submitted so easily.

"Who doesn't?" she shrugged, ignoring the vague taunt.

"In one way or another, the spouses generally go

through as much as the patients do," Bill commented almost absently.

Stacy tensed. Was it an idle remark, or had Bill caught the stinging inflection in Cord's voice? She glanced warily at Cord. A muscle was twitching along the bronze jaw.

He was upset about something; she knew him too well not to recognize the signs.

A glass of iced lemonade was held out to him. Cord stared at it for several seconds before taking it and setting it on a wrought-iron stand near his chair. He impatiently waved aside the plate of cookies and let his gaze slice to Bill.

"How much longer is it going to be before someone finally admits that I'm not going to walk again?" he challenged.

Bill's blue eyes narrowed thoughtfully in the crushing silence that followed. "That depends," he said finally.

"On what?"

Cord tipped his head back, aggressively thrusting his chin forward.

"On whether you've decided that you can't walk," was the calm reply. "Miracles are in short supply, like everything else. A doctor can't snap his fingers and have you on your feet. It takes a combined effort of doctor and patient, with a bit of grace from God thrown in."

"Which doesn't answer my question." One corner of the hard mouth quirked cynically, as if he expected the question to be dodged.

"Clinically speaking, the odds are still there that you will walk, but it isn't going to happen overnight."

A sound, something between laughter and contempt, rolled from Cord's throat. "That's a relief! For a minute there, I thought you were going to tell me this paralysis was psychosomatic."

"If I believed that," Bill said briskly, "I would have suggested a psychiatrist, not a—"

"Of course," Cord broke in sharply. His hands gripped the wheels, knuckles turning white under the strain of his hold. "Excuse me."

Before any of the three could speak, he was rolling his chair into the house.

The rigidity left Stacy in an uncontrollable shudder at his bitter display.

Bill's gaze swerved to her with professional sharpness.

"How long has this been going on?"

"Since shortly after he came home from the hospital this last time, almost constantly this last month," Stacy admitted.

Her eyes smarted with tears as she stared toward the house where Cord had gone.

"This ordeal would be rough on any man. As self-sufficient and independent as Cord has always been, I should have realized it would be even more difficult for him," the doctor murmured grimly.

Swallowing, she glanced nervously at him. "You suggested something to Cord. An operation?" She wasn't certain she could go through the anxiety of another operation and convalescence.

"No, I suggested a physiotherapist," he replied. "The simple exercises he's been doing have probably taken him as far as he can go on his own."

"What was Cord's reaction?"

She held her breath.

"Shall we say less than enthusiastic," Bill answered dryly.

"I'd like to shake him until his teeth rattled!" Mary declared. "Either way I don't envy the person who has to work with him. He can have a scorching tongue when he wants to cut somebody down to size."

"That's why I'm arranging to have Paula come." A faint smile of agreement with his wife's opinion curved his mouth. "She's the best I know."

"Paula? Paula Hanson?" Mary was suddenly alert. With an approving toss of her Titian hair, she turned to Stacy. "You'll like her."

"The question is—will Cord?" Stacy sighed.

"I doubt it." Bill chuckled. "But don't worry, Paula will be able to handle him. That girl not only knows her job, she also has an uncanny knack for knowing what tactics to use on her patient."

"She isn't exactly a girl, Bill," Mary corrected teasingly. "I think twenty-eight would qualify her as a woman."

"Is she married?"

Stacy glanced curiously at the two.

"So far, only to her career. She specializes in strictly the difficult cases, which is why I want her," Bill explained. "Paula once told me that by the time she gets acquainted with a new locale, it's time to move on to another case. You can tell that she finds her work very rewarding."

"Will she be living here—with us?" For some reason, Stacy found that thought unsettling. She couldn't say exactly why.

A frown creased Bill's forehead as if he had considered the answer a foregone conclusion. "It would be easiest, if it wouldn't be too much trouble for you."

"I'm sure it wouldn't," she hastened. "I was only wondering what arrangements you'd been making."

"I'm sorry, I feel as though I've stuck my foot in my mouth," Bill apologized. "I should have consulted with you first before telling Paula that she could stay here. It wasn't very considerate of me."

"I'm in favor of anything or any arrangement that helps Cord," Stacy assured him.

"I suppose I was so delighted when she called me this morning to say she was released from the case she was on and would be available to come here after a few days of rest that I never gave a thought to calling you first to clear things," he said ruefully.

"Bill, it really doesn't bother me. She's more than welcome to stay here." Yet there was an uncomfortable twinge of doubt. "I'm sure we'll get along."

"Don't judge her too quickly," he warned her. "Sometimes she comes on a little tough and blunt. But, if the saying was ever true that someone has a heart of pure gold, it fits Paula. She'll take some of the load of caring for Cord off your shoulders."

"Of course," Stacy smiled.

Inwardly she realized she was suffering from the pangs of jealousy. It was foolish and selfish to resent a woman she hadn't even met because she would be doing all the little things for Cord that Stacy was doing now.

It was difficult to get close to him. Paula Hanson's arrival would deny Stacy the few chances she had for closeness.

Recognizing the reason for her resentment also enabled Stacy to remember why Paula was coming. She was willing to sacrifice those moments with Cord if it would make him well again.

Mary and Bill Buchanan stayed for another hour. The conversation shifted from Cord to Josh and his visit with them.

Cord didn't return. When Stacy walked with the Buchanans to the front door, she noticed the door to his bedroom was closed.

He was still in there when Maria announced that dinner was ready. Stacy knew that if she went to the door he would simply say he wasn't hungry, so instead she sent Josh.

Cord wouldn't refuse his son.

The ploy worked as the three of them sat at the table together. Josh's nonstop chatter couldn't cover the brooding silence of his father, although Stacy was the only one to notice it.

"We played baseball, too," Josh declared, intent on relating everything he had done while he was gone. "Bill says I can hit pretty good. One time I hit a ball clear across the yard. That's a long way, huh?"

"It sure is," Stacy agreed, hiding a smile.

"Will you play ball with me tomorrow, dad?" Bright dark eyes were directed expectantly at his father. "And I'll show you the way I hit that ball."

Cord kept his dark gaze riveted to his plate, paling slightly beneath his tan. "It's difficult to play ball from a wheelchair, Josh," he responded with remarkable calm.

"I have an idea," Stacy spoke up quickly, trying to divert the sudden frowning look Josh was giving his father. "Why don't you and I play ball tomorrow? Daddy can watch while you show him how well you can hit the ball."

"I guess so," Josh agreed. He pushed the peas around on his plate for several silent seconds, and then he frowned again at Cord and tipped his head to the side. "Dad, don't you get tired of watching all the time?"

Cord's fork clattered to the plate at Josh's question and Stacy rushed to answer. "Of course he does, but it can't be helped." Trying to distract him, she said, "Eat your dinner."

"I'm full." The small shoulders shrugged indifferently. He set his napkin on the table and leaned back in his chair, swinging his legs in a rhythmic motion. "How much longer is it going to be before daddy gets better?"

Casting a sideways glance at Cord's grimly silent expression, she dodged the question.

"Long enough to make you ask questions. If you're through eating, you may be excused from the table.

Ask Maria if she'll fix you an ice-cream cone to eat on the veranda."

Josh slid from his chair and walked unenthusiastically toward the kitchen. He left the room charged with tension. Stacy stared at her plate for several seconds. Pushing thick chestnut hair behind an ear, she looked at Cord.

"He's just a little boy. He doesn't understand about these things," she offered nervously, not knowing how to ease the pain her son's innocent remarks had caused.

"Doesn't he?" His gaze pinned her, arrogant and aloof. "I thought Josh put it very succinctly. I am bored and tired of watching all the time." Cord crumpled his napkin and tossed it onto the table. "Excuse me."

"Cord, the therapist who's coming—" Stacy began as he pushed himself away from the table.

But he interrupted her attempt to restore hope. "I don't want to talk about it," was his caustic reply.

CHAPTER THREE

STACY LIFTED HER HEAD from the pillow and listened. She was certain she had heard something. She waited. Had it been Josh crying out for her? There wasn't a sound in the quiet house.

She glanced at the luminous dial of her clock. One in the morning.

Nibbling at her lower lip, she waited a few more seconds, then with a sigh, she slipped out of bed. It was no use.

She wouldn't go back to sleep until she had made certain Josh was all right.

It was crazy, but all the while he had been staying at the Buchanans', she hadn't woken once during the night to check on him. Yet this was only his first night at home and she was already instinctively listening for him.

Her peach-colored robe was lying near the foot of the bed. Throwing it around her shoulders, Stacy walked barefoot to the hall door. Silence greeted her as she entered the corridor. She relied on her memory to make her way in the darkness to Josh's room across the hall from hers.

She opened the door quickly, stepping in to see him

sleeping peacefully beneath the red and blue covers of his spread. Moonlight streamed in from the window, touching his black hair and magically lacing it with silver.

As she started to close the door, she heard what sounded like a low moan. Was it the wind rubbing a branch outdoors, she wondered. But there wasn't a strong wind, only the gentlest of breezes.

Then it came again. From downstairs, Stacy thought. Was it Cord? Her heart skipped a beat in fear that he might have fallen and was unable to pull himself up.

Her feet barely touched the steps as she raced down the unlit staircase to the master bedroom she had shared with Cord until the accident. A low, deep moan sounded on the other side of the door and she flung it open.

A small night-light illuminated his long shape in the bed. It glistened over the golden tan of his complexion. The black of his hair contrasted sharply with the white pillowcase.

His head rolled to one side. A tortured sound came from his throat, escaping his lips in the low moan that Stacy had heard. Swiftly she moved to his side, pausing for a frightened second when she saw the perspiration beading his face. Again his head moved restlessly to the side.

Stacy realized with relief that he wasn't ill or fevered. He was dreaming, it was a nightmare. Lightly she laid a hand on his shoulder.

"Cord, wake up," she whispered softly. "You're

dreaming. Everything is all right. It's just a dream. Wake up!"

His face was twisted as if in pain. He shook his head as though trying to chase away the image that frightened him. Her hand tightened on his shoulder.

"Cord, wake up," she repeated.

Sooty lashes raised as Cord stared at her blankly. His fingers closed over the wrist of her hand resting on his shoulder. She could feel him trying to fight through the misty waves that still gripped his consciousness.

"Josh?" he frowned harshly. "Is he all right?"

"He's fine," she nodded, smiling to reassure him.

"Are you sure?" Cord lifted his head from the pillow.

"I'm positive," Stacy said. "I just looked in on him before I came downstairs. He's sound asleep."

Cord sank back against the pillow, breathing shakily. "My God!" he shuddered. "I had this nightmare."

His fingers were biting so tightly into her wrist that he was nearly cutting off the circulation. Stacy leaned against the bed, half sitting on the edge. With her free hand, she took a tissue from the bedside table and began wiping the perspiration from his forehead.

"It was only a dream," she repeated.

Cord sighed heavily. "He was in the swimming pool and he couldn't swim."

"You know that Josh swims like a fish," she chided him gently.

"I know, but this time he couldn't. I don't know why." Cord shook his head wearily and gazed into a dark corner of the room. "He kept crying for me to stop watching and save him. But I couldn't move. I—"

"Sssh!" She touched a fingertip to his lips and he turned to look at her. His dark eyes mirrored the tormenting anguish that consumed him. "Forget about the dream."

Cord loosened the grip on her wrist without releasing it.

With his other hand, he stilled the wiping motion of her free hand, making it rest along the hard line of his jaw.

Sighing heavily, he seemed to banish the last remnant of the nightmare.

As if he needed her nearness to keep it from coming back, he slowly slid his arms around her and pulled her down to his chest. Her head was nestled near the hollow of his throat.

"It was so real," he murmured, wrapping his arms around Stacy to hold her there.

"I know." There was a slight catch in her voice.

Beneath her head, she could feel the uneven thud of his heart. The cloud of dark, curling hair on his chest tickled her cheek. Her arm was curved across his chest, her hand resting on the silken hardness of a bare shoulder.

The heady male scent of him was heightened by the perspiration that had flowed through his pores at the peak of his nightmare. It filled her senses with sensual intoxication.

Her heart skipped several beats at the caressing warmth of his breath stirring her hair. Almost of its own volition, her hand began lightly exploring the smooth muscles of his shoulder and the strong column of his neck.

A large, well-shaped hand moved down her spine, drawing her closer to him. Then lazily it began rubbing the curve of her waist. A searing contentment swept through her and Stacy sighed. There was no barrier between them now.

Cord pressed his mouth against the side of her hair for an instant, then rubbed the roughness of his cheek against the silken strands.

"Sometimes," he murmured huskily, "I lie awake nights remembering how it was when you lay all soft and warm beside me."

He slid a hand beneath her thick chestnut hair, curling it gently on the side of her neck. His thumb moved in a rhythmic circle on the sensitive cord. Shivers of joy danced over her skin as her heart quickened its pace.

"I remember the clean fragrance of your hair." Cord nuzzled the side of her head. "And the way you trembled when I touched you, your breasts swelling hard in my hand. I can still see the golden glow of your warm skin when you lay naked beside me, waiting, your eyes shimmering like brown silk with the fire we'd kindled."

Stacy was trembling, the same liquid fire racing again through her veins. The seductive pitch of his voice was arousing more than just a memory. Her head was tipped back over the curve of his arm. Her lashes closed as Cord softly brushed his lips over her eyes, teasing the corners and kissing the gold dust of freckles over the bridge of her nose.

"And your lips." He tantalized their quivering moistness. "The taste of your mouth, like a honeyed nectar that drugs the senses and never satisfies the thirst. I would drink and drink and drink and come back for more."

A soft moan of aching desire rolled over her tongue, his words teasing and stimulating her until she thought her reeling mind would never be sober again. She felt the crook of his smile against her skin.

"Most of all I remember the catlike sounds you made in your throat. What I don't remember—" there was an amused tone of gentle mockery in his low voice as he slid a hand to the neckline of her robe "—is you wearing so much to bed."

"That's because it wasn't on long enough for you to notice," Stacy murmured with a sighing laugh.

Her fingers wound themselves into the raven thickness of his hair. With the slightest pressure, she ended the exquisite tortore of his teasing mouth. Her heart rocketed under the commanding hardness of his kiss.

His mouth opened over hers, tasting the sweetness of her lips before parting them to familiarly explore her mouth. Deftly Cord untied her robe and cast it to the floor.

The narrow strap of her nightgown left her smooth shoulders bare to his caress.

The passionate embrace was a catalyst that released all the pent-up longings they had held in check for so long. The intimate touch of his hands made her feel more alive than she had in ages.

The days, the months, the strain of being together yet apart fled on silver wings as Stacy gave herself up to the joy of the moment that transcended a mere physical response.

Twisting a handful of hair, Cord tipped her head farther back to expose her throat to the bruising ardor of his mouth.

Stacy shuddered as he moved inexorably closer to the shadowy cleft between her breasts and arched toward him. Her fingers dug deep into the hard flesh of his arms.

In the next second, Cord was pushing her away from him with a groan.

A bare foot touched the cool tile of the floor to keep her balance. Still quivering from his lovemaking, she gazed at him numbly, her eyes luminous and very soft.

"I love you, Cord."

Her voice trembled.

His breathing was labored, and Stacy knew he was shaken as she was. In the dim light, she could see the frown creasing his wide forehead.

His eyes were tightly closed as if trying to shut out the sight of her.

With a nearly inaudible moan she glided back to the broad chest, sliding her arms around his shoulders to cling to him.

But his hands closed punishingly over the soft flesh of her upper arms and shoved her away.

"Stacy, don't," Cord demanded in a tormented groan.

Her fingers trailed over the rigid muscles in his arms as they held her away. She made them take her weight in with effort to lessen the distance between them.

"I want you to hold me," she protested in an aching murmur. "Just hold me for a little while. It's been so long since I've had your arms around me or known your kisses."

"And what about the agony of an unfulfilled embrace?" he taunted in half-anger. "Don't torment us with that."

"You're wrong, darling," Stacy cried softly. "I can be satisfied with kisses. It's better than going without touching you or feeling you caress me."

"I know you better than that," Cord breathed. "We've spent too many nights together for me to forget that core of passion inside you. A touch—a kiss— isn't enough for either of us, not ultimately."

His words chilled her.

"What are you saying?" She frowned warily, almost afraid to hear his answer.

"That I don't accept crumbs," he answered crisply. "I would always be tasting the whole loaf and wanting it."

Stiffening, Stacy pulled away from his iron grip. "What about what I want? What I need?"

"Dammit, Stacy," he swore softly in frustration. His jaw was clenched, the line of his mouth grimly forbidding. "I can't come to you half a man."

Her chin quivered as she straightened away from the

bed. "So you won't come to me at all, is that it?" she accused tightly. "And I'm not supposed to touch you or kiss you no matter how much I want to, is that what you're saying?"

"What I'm saying," Cord snapped, "is that if you go without food long enough, you stop being hungry."

"Do you, Cord?" flashed Stacy. Her heart was nearly bursting with pain. "Or do you just die?"

A muscle leaped in his jaw. "Not entirely." He scowled and looked away from her, his gaze again seeking the dark recesses of the room. "Although I've wished for it." He rubbed a numb thigh with his hand. "I have learned how a wild animal feels when he's caught in a trap and can't escape."

"But you aren't going to be trapped forever," she retorted. "You will walk again. Why can't you accept that? Why can't you believe that?"

"And why can't you accept the possibility that I may never walk again?" Cord growled.

"If I did, then what? Do you expect us to go on the rest of our lives with you sleeping in one room and me in the other? Never touching? Never kissing? Never showing our love for each other?" she challenged.

"I expect you to understand," he snapped impatiently. "My God, don't you know what it's like? Don't you know what it is remembering what we once shared? Then you ask me to love with virtually half of my body dead. I would prefer endless nightmares to that."

"It isn't dead," Stacy protested angrily.

The faint glow from the night-light glistened over

the golden tan of his naked physique. Always leanly muscled, there was now a sinewy look about him, a result of the weight loss he had suffered.

Yet it didn't detract from his dark looks. He still possessed vitality, an aura of virility, a touch of aloof arrogance, a dozen other indefinable qualities that singled him out as something special.

One corner of his mouth lifted in a cynical sneer. "Are you denying that I can't use my legs?"

"You can't use them now, no, but—" she brushed the hair away from her face, helplessly searching for the words to put forth her argument "—that doesn't mean it will always be that way."

"And it doesn't mean that it won't," he countered.

"The therapist Bill is sending here—he wouldn't have her come if he didn't think she could help you. Don't you realize that?" Stacy pleaded in a desperate kind of anger.

Cord breathed in deeply, a brooding look in his dark eyes.

"Sometimes I have the feeling that I'm a human guinea pig. Or a jigsaw puzzle that was put together in the wrong order and now the pieces don't fit so they're trying to force them."

The weary despair in his voice touched her. Stacy couldn't help flinching at the strong undercurrent of monotonous pain that made his tone sound dull and flat.

"You mustn't feel that way," she protested.

"Why?" A dark eyebrow lifted in dry amusement.

"For nearly a year, I've listened to one person after another telling me how good my chances are that I'll walk again. I keep hearing it and hearing it, but I'm still either in a wheelchair or a bed. Hopeful words are wearing thin."

"Maybe the therapist will help," Stacy offered weakly.

"There goes another maybe," he laughed without humor. "Maybe the therapist. Maybe the operation," Cord mocked. "It will be another blind alley that the wheelchair will take me out of."

"But what's the alternative?" she protested. "Not to try at all? Don't you want to walk?"

"That's not the point." His mouth thinned grimly.

"Forgive me, but I don't understand." Stacy walked to the end of the bed, her fingers gripping the bedrail until her knuckles were white. "What is the point?"

"I'm tired of constantly having hope build up like air in a balloon, then watching it slowly deflate when it comes to nothing. Not just my own, but yours and Josh's, everyone's. I don't want you to be hurt anymore because of me." Cord stared at her for a long moment, a silent ache in his eyes. "I've seen it happen and I've seen the way you try to hide it so I won't see. But I do."

Stacy shook her head. "Forget about what it's doing to Josh and me. Look what it's doing to you!" she argued. "You've become hard and embittered. I can't even come near you anymore. You don't want me to touch you or kiss you. You just keep retreating farther and farther away, living in your own little world. It must be terribly lonely there. Maybe you're tired of fighting, tired of trying and failing—I don't know."

"You haven't listened to anything I've said," Cord declared irritably.

"I have," she nodded. "You're trying to tell me that the chances are you won't walk again. You want me to admit that. All right, I do." Anger was building inside her, an anger born because he persisted in looking at the negative side. "You're a cripple, Cord. A cripple! Do you hear?" Suddenly Stacy wanted to hurt him with words as he had hurt her. "You'll always be a cripple! If that's the way you want to look at life, that's the way I'll look at it, too!"

Moisture was dampening her cheeks, and Stacy realized she was crying. Her vision had blurred to the point where she could only make out a dim shape of him.

She caught back a sob of pain and pivoted sharply around.

"Stacy!"

But she was flying from the room, sobs wracking her body with each racing, stumbling step. In her room, she threw herself onto the bed, drowning her pillow with tears.

She had held them back for nearly a year, but now the deluge had begun.

The ravages of the storm were visible in her face the next morning. Maria clucked anxiously around her, certain the swollen eyes, red nose and pale complexion were the symptoms of a cold. Stacy insisted she was fine, but her gaze kept straying to the closed door of the master bedroom.

Only Josh shared the breakfast meal with her. Cord remained in his room. On her way out of the house, she paused at the door, wanting to go in and apologize yet not knowing what to say. Finally she walked out to meet Travis.

There was so much that had to be done in preparation for the annual quarter-horse sale the ranch held. Stacy wished she had broken the tradition and postponed it.

She was a trembling mass of nerves, unable to concentrate. She kept remembering the first sale she had organized for Cord. It had been that day—the day of the auction—when she had been on the verge of leaving that he had told her he loved her and asked her to marry him.

Finally Travis had told her he would take care of the rest of the duties and suggested that she take the morning off. Stacy couldn't bring herself to go back to the house.

She didn't want to face Cord until she had control of herself.

If anyone looked at her crooked, she felt she would burst into tears.

Not once had she broken down when she had learned of Cord's plane crash, nor during her flight to his side, nor during the harrowing hours and days after surgery. When he had regained consciousness, Stacy had rejoiced with laughter and warmth. Now it had all caught up with her and it seemed she couldn't stop crying.

A tear slipped from her lashes. She wiped it away with a shaking hand. Releasing a sobbing sigh, she turned away from the house and walked toward the stables.

Hank ambled forward to meet her, his sharp eyes missing nothing.

"Hi, Hank." Stacy greeted the man with forced brightness. "Would you saddle my mare for me? I thought that I'd take a ride and chase away some of the tension."

"Sure will," he agreed.

Minutes later he led the chocolate-brown mare from the stable, saddled and bridled and ready to go. The breeze stirred the horse's flaxen mane as it nosed Stacy affectionately.

With Hank holding the bridle, she stepped into the saddle and gathered the reins in her hand. Hank remained at the horse's head, his wizened face inspecting her.

"The boss don't like for you to go out ridin' by yourself," he said quietly.

"I promise I won't go far."

Stacy smiled, but her voice broke at the end of her sentence.

There was only one person that Hank ever referred to as the boss, and that was Cord. She touched her heels to the mare's flanks and reined it away before Hank saw the shimmer of tears in her eyes. The sorrel stallion in the stud pen whickered forlornly as she rode away.

CHAPTER FOUR

A TEXAS SPRING was impossible to ignore. After leaving the ranch buildings, Stacy had given the mare her head.

They cantered through the meadow where the brood mares with new colts were pastured. Colorful blossoms of bluebonnets, Mexican hats and prickly poppies nodded and bowed their heads as Stacy and the mare went by.

Bees buzzed from blossom to blossom while bright butterflies lazily flitted along.

The creak of saddle leather and the dull thud of cantering hooves were soothing sounds to Stacy's jangled nerves.

To the west were the mountains, once the stronghold of the Mescaleros. A dusty haze obscured them.

Although raised in the city, Stacy was still a country girl. The land rejuvenated her, especially this land where she lived with Cord. It was her home and she loved it.

She could ride for hours over its vast reaches and never tire of it.

Sighing, she reined the mare in and turned her

toward the ranchyard. Unfortunately she didn't have time for such indulgences. There were a hundred and one things to be done at the ranch today. Stacy decided she had better get them done while her eyes were dry and the pain in her chest had been reduced to a funny little ache.

Hank was waiting at the pasture gate to let her through.

She guessed he had been watching for her for some time, although it seemed she had barely left. His concern touched her.

"You see, I made it back all in one piece." Dimples appeared in her cheeks as she teased him affectionately.

"You shore took your time about comin' back," he declared with mock gruffness. He took hold of the mare's bridle and held her while Stacy dismounted. "I was about to send someone out to look for you when I saw you in the meadow."

"You're worse than a mother hen," she chided.

"Yeah, well, it'd be my back the boss would climb on if anything was to happen to you."

"What could happen riding Candy Bar?"

She handed the reins to him, patting the mare's neck.

"I was beginnin' to wonder that myself," Hank grumbled.

"Would you mind walking her out for me?" she asked.

At his agreeing nod, Stacy angled toward the ranch house sitting on a slight knoll above the other buildings. Josh was playing in the front yard. When he saw her coming, he hopped on his tricycle and rode down the graveled driveway to meet her, varooming all the way.

"Where have you been, mommy?" he asked as he wheeled along side of her.

"I went for a ride," she smiled into the darkly bright eyes.

Josh immediately scowled at her answer. "I wanted to go, too," he protested.

"Another time, maybe," she suggested.

"That's what you always say," he grumbled. "You'll forget, I know you will."

"How could I possibly forget you!" As they started up the knoll, Stacy slowed her steps as Josh's small legs pedaled harder to keep up.

"Will you play ball with me?" He glanced up at her quickly, the scowl leaving his face. His foot slipped off a pedal and he nearly rolled down the hill before Stacy could grab the handlebars. "You said you would," he reminded her.

"I can't now, Josh." She shook her chestnut hair in a rueful gesture. "I have work to do. Later, okay?"

"Promise?"

"I promise."

Stacy crossed her heart with her fingers and he was satisfied.

"I hit grounders best of anything," he told her importantly.

"I'll bet you do." She hid a smile and nodded. They

had reached the sidewalk to the house. "You stay outside and play until lunchtime, okay? But don't go out of the yard."

"Okay, mom."

The level sidewalk offered a perfect straightaway and Josh was already careening down it as he shouted his answer.

A faint smile played on her lips as she opened the front door.

Walking in, she turned to close it, darting a tenderly maternal glance at her son.

"It's about time you got back!" a harshly censorious voice growled behind her.

Her shoulders stiffened under the piercing regard of Cord's gaze, then slowly she turned to meet it. Her barely healed nerves were suddenly fraying again, disintegrating from the sharp undercurrents slicing the air.

Cord's wheelchair blocked the foyer entrance into the living room. A clenched jaw made his lean features taut and forbidding. His narrowed black gaze pinned her.

Somehow she managed to close the door.

"Were you looking for me?" she inquired with forced calm.

"I wasn't looking for you," he informed her in a steely voice. "I was listening to everyone else tell me how ill you looked."

His gaze raked her mercilessly, nearly stripping away the thin veneer of composure that she had attained. Her mouth tightened, guessing that Maria was the talebearer and wishing the woman had kept silent.

"I hardly think it was everyone," she murmured, avoiding direct contact with his gaze.

"First Maria, then Travis, then Bill," Cord enumerated tersely.

"Bill?"

Stacy frowned at the name.

"The good doctor telephoned a little while ago to let you know that this Hanson woman will be arriving here on Friday." The sarcastic explanation was snapped out.

"How did he know about me?"

Immediately she wished that she hadn't worded the question that way.

It was an admission that she hadn't been herself when she had risen this morning. Despite her embittered statements last night, Stacy didn't want Cord becoming concerned about her.

Because right now he needed to concentrate on his own recovery.

"Maria answered the telephone," Cord explained. "By the time I talked to him, he was more worried about where you were."

"I went for a ride."

Stacy flipped her long chestnut hair away from her neck, striving for a nonchalance that she just didn't feel.

"Alone."

The accusation was sharply hurled at her.

Her head jerked slightly. "Who told you?" Surely Hank wouldn't have.

The strong, male line of his mouth tightened grimly. "I saw you leave the stables." With suppressed violence, he swung the wheelchair around toward the living room. "Dammit, Stacy, you already know how I feel about you wandering out on the range by yourself!"

Stacy flinched. "Yes, Hank reminded me," she said in a low voice.

He pushed the chair a few feet into the room and stopped.

"Suppose your mare had fallen or you'd been thrown. Do you want me to start having nightmares about you lying unconscious in some remote place? Is that why you did it?" he challenged tightly.

"No." Stacy followed him, her hands clasped nervously together. "I had to get away for a while, to be by myself and think."

"Alone on a horse?" he jeered. "I didn't realize that was a necessity for thinking."

"You don't understand. I had to get away," she began desperately.

"No, I don't understand!" Cord interrupted. "If you wanted to be alone, you could have just as easily gone to your room. There would have been considerably less danger than riding alone."

"I couldn't stay in the house. Everything closed in around me. I had to get away from—" She stopped abruptly, glancing at him.

A sardonic eyebrow shot up.

"From me?" Cord finished the sentence for her.

Stacy hesitated, then admitted, "Yes, from you. Last night—"

She wanted to say that she had said some things that she regretted, but her tongue tied itself in knots over the words.

"What about last night?"

His dark head was tilted to one side at a watchful angle.

She couldn't meet his alert gaze and turned her back to him. Her stomach was twisted into knots. There was a throbbing pain in her temples as her poise began to splinter.

"I can't take many more of these bitter arguments. I need to get away from this brittle atmosphere—"

A sob rose in her throat and she had to stop to swallow it. She didn't want to break down in front of Cord again.

"I thought that was what this was leading up to," Cord declared, exhaling harshly. "I should probably be surprised that it's taken you so long."

Stacy pivoted to look at him blankly. The disgust etched in his drawn features nearly took her breath away.

A smoldering fire darkened his eyes to the shade of hard black diamonds, just as sharp and cutting.

"There's no need to look so puzzled," he mocked with contemptuous sarcasm. "Bill has already paved the way for you. Did you cry on his shoulder last night?"

"I don't know what you're talking about."

She frowned in genuine confusion.

"Don't you? Didn't you just say that you needed to get away?" he countered arrogantly.

"Yes, but—" Her shoulders moved bewilderedly.

"It was Bill's medical opinion, too, that you needed a few weeks' rest away from me and the ranch." Cord breathed in deeply, his chin thrust forth in challenge. "He seemed to think you were under too much stress. Your nerves were becoming strained, on the verge of collapse, he said."

Stacy opened her mouth, wanting to deny it, yet secretly she feared the same thing. At this moment, she was trembling badly and she couldn't make herself stop.

"It hasn't been easy for me," she murmured finally.

"Did you stage that outburst last night so I would be convinced when Bill talked to me today, knowing all the while that he would call?" Cord accused.

"No!" she gasped in wounded outrage.

"And you made certain this morning that others saw how upset you were," added Cord, totally ignoring her denial.

"You were the one who had the nightmare," Stacy reminded him indignantly. "You woke me—that's why I came to your room. And you were the one who started the entire argument with your stupid pride and self-pity, and your insistence that there mustn't be any physical contact between us. Did you expect me to just bow my head and say whatever you wish, my lord?" she flashed.

"Don't pretend with me, Stacy!" There was a savage

note in the controlled anger of his reply. "I should have known that it wouldn't last. I should have guessed why you kept clinging so desperately to the vain hope that I might walk again. I have to give you credit for trying."

"Pretend? Trying? What are you talking about?" she demanded, now thoroughly confused. "Everything I've said is the truth. I didn't ask Bill to tell you I should have a few weeks' rest. When he suggested it to me, I told him no."

Cord laughed coldly.

"Whatever you do, don't destroy the image of a loving wife," he mocked bitterly. "Be sure to twist things around and make it look as if you're the injured party."

"I never claimed to be the injured party," Stacy cried helplessly.

"Others will do it for you."

The grooves around his mouth deepened with cynicism.

"Why?"

"Out of sympathy because you're married to a cripple, a man who's become short-tempered and embittered," Cord replied.

"At least you admit that," she muttered beneath her breath.

"Yes, I admit that," he said grimly. "Why won't you admit that what I'm saying is true?"

"But I don't know what you are saying." There was a frustrated ring to her protesting cry.

"You've finally become bored with ranch life,

haven't you?" Cord studied her with freezing aloofness.

"What?" She was stunned.

"It wasn't so bad before the crash, was it?" he taunted. "We traveled around a great deal, a horse-buying trip or an odd weekend to shop. Josh kept you busy when he was a baby. And the ranch life was still a new experience for you at first. Then—" he reached down and gripped his leg, his mouth quirking "—the accident happened."

He lifted his gaze from the wheelchair to her. Stacy was so shocked by what he was implying that she couldn't speak.

She stared at him in disbelief.

"This past year, it's been different. You've been chained to either the ranch or the hospital," continued Cord. "Life has become tedious, with no side trips to break the monotony. You're bored. Being young, you want some excitement in your life. You want to see and do things, just have fun once in a while."

"My father took me all over the world with him," she protested, remembering her travels with him as a freelance photographer. "I've seen everything."

"Which makes it all the more understandable why you can't settle for the dull routine of a ranch, miles from any cosmopolitan center." For all the unemotional quality in his voice, the cold glare of his eyes was condemning. "You don't want to accept the possibility that I might be an invalid for the rest of my life because that would mean the boredom would never end. There wouldn't be any more quick trips, no vacations, no dancing, no fun. Just a lifetime of taking care of me."

"I don't mind," Stacy insisted.

"For how long?" he questioned arrogantly. "Right now you feel guilty about leaving me alone. That's why you've contrived this incident where someone else suggests that you go away for a rest. It wouldn't be your idea that way."

"I didn't do anything of the kind," she denied angrily, wondering how he could make such an accusation.

"Yes, you did, dammit. Now admit it," Cord snarled. "You think that if you leave me for a few weeks, it wouldn't be so bad when you come back. But in six months, you'll be bored again and want to leave for another 'short' respite. A couple of months after you come back from that, you'll want to go again until finally you won't want to come back at all."

"That's not true. This is my home!" Her temper flared at the continued injustice of his remarks. "You don't know what you're talking about!"

"Yes, I do!" He was virtually shouting now, his voice rolling like thunder over her. "You're forgetting my mother! She was accustomed to the luxuries of life the same as you were. She was pampered and spoiled. At first the roughness, the earthiness of ranch life appealed to the adventurous side of her nature, too, but she soon tired of it, and eventually she went back to the so-called civilized world."

"I'm not like your mother was!"

Stacy denied it vehemently, her brown eyes flashing.

"Aren't you?" he jeered. "I'll bet you didn't even intend to take Josh with you when you went on Bill's medically recommended vacation. You would leave him the same way my mother left me."

"I would not leave him! And I'm not going on any vacation!" she cried.

"You're damned right you're not!" Cord agreed savagely. "Because I'm not my father! I won't let you go. You're going to stay right here with me."

"I'm staying here of my own free will!" Stacy declared. "Not because you order me or command me to stay!"

His hands gripped the arms of the wheelchair, the muscles rippling in his forearms at the strangling hold. It was difficult to believe he wasn't able to get out of the chair and have those long strides of his carrying him to her side.

"You will stay here and be my wife." He gave no indication that he had heard what she said. "You will abide by the vows we made to each other. In sickness and in health."

"One of them we said wrong." Her voice was starting to break, an uncontrollable anger trembling on the edges. "It should have been for *bitter* or worse!"

Pivoting, Stacy would have run from the room. A small, dark-haired boy stood in the opening to the veranda.

His rounded eyes were black pools of agony as he gazed from the glowering face of his father to Stacy's whitened features.

The crushing silence lasted only a few seconds, but they were tortuous ones as both Stacy and Cord realized Josh had overheard their heated argument. Stacy recovered her wits first, taking a sharp step toward him.

Josh immediately started to retreat, half turning as if to run.

"Joshua!" Cord's commanding voice checked his flight. He darted a frightened look at his father. When Cord spoke again, the bite of anger was out of his voice. "Come here, Josh. It's all right." Although said calmly, it was no less imperative.

Josh hesitated, glancing at Stacy. "It's all right." She added her reassurance to Cord's and held out a hand to her son.

With obvious reluctance, he walked toward her, his feet dragging. The silken black head was tilted downward, but his troubled dark eyes warily watched both his parents, peering at them through thick curling lashes.

There was a scalding ache in Stacy's heart when he stopped cautiously in front of her, ignoring her outstretched hand.

Kneeling, she placed her trembling hands on his small shoulders. They were stiff and silently resistant to her touch.

"It's okay, Josh," she reassured him again in a shaky voice. "We were arguing, that's all. You've heard mommy and daddy quarrel before."

"You were yelling at each other," he accused, his lower lip jutting out slightly.

He could tell that this time it was different, more than a mere disagreement.

Nibbling at her lower lip, she glanced at Cord. His expression was grim, his mouth clamped shut in a tight line.

He had clasped his hands in his lap. They gripped each other with punishing fierceness.

'Y—Your daddy was upset with me," Stacy began, trying to give him an explanation he would understand.

It was difficult. The emotionally charged scene with Cord was still whirling in her mind.

The thousand tiny knife cuts inflicted by his words dulled her thinking.

"Why?" Josh prompted in an unconvinced tone.

"Because—I'd gone riding by myself." She smiled tightly, running a hand over the sleeve of his shirt, wanting to draw the little boy into her arms. "You see, daddy became upset because I might have fallen and got hurt. Since I was all by myself, no one would know. And sometimes, when you're very upset because you care about someone, you start yelling."

Josh looked at Cord out of the corner of his eye, seeking confirmation of her explanation. Cord breathed in deeply, relaxing the death grip of his hands.

"That's true, Josh," he agreed.

Turning back to Stacy, Josh inspected the brittle calm of her expression. A niggling uncertainty remained in his dark eyes.

"Are you going away, mommy?"

"Of course not." She quickly busied her hands, straightened the collar of his shirt. "Why, if I went away, who would tie your shoes?" she teased wanly.

"Daddy said you were," Josh reminded her.

"Daddy said—" she swallowed the lump in her throat "—that I was going to stay here with you and him forever and ever and ever. Because we're a family."

"Are you sure?" he blinked.

"I'm sure," Stacy nodded.

"Okay," Josh grinned in satisfaction.

"Say, I have an idea." She brushed a forefinger across the tip of his nose in play.

"What's that?" his eyes were again bright and clear as he cocked his head to the side curiously.

"Instead of waiting until this afternoon, why don't we play ball now?" she suggested.

"Yeah!" he breathed excitedly. "And daddy can come outside with us, too, huh?"

"Ask him," Stacy smiled stiffly.

There was a time when she could have answered for Cord. But after the things he had said to her, he seemed practically like a stranger. She didn't seem to know him at all.

Josh turned eagerly to Cord. "Will you come watch us, dad?"

"Yes," he agreed with a curt nod.

Straightening, Stacy ruffled the silky soft hair on top of her son's head.

"Go and find your bat and ball," she said. "We'll meet you outside in a few minutes."

Not needing a second invitaton, Josh was off with a rush. Stacy's gaze followed him, watching the doorway for several seconds after he had disappeared from view. Wearily she slid her fingers through her hair, lifting it away from her face, and turned to walk toward Cord.

She felt drained.

"I'll help you outside," she muttered, heading toward the back of his wheelchair.

As she drew alongside of him, his hand closed over her wrist to halt her. She glanced down, stoically meeting his hooded look.

"I owe you an apology," Cord said quietly. A new life started to flow in her veins, only to be aborted by his next statement. "You could have easily used Josh as a weapon against me, but you didn't."

Stacy twisted her wrist away from his hand. "That's a hateful thing to say," she accused in a choked voice. "He is *our* son, not mine or yours. I would never make him take sides."

"I did apologize for thinking it," he reminded her tautly.

"Lately I don't know you." She stared at him almost fearfully. "I feel as if I'm living with a stranger. I don't see how you can imagine for one minute that I feel about you or our home the way your mother did."

Cord studied her silently, his lips twisting cynically. "But you were the one who told me yourself that you couldn't take much more and that you needed to get away. I didn't imagine that."

"But—" The beginnings of another argument

formed on her tongue. Stacy paused and shook her head hopelessly. "Don't let's start this all over again."

"We won't," he stated. "I only want to remind you that you're my wife and I'm never letting you go."

Stacy bridled at the ring of possession in his voice. It was the same tone that had once thrilled her when it was spoken with love instead of ruthless determination. So much had changed.

"We'd better go outside." She stifled the urge to make a cutting retort and stepped behind his wheelchair. "Josh will be waiting for us." She pushed him toward the opened veranda doors.

CHAPTER FIVE

"MARIA." Stacy stepped into the kitchen, adjusting the wide-brimmed hat on her head.

"*Si.*" The plump Mexican woman was standing in front of the sink, washing the breakfast dishes. She glanced over a shoulder at Stacy without pausing in her work.

"I'm leaving now with Travis to check on the cattle the boys are moving to the summer range," she told the housekeeper. "I should be back shortly before lunch if anyone calls. Josh is playing out front."

"I will keep an eye on him," the older woman promised.

"Thanks, Maria." Stacy turned to leave, then pivoted back.

"Oh—Miss Hanson, the woman Dr. Buchanan has hired to help Cord, should be arriving sometime today. If she comes while I'm gone, you can put her things in the room down the hall from mine."

"I have it all aired and cleaned for her," Maria assured her.

"Good. I'll see you later." Stacy waved briefly and hurried down the hallway to the front door.

As she passed Cord's room, she heard the radio

playing, but she didn't stop to tell him she was leaving. If he wondered where she was, he could ask Maria.

The barrier between them was as solid and as cold as a polar ice cap. There wasn't a thaw in sight.

Cord's embittered accusations had wounded Stacy deeply. She wasn't able to discount them or shrug them aside.

It was impossible to ignore the things he had said by chalking them off to frustration; her feelings had been hurt too severely for that.

If he believed any portion of what he said, he couldn't possibly love her as she loved him. And that was the cruelest blow of all. Pride wouldn't let her go to him and try to undo the damage their heated argument had done.

Nor was she going to pretend that the traumatic scene had not taken place. If there was any tearing down of the barrier to be done, the first move would be made by Cord, not by her.

The music filtering through the closed door followed Stacy as she walked out the front door, stopping when she shut it securely behind her. It wasn't as easy to block out the haunting memory of Cord's unfounded accusations.

The pickup truck was parked in the driveway. Travis was kneeling beside the red tricycle on the sidewalk and Josh was beside him supervising the tightening of the handlebars.

Both had glanced up at the closing of the front door. Stacy forced the strained line of her mouth into a smile of greeting.

"If you start adjusting all of his toys to Josh's personal satisfaction, Travis, he'll never give you a minute's peace," she declared, teasing her son's near obsession for things to operate smoothly, a trait of his father's.

"I don't mind," Travis insisted with a slow smile, straightening to his full height. He ruffled the mop of shining black hair on Josh's head. "After all, a person can't steer a tricycle properly if there's too much play in the handlebars, right?"

"Right." Josh bobbed his head emphatically.

"It's no wonder he's becoming spoiled," Stacy sighed, but with loving indulgence. "Everyone on the ranch caters to him."

She glanced pointedly at her son. "Have you thanked Travis for fixing your tricycle? He wasn't obliged to do it."

White teeth bit into his lower lip as Josh cast a quick sideways look at the tall man. "Thank you, Travis," hurriedly expressing the gratitude prompted by her words.

"You're welcome," Travis rejoined.

Stacy breathed in deeply. "We'd better be going," she said to Travis. Then to Josh, "You behave yourself."

"Can't I come along?" he frowned.

"Not this time." She shook her dark head in a definite refusal. "And you stay right here in the house yard so Maria won't have to worry about where you are."

"Ah!" Josh grumbled, grimacing at the sidewalk.

"Travis said there were two new colts in the barn. Can't I even go down and see them?"

"No, you can wait until after lunch and we'll go down to see them together. In the meantime you stay here where Maria can keep an eye on you. Do you understand?" Stacy repeated.

"Yeah," he mumbled.

"Yes what?" She prompted a more respectful reply.

"Yes, ma'am, I'll stay here," was his unenthusiastic response.

"I'll be back around lunchtime," she told him, and walked toward the pickup truck with Travis following her.

"He's quite a boy," Travis commented as he slid behind the wheel.

"Yes, he is," Stacy agreed quietly with a note of pride in her voice.

At the starting of the engine, she waved goodbye to Josh. The sight of the small figure watching her leave made her heart ache afresh. For Cord to think she wanted to leave him because of his confinement was one thing, but for him to accuse her of wanting to leave their son as well was unforgivable.

Hopelessness slumped her shoulders. Her elbow rested on the threshold of the truck window, the knuckles of her hand pressed fiercely on her trembling lips. She stared out of the window, her mind registering nothing that her eyes saw.

"I wish you hadn't let Cord talk you out of getting away for a few days," said Travis after several minutes of silence.

"What?" Her head jerked toward him in surprise and confusion.

Briefly his dark gaze left the rutted track to meet her stunned look of question. "Josh told me about it while I was fixing his tricycle," he explained. "I filled the odd parts in myself."

"How . . . how much did he tell you?" Stacy faltered.

"That he overheard the two of you arguing the other day about your leaving." They were approaching a fence gate and Travis geared the truck down. "Josh said that Cord refused to let you go."

When his gaze again swung toward her, Stacy averted her head, unwilling to meet his discerning look. He was much too perceptive.

"I see," she murmured the noncommittal remark.

"This is one time you should have stood your ground, Stacy," he observed grimly. "You need a break from the pressure of the ranch and Cord. Everything in general."

Stacy had two options. One was to deny that she had been the one to suggest to Cord that she wanted to get away for a few days. But that would mean explaining how Josh had misunderstood the argument. The second choice was to let Travis believe that she had asked Cord and he had refused to agree to a short vacation. She chose the second, not wanting to discuss the real argument that was still so very painful.

"I suppose I should have." The deliberately indifferent agreement was offered as Travis braked the truck to a stop at the fence gate. Immediately she lifted the door handle. "I'll open it."

Hopping quickly from the cab of the truck, she walked to the gate, unlatched it and swung it open for Travis to drive through. When the rear of the truck had cleared the gate, she closed it securely and walked back to the passenger side. With her fingers crossed that the subject was ended, she climbed back into the truck. For nearly a mile, there was silence.

"You didn't ask Cord if you could go away for a few days, did you?"

Travis stared at the ranch road, a grimness about his mouth.

Out of the corner of her eye, Stacy studied him, the strongly etched profile and the silvery streak of hair visible beneath the band of his stetson hat. His perception was too acute. When his keen gaze swung to her, she looked away.

"What makes you say that?" She tried to sound casual.

"You've been too adamant about leaving Cord," he replied. "And if you had changed your mind, you can be as stubborn as he is. You wouldn't have let him dissuade you. That means Josh didn't understand the argument, did he?"

"Does anyone really understand arguments or how they get started?" Stacy responded ambiguously.

"Very seldom," Travis admitted. "Do you want to talk about it?"

Her shoulders lifted in a shrugging sigh. "Cord was just a little more unreasonable than usual, that's all."

"Was it his suggestion that you should leave?" he asked quietly.

"Something like that," she answered, again non-committally.

There was a frowning arch of a thick brow in her direction. "Don't tell me he gave in to a quixotic impulse that you should leave him permanently rather than be tied to a supposed invalid the rest of your life?"

"Actually—" her mouth twisted wryly "—he believed that that was what I felt and what I wanted. He was reminding me of our marriage vows—in sickness and in health," her own paraphrase slipped out, "for bitter or worse."

"I don't believe it!" The words came out in an explosion of disgust.

"Unfortunately, it's true," she murmured.

"How—" Travis began in controlled anger.

"Please," Stacy interrupted in a strained voice. "I really don't want to talk about it. It won't change anything."

"I could certainly go talk to Cord and straighten him out on a few facts," he declared through clenched teeth.

"No," she refused his suggestion immediately. "I shouldn't have told you about the argument."

"You didn't—Josh did."

"That's a fine point since I explained what it was really about," Stacy smiled ruefully. "I shouldn't have. Our personal problems are something that Cord and I will have to work out alone."

At the conclusion of her statement, they both lapsed into silence. It wasn't broken until they reached the noon holding ground for the cattle drive. Then their conversation was centered around the spring calf crop, the drive, the condition of the pastures and the water levels of the various wells.

When the main herd topped a distant crest, Stacy's mind wandered from the conversation between Travis and Ike, the trail boss. The dusty haze that obscured the cattle and their faint lowing held Stacy in the trip of nostalgic memories of other drives. She remembered the first drive when she and Cord had been virtually at war with each other.

After they were married, they had sentimentally spent at least one night on the trail during the drive. Sharing a bedroll, they had lain beside their camp fire isolated from the main campground. They had laughed and teased each other about that first drive when she had accused him of being an arrogant tyrant and he had declared her to be a pampered, spoiled city girl.

Closing her eyes, Stacy could remember the way their laughter and soft voices had inevitably faded into silence. For a few minutes they would simply gaze into each other's eyes. In the few seconds before Cord would draw her into his arms, the stars had always seemed to grow brighter, just as if they knew what was on the minds of the two lovers below.

They had been so close, spiritually and physically. An invisible knife twisted inside Stacy at the knowledge that they were further apart now than they had ever been.

Suddenly she wished she hadn't felt the necessity to personally check on the cattle drive. The bittersweet memories from previous ones were just too overwhelming.

Moving away from the windmill and its watering tank, Stacy joined the conversation between Travis and the trail boss, needing to lose herself in the present in order to forget the past. It was not an altogether successful attempt, she realized when Travis suggested some time later that they should be getting back to the ranch house. Her relief was too great.

Travis reversed the pickup onto the ranch road as the remuda vans arrived with fresh horses for the riders. During the drive back to the ranch house, Stacy felt his gaze dwelling on her several times. Yet, invariably when he spoke, the subject was only ranch business.

A small economy car was parked in the house driveway when they arrived. Stacy gazed at it curiously, not remembering for a brief instant that Paula Hanson, the physiotherapist, was expected today. There was an odd mixture of anxiety and hope that the woman was here.

"Do you suppose that's the therapist's car?" Travis stopped the pickup behind it.

"I imagine so," Stacy nodded. "I don't know of anyone else who was expected today."

Her hand gripped the door handle and hesitated before opening it. "Why don't you join us for dinner tonight, Travis?"

Brown eyes studied her thoughtfully. It wasn't uncommon for Travis to have dinner with them. Stacy had invited him often.

"What is Cord's attitude toward her?" He ignored her invitation for the moment.

She glanced at the door handle. There was no sense hiding the truth. Cord would be quick enough to tell it if the occasion arose.

"He's nearly convinced himself that it will be a waste of time." She was afraid Cord's opinion was more definite than that.

"So you want me to act as a buffer tonight?" There was an understanding quirk of his mouth.

"Something like that," Stacy smiled faintly. "I would like to make Miss Hanson's first night here as cordial as possible."

"She isn't married?" Travis questioned.

"No." Stacy shook her head negatively.

"Then I'll be there," he said, winking.

Despite his teasing inflection, there was a lack of any real interest in the woman's apparent eligibility. Stacy was reminded again of the heartbreak Travis concealed.

"Thanks." She opened the cab door and stepped out. "Is seven too early for you?"

"I can make it," he assured her as he shifted the truck into gear.

With a saluting wave of one finger, he pulled around the car and started toward the ranch buildings beyond the house. Stacy glanced at the lime-green economy car again and walked toward the house. Unconsciously she squared her shoulders as she walked through the front door.

In the living-room arch, she paused, staring at the

woman seated on the sofa. Her hair was ash blond and long, swept away from her forehead and secured at the nape of her neck with a knotted scarf in a blue silk print.

Slacks of azure blue covered her long legs. Cajun's graying muzzle was resting near the toe of her white sandals. A sleeveless knit top in the same shade of blue as her slacks revealed a set of wide shoulders. The woman's stature was definitely one that could be described as Junoesque.

"Well, Mrs. Harris?" Paula Hanson spoke clearly when Stacy's slow study was completed. "Do you think I can handle him?"

She smiled slowly, and the action suddenly made Stacy forget that the woman's features were too forceful. The line of her brow was too straight. There was a slight crook in her nose and her chin jutted out from a strong jaw.

But the smile brought an animation to the face, a smile that was without guile. Even the woman's blue eyes seemed to sparkle a bit.

"What?" Stacy asked, forgetting the question that had just been put to her.

Paula Hanson's expression immediately became serious again as she rose to her feet, confirming Stacy's estimation that she was tall.

"You are Mrs. Harris, aren't you?" She tipped her head to the side, an end of her silk print scarf trailing over one shoulder.

"Yes, I'm Stacy Harris," she asserted with a quick smile. She walked into the living room, extending a hand toward the woman. "You obviously are Paula Hanson. I'm sorry I wasn't able to be here when you arrived."

"It's all right, I understand." Long fingers firmly clasped Stacy's hand in greeting. "Maria—that is your housekeeper's name, isn't it—showed me my room and helped me settle in. She indicated that you would be back for lunch."

"I hope everything is all right." But Stacy had noticed the omission of any reference to Cord. Hadn't they met yet?

"It's fine," Paula insisted.

She sat back on the sofa and reached for a glass filled with red liquid and ice cubes that was sitting on an end table. "Tomato juice with a dash of tabasco," she identified the contents with dry amusement in her voice. "Maria wanted to fix me something stronger, but I didn't want you to think you suddenly had a lush living in your home."

Stacy's smile became genuine and relaxed, her faint wariness toward the stranger leaving. "You're welcome to something stronger if you like," she assured her.

"Do you think I'll need it?" she asked Stacy.

A straight brow arched slightly as Paula's gaze swung pointedly in the general direction of the master bedroom.

"You haven't met—" Stacy breathed in deeply "—my husband yet, have you?"

"No." Her gaze ricocheted from Stacy to study the clear cubes in her glass. "I have the feeling that he would like to ignore me as if I were a bad dream, in the hopes that I'll go away."

Stacy didn't attempt to deny the comment. "He is aware that you have arrived, isn't he?"

"Oh, yes," the physiotherapist confirmed. "Maria knocked on his door and told him, but he was somewhat unexcited about the news."

"I'm sorry—"

"There's no need to apologize," Paula Hanson hastened to interrupt. "Bill—Dr. Buchanan—explained the situation. Believe me, it's nothing I haven't encountered before."

Stacy turned. "I'll see if he'll join us for lunch."

"Don't bother on my account," the woman shrugged indifferently and sipped at the tomato juice. "He has to come out of the room sooner or later."

Looking over her shoulder at the blond-haired woman, Stacy felt confused by her attitude of unconcern and disinterest toward her patient.

"I thought you would want to meet Cord as soon as possible," she explained.

"There's time enough to beard the lion without doing it on an empty stomach," Paula Hanson declared dryly. "I tend to speak very bluntly, Mrs. Harris. So I don't intend to offend you when I say that all I've learned so far about your husband makes me believe that he'll be an abominable patient. I don't mind putting off meeting him for a few hours."

"I think you might be right." Stacy's lips twitched with amusement as she pivoted back toward the woman.

How long had it been since she had found humor in the situation? A very long time, if ever, she was sure. She had the feeling that she needed Paula Hanson's caustic wit as much as Cord needed her professional help.

"And please, call me Stacy," she added.

"Thank you, I will." The blonde leaned over and scratched behind the ears of the German shepherd lying near her feet. "And what would be this fellow's name?"

"Cajun." At the sound of his name coming from his mistress's lips, the dog thumped his tail against the floor and gazed adoringly at Stacy. "He seems to like you," she observed.

Again there was the dry curve of Paula Hanson's mouth. "All manner of beasts end up liking me."

The innuendo to Cord was not missed by Stacy. It was also a prophetic-sounding statement that she hoped would come true. Now that she had met Paula Hanson, Stacy didn't feel any of the jealousy that had been her initial reaction. Already the physiotherapist was like a breath of fresh air in a house that had become stagnant with bitterness.

Maria's plump figure rolled into the living room. "Lunch will be ready in a few minutes," she announced.

"Thank you," Stacy smiled, then glanced toward the dining room. "Where's Josh? Have you called him to wash yet?"

"He is outside. I fixed him a picnic lunch," the housekeeper explained. "What about Mister Cord? Is he coming to the table or should I fix him a tray?"

"You'll have to ask him. I haven't spoken to him since I came back," Stacy answered.

As the housekeeper's rolling walk carried her toward the master bedroom, Stacy turned to the blonde sitting on the sofa. "It might be a good thing that I made it back for lunch or you could have been eating your first meal here alone. Have you met our son, Josh, yet?"

Paula Hanson nodded that she had. "He was playing outside when I drove in. That boy is going to be breaking women's hearts when he grows up. I like almost all children, but he's a real charmer."

"Like his father was." The smile suddenly faded from Stacy's lips as she realized she had used the past tense. But it had been a very long time since Cord had been charming about or toward anything.

"My specialty is ill-tempered brutes. I'm accustomed to them snarling instead of charming, so don't feel self-conscious about the fact, Mrs. H— Stacy," Paula Hanson corrected. "It's my job, I hope, to change them back to what they were."

Stacy couldn't respond to that. Too many of her prayers were riding on those same thoughts. Instead she smiled weakly in acknowledgement of the comment.

"Would you excuse me, Miss Hanson?" she apologized, expressively rubbing her hands together. "I'm dusty from the drive. I'll have a wash and join you at the table in a few minutes."

"Fine," the blonde agreed.

Stacy was climbing the stairs to her room when Maria stepped out of the master bedroom, closing the door behind her. Stacy didn't pause to ask if Cord was joining them for lunch.

As Paula had said, he was trying to ignore the physiotherapist's presence in the house, and the best way to do that was to remain in his room. Stacy sighed at his stubbornness.

CHAPTER SIX

As she started down the steps to rejoin Paula Hanson, Stacy saw the back of Cord's wheelchair as it disappeared into the dining room, and she paused in surprise. She had been certain he would insist on having a lunch tray in his room. Her heart quickened at the thought that he might have changed his mind about the new therapy.

Hurrying down the stairs, she entered the living room as Cord wheeled his chair into the dining room. He stopped just inside the archway, obviously gazing at the blonde. For some reason Stacy hesitated for a moment, wanting to witness the meeting unseen. Unconsciously she held her breath, able to see his carved profile.

"So you're the miracle worker," he commented in a low, cynically mocking tone. His skepticism hadn't relented an inch and Stacy's bubble of hope was pricked.

"So you're the cripple," Paula Hanson returned the dry challenge.

Cord's nostrils flared whitely. "That's right," he agreed sharply. "And I'm lucky to remain one, so you might as well plan on leaving."

"One of the advantages of my position," Paula replied smoothly, "is that once I'm assigned to a case, only the doctor in charge tells me when to leave. I don't take orders from you, Mr. Harris. In fact, the opposite is true. You take orders from me."

"Like hell I will!" A muscle was jumping along his jaw.

"Oh, you will," the blonde assured him in a silky voice. "You see, your muscles are weak from sitting all day in a wheelchair, whereas I'm as strong as a horse. Plus I'm mobile and you're crippled. So if you don't obey orders, I'll make you."

"I doubt that," he jeered.

"I've tossed around bigger men than you," she said with a shrugging inflection.

Cord tipped his head to one side, raven black hair gleaming in the light. "I wouldn't think that would be something a woman would brag about." There was sarcastic emphasis on her gender. "Is it a defense mechanism because you haven't got what it takes to attract a man?"

"Cord!" Stacy was aghast that he could be so cruelly insulting. Paula Hanson was an attractive woman. She rushed into the dining room, stunned also that he was so lacking in manners as to be rude to a guest in their home. Her gaze swerved apologetically to Paula Hanson. "I'm sorry, Miss Hanson."

"Don't be." The blonde showed no sign that the barbed comment had stung. "I've received more cutting insults than his made by children. His words only reveal his own fear of being unable to attract the opposite sex when he's confined to a wheelchair."

"You're insolent!" Cord snapped savagely.

"I'm impertinent and sassy, too!" Paula returned quickly, yet showing no sign of anger. "So it won't do you any good to try to browbeat me because I'll give it back just as fast as I get it."

The line of his mouth thinned forbiddingly. "You're fired!"

"You've forgotten something—you can't fire me. I don't work for you, I work for Dr. Buchanan," she reminded him.

"You've overlooked one fact," Cord responded with grim complacency. "All I have to do is discharge Bill from the case to get rid of you."

"Stop it!" Stacy protested angrily. "How can you throw away this chance simply because your stupid pride has got in the way, Cord?"

With a violent push, he propelled the chair away from Stacy toward the table.

"When are you going to admit that this whole therapy thing is a waste of time?" he demanded beneath his breath.

"When did time become such a valuable commodity?" Fire flashed in her brown eyes. "All you do all day is sit in your chair and watch the second hand move on your wristwatch. Since you haven't anything better to do, you might as well try the therapy. You certainly don't have anything to lose."

"That's a valid point, Mr. Harris," Paula inserted as Cord glared at Stacy. "Although I doubt that you have the guts to admit it. But take your time about thinking it over. I don't object to spending a few days' paid vacation in your home while you do. Eventually I get bored doing nothing, though, don't you?" she challenged with arching sweetness.

"Don't try to put words in my mouth," warned Cord.

"If I did, I'd make you eat them," the blonde shrugged.

He pivoted the wheelchair toward Stacy.

"Get her out of here," he growled. "I've gone through enough hell without enduring a pain in the neck like her."

Outraged by his statement, Stacy stared at him in disbelief. But Paula only laughed at his derogatory comment.

"Haven't you learned that it doesn't do any good to lose your temper? Your wife or I might find it and give it back to you tenfold."

"One more remark out of you and I'll throw you out of this house myself!" Cord muttered.

Paula was standing several feet to the side. She walked to a point two feet in front of his wheelchair and placed her hands on her hips. Five foot eight in her stockinged feet, she towered above him.

"Why don't you do that, Mr. Harris?" she said in an agreeing voice. "Why don't you get out of that wheelchair and do it? *If* you think you're man enough?" His hands gripped the arms of the metal chair in impotent rage. "But you can't, can you?" she smiled slowly.

The harsh line of his mouth was compressed tightly, a black rage spreading over his dark features. He wheeled the chair around and rolled it toward the green telephone on the bureau.

"Don't bother to telephone Dr. Buchanan," Paula said quietly as he picked up the receiver. "If you take him off the case now, your wife can simply hire him back with the claim that you aren't capable of making the decision yourself. You're stuck with me, Mr. Harris."

Cord glared at Stacy, daring her to take sides against him. "I would do it, Cord," she stated emphatically.

He slammed the receiver back in its cradle. "I should have known I could not trust you," he snapped at Stacy.

"Look at it this way, Mr. Harris," Paula reasoned. "If after a few weeks of therapy, you're able to get out of that wheelchair, think of the satisfaction you'll have in throwing me out. Surely that's something you can look forward to?"

"It would be a joy," Cord declared through clenched teeth.

"Good. That's settled," the blonde nodded, and walked toward the table. "Now why don't you run along to your room like a good little boy? A meal always tastes better when there isn't a pouty child at the table."

"I'll be damned if I will," he breathed harshly.

"You'll have to behave if you stay here." Her mouth quirked in a mocking smile. "Remember, I'm the one who's boss and you're the one who takes orders."

Stacy watched Cord's blazing dark eyes bore into the tall blonde, but Paula's serenely challenging composure didn't falter one whit. After crackling seconds, he propelled the chair angrily from the room. Stacy wasn't deceived that he was obeying the order. He was simply leaving before he gave in to the urge to kill.

"Whew!" Paula breathed with a silent laugh when he was out of hearing. "I thought I was going to need a whip and chair there at the last to keep him at bay. He's a hell of a man."

The long clump of ash-blond hair brushed back and forth between her shoulder blades as she shook her head in respectful admiration.

A lump entered Stacy's throat as she gazed at the point where Cord had disappeared. "He was," she murmured in quiet agreement.

The rude, embittered man was not the same one she had married, nor even the arrogant, mocking tyrant that she had first met.

"Not was," Paula corrected. "He is a hell of a man. My problem is to channel all that ferocity and spirit into the exercises."

Sighing, she pulled out a chair and sat down at the table. "There went my resolve to stop falling in love with my patients."

Stacy stared at her incredulously. "I beg your pardon?" She couldn't have heard correctly.

Round blue eyes returned her look. "You might as well know it up front that I end up falling in love with my patients. I just can't keep from getting involved with them. Admittedly—" an impish light entered her eyes "—most of them haven't entered their teens yet. So my feelings have seldom been reciprocated except on the most platonic level. Considering everything your husband has to offer, I know I won't be immune to him." Paula paused, tipping her head to one side. "Do you want to reconsider taking me off the case, Stacy? I'll understand if you do. I would certainly be jealous of any woman who came near him if he was my husband. Not that I'll ever make a fool of myself and let him see the way I feel."

Stacy's mind ran through a whole gamut of thoughts as she hesitated before answering. There was admiration for the blonde's honesty, the knowledge that she instinctively liked Paula, and confidence that she had the ability to help Cord.

Also, there was the fear that Cord might fall in love with her. Patients had fallen in love with their nurses before and Stacy was not secure anymore, not after the last few weeks.

"No, I won't reconsider," she said finally, refusing to give into the selfish fear. "I want you to stay."

"I'm glad you thought about that before answering," Paula stated decisively. "Because I'm going to need your trust as much as I need his. I don't want to divide my energies by fighting for it from the two of you."

"Don't worry," Stacy smiled faintly. "Besides, I've

invited our foreman to dinner tonight. He happens to be a tall, dark and handsome bachelor. Maybe we can channel your emotions to him instead of Cord."

"That's an idea," Paula laughed good-naturedly. "Ah, here comes Maria with lunch," she said, glancing up as the housekeeper came from the kitchen. "I'm afraid that as well as being as strong as a horse, I also have the appetite of one."

True to her word, Paula cleaned her plate with the gusto of one who enjoys good food. Josh wandered into the dining room a few minutes before Maria served a fresh fruit with cheese dessert and succeeded in wheedling a second helping from the housekeeper.

"You promised to take me to see the baby colts, mom," he reminded Stacy between spoonfuls.

"As soon as we have all finished with lunch," she agreed.

"Would you like to come too, Paula?" he asked brightly. "They've just been borned."

"The colts were just born," Stacy corrected his grammar.

"That's what I said." He looked at her blankly.

"And did you ask Miss Hanson's permission to call her by her first name?" Stacy inserted.

"She said I could," he nodded, and glanced at the blonde for confirmation.

"I did tell him he could."

The slow smile spread across Paula's strong features again.

"I'm accused often enough about being an old maid

without a little boy calling me Miss Hanson. Please, you call me Paula, too, Stacy."

"You're welcome to come to the stables with us if you would like to," Stacy repeated Josh's offer.

"I would like to," she agreed. "I'm a native-born Texan, but the truth is I've never been on an honest-to-goodness ranch before. A few ranch-type farms, but nothing ever of this size."

"Josh and I will give you a grand tour, won't we, Josh?"

"You bet!" His bowl was scraped clean. He let the spoon clatter on the bottom as he hopped from the chair. "We can show you everything. We've got sheep and goats and horses and cattle and— Can you ride?" He interrupted his list with a quick question.

"Sorry, I don't know the front of a horse from the back." The blonde lifted her hands palm upward, hiding her smile at his excitement.

"The back is where the tail is," he frowned at her ignorance.

"You'll have to show me." Paula offered him her hand and he grasped it immediately, eager to be off on the tour of the ranch.

"At a walk, though, Josh. I'm not as young as you are."

"You two go ahead." Stacy waved them on. "I want to have a word with Maria. I'll meet you outside in a few minutes."

During the tour of the ranch, Paula continually expressed her amazement at the size of the operation.

Seeing it through a stranger's eyes, Stacy was actually a little stunned by it herself. She had become so familiar with it over the years that she had taken it for granted.

"You're really in charge of all this?" Paula queried again as she paused on the rise leading to the house. She looked back at the ranch property sweeping endlessly to the horizon.

"Yes." Stacy smiled, bemused by the fact, as well. "With Travis McCrea, our foreman. I'm not so foolish that I think I could run it without his help."

"I didn't mean anything chauvinistic by that remark," the blonde hastened. "There isn't any reason why a woman isn't just as capable as a man of operating a ranch. I was just wondering what your husband's reaction is to it."

"Cord's?" Stacy frowned in faint bewilderment. "I'm not sure I know what you mean."

"I was thinking it must have deflated his ego a bit to have everything running so smoothly without him. As proud and independent as he is, I bet he wished it had fallen apart—secretly at least."

Her thoughtful gaze swung to Stacy, a questioning light blue. "Or has he taken part in some of the decisions?"

Remembering how Cord had accused her of patronizing him, Stacy shook her head and looked away. "Travis and I have tried to involve him in the running of the ranch, but he refused to take any interest."

"I see," Paula mused absently.

"Aren't you coming?"

Josh was waiting impatiently at the sidewalk, anxious to enter the house and have the afternoon snack of milk and cookies he knew Maria would have ready for him.

"I appreciate your taking the time to show me around," said Paula as they jointly turned to accompany Josh into the house. "It was a revelation for me. I hope it didn't interfere too much with your schedule?"

"It didn't," Stacy assured her. "The heat of the afternoon I generally spend in the office doing the book work after devoting a couple of hours to Josh." She glanced at her watch as Paula opened the front door. "I still have time to do the biggest share of the book work before dinner. Incidentally, I've asked Travis to come at seven and Maria is planning dinner for seven-thirty."

"While you're working, I can take all the time I need to get ready for dinner and—" the blonde laughed with self-mockery "—I hope, impress your bachelor foreman tonight!"

The door to the master bedroom was ajar. As Stacy was about to respond to Paula's comment, Cord's voice barked her name.

"Stacy!"

In the rolling arc of her gaze to Stacy, Paula's blue eyes seemed to say that the beast had roared a summons for her presence at his throne. It was an expressively mocking look that made Stacy smile.

"Excuse me. I'll see you later, Paula," she murmured, and moved toward the partially opened door.

"Where have you been?" Cord demanded when she entered the room.

"Josh wanted to see the new colts after lunch. And since Miss Hanson had never been on a working ranch before, I took her on a tour." It was difficult to reply calmly and keep the edge of temper from showing at his peremptory tone.

"That viper-tongued witch!" he jeered.

"She was no more rude and insulting than you were," Stacy reminded him sharply. "If you'd seen her this afternoon with Josh, you would know how terribly you misjudged her. She was completely at ease with him, more natural than a lot of parents are with their own children. Miss Hanson knows exactly how to handle children."

"Is that some snide endorsement of her ability to handle me?" he asked. His mouth thinned sardonically.

"It wasn't," Stacy flashed. "But I won't deny that you behaved like a boorish brat this noon. You deserved to be put down."

"You made it very clear earlier that you'd sided against me." His gaze narrowed with piercing censure. "Is this your way of taking revenge because I won't allow you to go away?"

"Why do you have to be so unreasonable?" she protested bitterly. "It wasn't a question of taking sides—I was doing what I believed was right for you.

That was my only motive." She avoided the battleground of disclaiming she had ever suggested she wanted to go away.

"Since it's my life and my body, I should have some decision in what's done with it," declared Cord. "Not you."

"As long as your life affects mine and Josh's, I do have a right," Stacy asserted.

"I didn't realize you were so bored with your life here that you would welcome the company of that blond viper."

He wheeled his chair to the window and apparently unable to find a valid argument to her comment, he had altered the subject instead.

"I'm too busy to be bored. Tired, yes, but not bored," she sighed. "Miss Hanson is a working guest, but she still is a guest in our home. I'd like you to remember that tonight at dinner and treat her accordingly."

"Do you mean she gave me permission to come to the table?"

Cord glanced over his right shoulder, a contemptuous lift to a black brow. "Am *I* supposed to feel honored that she's willing to endure my presence at the table? Or grateful that she didn't order me to stay in my room without supper?"

His fingers ground into the arm of the chair. "That woman really has gall, ordering me around in my own home!"

"She would have to have gall to stand up to you,"

Stacy returned. "I don't want to quarrel about this with you anymore—I have more constructive things to do with my time. I've invited Travis to dinner tonight. He'll be here around seven."

"What did you do?" Cord breathed contemptuously. "Turn tonight's meal into a dinner party for that witch? Why didn't you roll out the red carpet and hire a brass band?"

"Her name is Paula Hanson," she corrected tightly. "Would you please remember that? And it isn't exactly a dinner party. I hope it will be just a cordial evening without any embarrassing scenes."

"Now I embarrass you." There was scorning amusement in his voice. "What comes next, Stacy? Will you become sick of the sight of me?"

"For heaven's sake, Cord!" she exclaimed in disgust. "Don't twist everything I say. I only meant that I didn't want you hurling any more insults at Miss Hanson during dinner this evening."

"Is that why you invited Travis?" he mocked. "Is he to provide Miss Hanson—" stressing her proper name sarcastically "—with some male companionship or to keep the conversation on safe topics?"

"Both, I hope," Stacy agreed.

For an instant, there was silence.

Then Cord sighed wearily, all of the sarcasm and bitterness seeming to flow out of him. He rubbed the back of his neck for several seconds.

"I didn't call you in here to taunt you, Stacy," he muttered thickly. "I don't even know how it got started. I lash out at everyone these days."

"Why did you call me?" she asked, trying to adjust to the change in the atmosphere.

"I was worried about you. You were gone longer than I thought you would be and Maria said Josh was with you. I—"

Cord hesitated, still staring out the window. "Don't worry about tonight. I'll be pleasant to your miracle worker."

"Thank you, Cord," Stacy murmured, biting her lip at the cynical tone of his voice. "If you need me, I'll be in the study. I have some book work to do before dinner."

The congenial atmosphere that dominated the evening meal was a welcome change from the taut, uneasy silences of previous ones.

It was due in part to the immediate rapport between Travis and Paula, an instant and mutual liking and respect for each other.

The polite phrases of two strangers meeting were bypassed, eliminating the tension of a getting-acquainted period.

Conversation at the dinner table was centered mainly between Travis and Paula, with Stacy joining in frequently. Paula's brief tour of the ranch that afternoon had whetted her curiosity to learn more about the workings of the ranch and especially the cattle drive being carried out. Travis obligingly explained it to her.

Cord, who had grown to detest any discussion of the ranch operation, exhibited commendable restraint and remained silent during much of the dinner. Covertly

Stacy studied his expression, trying to discern some small crack in his mask of indifference. Nothing revealed that he listened as eagerly as Paula did to the activities going on now.

There didn't seem to be a glimmer of interest. Cord was keeping to his promise to be pleasant this evening. More than that Stacy couldn't read into his silence no matter how much she wanted to try.

She attempted to feel grateful that he wasn't sniping away at the blond physiotherapist, but there wasn't much comfort in that. Stacy was becoming as difficult to satisfy as Cord. She sighed inwardly as Maria cleared the dessert dishes and brought in the coffee.

A cup was set in front of Cord.

"No!" he sputtered. The word seemed to explode from him, almost involuntarily. With suppressed violence he pushed his chair away from the table. Controlling the faint snarl in his voice with an effort, he muttered, "I'll have my coffee on the veranda, Maria."

He did not invite anyone to join him as he wheeled his chair toward the sliding glass doors. The omission was too blatant for any of them to miss.

Paula made a slight face and murmured, "Why didn't he come right out and say he didn't want our company? I could have taken the hint."

Travis chuckled softly at her dry wit. Stacy smiled stiffly. There was no point in apologizing to them or making excuses for Cord's behavior. Yet something inside her wouldn't let him exile himself to the veranda alone.

Glancing at Maria, who was setting Cord's cup back on the tray, Stacy said, "I'll have my coffee on the veranda, too, Maria." Briefly she nodded to Travis and Paula, "Excuse me," she said, and rose from her chair.

CHAPTER SEVEN

THE NIGHT AIR WAS SULTRY from the afternoon's heat. The starfire shimmering from the sky cast soft shadows on the whitewashed arches of the veranda.

Cord murmured a terse "thank you" when Maria set the tray on a table near his wheelchair. His gaze riveted itself on the two cups sitting on the tray, recognizing the significance of them and knowing he wasn't alone.

Stacy paused behind him, feeling the invisible crackle of electricity in the still air. Her heels clicked loudly on the cobblestones as she ignored his silent demand to leave and walked to a chaise longue beside him.

"What are you doing out here?" he muttered impatiently, then continued without allowing her an opportunity to reply. "If you've come to tell me that I've rudely left our guests, you can save your breath." His voice curled sarcastically around the word "guests." "If I'd stayed inside, I doubt if I would have kept my promise. So be grateful for a small show of bad manners."

"I am." Stacy leaned back in her chair and sipped at her coffee, refusing to respond to his baiting tone.

The starlight glittered over the tightly clenched line of his jaw. "Shouldn't you go back inside with our guests?" There was a savage undercurrent in his biting mockery. "One of us should be in there to entertain them."

"Travis isn't exactly a guest," she replied evenly. "He can keep Paula company for a while."

"You make it sound as if he's practically a member of the family instead of the foreman," Cord jeered with disdain.

"I guess I do think of him in that way," Stacy admitted. "I don't believe you realize how much help he's been to us through all this."

"To you, you mean," he corrected. His mouth quirked bitterly. "Do you confide all your troubles to him and cry on his shoulder?"

"I don't cry on anyone's shoulder."

She was too independent to do that and she knew it, even if at times she wanted to pour out her troubles to someone. "The help I referred to that Travis had given us was shouldering the bulk of the ranch operation. I didn't mean help that he had personally given me," she explained.

Travis's knowledge of her problems was gleaned from what he had witnessed or guessed and not from any confessions from Stacy, regardless of Cord's accusation to the contrary.

"And you're so grateful for his assistance that you've left him in the house alone with that barracuda," Cord jeered.

Stacy breathed in deeply, fighting to control the spark of temper before it burst into flame. He seemed determined to incite an argument and she was just as determined not to oblige.

"Cord, I came out here for some fresh air," she said slowly and distinctly, "certainly not to become embroiled in a bitter dispute with you. If you don't want to enjoy the peace and quiet, then I'll move to another part of the veranda where I can."

His cup clinked loudly in its saucer. Stacy's heart thudded rapidly in the heavy silence that followed. It was not a desire for fresh air that had brought her outdoors but the sensation that Cord had wanted her company. She wanted his, but not if it meant arguing. She had endured all the embittered and angry exchanges that she could stand for one day.

Gradually the prickles at the back of her neck eased and Stacy relaxed, resting her head against the back of the chair cushion. Miles away, a coyote yipped. The sound echoed clearly to her ears.

Her thoughts drifted to the cattle drive as she gazed at the stardust sky. Somewhere out there a night rider was watching over the herd, taking his turn while others slept in bedrolls around the campfire. A lump entered her throat as Stacy remembered again the nights she and Cord had camped out.

Eager to rid her mind of the haunting image, she focused her attention on the mechanics of the drive and Travis's recounting of the drive's success so far this year. It had been almost unbelievably smooth and without incident.

"It's a relief that the cattle drive is going so well." The absent comment was out before Stacy realized that it was her voice that had broken the silence.

Darting a quick, sideways glance at Cord, she held her breath. There wasn't any tightness to his smooth jawline that was usually present whenever any mention of the ranch's operation was made in his hearing.

He appeared relaxed and calm as he gazed heavenward at the stars.

The tensing of her nerves eased. Stacy decided he hadn't heard her inadvertent remark and breathed a silent sigh of relief. She let her gaze swing back to the stars.

"I can almost smell the smoke from the camp fire," Cord murmured softly.

The starlight seemed to glow more brilliantly, filling her brown eyes with hopeful light as his warm voice rolled caressingly over her. Hesitantly she glanced at him, wondered if he, too, was remembering the nights they had spent alone on the trail. The affirmative answer was in the glittering darkness of his gaze on her face.

No words were spoken as they gazed at each other. Sometime during the eternity of seconds, his wheelchair glided silently to the side of her chair. Stacy wasn't aware of its actual movement. She wasn't certain that Cord knew he had done it.

He was simply there, near enough that she could have touched him with only the slightest movement of her hand. But she didn't. His previous rejections of any physical contact with her were too painfully branded in her heart. Any touch or caress would come first from Cord or not at all.

As he remained motionless for several more seconds, Stacy quivered with the aching longing to be in his arms. He leaned forward, his hands clasping her rib cage to draw her toward him. She didn't need the assistance to move to the hard male line of his descending mouth.

The searing possession of his kiss burned the softness of her lips. Fire rocketed through her veins as she responded to his hungry demand. Her hands cupped the powerful line of his jaw, hard and firm beneath her fingers.

Too soon, his hands were decisively but slowly pushing her away from him. Her own hands retained the shape of his face, suspended in air, as Cord set her back in her chair. Unwillingly her lashes fluttered open. His eyes were black, fathomless pools of torture.

"Stacy, my life," Cord whispered with agony. "What am I doing? I'm destroying both of us. For bitter or worse, you said. But how much more bitter can either of us take?"

He turned away, his profile hardening into an unrelenting silhouette in the starlight. "God help me, I can't let you go. I'll never let you go!"

"Cord, I don't want to go," she murmured huskily. "I only want you to stop shutting me out. I want to share in your life."

A dark eyebrow arched with bitter cynicism. "I can't

share. What is there for me to share? My wheelchair?
It's my prison." His mouth twisted in sardonic
amusement. "The wheelchair is my prison, yet I'm
your jailer. I'll never let you go free."

"I don't want to be free," Stacy protested with a faint
catch of pain in her voice.

"Do you know what I'm afraid of?" There was no
humor in his chilling smile. "That some day you'll say
that so often I'll finally believe you—even though I
know it's not the truth."

"No." It was an inaudible denial, lost in a choked
sob that Cord didn't hear.

There was the quiet swish of his wheels turning.
Stacy's head was bowed so she didn't see him reenter
the house. Her hands were clasped tightly in front of
her in desperate prayer. Pain reverberated through her
body, racking her muscles until she wanted to cry away
the hurt, but she held the flood of tears in check.

It was several minutes before she was in sufficient
control of herself to join Travis and Paula in the living
room. A hand wearily pushed the hair away from her
forehead as she walked into the house.

The sight of Cord in the living room brought her to
an abrupt halt. She had been certain he would retreat
to his bedroom.

The impregnable hardness of his gaze swept over
her, noting the ravages of her storm within. A cigarette
was in his hand, and the gray smoke outlined the
ebony blackness of his hair.

Not a sound had betrayed Stacy's entrance into the

living room, yet Paula glanced up, as if sensing a change in the atmosphere. Her azure eyes narrowed briefly on Stacy's wan cheeks, and a split second later a smile of warm greeting was rimming the blond woman's face.

"You're just in time, Stacy," Paula declared, darting a fleeting sideways glance at Travis. "I was just trying to find out more about this annual horse sale you have from Travis. He said you were in charge of that, and that it had been your personal project for the last several years."

"That's true."

Stacy started forward, grateful for the safe topic of conversation and the lack of any comment about where she had been. "What did you want to know about it?"

"Well, I—" Paula began.

"Isn't there something else we can discuss?" Cord interrupted with a snap. He ground his cigarette out in an ashtray, suppressing anger in the action.

There was a challenging tilt of the physiotherapist's head in his direction. "I was only going to ask Stacy what she was doing now—in connection with the sale."

"What difference does it make to you?" Cord met her look and returned the challenge.

"It doesn't make any difference to me," Paula shrugged. "I was just interested."

"Well, I'm not!" he retorted.

"Do you mean you're not interested in what goes on here at the ranch?" she asked with a long considering look,

"That's precisely what I mean," Cord replied sharply.

"I understood it was your ranch." Paula tapped a cigarette from the pack sitting on the table in front of her.

As she placed the filtered tip between her lips, Cord's gold lighter was there to touch a flame to the tobaccoed end. Stacy saw their gazes lock above the yellow flame.

"It was," he agreed, stressing the past tense. "Since my accident, Stacy and Travis have taken over the operation of it. It's not my affair anymore."

"Why?" Paula blew a stream of smoke into the air.

"They make all the decisions," was the answer.

"Why don't you, if it's your ranch?" she challenged.

"In case it hasn't occurred to you, Miss Hanson—" there was a sarcastic inflection in his voice "—it's difficult to oversee an operation of this size from a wheelchair."

"Difficult but not impossible, Mr. Harris," returning his cutting formality in kind. "Other men confined to wheelchairs have controlled holdings larger and more complex than yours."

A muscle leaped in his jaw, the only indication of his severely checked anger. "Really?" he drawled with indifference.

"When I first met you, I thought you were that kind of man," Paula continued. "It never occurred to me that you would let a woman rule your life, even if she is your wife. Of course—" she shrugged nonchalantly "—initially I thought you were a man."

"Meaning?" he demanded coldly.

"Surely I don't have to explain." Paula blinked her widened eyes. "You're the one who's hiding behind your wife's skirt and letting her make all the decisions. You could hardly be described as the master of your own destiny."

Stacy had apprehensively sunk her teeth into her lower lip at the insult to Cord's masculinity in Paula's last remark. She took a step forward, but Travis caught her eye and shook his head.

Stacy breathed in sharply in surprise when she saw Cord lean back in his chair and laugh silently, admittedly without humor.

"You're not opposed to hitting below the belt, are you?"

The grooves around his mouth deepened with satirical amusement as his gaze narrowed on his blond adversary.

"Why should I be?" Paula countered. "You don't seem to be bothered when you hurt people who care about you."

Just in case Cord didn't understand her vague reference to Stacy, Paula glanced pointedly at her, dwelling on the lines of strain around her mouth and eyes.

Cord followed her look. There wasn't even a glimmer of guilt or remorse in his impassive features. He turned back to Paula, a suggestion of arrogance in the tilt of his head.

"You can do all the hitting below the belt that you want, Miss Hanson," he said calmly. "It doesn't bother me in the least. As for my wife—" his gaze slashed to Stacy; its mockery chilled her "—Stacy and I understand each other. I'm perfectly aware of what she wants. I doubt very seriously, Miss Hanson, if you do. Now, I'll bid all of you good night and relieve you of my uncomfortable presence."

As he started to move his wheelchair forward, Paula suggested smoothly, "I think you're the one who is uncomfortable, Mr. Harris."

Cord paused, met her challenging glance, and smiled.

"I'm bored, but not uncomfortable." His smile deepened, carving grooves near his mouth. "As a matter of fact, Miss Hanson, I'm now beginning to realize that these little battles with you just might relieve my boredom."

A silence followed his departure from the room, with all three pairs of eyes watching him leave. All of them were a bit stunned by his curious about-face and what it meant.

"Round two was a draw," Paula breathed finally. "I think I'm going to have to be on my toes tomorrow morning if I expect to come out on top."

"Cord isn't the type to let anyone else stay on top for long," Travis commented idly, unaware that he had spoken his thoughts aloud. "He always lands on his feet, like a cat."

"I hope I'm just as agile," Paula tacked on thoughtfully.

An icy finger trailed down Stacy's spine and she shivered. Her world was being turned upside down and there seemed to be nothing she could do or say to put it right. Earlier Cord had called her his life. In the next breath, he had declared he didn't believe her when she said she never wanted to leave him.

Time was on her side and she could overcome that. But that wasn't what was making her blood run cold. It was his comment that Paula would provide a diversion to his boredom. Stacy was afraid of what that might mean. Cord was virtually a stranger to her. She didn't know him anymore.

A lump rose in her throat. Her stomach churned sickeningly, and rubbery legs threatened to give way beneath her. She swayed unsteadily, a hand pressing itself against the flat of her stomach to quell the convulsing muscles.

"I—I think I'll check on Josh."

She needed to escape, so she grabbed at the first logical excuse.

"Stacy."

Paula's voice checked her first awkward step from the room. "Before I forget, will you be here at the house tomorrow morning?"

"I—" She couldn't think. Tomorrow was an eternity away and her mind couldn't seem to focus on it.

"You mentioned something about going into town in the morning," Travis prompted gently.

"Oh, yes, of course," Stacy laughed brittlely, running a trembling hand along her temple. "I have to take the yearling list for the sales catalog to the printers in the morning." Her nerves were threadbare. "Was there something you wanted, Paula?"

"No." Paula inhaled briefly on her cigarette and snuffed it out in the ashtray. "I was going to start initiating your husband to his exercises and I just wondered where you would be."

"I can postpone going into town until the afternoon if you'd like me to help." The offer was made almost desperately as Stacy turned, her chestnut hair swinging silkily around her shoulders. She wanted to maintain any link with Cord regardless of how rusty the connection might be.

"Don't do that." The blonde shook her head.

"I don't mind. I—I want to help."

For the first time, Stacy noticed a flash of uncertainty in the woman's face. The blue eyes looked in her direction without looking directly at her.

"Actually, Stacy, it would be better if you weren't here—at least in the beginning," Paula hastily added. "I'm afraid you would be more of a distraction than a help, however good your intentions. The therapist-patient relationship is very important, especially in your husband's case. Besides, the first few days or more will probably be pretty rough on Cord. Caring about him the way you do, your instinct would be to try to make it easier for him. I'm sorry, but it's nothing personal."

"I understand."

Did she though? Stacy didn't know. There were so many things she didn't know or understand anymore. Not the least among them was Cord.

"Excuse me," she murmured, and this time made her exit from the room.

The next morning Stacy had genuinely intended to be gone from the house before Paula started her exercise and therapy program with Cord. But one minor interruption after another kept her in the study until half-past nine.

With the list in her hand of the yearling colts and fillies to be sold, Stacy walked out of the study. The door to the master bedroom was ajar. It drew her gaze like a magnet. A muffled exclamation of pain made her hesitate.

"Dammit, that hurts!" she heard Cord mutter savagely.

"Well, dammit, it's supposed to," was the unruffled response from Paula. "It's going to hurt a lot more before we're through."

"I don't like it when a woman swears," he retorted with a muffled undertone of discomfort.

"For once we share a similar viewpoint, Mr. Harris," Paula declared. "I find it offensive when a man swears."

Suddenly Stacy realized that she was eavesdropping. That realization was followed immediately by a niggling doubt that she had allowed herself to be detained at the house when she could have left earlier as planned.

With a guilty start, she hurried toward the front door before her presence was discovered.

The next day Stacy made certain that she succeeded in leaving the house early in the morning, not returning until lunchtime. Insecurity had allowed twinges of jealousy to enter her, and she overcompensated for them by staying away rather than turning into a suspicious, prying wife.

True to Paula's prediction, the first week was miserable. Stacy's self-imposed exile in the mornings had begun to make her feel like an intruder in her own home, as if she should ask permission whenever she wanted to spend any length of time there during the day.

The mental and physical exertion had made Cord ill-tempered. His moods varied from brooding silence to snarling sarcasm. It seemed to Stacy that she was his favorite target, although Paula received her fair share of his scathing remarks.

Maybe it only seemed that Cord singled Stacy out because her love gave him such an overwhelming power to hurt. Inwardly she cringed when his slashing tongue cut her heart to ribbons, but she didn't let her wounds show. She tried to mimic Paula by pretending his acid comments bounced off her as they appeared to bounce off Paula.

As her fork played with the tuna-salad stuffing of her tomato, Stacy searched for something to say. The heavy atmosphere at the lunch table was oppressive, induced by Cord's brooding silence. The prong of her fork made a scraping sound on the plate.

Jet dark eyes pierced her. "Are you going to eat that or just keep pushing it around on your plate?" Cord snapped.

His sudden attention disconcerted her. Awkwardly she laid the fork down and clasped her shaking fingers in her lap, out of sight of Cord's penetrating gaze.

"I'm not very hungry," she answered with forced calm.

"Then stop playing with your food," he growled.

Silence descended again. Stacy glanced at Paula, wondering how the blonde could be so indifferent to the brittle tension. Or was she simply a better actress than Stacy?

"How is the—the therapy coming along?" Stacy faltered over the question, again drawing Cord's dark gaze.

"Don't ask me, ask Paula." There was an arrogant flare of his nostrils in scorn. "She's supposed to be the expert."

The physiotherapist's knife sliced through the red tomato. "It's Miss Hanson to you, Mr. Harris," Paula corrected him smoothly. "When you become a person I can like and respect, then you have permission to call me Paula, but not before."

"Miss Hanson—" the strong line of his lip curled sarcastically over her name "—I don't particularly care whether you ever like me or not."

"And vice versa, Mr. Harris," Paula returned with a saccharine smile. When the blue eyes turned to Stacy, they held a twinkling light of mock despair. "To answer your question, Stacy, it's slow when you have to fight every inch of the way."

"Translated, that means a lot of pain and little progress," Cord inserted dryly.

"When did you become such an optimist, Cord?" Stacy's mouth curved into a humorless smile.

"What?" He looked at her blankly.

"You just admitted there was a little progress, which is better than none at all," she retorted.

He exhaled a short, angry breath. "Damned little," he muttered in a savage undertone. Almost instantly a black eyebrow arched in Paula's direction. "Pardon me, Miss Hanson."

"I'll be damned if I should, but I will, Mr. Harris." A smile twitched at the corners of her full mouth.

Jealousy flamed with emerald green fire inside Stacy at the exchange. Before it consumed her with its self-destructive force, she pushed her chair away from the table. The suppressed violence of her action nearly tipped over the glassware.

"Excuse me, I have work to do," she muttered as she started to flee from the surprised glances.

Inside the study, she shut the door and leaned against it. If she hadn't overheard their conversation the other day, she wouldn't have understood the teasing subtlety regarding swearing that had passed between Cord and Paula.

Now they were sharing secret jokes. In the green-eyed throes of her misery, she wondered what else they shared during all the mornings she left them alone.

She walked to the desk. At this time she knew she wouldn't be able to concentrate on paperwork. Her mind would be wondering what was going on in the rest of the house.

Her wide-brimmed Western hat was sitting on top of the letter basket where she had left it this morning. Picking it up, she hurried from the study and out of the house.

At the stable, Hank stared at her in astonishment. "Saddle the mare?" He repeated her request. "You want to go ridin' in the heat of the day?" He peered at her closely, his weathered face crinkled by the sun. "Are you all right, Miss Stacy?"

"Of course," she answered sharply. She sunk her teeth into her lip for an instant to check any further venting of frustration on Hank.

"If you're too busy, Hank, I'll saddle Candy Bar myself."

"I'll do it," he grumbled, and shuffled toward the corral. But Stacy heard him mumble as he left, "Somebody around here is tetched in the head, and it ain't me!"

CHAPTER EIGHT

THE GREEN PICKUP TRUCK rumbled down the lane toward the stables, slowing down as it approached Stacy walking toward the house. She waited until it stopped beside her, and smiled tiredly at the dark-haired man behind the wheel. His arm was crooked over the open window of the cab.

"Hello, Travis," she greeted him. "It seems like I haven't seen you for ages." He was the one person with whom she didn't feel she always had to be on her guard.

"We've both been pretty busy these last three days," he agreed. He kept the truck in gear, the engine idling eagerly.

"How are the preparations for the horse sale going?" he asked.

"Fine," Stacy nodded with a wry smile, "I think," she added the qualification.

"And Cord?" The brown eyes were thoughtful as they ran over her wholesomely attractive features, drawn and tired, the signs of weight loss visible in the accented hollows of her cheeks. "Paula has been here almost two weeks now. Has there been any improvement?"

"None that I know about." Stacy glanced self-consciously away.

The information hadn't been volunteered to her regarding Cord's progress, or lack of it. It had been on the tip of her tongue several times to put the question to Paula, but the very fact that Stacy hadn't been kept informed held her back.

"It takes time, I guess," Travis shrugged.

"Yes, of course," she agreed. "I was just going up to the house for lunch. Would you like to join me?"

He frowned curiously. "Won't Cord and Paula be there?"

"Sure," she smiled nervously.

It had been a slip of the tongue to say "me." The truth was that Stacy felt like the unwanted third at the table. The thought of Travis joining them for lunch had been a means of being included for once instead of feeling left out. She realized that it was all in her imagination, but she still felt uncomfortable.

"I'd like to," Travis hesitated, "but—"

"I understand," Stacy inserted, stretching her mouth into a smile. "Work," she offered him an excuse. "Another time."

"I'll hold you to it," he smiled, and the truck began rolling forward.

If only something had developed between Paula and Travis, Stacy sighed wistfully. But it hadn't. They were friendly toward each other but nothing more.

When her path was clear, she started toward the house again. The closer she got, the more taut her nerves became. Her throat and mouth were dry. The food would be tasteless again.

Lately she had had to force herself to eat, but the portions that she had succeeded in swallowing had been small.

"Hi, mom!"

Josh came racing down the sloping lawn toward her. Water glistened on his chest, browned by the sun. His red swimming trunks were plastered to his slender form. Shining wet hair gleamed as black as a raven's wing in the sunlight.

"You've been playing with the water hose again, I see," Stacy smiled indulgently.

"No, I've been swimming," he corrected her brightly.

The smile vanished completely.

"Joshua Stephen Harris!"

She grasped his shoulders and gave him a hard shake. "You've been told and told and told never to go swimming by yourself! You are not to be in that pool unless y—" Stacy had been about to say "your father or I," but she quickly changed it "—there's an adult in the pool with you. Now you can spend the afternoon in your room."

His dark eyes flashed resentfully at her.

"But daddy and Paula were in the pool with me!" he declared.

"I don't like it when you lie to me, Josh," scolded Stacy. Her frayed nerve ends had armed her temper with a short fuse.

"I am not lying. It's the truth!" Josh insisted. "We all went swimming together."

Her chestnut head tipped to one side in doubt.
"Your father, too?" she questioned skeptically.

"Paula said it was 'therpy'—" he mispronounced the
unfamiliar word "—to make daddy stronger. They've
been swimming every day and today Paula said I could
come in, too."

The brisk nod of his chin added a very definite "so
there!" to the end of his explanation.

"I—" Stacy was flustered. She had heard of
swimming used in therapy, but she hadn't realized
Paula was employing it. "I didn't know. I'm sorry,
Josh."

He accepted her apology somewhat sullenly, his
lower lip jutting out in a pout.

She should have realized he wouldn't deliberately
disobey her. Or if he did, he wouldn't brag about it.
She was just too keyed up. She shouldn't have jumped
on him without allowing him to make an explanation.

"I was wrong and I take back everything I said.
Naturally you don't have to stay in your room this
afternoon," she added.

Then trying to change the subject, she said, "Do you
suppose Maria has lunch ready yet? Shall we go and
see?"

A bare toe dug into a clump of grass. "I guess so," he
agreed without enthusiasm.

But he didn't walk beside her. Instead he raced
ahead, a faint droop to his shoulders. Her unwarranted anger had taken his enjoyment out of the
morning swim and he wasn't going to let her forget it

immediately. Knowing that she had been wrong only made Stacy feel worse.

If only Paula or Cord had mentioned the morning swims, Stacy defended her action silently, none of this would have happened. Resentment smoldered, as it had done in Josh.

Entering the house, Stacy walked directly toward the master bedroom. It was time she found out all that was going on in her house. She had a right to know what was being done, when, where, and why.

The door was opened. A half step through the frame, Stacy halted, stopped by the sight of Cord lying nearly half-naked on a sheet-draped table. A blue towel was wrapped around his waist. The narrow width of the towel revealed the rippling muscles of his shoulders and back, and the dark curling hair on his thighs and legs. Lying on his stomach, his head was resting on his hand, his face turned away from the door. Dampness changed his hair to midnight black, inclining it to wave.

Stacy's view was blocked by a tall, slender shape as a pair of strong hands began spreading a glistening oil all over Cord's naked back. Her gaze swept over the woman.

Ash-blond hair was swept on top of her head in a disheveled coil. Wet tendrils had escaped to curl attractively on the slender column of her neck. A white lace beach jacket veiled a two-piece swimming suit, revealing the stunning length of golden legs.

Long fingers supply massaged Cord's back, polishing the bronzed tan of his skin with the oil. How unobservant she had been these past days, Stacy thought silently. Not once had she noticed the deepening shade of Cord's sunbrowned skin. Her pulse stirred at the virility stamped in the totally male figure. There was an ache in the pit of her stomach, a yearning emptiness that wanted to be filled.

Envy crushed her heart into a painful ball as Stacy watched Paula's hands moving with familiar intimacy over his naked back and shoulders. A cry of jealous anger rose in her throat that Paula, and not herself, was the one touching him, caressing him. Smothering the tortured sob with the back of her hand, Stacy retreated from the doorway on trembling legs.

It was either retreat or she would have raced into the room, screaming and clawing at Paula. The violence of her raging emotions dazed her. Not even with Lydia, whom Stacy had once thought Cord might marry, had she ever wanted to start a spitting, hair-pulling fight. It was crazy, because she had despised Lydia while she actually liked Paula. But not with Cord—never with Cord!

Three steps backward into the hallway, she heard Cord speak and stopped to listen, despising herself for listening.

"You could make a fortune with your hands, Paula," he murmured in a husky, caressing voice that had so often quickened Stacy's heartbeat and sent flames of desire shooting through her limbs.

Paula! A jealous voice screamed in her head. He had called her Paula!

The physiotherapist's words at the table came back

to haunt Stacy—"When you become someone I can like and respect, then you have permission to call me Paula." Would she correct him now? Stacy held her breath, grinding the back of her hand against her teeth.

"I'm not interested in making a fortune," the blonde replied quietly.

There was no correction. A searing pain plunged through Stacy's heart, nearly doubling her in half.

"What do you want?" Cord spoke again. His decidedly interested tone indicated that the question was more than idle curiosity.

"What every woman wants. A satisfying and rewarding career, a home and a man." An instant of silence followed before Paula added, "Not necessarily in that order."

Not Cord. You can't have Cord, Stacy cried silently.

"Are you hard to please?" he mocked.

"Very," Paula agreed in what sounded like a deliberately light tone.

"The man who gets you will have his hands full." His voice was rimmed with amusement.

"But he'll be man enough to handle me." Despite the smiling sound in Paula's answer, it carried an inflection of complete seriousness.

"That sounds like a challenge," Cord chuckled.

"Are you going to pick up the glove?"

Stacy couldn't tell whether Paula was teasing or trying to make her interest in Cord apparent to him. Paula had warned Stacy the day she arrived that she always fell in love with her patients.

Her eyes burned, but they remained dry as Stacy hastily stumbled into the living room. She was afraid to hear anymore. A chilling dread froze her senses to everything but the image of the two semi-clad people in the master bedroom, and the feminine hands that so freely touched Cord's body when he had denied Stacy the right.

Her white teeth bit into the back of her hand as she sank onto the couch. Sightlessly she stared over the rear cushion at the blue sky visible through the glass doors to the veranda. Something inside her shattered, splintering into a thousand pieces. What was it? Her heart?

Deaf and blind to the world around her, Maria repeated her name several times before Stacy realized she was not alone in the room anymore. She turned blankly to the housekeeper.

"What was it you wanted, Maria?" she asked flatly.

"There is a phone call for you."

Stacy resumed her former position.

"Take their name and phone number and tell them I'll call them back. I don't want to talk to anyone right now."

"I will tell them you will call back this afternoon," Maria agreed.

"Not this afternoon. I won't be in this afternoon," Stacy replied in the same emotionless tone.

"You are never at the house anymore," the housekeeper chided in a sadly scolding tone.

"No, I'm never at the house anymore." It seemed to be a pronouncement of her fate.

Stacy roused herself sufficiently to inquire; "Is lunch nearly ready?"

"A *momento* only," Maria answered.

As Maria left the room, Stacy rose from the couch to mechanically go through the motions of washing up for the meal. She felt very much like a robot sitting at the table silently eating the salad of avocado and grapefruit sections coated with a sweet syrup. Her tongue tasted neither sweet nor sour.

Yet it wasn't her silence that drew comment as Paula, dressed in slacks and a top, glanced curiously at the unnaturally silent Josh seated across the table from her.

"You're very quiet this noon, Josh. Are you tired?" she queried lightly.

His small dark head moved in a negative shake, his gaze never leaving his plate.

"You generally always chatter like a chipmunk," Paula teased. "Something terrible must be bothering you."

"I scolded him for going swimming this morning," Stacy explained blandly when Josh remained silent. Her features were stoically void of any expression as she glanced at the blond woman. "I wasn't aware until afterward that you and Cord had been making daily use of the pool for therapy and that Joshua was supervised and not swimming alone as I'd first supposed. My apologies haven't been fully accepted so far."

"I'm sorry, Stacy. I thought you knew," Paula apologized.

"It doesn't matter," Stacy shrugged. "I know now. Has the, er, swimming been useful?"

She glanced up in time to see the brief look exchanged between Cord and Paula, and her stomach somersaulted sickeningly at the intimately private secret the look implied.

"It hasn't done any harm," the therapist replied diffidently.

A shudder of pain quaked through Stacy. "Excuse me," she murmured. "I just remembered Maria told me there was an important telephone message for me. I was supposed to return it immediately."

It was a feeble excuse, but it was the only one she could think of to leave the table in the middle of a meal. Her retreating footsteps were haunted by how many other secret glances they had exchanged when she wasn't looking.

She cursed her vivid imagination, but it was fed by the vague glitter of contentment in Cord's dark eyes and the lack of any bitter cynicism around the edges of his mouth.

Slipping out through the front door, Stacy knew she would never be able to share another meal with them without wondering what silent message was being transmitted. She resolved not to subject herself to that torture.

Over the next few days she began rearranging things. Travis became her link with sanity, and she used him shamelessly as a buffer. Since Paula had arrived she had invited him over several times each week for dinner. Now she scheduled their ranch meetings at lunchtime. If Travis thought her behavior was odd, he took care not to mention it, treating her almost constant demand for his spare time as natural.

The question Stacy kept ignoring was where would it all end? This day-to-day survival couldn't continue forever.

How long could she avoid acknowledging the relationship that was developing beneath her nose between Cord and Paula?

But what was the alternative? Should she confront Cord with her suspicions and make herself look the fool if she was wrong? Or should she accuse Paula and warn her to stay away from Cord?

Sighing dispiritedly, Stacy looped her chestnut hair behind her ears. Her boots continued carrying her toward the house, her troubled brown eyes staring at the ground.

A squeal of childish delight came from the direction of the house followed by a resounding splash of water. Nearing the slight knoll that permitted her a view of the pool area on the west side of the hacienda, Stacy paused. The red-tiled roof gleamed dully against the whitewashed adobe walls.

Two more steps and she could see the swimming pool and its three occupants. Cord's rolling laughter carried across the distance to her ears. Her chest contracted as she tried to remember the last time she had heard him laugh with such happiness. It must have been shortly after his accident when he had been simply glad to be alive.

She could see Paula's blond head in the water near Cord's. When the physiotherapist turned and said something to him, Cord laughed again. Stacy bit her lip until the salty taste of blood was in her mouth. She had not been able to make him laugh like that, but Paula had.

Jealousy scored another blow. The scene of man, woman and child playing in the swimming pool was an ideal picture of a family unit. The picture was wrong because Stacy should have been there to portray the mother, not Paula. Why did they have to look so happy together, she cried silently.

"They look like they're having fun, don't they?" The male voice jerked Stacy's head in its direction, alarm registering in her widened eyes, and in the sudden draining of color from her face. Concern darkened Travis's gaze.

"I didn't mean to startle you," he said.

"I . . . it's . . . okay. I . . . I just didn't hear you walk up."

Stacy fought to regain her composure with limited success. "You're early. I wasn't expecting you until lunch."

Jerkily she started toward the house, anxious to take his attention away from the occupants of the swimming pool. She didn't think she could talk about them with any degree of poise.

"I can't make lunch today. That's why I stopped now on the off chance I would find you." Travis fell in step beside her. "If you aren't busy now, I thought we could go over those grain invoices together and see if we can find the reason for the discrepancy with our records."

"I'm free," Stacy agreed, grateful she would not have the opportunity to dwell on the scene she had witnessed.

Unfortunately the office work didn't prove to be the distraction that she had hoped it would. Somewhere part way through her stack of papers, she forgot to concentrate on what she was doing. Her gaze wandered instead to the window and the driveway beyond the panes. The laughter and voices from the pool area had ended some time ago, yet the sounds echoed endlessly in her mind.

"Stacy, what's wrong?"

Her reaction was in slow motion as she turned to Travis. "What?" she asked blankly, hearing his voice without hearing his question.

His frowning gaze inspected her face. "I said, what's wrong? Why are you crying?"

Stacy lifted a hand to her cheeks, surprised by the moistness she found there. Hurriedly she wiped the tears away, only to feel the rivulets of more tears retracing the paths of the first. In agitation and embarrassment, she rose from her chair, turning her back to Travis.

"Nothing—really." Her voice quivered, revealing her lie, and more tears slipped from her lashes.

There was the scrape of a chair leg as Travis straightened. Stacy knew she hadn't deceived him. She wiped frantically at the tears and tried to laugh. It was a choking sound.

"I don't know what's the matter with me. I'm sorry, Travis," she muffled the words through her hands, trying to still her quivering lips and chin. "You must think I've lost my mind." It was what Stacy was wondering.

"I think something is wrong," he said quietly. "Will it help to talk about it?"

"Yes—no." She slid her hands behind her neck, letting them rest there for an instant. "I'm so mixed up." A sighing sob accompanied her admission. "I'm such a fool, I know, but you saw them out there."

"Cord and Paula?"

"Did you hear him laugh?" Stacy glanced at Travis's handsome features and the wings of silver lacing the temples of his curling black hair. She turned away from his thoughtful gaze. "I wanted to be the one to make him laugh again. It . . . it sounds selfish, doesn't it? Selfish and jealous?"

Again she wiped at the tears on her cheeks. "I am." Her voice was low and defeated. "It's just that they have become so close—so friendly. I know . . . I'm sure they . . . ." Stacy couldn't put her suspicions into words.

Her throat tightened and silent sobs shook her shoulders. Breaking down like this in front of Travis was too humiliating.

His large hands closed over her shoulders and turned her into his chest. The inviting expanse of shirt snapped what little remained of her control, and she buried her face in his shirt and cried. Travis rocked her gently like a child, stroking the silken length of her chestnut hair, highlighted with gold. Over and over again Stacy sobbed that she was sorry.

"Ssh," Travis soothed. "You've been living on your nerves for too long, bottling everything up inside. This was bound to happen."

"I didn't want it to," Stacy mumbled brokenly.

"That's beside the point now," he smiled gently.

"If only I didn't think that Cord : . . Paula . . . ." She shook her head, pressing her lips together.

"If you think something is going on between Cord and Paula, then you're letting your imagination run away with you," Travis scolded gently.

"I want to believe that." Desperately she wanted to believe that.

Travis crooked a finger under her chin and raised it to smile into her face.

"It's just a matter of time."

The little breath she exhaled was wistful. Tremulously she curved her lips into a smile, appreciating his encouraging words and hoping he was right. Uncertainty lingered in her tear-wet eyes. Tenderly he wiped the tears from her left cheek, a soothing roughness to his callused hand.

Blinking, her gaze swung from his roughly hewn face toward his wrist. Halfway through the arc, her gaze was stopped. The study door was opened and a tall figure stood within the frame. The jubilant light in the jet dark eyes flamed into menacing rage, piercing Stacy with their fury.

Her mouth opened incredulously as she stared at Cord. He was standing upright, leaning heavily on a horseshoe-shaped walking aid. But he was standing! She wanted to cry for joy, but she couldn't speak.

At the shining change in her expression, Travis glanced over his shoulder, and instantly his hand fell away from her face. There was an instant when he mirrored the same surprise and gladness as Stacy. But Travis noted, too, the chiseled coldness in Cord's patrician features. Stacy was still too overwhelmed by Cord's recovery to notice the sudden tensing of the man standing next to her.

"First it was Colter's wife, now it's mine, is that it, McCrea?" Cord jeered coldly. "Can't you find a woman who doesn't belong to someone else?"

"You've made a mistake, Cord," Travis replied quietly.

Stunned by the violence in Cord's voice, Stacy finally registered in her mind the construction Cord had built out of the situation. Unhurriedly Travis set her away from him.

"The only mistake I made was being fool enough to trust you!" Cord snapped. "Get out of here at once, McCrea!"

Lifting the horseshoe frame that supported him, he set it inches forward into the room, half dragging his legs after it. After several repetitions of the procedure, the doorway was clear.

"It's not at all true what you're thinking, Cord," Stacy protested as he continued to glare savagely at Travis.

"It's all right, Stacy." But she could see Travis was

controlling himself with an effort. "I'll leave for now."

"You're damned right you will!" was Cord's growling agreement.

With smooth strides, Travis walked from the room. When the front door had clicked shut, Cord shifted his diamond-black gaze to Stacy. She shivered at the contempt in his expression.

"I was upset," she defended. "Travis was only trying to make me feel better, that's all."

"Do you expect me to believe that?" he jeered.

"It's the truth."

She shook her head helplessly, her gaze running over his erect figure. "Oh, Cord, you're out of that wheelchair! I can't get over it." She moved blindly toward him, wanting to forget the stupid misunderstanding over Travis and rejoice in Cord's recovery. "I—"

"It was meant to be a surprise. Some surprise!" His mouth thinned bitterly.

The darkening fires in his eyes made Stacy realize that he was revisualizing the scene with Travis when he had opened the study door.

"Please, don't let's argue," she pleaded softly.

The tips of her fingers hesitantly touched his hand on the walker. "This is a time to be happy you're on your feet again. How long? When did it happen?" she asked.

Cord shifted his hand away from her touch. "Does it matter?" he mocked. "Tell me, Stacy, how did it feel to have a man's arms around you?"

His rejection of her tentative caress stung. Stacy drew back, tilting her chin forward. He towered above her, aloof and arrogant.

"Tell me how it feels when Paula touches you, rubbing your shoulders and neck?" she challenged.

"That has nothing to do with what we're talking about!" He became angry at her question. "Don't try to justify your unfaithfulness with her."

"Where's the difference?" She stood stiffly in front of him. Her heart kept waiting for his denial, the few words necessary that would tell her she had simply been imagining that something was going on between him and Paula.

But he ignored the question. "I knew you'd become bored with ranch life and being tied down to one place, but I never suspected for one minute that you would seek a diversion in the arms of another man," he declared in disgust.

Stacy flinched uncontrollably, then recovered. "Would you believe me if I told you that Travis and I are only friends?"

"I'm not blind!" The hard line of his mouth crooked cynically. "I saw the two of you embracing when I opened the door!"

"And you believe everything you see? So do I, then! I guess there's nothing more to say, is there?" She sounded quite calm, but her legs were shaking as she started walking toward the door.

"I want Travis off this ranch within the hour," he snapped.

Her hand rested on the doorknob. She turned, meeting the freezing blackness of his gaze. "I'm the one who's running this ranch, Cord, not you," she replied softly to keep her voice from betraying the quaking of her body. "I was the one who hired Travis and I'll be the one to tell him to leave. And I have no intention of doing so."

Without another word, she opened the door and walked into the hall. She could hear Cord cursing under his breath as he tried to follow her, laboriously dragging each leg a step at a time. She trembled at the raging anger she had incited. Quickly she closed the front door and hurried from the house.

CHAPTER NINE

TRAVIS WAS LEANING against the fender of the pickup, the crown of his dusty stetson pushed back on his head. A cigarette was cupped in his hand as he impassively watched Stacy's approach.

"Did you explain?"

His brown eyes ran over her grim expression and the defiant thrust of her chin.

"Cord was too convinced of his own conclusion to listen," Stacy replied stiffly.

"I'm sorry." Travis flipped his cigarette to the ground and then crushed it beneath the heel of his boot.

"Neither of us has done anything to be sorry about," she retorted with a rush of indignant pride.

"I know that." He stared down the winding lane leading through the broken Texas hills to the main road. "But just the same I think Cord was right when he told me to leave. It would probably be best all the way around. With me out of the picture, he'll be more apt to listen to you."

"No!" Stacy violently rejected the idea. "Under no circumstances do I want you to leave unless I personally ask you to go."

Shaking his dark head, Travis looked back at her and sighed. "You're only complicating a difficult situation. His jealousy proves that there's nothing going on between him and Paula. You were only imagining it."

A lump entered her throat. "That's where you're wrong," she said tightly.

His mouth tightened grimly in exasperation. "Stacy, you can't still believe it's possible."

"I confronted Cord with it." Tears burned the back of her eyes, and she bent her head so Travis wouldn't see them. "It's the old case of what's sauce for the gander isn't sauce for the goose. It's one thing for Cord to be unfaithful, but it's unforgivable in his eyes that I should be."

Travis frowned, studying her intently. "I don't believe it."

"It's the truth." Swallowing back the tears, Stacy lifted her gaze. "Travis, I want your word that you'll stay."

He hesitated, carefully considering her request. "I'll stay for the time being." His reluctant agreement indicated that he thought she was making a mistake by asking him to remain.

"Thank you," she murmured gratefully. Pausing for a second, she added, "And I'm sorry about the reference Cord made to Natalie."

Travis took a deep breath and stared into space again. "I love her."

His mouth crooked wryly. "I'm afraid I haven't got to the point where I can say it in the past tense.

Maybe I never will. But there was never anything physical between us. She was always Colter's. She was never mine to take. They're happy now and I couldn't wish any more than that."

Abruptly he turned and walked to the driver's door of the pickup. "Since I'm still on the payroll, I'd better get to work."

Stacy didn't attempt to stop him. "I'll see you later, Travis, and thanks—for everything."

When she returned to the house at lunchtime, Stacy expected another confrontation with Cord, but there was nothing but glacial silence as they faced each other over the table. Before the meal was over, she wished there had been a volcanic eruption instead.

His chilling attitude didn't change one degree during the next three days, and Stacy didn't make any attempt to begin a thaw. She had tried to explain once and Cord wouldn't listen. She was too stubborn and proud to try again.

Cross-legged on the end of the bed, she methodically brushed her long hair, electricity crackling through the silken strands.

Once she had thought things couldn't get any worse between herself and Cord. How very wrong she had been!

There was a light rap on her bedroom door, and she tensed, her heart quickening in hope.

"Who is it?" She hadn't heard the labored sounds of Cord's footsteps, but the carpet might have muffled them.

"It's me, Paula. May I come in?"

"Come in." It seemed almost like admitting a traitor into the camp. As the door opened, Stacy resumed the rhythmic strokes of the brush through her hair, not glancing up. "What was it you wanted, Paula?" she asked briskly.

"I hoped you weren't in bed yet. There was something I wanted to talk to you about." There was no indication that Paula had noticed the absence of welcome in Stacy's voice.

"What is it?" Deliberately she didn't suggest that the physiotherapist take a seat in the velvet-covered chair in the corner.

"It's about Cord."

Paula didn't wait for an invitation and settled her tall frame on the chair.

"Yes?" Stacy prompted coolly.

"Lately he's reverted to his old snarling self."

Uncurling her legs from beneath her, Stacy walked to the vanity table and stood in front of the mirror.

"So I've noticed," she responded indifferently. Actually Cord hadn't spoken a word to her, but she had heard him snapping at everyone else.

"In a way, I expected it," Paula said.

She rose from the chair and moved to join her reflection with Stacy's in the mirror. "He's on his feet again and replaced the walker with crutches, but he's not as mobile yet as he wants to be. When I first came here, I had to bully him into the therapy. Now he's trying too hard."

"I see," Stacy murmured, but she kept all of her attention focused on fluffing her hair into its style.

"If I don't find some way to distract him, he'll over-do it."

There was a second's pause as Paula waited for Stacy's comment, but she made none. She sensed that the therapist had a suggestion to make and she, in turn, waited for it. "There's no reason why he can't begin taking part in the operation of the ranch. I want you to talk to him about it."

"No!" The word exploded from Stacy as her flashing gaze swung to Paula's reflection. She wouldn't seek Cord out for any reason. Placing the hairbrush on the table, she moved toward the window. "It wouldn't do any good. Travis and I have tried many times before."

"You have to try again," Paula declared quietly but firmly.

"He—he wouldn't listen to me," Stacy argued. "You would be much better off to suggest it to him yourself."

"He might not listen to you, not if—" Paula conceded, qualifying the admission with "—he still thought you really didn't need his help and were trying to patronize him. But anyone taking a look at you, Stacy, would realize that you're overworked. All you have to do is plead that you can't cope with all of it anymore. It's unarguable fact."

Stacy had seen her reflection in the mirror. Blue shadow rimmed her eyes, eyes that had become a dull, flat brown except when she was roused to anger. The hollows of her cheeks accented her bones and hardly a glimmer of happiness remained in her features. Even the gold-dust sprinkle of freckles across her nose lacked the usual appeal.

Although Paula's words were valid, Stacy couldn't bring herself to agree, and she felt mean to refuse, so she made no reply.

"Stacy, what's the matter with you?" Paula demanded. "You almost act as if you don't want Cord to recover completely."

"That's not true!" she denied, spinning to face the tall blonde.

"Something has happened between you and Cord, hasn't it?" Blue eyes watched Stacy alertly. "What is it?"

Stacy turned away from the scrutiny. "You'll have to ask Cord," she answered stiffly.

"I have. He told me to mind my own business."

"Then that's my answer, too."

"I won't accept that from you," Paula responded. "I don't care whether you think I'm sticking my nose in where it doesn't belong or not. My only concern is Cord and what's best for him. I thought that was your only concern, too, regardless of any petty misunderstanding."

Staring at her twisting fingers, Stacy cried inwardly at the unfairness of being blackmailed by her love.

"I am concerned." Her voice was barely above a whisper.

"If you are, then talk to him," the blonde challenged. "Persuade him to take some of the work off your shoulders. Give him something to do other than brood all day long."

"All . . . all right."

The reluctant agreement was released through gritted teeth as Stacy brushed a hand across her temple and gazed sightlessly at the ceiling. "I'll talk to him tomorrow," she frowned.

"Tonight," Paula stated unequivocally. "Putting it off until tomorrow won't make it any easier."

Stacy pivoted, meeting the directness of the blue gaze. The angry protest rising in her throat was checked by her tightly compressed lips. Without a word, she swept past the tall blonde through the door and down the stairs to the master bedroom.

There her own courage faltered. She stared at the closed door for a hesitating second, her hand clenching nervously. Quickly she rapped once and opened the door without waiting for permission to enter. Cord was standing freely at the end of the bed, a hand clutching the sturdy post of the Spanish style bed. His expression was grim with determination as he glanced up. At the sight of Stacy, he drew his dark head back in aloof arrogance.

"What do you want?" he challenged.

Skirting his cold gaze, Stacy glanced at his crutches some distance away. "What are you doing?" she breathed, alarm surfacing at the obvious unsteadiness of his legs.

Half dragging and half lifting one leg forward to put himself at a better angle to face her, Cord lifted one corner of his mouth.

"Don't you recognize the movement?" he mocked cynically. "It's my version of walking."

"But you could fall," she protested, realizing what Paula had been talking about. Cord was trying to push himself beyond the limit of his capabilities at this moment.

He leaned a hip against the bed railing. She could see by the rippling muscles in his arms the effort was costing him to remain upright. He was clad only in dark trousers, his shirt discarded. Perspiration curled the dark hairs on his naked chest.

" I'm not interested in listening to your false gestures of concern," he jeered. "Get to the point of why you're here. I know it's not a desire for my company that's brought you."

Stacy's mouth opened to deny his cutting remark, but she closed it without speaking. It would be a waste of breath. He wouldn't believe her.

"I need your help," she said finally.

A black eyebrow arched in arrogant disbelief. "For what?"

"The ranch work has become too much for me. I can't handle it all anymore," Stacy rushed.

There was more than a grain of truth in the statement. Managing the ranch was a full-time occupation without the added burden of the coming horse sale.

"What's the matter?" Cord mocked harshly. "Don't you have enough free time to sneak off to meet Travis? Are you expecting me to provide it?"

Stacy flinched at the physical blow to his sarcasm. In agitation she moved with no direction to her steps, a release of the frustration and pain that consumed her.

"Travis has nothing to do with my request in any way," she denied in a low, trembling voice.

"Doesn't he?" Cord snarled.

His sunbrowned fingers closed savagely around her wrist and yanked her to him. The force of the sudden contact with his hard male shape momentarily took her breath away. Her wrist was released as his hand gathered a handful of her gleaming hair and viciously twisted it to pull her head back. Stacy gasped, wincing at the pain in her scalp.

Her eyes opened to focus on the glittering fire in his gaze. The thud of her heart sounded like a hammer pounding in her chest. His gaze centered on the parted moistness of her lips.

"Is Travis a good lover, my passionate Stacy?" he hissed.

His gaze traveled downward to the exposed curve of her neck. "Do you make those kitten sounds in your throat for him?"

Relentlessly he bruised the sensitive cord of her neck as if intent on destroying any trace of another man's caress. He paused near her ear to nibble cruelly at its lobe.

Hot fire raced through Stacy's veins, melting her bones. Her fingers spread over the hard flesh of his shoulders, muscles bunched and flexing beneath her palms. The scent of his body was musky and warm, arousing her senses with familiar desire. But it was not desire driving Cord, only a ruthlessness to claim what was his.

"Don't do this, Cord. Please," Stacy begged.

Her protest was instantly smothered by the grinding force of his mouth. Yielding against him, she knew she couldn't deny him his way. The bitter truth was that she wanted his caresses even if they were prompted by anger and contempt.

As she leaned against him, his knees buckled. He was forced to release her to let his arms grip the bed, taking the bulk of his weight away from his still weak legs. Instantly Stacy reached forward when she realized what had happened, anxious to lend him her support.

"Let me help you," she said.

Cord turned away from her, struggling to keep his balance. "I don't want your help!" he hurled savagely. "Just get out of here!"

Biting into her lower lip, swollen from the cruel mastery of his kiss, Stacy took a step backward. Then she turned and hurried blindly toward the door.

His voice snarled after her. "And you can tell your precious Travis that you weren't able to trick your husband into allowing you more time for your rendezvous!"

Stacy stopped at the door. "For the last time, Cord, Travis had nothing to do with my coming here." Her voice quivered with pain. "The quarter-horse auction is only a week away. I can't cope with everything there is to do."

She made one last attempt to fulfill the purpose that had brought her to the room. "I talked to Paula and she said that your helping with the ranch probably wouldn't interfere with the therapy."

Her back was turned to him as she reached for the doorknob. It turned beneath her hand before he replied to her statement.

"When did you talk to Paula?" he demanded quietly.

A frown marred her forehead. "A few minutes ago. She's upstairs."

She released the knob and faced him. "What difference does that make?"

"Was this her idea or yours?" His gaze narrowed.

"It was Paula's idea," she answered truthfully. "But it doesn't change the fact that I need help, Cord, your help. I once said I would ask for no quarter from you, but now I'm begging for it. I can't make it without you." Stacy meant that in every sense of the word, but she qualified it almost instantly out of pride. "At least, you could do the bookwork if nothing else."

He seemed to weigh her appeal, testing its sincerity, then nodded grudgingly. "I'll do the bookwork. Now go away and leave me alone."

He began the slow task of walking beside the bed, his arms bearing most of the burden as he made it clear the dismissal was final.

Knowing any offer of assistance would be summarily rejected, Stacy left the room. Listlessly she climbed the stairs, walking past her room to Paula's. The door was opened and she paused in its frame.

"Cord has agreed to help," she said simply.

"I knew you could persuade him," Paula smiled.

One corner of Stacy's mouth lifted in a bitter movement. She felt that Paula's name had lent more weight with Cord than her own plea for aid. She made no reply to the comment as she turned and retreated to the emptiness of her bedroom. Her body was haunted by the memory of Cord's. There would be no rest tonight. Nor the next two nights.

WEARILY SHE PUSHED the front door open, wondering why she had bothered to come to the house for lunch. She was too tired to eat and felt as brittle as an eggshell.

There was a rustling of papers from the study. The door stood open and Stacy guessed that Cord was in the room working. She started to hurry silently by, not wanting to see him when she was so vulnerable to his barbs.

"Stacy! Come in here!"

His imperious order checked her in mid-stride. She hesitated, then moved into the doorway. He was sitting behind the desk, his patrician features darkened in anger.

"What do you want?" Her brisk question was intended to imply that she was busy and impatient to be on her way.

"I want an explanation for this." Lifting his hand to indicate the papers he held, he tossed them to the front of the desk for her inspection.

Stacy paused, wanting to flee. Resolutely squaring her shoulders, she walked to the desk and picked up the papers. A quick glance identified them as the catalog of the yearlings to be sold.

"What do you want explained?" she frowned, seeing nothing that was in error.

"Why are the two stud colts sired by Lije Masters' stallion listed for sale?" he demanded.

Stacy shrugged her shoulders in confusion. "Neither Travis nor I saw any reason to keep them. We already have three two-year-old stallions for stud prospects as well as the proven stallion you bought last year. That's not even mentioning the two we already use for breeding."

His mouth tightened grimly. "You knew I wanted to add the Malpais bloodline to my stock. This one yearling out of the Cutters' mare I especially wanted to keep."

"How in the world could I know that?" Stacy protested angrily. "Am I supposed to read your mind?"

"You could have used some common sense," he retorted.

"I asked you to help choose the yearlings to sell!" she shouted in defense, her raw nerves unable to tolerate his anger. "Travis told you he didn't know anything about horses, only cattle. You refused to help, so don't blame me if there are horses listed that you don't want to sell. It's your own fault."

"How was I supposed to know you would do something as stupid as this?" Cord waved angrily at the catalog.

Hot tears spilled over her lashes, flaming her cheeks with their scalding warmth.

"I can't do anything to please you anymore!" she declared in a choked voice. "If you think I'm doing such a lousy job of running things, then you can do it all from now on! I'm handing in my resignation as of this moment!"

Pivoting, she raced from the room, half-blinded by her tears. A hand covered her mouth to stifle the sobs that wrenched her throat.

"Stacy, come back here!" Cord shouted.

She slammed the front door on his order. Her headlong flight took her down the sloping grade to the stables. Throwing open the door to the tack room, she pulled a bridle from the wall and her saddle and blanket. Indifferent to the weight, she walked swiftly to the corral, but there was no sign of the chocolate-brown mare.

From a sturdy enclosure apart from the others came a whinny of greeting. Stacy glanced in its direction, her gaze focusing on the sorrel stallion. His delicate head was over the top rail, luminous brown eyes returning her look, pointed ears pricked forward.

"Diablo," Stacy murmured with decision, and moved to his corral.

Docilely the red horse nuzzled her arm, playfully nipping at her blouse as she entered his corral. He bent his head without argument to accept the bridle, and swished his flaxen tail contentedly as she laid the saddle blanket on his back.

Minutes later Stacy was swinging into the saddle, mentally thumbing her nose at Cord's long-standing order not to ride the high-spirited stallion. With her weight on his back, the sorrel pranced eagerly. His four white feet stirred up the dusty ground.

Running a soothing hand over his arched neck,

Stacy turned him toward the corral gate. From the corner of her eye, she saw the wizened figure hurrying to intercept them. She leaned forward and unlatched the gate only to have Hank reach it before she could swing it open.

"You get down off that horse!" He held the gate shut as he frowned at her, certain she had lost all her senses.

"Get out of the way, Hank," she ordered.

"You know you ain't supposed to ride that stallion."

"He's my horse and I'll do what I want."

Stacy nudged the sorrel forward until his shoulder was pushing against the gate. Her hand joined the effort to swing the gate open. "Move, Hank," she warned.

"The boss gave strict orders none of us was to let you ride that horse!" He strained to keep it closed, but the combined strength of horse and rider was more than he could stop, especially when the sorrel saw the narrow opening and pushed to enlarge it.

"I don't care what the boss says!" Stacy declared.

Hank was knocked to the ground as the horse burst through. Stacy had only a second to glance back to make certain the old man was getting to his feet unharmed. After that, all her efforts were directed to controlling her mount.

Reining him away from the fenced enclosures of the other horses, she guided him toward the house and the winding lane that would take them to open range. In a lunging canter, the sorrel threatened to bolt with each stride. The leather reins bit into her hands as she tried to hold him.

Cord was on the sidewalk when the stallion plunged by the house. One look at Stacy fighting to hold the horse and he began shouting orders to the stablehands emerging from the buildings. A smile curved her mouth, guessing his anger at seeing her astride the horse he had forbidden her to ride.

Her pleasure was short-lived. She had to concentrate on mastering the spirited steed beneath her. It had been so long since Diablo had tasted freedom and he wanted to drink his fill. Lack of sleep and loss of weight had depleted Stacy's strength, and the muscles in her arms began to tremble at the effort of holding the stallion in a controllable canter.

With a determined shake of his head, the sorrel loosened the hold on the reins and gained the bit between his teeth. In one bound, he was at a dead run, breaking away from the driveway to veer across the rolling plains racing toward the eastern mountains.

The wind whipped Stacy's breath away. A blackness swam around her eyes as she buried her face in the flaxen mane and gripped the saddle horn to stay on. Dodging patches of prickly pear cactus and skimming over the top of sagebrush and range grass, the stallion ran with ecstasy.

Somehow Stacy managed to stay in the saddle, aboard the runaway, mindless to the wild ride. Not until he slowed to a bone-jarring trot miles from the ranch house did she take notice of her surroundings. His flanks heaved as he blew the dust from his lungs and finally obeyed the pressure of the reins when she drew him to a stop.

Weakly, she slipped from the saddle, a death grip remaining on the reins. Her knees buckled beneath her and she slumped to the ground. Diablo was content to munch the long strands of grass. For the moment Stacy didn't care if he broke away. She lay there on the ground, strength gradually flowing back into her limbs.

But it was nearly an hour before she climbed back into the saddle and turned the horse toward home.

CHAPTER TEN

BOTH STACY AND DIABLO were hot and tired by the time they gained sight of the ranch yard. Pausing beside the wrought-iron fence enclosing the family cemetery on a knoll west of the house, Stacy indifferently watched the activity below. The circuitous route she had taken had been necessary in order to get her bearing after the wild ride.

Travis's green pickup truck was parked in the driveway in front of the house. The door to the driver's side was opened. The broad-shouldered figure sitting half in the cab and half out was undoubtedly Travis.

There was also no mistaking the identity of Cord leaning on his crutches and gazing in the direction Stacy had originally gone. Paula was there, too, her hands on her hips conveying an attitude of troubled concern.

A search party had obviously been organized for her. Stacy guessed that Travis was probably in contact with it now, via the radio in his truck. She supposed she hadn't run into it because of the different route she had taken back.

Touching a heel to the sorrel, she started down the small hill toward the truck. There was no thought to

Cord's anger at her deliberate disobedience that would await her return. She seemed invulnerable to everything but her own tiredness.

She was a hundred feet away before Travis glanced around and noticed her approach. He stepped quickly out of the truck, saying something to the other two. With a jerk of his head, Cord looked at her, a taut alertness about him like a lion ready to spring.

It was Travis who moved forward to intercept her, his hand grasping the reins near the cheek strap. Diablo tossed his head, disliking the touch of a man's hand.

Travis ignored the stallion, his gaze sweeping over Stacy's disheveled appearance. Dirt clung to the shoulder and sleeve of her blouse where she had rested on the ground.

"Are you all right, Stacy?"

"Yes," she smiled wanly.

Looping the reins around the saddle horn, she swung her right leg over the horn, kicking her other foot free of the stirrup to slide to the ground. But Travis's hands were around her waist, lifting her down. For a brief instant she stumbled against him before regaining her balance.

Almost absently her gaze met the blaze of Cord's dark eyes, blistering hotly over her. She stepped away from Travis's supporting hands.

"Get that stallion out of here, Travis," ordered Cord. "And as for you, Stacy—" His voice was ominously low.

Paula placed a restraining hand on his arm. "Let her

be, Cord," she murmured. Her blue eyes moved sympathetically to Stacy's exhausted expression. "She's hot and tired. She needs a shower and a rest, not a lecture."

A muscle worked convulsively in Cord's jaw as if he wasn't entirely convinced of Paula's statement. Before he could complete his interrupted sentence, Paula walked around him and curved an arm around Stacy's shoulders, turning her toward the house. "Come on, Stacy."

In other circumstances, Stacy would have resented the other girl's proprietorial air. At the moment she was too tired to care. It didn't even matter that she had been rescued from Cord's wrath. She was numbed beyond emotion.

The sting of the shower spray eliminated that protection. Wrapped in a cotton robe, Stacy stood at her bedroom window watching the search party that had just ridden in, recalled by either Cord or Travis. Guilt nagged her at the amount of work undone because they had searched for her. Riding Diablo had been a childish gesture of defiance.

A peculiar thudding sound came from the staircase, and Stacy tipped her head in absent curiosity. It stopped outside her door, and a wave of certainty washed over her that it was Cord outside. A second later the door opened to reveal him, anger darkening his face with a thundercloud warning.

"Did you think by staying in your room you would avoid facing me?" he challenged.

She shook her head without verbally answering and

stared out the window. A whole gamut of painful sensations returned.

"You deliberately rode that horse knowing how I felt, didn't you?" His harshly condemning voice scraped at her barely healed nerves.

"Yes," she admitted quietly.

"You realize you could have been very seriously hurt, don't you? And don't pretend that you had control of that horse, because he was running away with you."

"But I wasn't hurt," she defended with forced evenness.

"That's beside the point," Cord snapped.

Irritatedly she swung away from the window. "There's no reason to go into all this. It's over and done with and I admit it was foolish. I was . . . I was just upset."

"You're right," he said tightly. "It is over and done with. And it won't happen again. Diablo will be off this ranch before nightfall."

It was a full second before his statement penetrated. "What do you mean?" Stacy demanded.

"I'm selling him," declared Cord flatly. "Never again am I going through what I did this afternoon."

"He's not yours to sell!" Temper flashed in her brown eyes. "Diablo belongs to me!"

There was a complacent curve to his firm mouth. "The ranch belongs to me—you even handed the running of it over to me this morning. And I refuse to have that stallion on my property. You can fight the sale, but you can't fight that."

"How can you do this?" Her chin quivered with anger.

"How could you do what you did?" he countered.

"I told you I was upset!"

"And I'm insuring that the next time you get upset, you don't go riding off and breaking your foolish neck!"

"You can't sell him. He's mine," Stacy repeated.

"He'll not stay another night on this ranch," Cord reiterated just as forcefully as Stacy.

"If he goes, I leave with him!" she threatened.

To add credibility to her words, she pivoted away from Cord with a defiant flourish, but before she could take a step, his hand encircled her wrist and spun her back.

"You are not leaving here!" Cruelly he gripped her wrist.

Needing a hand on a crutch to remain upright, there wasn't any way Cord could check the open palm of Stacy's free hand as it swung toward his cheek. It struck its mark, his tanned skin marked with white then filled with red. For a cold instant, she thought he was going to retaliate in kind.

Stone-faced, Cord released her hand and maneuvered himself in awkward steps to the hall door. There he paused, the glowing dark coals of his eyes seeking her.

"I'm not letting you go, so don't try." It wasn't a warning. It was an unequivocal statement.

As the door closed behind him, Stacy slumped on to her bed, rubbing her bruised wrist.

After several minutes she went to the bedroom window and waited to see if Cord was really going to get rid of Diablo.

If he did, she wasn't certain what she would do. She was afraid that temper had brought them both to an impasse and pride wouldn't allow either of them to back down.

There was no activity in the driveway below, no movement of horse trailers or vans. Perhaps Cord had reconsidered, she thought hopefully.

Then an almost imperceptible click of the doorknob turned her head. Very slowly the door swung partially open. Stacy watched it warily. Josh peered around the door.

His round dark eyes found her and he asked, "Are you sick, mommy?"

"No, I'm not sick," she smiled with loving indulgence. "Come in."

Still he hesitated. "Maria said I wasn't to bother you and I thought you were sick."

"I was just very tired and thought I would rest for a while," Stacy explained more fully to her doubting son.

"Are you all rested now?" Josh inquired, stepping just inside the door. His expression was expectantly bright.

She inclined her head towards him in amusement. "Why?"

"Cause," he shrugged, "I got nothing to do. I thought you might think of something."

Gazing at the hopeful light in his nearly black eyes,

Stacy knew she had spent little time with her son lately. There wasn't any reason not to make up for it now.

"Any suggestions in particular that you wanted me to make?" she teased.

An impish smile curved his mouth. "We could play ball."

"How about something less strenuous like swinging?" she suggested.

"Okay," Josh agreed readily.

"Give me five minutes to get dressed and I'll be down," Stacy promised.

With a nod of his head, he darted into the hall. She wasted no time changing into a pair of shorts and a cool top.

At the door, she glanced to the bedroom window, then walked out. There would be plenty of time to find out what Cord was doing about Diablo. She didn't mind postponing her own decision.

It was a carefree afternoon Stacy spent playing with Josh, pushing his swing high in the air and listening to his shrieks of delight. She ruffled the top of Josh's head affectionately as they approached the house.

"Why don't you see if Maria has anything cold to drink?" said Stacy.

"And cookies?" Josh added.

"And cookies," she agreed. "We'll have it out here on the veranda. You can help Maria carry it out, can't you?"

"Sure."

He dashed toward the sliding glass doors as Stacy settled contentedly on a chaise longue. The glass door wasn't completely closed by Josh, and with a sigh at his impatience, Stacy rose to close it.

The loud impact of something falling stopped her hand from sliding the door shut. Identifying the location of the sound as the study, she pushed the door open and darted inside. Her heart kept skipping beats at the thought that Cord might have fallen.

She was not alone in her fear as she spied Paula already racing from the living room toward the study. The physiotherapist's haste lent wings to Stacy's feet. She followed the girl with no hope of reaching Cord first. As she entered the hallway, Paula disappeared through the study door.

"You crazy, idiotic darling!" Stacy heard Paula exclaim in mock reproof. "What on earth were you trying to do?"

The unconsciously murmured endearment slowed Stacy's feet.

A cold chill ran through her veins, reducing her pulse to a dull thud.

"I was trying to get some papers from the file." Cord muttered his answer. His voice was low and strained as if from physical effort.

"Yes, you were trying to get them without your crutches," Paula reprimanded. "When are you going to learn that you have to take things by stages? You'll walk soon enough if you don't break a leg first. Are you hurt anywhere?"

Stacy paused near the door, giving herself a limited angle to view the room. Jealously she watched the tall blonde kneel beside Cord, the contrast between his dark looks and Paula's fairness crushing the life from her heart.

"I think I'm only suffering from a gravely wounded pride," he answered, levering himself into a half-sitting position with one arm and struggling to persuade his uncoordinated legs to shift him to his feet.

"Let me help you," Paula stated.

Without waiting for his agreement, she hooked his arm around her neck and shoulders. The physical effort of both of them brought Cord upright, and he wavered unsteadily for a few seconds, trying to regain his balance.

Razor-sharp claws sliced at Stacy's heart. Paula's height brought the top of her head even with Cord's dark eyes. The fullness of her lips was just below the jutting angle of his chin.

They stood so closely together with Cord's arm around her shoulders that tears of impotent rage welled in Stacy's eyes. When the grooves around his mouth deepened and Cord looked so warmly into the pair of blue eyes, Stacy held her breath to keep from crying out in pain.

"You're one in a million, Paula," he said.

"I'm glad you finally recognize that," she responded lightly.

"Oh, I've recognized it for a long time," Cord nodded.

The half-smile deepened the corners of his mouth. "I just haven't got around to saying anything until now."

Paula's ash-blond head moved downward as if

glancing at the floor. Stacy knew the impact of Cord's charm, especially at such close quarters. Cord placed a thumb and forefinger beneath Paula's chin and turned her face toward him again.

"Do you know something?" he asked rhetorically. "I don't think I'll throw you out of the house when all this is finished."

"Careful," Paula warned huskily, "or I might make you live up to that statement."

Cord shook his head and smiled. "You're welcome to stay in my home for as long as you want."

Paula seemed to catch her breath, then laughed with brittle lightness. "Stacy might have something to say about another woman taking up residence here," she reminded him.

His handsome, patrician features immediately hardened, the line of his mouth straightening. A guardedly aloof look entered his gaze as he released Paula's chin.

"Yes," he agreed quietly, "if Stacy is still here."

Reeling away from the study door, Stacy stumbled back toward the veranda. Jumbled thoughts whirled through her head. His enigmatic statement echoed and reechoed in her mind, its meaning no clearer than when he had spoken it. The only certainty in it was that Cord considered it a distinct possibility that she, Stacy, would be gone. The question unanswered was would she leave at her instigation or his?

For two days, Stacy wandered aimlessly through each waking hour, waiting in dread for the death blow to fall. Diablo was still in his corral. She hadn't the courage to ask Cord if he had reconsidered his threat to sell the horse. She feared the result of such a confrontation.

The entire ranch was bustling with preparations for the quarter-horse auction on Saturday, only two days away. Only Stacy and Paula had nothing to do. Stacy's nerves couldn't tolerate the company of the woman who was stealing Cord's love as she restored his mobility.

The lovely old hacienda with its whitewashed adobe and red-tiled roof became a stifling prison, which she had to escape from for some part of each day. The shopping expedition that had brought Stacy into McCloud, Texas, had merely been an excuse to flee from the sword-of-Damocles atmosphere of the house.

Josh tugged at her hand. "I'm hungry, mommy," he said.

Catching back a sigh, Stacy glanced at her watch. It was nearly time for lunch. She knew Maria was expecting them back, but she had no desire to return yet.

"Why don't we have something to eat here in town instead of going home?" she suggested with forced brightness.

"Yeah!" he agreed with a wide grin.

As they entered the restaurant, one familiar face stood out from the others of the townspeople. Josh saw him at the same moment Stacy did.

"Look, mom, there's Travis!" His loud voice turned heads, including the foreman's.

Travis straightened from the table as Josh withdrew his hand from Stacy's and rushed forward to greet him. She would rather have avoided the discerning pair of brown eyes, but she followed her son.

"Hello, Josh." Travis playfully mussed the shining black hair of her son's head before lifting his gaze to Stacy, its look faintly probing. "Stacy," he nodded a greeting.

"Hello, Travis," she returned with a voice that she hoped sounded calm. "We didn't expect to see you in here."

"I had an errand in town and thought I'd have something to eat before going back. Would you care to join me?" He gestured toward the empty chairs at his table.

It would have been churlish to refuse. "Of course," she accepted with inner reluctance.

Travis had already ordered before they arrived. After the waitress had taken hers and Josh's order, Stacy fiddled nervously with the cutlery until she felt Travis watching the movement. Quickly she hid her hands in her lap and tried to fill the silence that had gaped alarmingly.

"How are things at the ranch?"

It seemed a strange question to ask, yet Stacy had had no contact with the operation of the ranch for nearly a week.

"Running smoothly," Travis replied. "Cord has taken charge as if he'd never been away."

"That's good," she nodded stiffly. Hesitating, she asked, "Has he said anymore about you—leaving?"

"Not directly." He lifted the coffee mug and held it in two hands, swirling the brown black liquid. "He said he needed my legs for the time being."

"I'm sorry for not warning you in advance that I was turning things over to him." Stacy glanced self-consciously at the table top.

"I guessed it was a sudden decision." Travis sipped the coffee. "How is it going with you two?"

"We haven't talked much." That was an understatement. "Before I was busy with the ranch. Now, Cord is."

She watched Josh flipping through the pages of the coloring book she had bought him, as she avoided the introspective gaze of the man seated opposite her. "And he still has to spend a lot of time with Paula," she added.

"You don't still believe—" The waitress arrived, interrupting Travis's impatient comment.

The arrival of the meal brought Josh's attention back to the table and Travis wasn't able to reintroduce the subject, to Stacy's relief. Her son's chatter covered her own lack of participation in the subsequent conversation.

"Are you going to the ranch now, Travis?" Josh wanted to know as the three of them paused outside the restaurant.

Travis adjusted his dust-stained stetson on his dark head and nodded affirmatively. "I have to go back to work."

"We're going back now, too," Josh said with certainty.

Stacy couldn't argue with his statement. They had exhausted the morning wandering through stores, and Josh's interest in the outing was over. She couldn't expect her son to understand that she wasn't eager to return to the ranch. It was his home, even if she had begun to feel uncomfortable in it.

"Where is your car parked?" Travis glanced at Stacy.

"Over by the lumber yard." She motioned in the general direction of its location.

"So is my truck." He winked at Josh. "How about a piggyback ride to your car, Josh?" At the boy's eager nod, Travis hoisted him onto his shoulders. "Watch the hat," he warned Josh's clasping hands, "and my neck."

With Josh giggling, Travis started walking toward the lumber yard. His large hands firmly held the small legs dangling across his chest.

"Giddy-up, horsey!" Josh laughed, moving back and forth across the shoulders to urge Travis to go faster.

"Careful or I'll buck you off." Travis tipped his head back in a mock threat.

Stacy laughed at the wide-eyed look on Josh's face as his hands tightly clutched the strong neck for a second before he realized that Travis was only teasing. As they were about to step off the sidewalk curb into the street, a small lime-green car slowed to a stop in front of them, blocking their path.

In disbelief, Stacy stared into the impenetrable mask of coldness that was Cord's face. He was sitting in the passenger seat, his tall frame looking cramped in the close quarters of the economy car. His unrevealing gaze was narrowed on the man carrying his son.

"I thought you were at the ranch, Travis," he said flatly.

"I had an errand in town," was the calm reply as Travis swung Josh down from his perch.

Stacy silently marveled at the way Travis ignored the underlying accusation in Cord's statement. The ruthless set of Cord's jaw made her shiver, yet nothing seemed to ruffle Travis, a trait he had probably gained through years of working for Colter Langston.

Her thoughts were jerked back to the present as Cord's gaze sliced from Travis to her with condemning force, silently accusing her of keeping an assignation with the foreman.

"Josh and I ran into Travis at the restaurant when we stopped for lunch," she explained, hating herself immediately for explaining why she was in Travis's company.

In the driver's seat, Paula bent her head to look past Cord at the threesome standing on the sidewalk. "You were in town shopping, weren't you, Stacy?" she asked.

"Yes," she agreed quickly.

"What did you buy?" Cord glanced pointedly at the thin paper bag in her hand.

Stacy's fingers tightened on it instinctively. "A coloring book for Josh."

"And you've been gone all morning?" Cord mocked.

"I—I couldn't find anything else I wanted," she

defended weakly, knowing she hadn't looked at anything but in the most abstract way.

"After spending such a futile morning, it was
fortunate you accidentally ran into Travis and weren't
forced to eat lunch alone."

An undercurrent of sarcasm and contempt laced
Cord's low voice.

"Yes, it was," Stacy agreed, shaking back her head
in a gesture of pride and sending her silken chestnut
hair dancing around her shoulders. Her defense was
shaky, so she tried to attack. "If I had known you and
Paula were going to be in town, I would have met you
for lunch."

"It was time for Cord's checkup," Paula explained.
"And Bill was too busy to get away to come to the
ranch."

"Then you haven't eaten," Stacy commented, glad
the image of the two of them sharing an intimate lunch
could be banished from her mind.

"Actually Mary talked us into eating with them,"
she said.

A fingernail broke through the thin paper bag as
Stacy tightly clenched it in her hand. Now Paula was
even usurping her position with Mary, one of her best
friends. The thought choked her.

"I see," she responded, tautly soft.

"We're on our way back to the ranch now," Paula
inserted.

"So are we." Stacy coupled herself with Travis in
deliberate defiance, uncaring of the diamond sharp
look from Cord.

"We'll see you there." Shifting the car into gear, Paula lifted a hand in goodbye, which Stacy managed to stiffly return.

With their way across the street cleared, Stacy took hold of Josh's hand. As they stepped off, Travis lingered for an instant on the curb staring after the car. Then he fell in beside them.

"When Cord gets an idea in his head, he doesn't let go," he muttered.

Stacy knew he was referring to Cord's belief that she and Travis were having an affair, but she didn't comment. There wasn't anything to say.

CHAPTER ELEVEN

THERE WAS A TIRED MOVEMENT of her mouth into a smile. The shining dark head on the white pillow looked so peaceful and happy. Long, curling lashes lay softly against Josh's tanned cheeks. He had been so adamantly opposed to the suggestion of a nap, yet he had fallen asleep before she had reached the last page of the storybook.

Quietly she closed the door to his room. She thought how blissful it would be to have the innocent, untroubled sleep of a child for one night. But then there were occasions when they had nightmares, too.

Halfway down the stairs, Stacy heard the thump of Cord's crutches in the hallway below. Freezing for an instant at the sound, she was motionless when Cord's frowning countenance glanced at her.

"Do you know where Travis is?" he demanded curtly.

"No." She started down the stairs.

"I though you kept track of him," Cord mocked.

"You think a lot of things that are wrong," she retorted.

"You're all sweetness and innocence, aren't you?" His mouth quirked.

"Just as much as you are," Stacy flashed.

"What's that supposed to mean?" he glowered.

"You figure it out." Impatient that she had allowed herself to become involved in a meaningful trade of innuendoes, she started to walk past him to the living room.

"Don't walk away from me!" Cord snapped, grabbing her arm and spinning her back.

Stacy's temper flared. "Of course not! That's unthinkable! I'm one of your possessions, am I not? Do you keep me around for decoration or for the sake of appearances?" she challenged harshly.

"It certainly isn't for decoration!" His gaze raked her thinning figure with scorn. "I can feel your bones beneath my hands. You're turning into a scarecrow, wasting away."

His contempt of her appearance hurt. "Dying for love from you." The words were torn from her throat before she could check them.

"Pining for your freedom is more like it." Cord dismissed her truthful admission with disdain. The crutches beneath his arms supported him as his fingers dug into the soft flesh of her upper arms, and gave her a violent shake.

"Isn't it? Admit it, Stacy. You want to be free, don't you?"

Free from what, her whirling mind wondered. Free from the agony of wanting his love and knowing she no longer received it? Free from the torture of wondering what he and Paula did when they were alone? Free from the pain of a broken heart?

"Yes. Yes! *Yes!*" The admission rose to a crescendo of emotion as her head moved insanely from side to side in denial.

His grip tightened on her arms, cutting off the circulation until the rest of her arms throbbed with pain. Then his hold loosened and he shifted back on his crutches. Stacy buried her face in her numbed hands to smother the sobs that racked her chest.

"I told you I would never let you go." His voice was ominously low, rumbling like thunger in the storm-charged seconds. "But I'm destroying both of us doing that. My father was right when he sent my mother away. Why ruin two lives? You're free, Stacy. I won't hold you here."

"Wh-what are you saying?" She raised her tear-wet lashes, trying to read the granite-hard lines of his expression.

"I'm saying that you're free," Cord repeated coldly. "You may leave whenever you want. Today, to-morrow, this minute, I don't care."

With painstaking movement, he pivoted on his crutches to leave her. Uncertainty plagued Stacy. Even in her darkest moments she had never really believed that Cord would send her away.

His back was to her, broad and strong. With laborious steps, balanced by his crutches, he began walking toward the study. Stacy couldn't let him go without knowing for sure what he meant.

Her fingers touched his arm to detain him. He stopped immediately, his muscles stiffening beneath her hand, but he didn't turn to face her.

"I gave you what you wanted," he growled. "What is it now?"

"I—I. . ." she faltered at the aloof profile she saw. "I want to know if it's what you want."

His jaw was clenched for an instant. "Stacy, you're free to do what you want. You can go or stay. But don't make me look at you again."

Her hand fell away from his arm, the nails digging into the palms. Stacy lifted her chin with a false attempt to react with dignity to his final, cutting statement.

"Tell—tell Maria to pack my things," she said numbly. 'I'll let her know where I want them to be sent."

"I will," he agreed tersely, and began walking toward the study again.

Stacy watched him for a painful second, then pivoted to race back up the stairs. She threw a few essential items into an overnight bag and hurried out of the room. Cord had made no reference to Josh and neither had she. She was leaving, but she was taking Josh with her.

In his room, she quickly added his things to her case. When it was locked and sitting beside the door, she walked to the bed to wake the slumbering boy.

He rubbed his eyes sleepily when she shook his shoulders. "I'm tired," he grumbled.

"You have to get up now," she coaxed, lifting him to a sitting position. "We're leaving."

The statement gained his immediate interest. "Where are we going?"

Stacy hesitated. This was not the time to tell him the truth, not when she wanted to get him out of the house without Cord being aware of what she was doing. She tucked the tails of his shirt into his pants.

"We're going on a trip." It was a half-truth.

"Where?"

Stacy had no idea. It didn't seem to matter where they went. "You'll see." She tried to make it sound like a mysterious adventure.

Taking Josh by the hand, she hurried down the stairs, carrying the suitcase. Silence came from the study. She didn't know if Cord was there or not and she didn't pause to find out.

Outside, Josh gave her a confused look. "Isn't daddy coming with us?"

"Not this time." Her throat constricted and she bustled him into the car.

Stacy didn't look back at the house as she reversed the car out of the driveway onto the lane. She didn't dare or she wouldn't have the strength to leave.

Chaos reigned over her thoughts, scattering them to the winds and leaving her without conscious direction. Road dust billowed from the accelerating car tires. She drove in a daze, not knowing or caring where she was going. Her eyes were dry, parched by pain that was beyond tears. Staring straight ahead, her mind registered nothing that she saw. She wasn't even aware when the car stopped.

"Mommy, why are we stopping here?" Josh laid a hand on her shoulder. Her hands were still gripping the steering wheel as she tried to shake off the stupor that paralyzed her. "Mommy, why have we come to Mary's house? Aren't we going on a trip?"

Mary's house. The words pierced the fog. With an effort Stacy focused her gaze on the familiar ranch-style home of Mary Buchanan. Something inside her began to crumble. It suddenly became imperative that she reach her friend before that 'something' caved in.

"Come on, Josh." She switched off the engine and stepped out of the car.

Indifferent to her son's bewilderment as he scrambled out, Stacy walked robotlike to the front door and rang the bell. A few seconds later it was opened and Mary's smiling face greeted them.

"Stacy, this is a surprise!" the redhead exclaimed in delight, swinging the door open wider. "Come in. You'll have to excuse the house. It's a mess, but I'm in the middle of—"

Stacy's grip tightened on Josh's hand. "Can you put us up?" There was a ring of despair in her voice as she interrupted.

Astonishment opened Mary's mouth. "Well, of course, but—"

"I've left Cord," Stacy answered the question that had been forming in her friend's mind.

"You've what?" Mary exclaimed incredulously. "Stacy, you can't mean it! Why, for heaven's sake?"

There was a shuddering collapse within. A black void swirled in front of Stacy's eyes. She didn't have to answer the question as she slipped into unconsciousness.

The dark world wrapped her in a protective cocoon,

insulating her mind from the pain it couldn't bear. Occasionally a haunting image of Cord would drift into the blackness. Her lips would form his name and she would call out to him. The masculine vision would look at her with silent contempt and fade away.

The last time his ghost appeared, he took her hand and looked at her gravely. "I'll always be with you, Stacy," the image told her. "I'll never leave you."

"No! No!" She protested the bitterness of her fate that she should always be haunted by his ghost.

"Ssh, darling," the familiar voice soothed. "You must rest."

Then the apparition dissolved into a mist, and oblivion claimed her again. She welcomed the black void, seeking its darkest corners to escape from Cord's specter.

For a long time Stacy remained safe in her vacuum, untouched by outside forces. Then a hand took her arm and lifted it, almost physically drawing her back into reality. Her lashes fluttered in protest, resisting the attempt to bring her back to the world she couldn't endure without Cord.

"Have you decided to rejoin us, Stacy?" a familiar voice inquired gently.

A frown creased her forehead. It wasn't Cord's voice that spoke to her. Nor was it Cord's patrician features Stacy saw when she was finally able to focus her gaze on the man standing beside her. The stocky figure belonged to Bill Buchanan. She stared at him bewilderedly for a minute, as he held her wrist in his fingers, checking her pulse.

"Wh-what happened?" she murmured in a disorientated fashion. Was she ill?

"You collapsed," the doctor informed her with a faint smile, "as I predicted you would if you didn't get away for a while." With her pulse taken, he let her arm lie back along her side.

"I don't understand," Stacy murmured with a confused shake of her head.

"It was a case of complete exhaustion," he explained. "When you wouldn't give your body the rest it needed, it took over. That's why you blacked out."

A movement near the window caught Stacy's eye, and her pulse rocked at the sight of Cord leaning on his crutches. Sunlight streamed over his shoulder, blinding her to the expression on his handsome face.

"What are you doing here?" she breathed, her heart fluctuating between fear and hope.

Bill Buchanan glanced from Stacy to Cord. "I'll leave you alone for a few minutes." He addressed the statement to Cord. "Only for a few minutes, though. She still needs a lot of rest."

There was a curt nod of agreement from Cord, followed by silence as the doctor withdrew from the room. Stacy's gaze searched the hidden recesses of his patrician features.

"Why are you here?" Stacy repeated. Instantly the answer occurred to her. "You've come to take Josh, haven't you?" She thought that subconsciously she had known that Cord would come after their son. "That's why you've come, isn't it?" Pain throbbed in her voice.

Cord moved out of the sunlight. His expression was an inscrutable mask that told her nothing. He stopped beside the bed.

"Mary phoned me to let me know what happened. I am still your husband," he inserted dryly. "I came because I wanted to make sure you were all right."

Stacy turned her head away.

"What difference would it make to you?" she muttered in self-pity.

"I haven't stopped caring about you, Stacy," he declared with a hiss of impatience.

No, she supposed he hadn't. He might have stopped loving her, but they had shared too many things for him to stop caring. A broken sigh quivered from her lungs.

"You won't take Josh, will you?" she asked weakly.

Cord exhaled heavily. "No, I won't take Josh." He seemed to hesitate. "You're going to need rest. You're welcome to come back to the ranch until you're better."

"I won't go back there!" Stacy violently rejected the suggestion and its implication of further torment at seeing Cord and Paula together.

"Very well," he nodded grimly, and turned on his crutches. "I have to be getting back to the ranch. There are a lot of things to be done."

"Yes." There was a poignant catch in her voice. "The horse sale is tomorrow, isn't it?"

Cord paused, not quite looking over his shoulder.

"You've been unconscious for a long time, Stacy. Tomorrow is today. The auction is going on right now."

Had she been unconscious that long? The discovery startled her.

"I'll see you later," he offered distantly and opened the bedroom door.

"No," Stacy responded abruptly. His concern for her welfare was not enough when she hungered for his love. "There's no need for you to come back," she added stiffly.

His shoulders squared slightly. "Perhaps not," was his noncommittal response. "I'll let Josh know you're okay. He's been worried." He moved out of the room.

The door closed and Stacy turned her face into the pillow. Shutting her eyes tightly, she held back the tears. Rest, Bill Buchanan had decreed. It seemed an impossible order. Yet within minutes, her exhausted body had induced sleep.

The opening of the door awakened her. Through half-closed eyes, she glanced at her visitor, not welcoming the interruption from her heavy sleep. At least in sleep she stopped thinking and feeling. When her gaze focused on Paula, she was even less glad.

"How are you feeling?" Paula smiled sympathetically.

Stacy ignored the question. "Why are you here?" To rub salt into the wounds, she added silently in resentment.

"I brought some things in for Josh," the blonde explained. "I thought I'd look in to see how you were while I was here."

"I'm fine." Stacy breathed tightly, raking the fingers of one hand through the sides of her hair. "Please go away. You've done enough damage already." Bitterness surfaced with a rush that she couldn't hold back. "Unless you've come to gloat over your victory."

Frowning, Paula exhaled a confused laugh. "What on earth are you talking about?"

"Stop the pretense, Paula." Her voice was strangled with emotion. "You know very well that I'm talking about Cord. To the victor belong the spoils. I've conceded that you're the victor. Now get out of here!"

A charged moment of silence followed Stacy's choked outburst. Then Paula advanced into the room, her blue eyes narrowing.

"I don't like what you're saying, Stacy. Mary told me some nonsense about you telling her you'd left Cord just before you collapsed yesterday. Or was it nonsense?" she accused.

"Hardly." Stacy blinked furiously at her tears, holding them back. "He's all yours now."

"That's wonderful!" Paula exclaimed with dry amusement. "Do you actually mean you left Cord because of me?"

"You surely didn't expect me to stay while the two of you carried on your little affair? I do have some pride left," Stacy declared tautly.

"An affair? Cord and me?" Paula's mouth remained open in astonishment.

"I saw the two of you together." Stacy hated Paula's show of innocence. "Laughing and smiling and sharing your secret jokes."

"The joke is on you, honey." Paula shook her head. "Not that I wouldn't give my eyeteeth to have an affair with your husband, because I would. Two things would stop me, though. One is that I happen to like you. And the second, and overriding reason, is that Cord and I are just friends. If you'll pardon the usage of an oft-used cliché, he regards me as a sister."

"I don't believe you," she said, because she wanted to believe it so desperately.

"Cord is a one-woman man and that one woman is you, Stacy."

"But he said—" Her head spun. Could it be true? "I thought—"

"How much more proof do you need?" Paula sighed. "The poor man never left your side the whole time you were unconscious. Mary said he was a man possessed, sitting beside the bed staring at you."

It hadn't been a dream. Those weren't ghosts and visions of Cord that had haunted her when she was unconscious. It had really been Cord.

"But—" Stacy pressed a hand against her temple in confusion. "Why did he tell me to leave?"

"Probably because he thought that you wanted to go." Paula shrugged. "It certainly wasn't because he'd stopped loving you. In fact, it was probably the reverse. He loved you too much to keep you against your will."

It was all too possible that everything Paula said was true. She had never been able to convince Cord after that argument that she had not grown bored with the ranch and its life-style as his mother had done long ago. And he still mistakenly believed that she cared for Travis.

Throwing back the bedcovers, Stacy started to rise.

The blackness that suddenly began spinning in front of her sent her reeling back against the pillow. When it receded, she tried to rise again.

"What do you think you're doing?" Paula was at her side, trying to halt her movement. "You're still too weak."

"I have to get to the ranch." Determinedly Stacy tried to sit up. "I have to see Cord."

"I understand that you have to straighten things out, but—"

The bedroom door burst open and Cord came swinging in, barely using his crutches. Joy leaped into Stacy's brown eyes at the sight of him.

"Cord!" she cried out to him, flinging open her arms as Paula discreetly stepped to one side.

He stopped just short of her reach, his dark eyes scanning her face. "I've just been talking to Travis." He glanced over his shoulder at the tall figure standing in the doorway. "He said—"

Stacy guessed what Travis had said. He had obviously cleared up the matter of her supposed affair with him and her fears that Cord had been having one with Paula.

She interrupted him with a laugh. "I've just been talking to Paula."

In the next second he was sitting on the bed, crushing her against his chest. Stacy clung to him without restraint as he buried his face in the curve of her neck.

"It is true, then." His voice was muffled by the

bruising kisses he trailed over the column of her throat. "You love me?"

"I love you," she whispered achingly against his ear.

Cord shuddered against her, raising his head to gaze at her upturned face, flushed and animated with her love. A mixture of tender devotion and fiery passion blazed in his dark eyes.

"I never thought it was possible to love you more than I did in the beginning," he murmured for her hearing alone. "But I do, darling."

Rapture quivered through Stacy. Her lips moved inexorably closer to the sensuous line of his mouth, hard and firm.

Their contact was prevented by a third voice dryly inquiring, "What's going on here? A lovers' reunion?"

With a faintly embarrassed start, Stacy moved away from the inviting male lips. Her glowing brown eyes swung to Bill Buchanan standing behind his redhaired wife in the doorway. Mary had a tray in her hands.

"It certainly looks that way, doesn't it?" Paula chimed in. "Travis and I were just wondering how we could disappear before it got too warm in here."

"I was bringing you and Stacy some hot tea," Mary smiled at Paula. "I thought it would give Stacy some strength. Obviously she doesn't need it."

Cord smiled at Stacy, stealing her breath with the sheer charm of it.

"Your timing is terrible, Mary." He wrenched his gaze from Stacy. "But since you are here, bring some more cups. I want my wife stronger soon."

"We're intruding," protested Paula. "The two of you should be alone."

"Bill warned me this morning about overexciting Stacy when she regained consciousness." The intimate light in his eyes danced over the sudden flush in her cheeks. "So I think all of you should stay or I'll forget about his advice."

"We'll stay for a few minutes," Bill agreed. "Long enough to drink to your happiness."

Minutes later they were all lifting their tea cups in a mock toast. As Cord touched the rim of his china cup to Stacy's, he gazed into her eyes.

"I'm the luckiest man in the world," he murmured. "To love you and be loved by you with no end in sight."

His head dipped slowly toward hers, drinking from her lips, barely controlling his insatiable thirst. Stacy felt positively weak when he lifted his head. Somehow she raised the tea cup to her mouth and sipped at the reviving liquid, her gaze unable to leave Cord as he did the same, sealing their private toast.

"This should be champagne," Cord declared regretfully.

"Isn't it?" she smiled, giddy from his kiss.

"When you can't tell tea from champagne, you're definitely in love," Bill laughed. His hand slipped under his wife's elbow. "I think it's time we made our exit, Mary."

"Me, too," Paula joined in.

This time Cord didn't protest. Only Travis lingered after the others had left. His hat was in his hand.

"I'll be leaving, too," he said finally when Cord

looked expectantly at him. "Now that the quarter-horse auction is over, the ranch work will be back to normal. You and Stacy can handle it."

"You don't mean you're leaving permanently?" Stacy breathed.

"You don't need me anymore." Travis shook his head and smiled.

"But we want you to stay," she protested, glancing at her husband. "Don't we, Cord?"

"Definitely," he agreed.

"Thanks, but—" again there was a negative shake of the dark head winged with silver tips "—I never planned to stay this long anyway. I started looking for a ranch of my own. It's time I found it."

"Travis, I—" a seriousness entered Cord's expression "—I was wrong about a lot of things that I'm sorry for now. I've never thanked you for all you did for us."

"It isn't necessary. You had your reasons at the time, so there's nothing to forgive. And as for thanks, well—" his mouth quirked as he placed the wide-brimmed stetson on his head "—I've had that today."

"Won't you stay for a few days?" Stacy asked as Travis walked toward the door.

"I don't like prolonging goodbyes," he stated, pausing in the doorway.

"When you buy that ranch," Cord told him, "let us know. I have a seed bull and thirty cows that belong to you."

"That isn't necessary—" Travis began firmly.

"It's a bonus," Cord announced. "Anyone else would have stolen that much from me in a year.

Besides, I'm giving you thirty-one headaches on the hoof!"

The grooves around his mouth deepened as he met Travis's gaze. A smile curved the foreman's mouth. He raised a finger to his hat brim and walked into the hallway, closing the door behind him.

"That was generous of you, darling," Stacy smiled.

"Generous?" Cord looked at her in a bemused way. "I'd give him my ranch for opening my eyes to the truth—if it didn't already belong to our son."

He took the tea cup from her hand and set it on the bedside table. It left her hand free to lightly caress the powerful line of his jaw.

"Cord," she whispered.

"I've been such a fool about so many things." He caught her fingers and kissed the tips. "Can you ever forgive me for the terrible things I said to you?"

"Of course," Stacy sighed.

"I loved you so much that I couldn't stand the thought of you staying out of pity for a cripple." Cord frowned at the memory of their bitter arguments. "Each time you came near me, I doubted that it was because you loved me. That's why I kept pushing you away, why I kept hurting you and destroying myself each time I succeeded."

Stacy slid her fingers inside his shirt, feeling the warmth of his body heat and the dark hairs tickling the palms of her hands. She tilted her head back, her lips moist and parted.

"Try pushing me away now, darling," she declared huskily.

Beneath her hands, she felt his heartbeat stop for an instant. Then he was pushing her away—back against the pillow as his mouth closed over hers.

"Mommy!" Josh's voice called from the hallway.

Stacy moved in a faint protest beneath his commanding kiss, and Cord smiled against her trembling lips. "Mary will find something for him to do for a little while. She's a married woman."

Sure enough, Stacy heard Mary's voice in the hall, and wound her arms around Cord's neck.

Janet
Dailey
THE
AUTHOR

From the moment she finished reading her first
Harlequin, this American author became hooked on the
romance genre. How fitting that she should go on to win
international fame by writing over fifty novels for the
Harlequin Presents line. Readers delight in learning
more about the individual states she uses as
backgrounds for her novels and are captivated by the
lively, memorable characters she creates.